Also by
Laurelin McGee

MISS MATCH
MISTAKEN (novella)

Love Struck

LAURELIN McGEE

St. Martin's Paperbacks

This is a work of fiction. All of the characters, organizations, and events portrayed in this novel are either products of the author's imagination or are used fictitiously.

LOVE STRUCK

3 1907 00355 5025

Copyright © 2016 by Laurelin McGee.

For information address St. Martin's Press, 175 Fifth Avenue, New York, NY 10010.

ISBN: 978-1-250-05919-2

Printed in the United States of America

St. Martin's Paperbacks edition / February 2016

St. Martin's Paperbacks are published by St. Martin's Press, 175 Fifth Avenue, New York, NY 10010.

10 9 8 7 6 5 4 3 2 1

For Bethany, the midwife to our story.

Chapter One

"A-D-Z-E?" Lance looked at the word on the Scrabble board, his brows furrowed. "What the hell is 'adze'? You're making words up again, aren't you?"

Lacy wrapped her arms tighter around the pillow she was holding—*his* pillow—and scowled in mock indignation. "Making words up *again*? I *never* make up words. That's you."

"I do not. Ever." But his grin would have been an admission even if they both didn't already know full well that he often just placed letters on the board, hoping they spelled something legitimate. "And if 'adze' is for real, then tell me what it means."

"It's . . . uh . . ." She was excellent at words, but not always at remembering definitions.

"If you don't know, it's not a word. I call foul." He shifted, stretching one leg out and jostling the mattress as he did.

"Careful." Lacy put her hands out to steady the board. It was the one problem with playing in bed—any movement threatened the integrity of the game.

"*You* be careful, missy. Cheating at Scrabble . . . who would have thought? From Lacy Dawson of all people."

"Are you officially challenging me?"

Lance dove across the board, sending wooden tiles flying.

Lacy squealed as he pinned her to the mattress. So much for Scrabble. Oh well, she was more interested in this new game anyway.

"Admit it. You made it up," he said as he stretched his body over her.

"It's a tool!" she said, suddenly remembering the meaning of the word. "An adze is a kind of tool. . . . I think."

"A tool? I'll show you a tool." Lance pressed his hips into hers, and she could feel his *tool* all right.

She pretended to pout. "This tool of yours better be worth it. I mean, I was winning, you know."

He let go of one of her arms so he could pull the pillow out from between them and toss it out of the way. "I'm sure you were. But guess what. I've already won."

Lacy wiggled, positioning herself better beneath her fiancé. "Oh, really. Just what have you won?"

"You. I've won you." He lowered his lips to hers, taking her to a place where words were no longer needed, where her solo turned to a duet. Eventually he trailed kisses up her jaw and to her ear. "Lacy?"

She closed her eyes, too enthralled in the passion of the moment to answer.

"Lacy?" he said again.

"Mm hmm?" she murmured.

"Lacy?"

What the hell? She'd already answered him.

"Lacy?" It was louder this time, and the tone sounded less like Lance and more like . . .

Her eyes popped open and she was no longer under-

neath the man she loved, no longer on her bed with a
Scrabble game in disarray around her.

Instead, she was in the recording studio, headphones on
her ears, guitar in her lap, her hands shifting automatically
through the chords of the song she was playing.

It was Darrin, calling her name from the recording
booth. Not Lance. Of course, it couldn't be Lance. Lance
was gone. He died months ago, and she still came back to
him in fantasy every time she got lost in song.

"Lacy Dawson."

She muted her strings and swallowed past the lump in
her throat. "Darrin Ortiz. I was in the zone. What do you
want?" She glared at her boss through the glass wall.

He glared back.

Dick.

They made it through almost three more seconds before he cracked up. He could never stay angry at her. She
joined in the laughter, not really feeling it but knowing it
was what she would have done . . . before.

"Get out here and talk to me and you'll find out. This
recording job was supposed to be finished an hour ago."

"Sometimes jobs go long." She played a riff that suddenly popped in her head. *Yeah, that's how Lance would
have liked it.*

Darrin rolled his eyes. "You and I both know you had
this on your second take."

At least, Lacy assumed he was rolling his eyes. She
didn't bother to look up and see, but she knew him well
enough to know his mannerisms, and eye-rolling was one
of his favorites.

She stuck her lip out stubbornly—one of *her* favorite
mannerisms. "I'm fine-tuning. It's an important part of my
process."

"Your *process* involves spending the last hour of every

workday 'fine-tuning' so you can get out of doing any paperwork."

She raised her head to see him staring her down. This time she didn't have a witty comeback. He was completely right about her fine-tuning, just not right about her reasons. She really didn't mind paperwork, but it wasn't in lead sheets and recording logs where she found Lance. She found him in the strum of her hands, in the harmonic vibrations of her instrument. So with the melancholy she always felt when she returned from the music in her head—the only place Lance still lived—to the real world, she set her guitar down and exited the booth.

She followed Darrin toward the office, taking a quick moment to stick her tongue out at Kat. The other girl was polishing the cymbals on a drum set and didn't notice. Lacy never knew exactly where she stood on Kat. She'd been a well-meaning friend through the last painful months. Well meaning and reliable. Sometimes, though, Kat's perfectly styled rocker look made Lacy want to push her into a mud puddle. Or an angry mosh pit. Or both.

But that was mostly because she had barely brushed her own hair for a year or so. It was surprisingly easy to resent the people who had it all together. Sometimes Lacy wondered if people used to resent her, too.

Kat looked up and grinned. Lacy blew her a kiss.

Kat held up her hand in the shape of a phone and mouthed, "Call me later."

Suppressing a groan, Lacy gave her a thumbs-up and hurried after Darrin, who was waiting in the doorway clearing his throat. As she walked in, he slammed the door behind her.

Which suddenly put Lacy on guard. The last time she'd been in Darrin's office with the door shut was when he'd told her that due to slow business, he had to cut her studio hours.

She didn't have many more hours left to cut. *Please, oh please, oh please, don't let it mean I'm getting fired.* She would die if she didn't have this job. Well, not die. She tried not to use that term loosely after Lance—*don't think about him, don't cry*—but it would be *near* dying. Playing around town and laying down background tracks had been the only things she'd lived for the last few months. The only times she could lose herself in fantasies of him without anyone questioning where she was in her head. She was able to get so few gigs these days, without the studio she'd be . . .

She couldn't bear to think about it. She'd wait until he said it outright, even if that was only seconds away.

Tightly gripping the back of the bar stool that Darrin had repurposed—aka, stolen—for his office guests, Lacy attempted to hide her trepidation. "What is it?"

Darrin slumped into his beat-up, faux-leather rolling chair, flinging a leg up on a file cabinet, nearly toppling the pile of sheet music on top. "I just got off the phone with the singer from Bitchy Ether. You know, the girl band from Harvard?"

It was Lacy's turn to eye roll. "I remember them. Bunch of women's studies majors, no real inspiration except to represent women in music. I am so not looking forward to mixing their album."

"Well, that's the thing." Darrin was practically bouncing, which was sort of funny considering that he was talking about some of the most annoyingly serious musicians ever to grace the booths of his studio. Also, it was strange for a guy with such a hardcore look. His tattoos were uncountable, his hair was perfectly coiffed in a rockabilly cut, and the spikes on his collar and wristband would intimidate a pit bull. Any behavior that was giddy in nature seemed completely out of place on him, but that was only if you didn't know the guy.

"What's the thing? Did they actually figure out how to play their instruments? Or write a song that isn't copied from the SCUM manifesto?" Lacy giggled a little. She only knew about that particular piece of literature from her feminist neighbor Jaylene. Jay loved Bitchy Ether. She might have been their only fan.

"No, none of that. Apparently, 'bitchy ether' is a life-style, not just a name. The band has broken up, and I was forced to listen to various reasons why for at least twenty minutes. Which brings me to my point, my darling."

Dammit, she knew it. Now he was going to tell her that since the schedule was empty, he didn't need her. At least he was giving her the news gently, with terms of endearment. Darrin was the only person she knew who could say things like 'darling' without sounding condescending.

Well, if he was going to be graceful about it, so was she. She could save the crying for home, like she usually did, where she could bury her face in Lance's pillow. "Out with it, beloved boss. I can take it. Tell me your point." She'd become amazingly good at false strength. He didn't even notice her wobbling knees.

"The point is, we suddenly have an opening for studio time. And I wouldn't dream of opening it publicly without offering it to you first."

Oh.

She blinked, surprise momentarily throwing her speechless. That was definitely not what she'd expected him to say.

Maybe she'd heard him wrong. "You're offering their studio time to *me*?" With the cut back to just one operating booth, the calendar had filled up quickly. Lacy wasn't on the books now to get in for months, and that was with staff preferential treatment.

"I know you were hoping to record *your* new album, and this gets you in ten weeks out instead of after the New

Year. . . . How much do you love me?" Now he actually *was* bouncing. It was so adorable, she could almost ignore that this was the last thing she wanted him to be saying to her.

It was also really amazingly kind. Lacy may have teared up. Only a tiny bit, though.

"I love you the mostest, D. Thank you." She really meant it, too. Despite the pit that had just formed in her stomach. She smiled extra big so he wouldn't notice her hand resting on it, trying to quell the sudden wave of nausea.

"You don't have to thank me. I just can't wait to hear what you've been working on. It's been a shit year for you, Lace, but I know your music is going to be amazing. I'm so proud of you. Get the heck out of here before I get emotional." He waved his hand toward the door. "And stop pretending to fine-tune. Go grab a drink or something. Have a good weekend. Tell your sister I said what's up!" He was practically shouting as she ran from the office.

Don't throw up, don't throw up. Lacy darted into the bathroom and leaned over the sink. What the hell was she going to do now? There was no way she'd have an album ready to record in ten weeks. She was doubtful she'd have one ready in four months. Dammit, she should just own up and tell Darrin the truth—none of the songs he'd heard her playing the last few months were anywhere near complete. And definitely nowhere near recording ready. Hard to record with no lyrics.

But after his speech about being proud and all that, she couldn't bear to see his disappointment. Couldn't bear to admit to total fraudhood.

No, better not make any rash decisions. She'd talk to Folx about it first. Right now she had to get through her panic attack. Deep breaths and a splash of cold water usually helped. That, and unloading on her writing group. She dug out her phone and used the group's app to send an urgent message to Folx. *Need to talk. Message me when you can?*

Lacy felt a little better already. Maybe even better enough to get through the rest of her shift.

Wait—Darrin said she could leave early. That helped her stomach subside. She'd wait for Folx's reply in the comfort of her own home. She'd probably be dragged into helping her sister, Andy, with wedding plans. Which was fine. As challenging as it was to hear endless conversations about linens and venue options, living with a bride-to-be was fantastic for keeping her mind busy—even though it did make her think of the wedding *she* was supposed to have with Lance. At least it was great for keeping her troubles to herself. Engaged women, especially ones engaged to prominent billionaires, were too busy to pry. Andy's preoccupation with her upcoming nuptials was the only reason she hadn't noticed that her precious baby sister was keeping secrets.

One more deep breath. Lacy peered in the mirror. She was a little paler than normal, but otherwise looked fine. She fluffed her long blonde curls and practiced a fake smile. The trick was squinting. If you squinted just slightly when you smiled, people thought you meant it. The things learned while hiding from the world. One day she'd write a book. When she got her words back, that was.

Opening the bathroom door, she almost walked smack into Kat.

"Um, oh my God!" Kat pursed her lips at Lacy and stared meaningfully.

" 'Um, oh my God' what?" Of course this chick was waiting outside the bathroom. Thank the lord she hadn't actually thrown up.

"Darrin told me you're taking Bitchy Ether's recording

time! I'm so stoked for you! I'm going to do your drums. It's my gift to you. Of course, Darrin said he'd pay me my normal rate, but I'm really doing it for you. Oh honey, come here!" She threw her arms wide, inviting Lacy to walk into her embrace.

Lacy did, but took another deep breath first, not because of her nerves this time, but because of her nose. It was her experience that Kat usually smelled like more patchouli than she was comfortable with. Some of the scent always clung to her post-hug, which was tolerable, but it was best not to do an inhale during the actual act. Inhalation led to choking fits.

And this hug was going on too long. She needed to breathe again. "I was supposed to call you?" she asked as she pushed away, using the question as a reason to extricate herself.

"Yeah! There's this band playing tonight that is like soooo good, I swear to God you will love them so much, so we have to go. Right?"

And that was another thing that sometimes bugged Lacy about Kat. She talked like a preteen. That was annoying as hell. Kat's taste in music was impeccable, and the fact that she was able to keep tabs on all that went on in the Boston music scene was even more annoying. Yet another area where Kat had it going on, and Lacy no longer did.

Lacy was torn on the invitation. She really needed to talk to Folx, but if he wasn't online, she'd just be sitting around home fretting and nodding at centerpiece options. Good music also might help resolve the tight knot in her belly. At the very least, it might be inspiring. And, man, did she need inspiration. "Fine. What's the club?"

"Tigerstripes."

Lacy sighed heavily. She'd have to change first, then. Tigerstripes was an über-trendy place, a total "see and be seen" for local musicians. Her yoga pants and tank top might be comfortable and fine for solo studio days, but she couldn't wear them somewhere cool, somewhere people might know her. It was her least favorite part of being a musician—she really couldn't go out in public without being "in character." Her sister usually wore pantsuits to work and then got herself casual and comfy when they went out, but Lacy didn't have that luxury.

When Lacy Dawson saw a band, she saw them as Up-and-Coming-Indie-Sensation Lacy Dawson. Which meant she needed to be in her uniform—full hair and makeup, plus trendy jeans and stylish shirt. In other words, clothes that didn't double as pajamas.

Chapter Two

Twenty minutes later, Lacy was at home applying copious amounts of black eyeliner and fending off her sister.

"This wedding guest list is impossible!" Andy was yelling from her bedroom.

Lacy ignored her, and started filling in her brows, but not without first glancing at her phone to see if she'd missed any notifications from the songwriter forum app. She hadn't. She tried not to be too disheartened.

"This process has made me realize—and don't be shocked—but I don't have a ton of close friends. Do co-workers count? Can I ignore them and elope?"

Lacy dabbed white sparkles on to her brow bone. She studied the effect, and added some more to the corners of her eyes. She told herself Andy wasn't looking for an answer, she just wanted to hear herself talk. That way she didn't have to feel guilty about not weighing in.

"Are roses or lilies hotter right now? We're bound to get covered in *Boston* mag. If I pick wrong, will I be lame, or trendsetting?" It was getting harder to pretend Andy didn't really want answers when she kept pestering for them like that.

"Look," Lacy yelled over her shoulder, "I'll go to your meeting tomorrow with the planner. Just stop stressing tonight, okay?" She wanted to be there for Andy, but she couldn't deal with the recording studio anxiety *and* her petty bridal jealousy. It took more energy than she had.

She left the mirror and stuck her head into her sister's room. "Do you want to come listen to a new band with me and Kat? It'll calm you down." Though Andy didn't live and breathe music like Lacy, they always enjoyed each other's company. Even when Andy was being a bit wedding-crazy, she was still Lacy's sister and best friend.

Andy glared. "Thanks, but no thanks. The last time I went out with you two I ran into that weirdo from the Irony and Wine bar. A night at home with Netflix and a bath sounds far more relaxing. Thank you, thank you, thank you for attending my meeting, though. Be awake and not hung-over by eleven, please!"

Lacy returned the glare, but Andy was right. The strangest people hung out at the coolest bars, and the Iron and Wine guy, or Eeyore, as Andy called him, had developed a fascination with the older Dawson sister. He was a recovering alcoholic who dropped trou after a single Jäger shot. It was weird.

Also, Andy and Kat were hard to bear when they got together. Kat got all cable show about wedding ideas, and Andy liked it. Maybe even loved it. It disgusted Lacy. Weddings should be reflections of the couple. So why all the hassle? Andy and Blake were Type A workaholics. They should have a courthouse ceremony followed by a formal sushi dinner and something fancy, like—port. Ob. Vi. Us. Weddings were overdone.

The doorbell rang, and Lacy was so grateful to stop the

holy matrimony talk that she almost jumped into Kat's hippie-reeking arms.

"Hey, let's go!" she yelped. She blew a kiss to her sister and off they went.

Chapter Three

An hour later, and Lacy was actually really happy she'd gone. Folx still hadn't responded to her message—she'd checked her phone several times—but, as she'd hoped, the music had eased her anxiety. This band was phenomenal. They had the folky sound of Mumford & Sons but the symphonic composition of Bastille. It was fresh and traditional at once. Lacy was entranced.

"Where did you hear about these guys?" she yelled in Kat's ear.

"I screwed the drummer!" Kat screamed back, through neon orange lips.

Dear God. I did not miss the single life. Lacy mimed getting a refill on her drink, and headed toward the back bar.

"G and T," she told the bartender, who seemed like a normal guy. It was a relief these days to find one who was clean-shaven. The last bar she'd played at, mustachioed patrons could actually order drinks in glasses with guards to keep their facial hair from getting damp. At that point, she thought that hipster bars had either jumped the shark . . . or she was too old. As Lacy had only just celebrated her twenty-sixth birthday, she hoped it was the former.

When her drink came sans any accoutrement but a lime wedge, she relaxed. Good music, good drinks. If Darrin and Andy were here, she might be having A Best Day Ever.

That was something Lance had taught her. Calling any one particular day your favorite was silly. There were a ton of tiny moments that added up to a great day, if you paid attention. Probably once a month you could find enough moments in a day to call it A Best Day Ever. Not *The*. But *A*. That made it possible to have them more often.

Lance had always been an optimist. Or at least he'd done a good job of pretending he was. It was the one thing she'd tried, on her grief counselor's suggestion, since his death. Lacy tried to honor him by having at least one great day per month. Most days she faked it, pretending to find joy in a BLT and a new Neil Gaiman book when all she really saw was the jarring absence of the one person she wanted to read aloud to over lunch. Sometimes, though, it actually worked.

This band, for example. She really meant it tonight. Their sound was new and fresh and very soothing at the same time.

"Aren't they totes amaze?" Lacy jumped when Kat's familiar shrill voice pierced her right ear. "Let's do shots."

Lacy considered. She wouldn't mind hanging out longer for the music, but she'd promised Andy she'd come home soon and sober. "Actually, I've got an appointment pretty early. I should probably go." Plus, even though Folx hadn't responded yet, she knew he would any minute, and she wanted to be able to talk to him freely. "Thanks for the offer, though. And for showing me this band. What are they called?"

"The Blue Hills! Just one shot? Come on. You never wanna have any fun." The other girl pouted.

"I really shouldn't." She stood up to leave.

Onstage the song finished and immediately launched into something else. Something somber and emotional that made Lacy look back at the stage. Then the lead singer began the verse, and the timbre of his voice drew her in. It was tortured and raw. Honest. But it was the lyrics that caught her up entirely, forcing her to sit back down and listen.

Flying out of Boston
December in mid-morning
Watching the world disappear below me
As I leave

Flying into background
In the air, an incomplete
The sun is rising right behind me
As I go

And so I journey from this place
Creating one more space
Leaving this galaxy for a new one
Hoping to find harmony

God, they hit home. From the haunting melody and arrangement of the words against the background instruments, it was obvious the song was a metaphor. It wasn't really about a flight but about someone feeling her whole life changing, her whole existence fading away below as she is jetted into a new state of being. A new journey. A new galaxy. She loved the dual meaning in some of the lines. Mid-morning, for example, also could mean mid-*mourning*.

It felt like a song that had been written about her. It was the mark of a truly exceptional lyric—capturing a universal emotion so adeptly that everyone could relate. This band wasn't just good. They were really good.

She studied the lead singer. He was enchanting with blond hair that had probably been highlighted, styled forward and up, à la James Dean. His face was scruffy, like all the alternative folk male musicians these days, and his deep-set blue eyes were wildly expressive. Yeah. He was hot. Rumpled in all the right ways. His pants were a little tight for her taste, but they still did the job of putting her hormones in overdrive.

Whoa. That was new. She hadn't been attracted to a man in . . . well, since Lance. Maybe it was time she thought about getting back out there.

Or maybe this guy just knew how to play to the women.

She continued to watch him, and when his gaze circled the audience, it landed on her and he winked. It startled her, but she gave him a half smile and looked away, not sure she was ready to give him the wrong impression.

And that's when she saw the musician playing the banjo.

Her mouth felt dry, and she was suddenly aware of every breath that entered and left her lungs. He was different than the lead singer. Just as eye-catching, but not as enigmatic. He was easier to look at, somehow. Softer. More real. His hands danced over his instrument, and the intent expression on his face conveyed his total love for what he was doing. While the lead singer was giving a performance, this guy was playing for himself. And in a way, it made for a more interesting show.

Now that she'd discovered him, in fact, she found her attention stayed on him nearly as much as the lead. Both of them were incredibly attractive, but unlike the singer, the banjo player was more *cute* than *hot*. He had that artsy look going on—dark disheveled hair, dimples visible even beneath his closely trimmed goatee, and penetrating brown eyes.

Oh, shit. She'd thought the word "penetrating" just as he looked up from his fingerpicking. Now she was thinking about penetration. And his fingers. She was certain her face gave away her inappropriate thoughts, but his eyes locked with hers and she couldn't look away, no matter what he saw. A shiver rippled down her spine at the intensity in his gaze. It was more than simply reading the lust on her face. It was like he was looking right into her mind. Into her soul. Like he was seeing something in her that she'd been certain didn't exist anymore.

It was unnerving and strangely intimate. It stirred her. Made her feel . . . things.

She shook her head, forcing herself to look away. She wasn't ready for an onslaught of emotion. She was just getting used to being numb.

It was definitely past time to go.

In front of her was a shot Kat had slipped over, despite the refusal. Lacy stared at it. If she took that, another would follow, and next thing she'd be trying to pick up one of the sexy men onstage. Not a good plan, even if she didn't have the wedding thing in the morning. She caught the eye of another girl sitting nearby and nodded to the small glass of dark liquid. "Cheers." The girl grinned her thanks and grabbed it.

"Good night, Kat." Lacy grabbed her purse and tossed a few bills on the bar. "See you at work Monday."

"Night, Anti-fun!"

Lacy rolled her eyes as she stood to leave. On her way toward the door, she threw one last glance over at the band. The singer was on his knees with the mike like he'd been practicing in front of a mirror. But the banjo player was still staring at her, with his dimpled half smile. She turned away quickly, before she started having capital-E emotions again.

Anti-fun. That wasn't what she was. Anti-*feel*, was more

like it. God, she used to be so different. She had been the girl who loved to sit around getting wasted in a bar with a coworker, hitting on delicious, talented musicians.

But now she didn't know how to flirt without crying, how to talk without depressing people. Didn't know how to engage or relate or connect. So she'd simply stopped trying.

Now her career was number one on her priority list. It was much easier to deal with than people, and it needed her since it had hit a devastating standstill. Any moment she could spare was devoted to getting her dream back on track and, except for participating in a handful of support groups, with as little social interaction as possible.

At home, Lacy sank into her desk chair and opened her Internet browser. The SoWriAn site was her startup page. Song Writers Anonymous. Her favorite support group. Her home. Her family. The only people she could really talk to because they didn't know what she had been through. They knew only what she told them. They didn't talk to her with pitying consolation. It was refreshing and exactly what she'd needed.

She'd stumbled upon the site accidentally in the wake of Lance's death, seeking a less traditional outlet to grieve. It wasn't that Lacy was anti-therapy. She'd even gone to that grief counselor a few times. No, it was that she'd been taught by the great masters since she was small: Joplin, Plath, Beethoven, Cobain, Poe, Winehouse. They didn't sit on a couch and talk about their struggles. They put them into their music, and she related to that. Music got her through everything.

She didn't plan to follow any of them into an early grave. Really, she didn't. But all of them produced their best works when they were at their worst. So she planned to follow suit, to channel the—"heartbreak" was such a tiny word to describe the yawning emptiness in her life.

But she *wanted* to channel the heartbreak, as it were, to turn it into a masterwork that would now and forever pay tribute to the love that she and her fiancé had shared.

She didn't want the rawness of her loss to leave her until she'd wrung every last drop out of it, made it not worth it—nothing could ever be worth it—but worthy, and hopefully healing as well.

The competing emotions in her brain left tracers of songs she could write. The desolation, confusion, loneliness, and if she were honest, anger, had all the makings of beautiful music. Yes, all the pieces were there.

If only she could access them . . .

She scrolled through a couple of message boards. One of her favorites was called *SadCore*, and she found it perversely hilarious. Songwriters posted links to news stories about people who died the night before their wedding, to disaster videos, to articles about the homeless. The idea was that it was a place people could come if they were too upbeat to write a "real" song. A few doses of depression later they'd presumably wander off to write something sad—and saleable.

It was perverse because she'd lived through the horror of finding her fiancé's lifeless body, and wouldn't wish it on anyone. It was hilarious because she completely understood the creative impulse.

Maybe she did need therapy.

The other board she tended to lurk around on was far more straightforward, *Write or Die*. If that were an actual option, Lacy was certain she'd fall into the wrong category. But it did sum up how she felt about music in general.

Ping. A private message came through. *Finally!* She tried to suppress the thrill that ran through her. It was the ping she'd been waiting for all night. She flushed as she took in the message.

Hey, you. Just got your message. What's up?

FolxNotDead27. Her online bestie.

Screw that, calling it an online friendship cheapened it. Folx and Lacy, or LoveCoda as she was known on the boards, were real friends. Real friends in a false environment. There was probably a song in there, too.

Hey, yourself. Did you have band stuff? Now that she had him online, she didn't want to rush to her drama. She enjoyed the easy banter too much. There wasn't anything she looked forward to more each day than their nightly conversations.

It was logical that Lacy had formed such a tight bond with a fellow musician, especially one as talented as this one. She'd read his words and tabs and given feedback on a number of them. Each one was better than the last, simple lyrics underscoring complex emotional stories. It was natural she'd enjoy talking to him. Natural for her to crush on his words.

What wasn't natural, not even a little, was the rush she got when they were messaging.

Yeah. Getting ready for tour. But you're avoiding the topic. What's going on?

Not natural at all, considering she didn't know his name, or what he looked like, or whether or not he chewed with his mouth open.

You're going on tour?

Here was where things started to get tricky. SoWri*An*. *An*, for "Anonymous." It was that component of the group that made it so successful, and the moderators enforced it above all. Designed to be a safe space, the forum attempted to eliminate all the hierarchies of fame and power and who-banged-whose-girlfriend by keeping the members identities sheltered. There were supposedly famous people on the site, as well as people on their way to being famous, and those hoping they were on their way. Complete privacy was a necessity. Personal details not allowed. To even join

the boards, musicians were required to sign a legal dis-
claimer agreeing not to share or request personal information in order to prevent lawsuits and slander as well as
petty jealousies and gossip. Writers helping writers—that
was all the forum allowed.

So FolxNotDead27 knew LoveCoda worked a full-
time day job and that she was in the industry, but nothing
more. Questions like the one she'd asked about his tour,
genuine among friends, were also somewhat charged. Even
though she was sure they wouldn't do it often, the moderators could read the PMs if they wanted. And who knew
what sort of information exchange they'd consider crossing
the line? Those decisions were made completely at their
discretion.

Stop dodging. Tell me your news, Love!

Of everyone she knew, this was the only person she
wanted to talk to about the studio session. The only one
who would understand, so even though it was delving into
the area of "not anonymous," she plunged in. *The recording session I had booked for January got bumped up due
to a cancellation.*

What?! That's fabulous! This was the intended beauty
of the forum. Shared celebration of successes was exactly
the sort of thing the founders had hoped for.

This, however, was not what Lacy would call a success.

*How can you say that? Think I can get away with
doing an album of American Standards? You know I
have nothing to record.*

He was the only one who knew that, actually.

And this was why the anonymity factor had drawn Lacy
to the forum in the first place. Only here, where she
wouldn't be judged or pitied or encouraged to start taking
an anti-depressant, could she admit her big secret. Could
admit that, since Lance's death, she'd been blocked. More
than blocked—she'd been paralyzed.

Every single morning since The Worst Day Ever (this one was an absolute, not a category), she'd picked up her favorite beat-up guitar, the one she'd named Lucky when she was fifteen and considered it to be. Lucky and Lacy had sat on the window seat overlooking Tremont Street and strummed and waited for the words to come, the words that would unlock the pain she carried inside. Every day she somehow lived while her love did not, the words dried up in her throat, becoming a knotted tangle of unrealized lyrics that grew until she set the guitar aside, gasping for air.

I won't let you do that. What kind of timeframe are we looking at?

This, this was exactly why she felt such an intense bond with this faceless man on the other side of the screen. He cared, enough to reach out a hand to her. Again. And again. It seemed like every time she'd lost it this year, wondering if she'd ever write again, or if her career was over before it began, he'd been there to pull her back up.

Her hands were sweaty as she typed. *Ten weeks.*

Easy. We got this.

We do? She loved how he attached himself to her problem with his "we." It gave her comfort, misguided as it was.

Yeah, we do. We just have to change our tactics. We were waiting for your block to disappear on its own. Now we'll have to be more aggressive with our approach to break through.

More aggressive. As if she hadn't already tried with every ounce of her being. Folx was well aware of her attempts. He wasn't trying to belittle her situation—she knew that. He was being supportive. It didn't change the truth, though, and she confessed her worst fears now. *I'm scared, Folx. What if I'm dry forever? What if inspiration never strikes again?*

It will. And I know you're scared, but we'll get through this. I'll make sure of it.

What are you going to do, exactly? She smiled at the monitor, waiting.

Anything it takes.

That night, she fell asleep with those words dancing across the backs of her lids, her soul a little more hopeful as the strains of the Blue Hills beat a soundtrack through her memory in time with her heartbeat.

Chapter Four

"Okay, I should warn you. My wedding planner is kind of terrifying." Andy glanced over at Lacy from her plastic Charlie seat.

"Right. Terrifying." Lacy was already wary about the outing. Only a little more than a year ago she was planning her own wedding. Though she'd been "fine" through the months since, was it really a good idea to spend the day reminiscing about her own choices? The group of singer-songwriter friends she'd chosen as her musicians, the daisies—the first flower Lance had ever given her—the old theater that she'd picked as her venue. They constantly sat at the edge of her conscience, haunting her. Though she was hopeful they'd one day pour out of her in song, she was also terrified that instead they'd explode when she least expected it. Like while sitting through her sister's planning meeting.

But wait—why was Andy scared? "Terrifying like how, exactly?"

Andy offered a hesitant frown.

"Hey, I've seen every wedding planner movie, including

the JLo one. And I've been to lots of weddings. Hell, I've played enough weddings to have the drill down pat. So I can say with authority that planners are just there to make sure your shit goes smoothly. No reason to be scared. If you're freaked, it's probably because you're freaked about the whole shebang. Which is natural."

Lacy hoped she sounded comforting, though she really wanted to say, *Sheesh, Andy, get it together.* The planner she'd hired was obviously good. Lacy had double-checked on all the online bridal boards and found he was by far the planner most recommended. It wasn't really fair for Andy to blame her insecurity on the poor guy just because her wedding was going to be widely reported. Which was what happened when you married one of the city's richest businessmen.

Luckily, bridezillas were almost Lacy's specialty at this point. She knew how to handle them. She wasn't exaggerating when she said she'd sung at enough weddings to know what they were like. At last count, there were almost thirty. It didn't mean she thought Andy would turn into a nightmare bride, exactly. Just that, if she did, Lacy was prepared.

"I wasn't freaked about the wedding until I met Tim. I know he's well meaning. But he's also terrifying."

Lacy doubted that. He wouldn't be the best in the city if he were honestly terrifying. But she didn't want to argue, so she closed her eyes for the remainder of the ride to avoid discussing it further. A sharp elbow to the ribs told her where they were at the stop, unnecessary since she wasn't actually asleep. She swallowed her irritation and held her sister's hand as they walked up the tiled path outside Boston Brides as she remembered another thing from her own wedding planning—getting married was the scariest shit ever.

She'd almost forgotten that. The little doubt-spiders that

had crept up her spine constantly. Forever? *Creep, bite.* With one person? *Bite, bite.* Putting the whole event together? *Bite, venom, coma.*

Even though she'd wanted it. Even though she'd known Lance was The One. There had still been the fear. She squeezed Andy's hand to reassure her. Or herself. Maybe they both needed a little squeeze.

But when they weren't even up the steps and the door burst open so forcefully that Lacy was concerned it would fly off its hinges, she started to wonder if she should have given Andy's remarks more credibility.

"There you are! It's about goddamn time. We're behind!"

Lacy drew up short, tightening her grip on her sister's hand. The man in the doorway was only about her height, five ten maybe, with beautifully coiffed blond hair, a pressed suit, and black-rimmed glasses. He looked like he should be the butler in a movie about an Italian fashion designer. The crass words that came out of his mouth, however . . .

"Told you," Andy muttered. "Tim! We're early, actually." She leapt up the steps and gave the man a kiss on the cheek. He wiped it off, semi-surreptitiously, and glared.

"Barely," he told her. "Who's the blonde?"

"My sister. Remember? I told you she'd be with me." Andy was much more patient with her planner than called for. Then again, he *was* the best.

"But you didn't tell me she was blonde." This time Tim's glare went past Andy to fall on Lacy.

"You're blond too," Lacy reminded him.

He narrowed his eyes further but directed his comment to Andy. "She'll throw off my color scheme! It was built around *your* hair. Are you dead set on involving her?"

Lacy's mouth fell open. Was he really suggesting cutting her from the wedding just because her hair was the wrong color? Maybe he just had an odd sense of humor. The kind that wasn't funny.

"Yes, Tim. That's a non-negotiable." So far Andy appeared to be perfectly capable of handling the man by herself. If Lacy wasn't so stunned by him, she might have suggested her sister take the meeting without her.

Tim sighed overdramatically. "Well, screw everything. We'll have to revise. You better come in."

Lacy fingered her scheme-destroying curls as Tim led them inside to a wood-paneled room filled with low tables, portfolios, and very expensive-looking rugs. With each step, he winced, as if he had hidden nerve endings in the carpets. He stopped at a table and flipped open a binder.

"You see this?"

Lacy and Andy leaned down to study the pictures before them. "You did the Jen Jankovich wedding?" Lacy asked, recognizing the elite heiress socialite celebrity in the photos. It had been one of the biggest events in recent Boston history.

Tim theatrically clapped his hand to his chest. "God, no. If I'd done that event, the city would still be talking about it. That planner had absolutely no taste. There's far too much white going on and far too few elephants."

"I didn't realize there were elephants at all." Andy seemed to actually be imagining how to incorporate pachyderms in her ceremony.

"There weren't. That's my point."

Lacy bit her lip. "Terrifying" wasn't the word Lacy would have used for him. "Hilarious" was better. He was so strange, so outrageous, so intense. It was hard to imagine that his plans for the big event wouldn't reflect those same attributes. Now *that* was terrifying.

"That was an example of what *not* to do." He slammed the portfolio shut. "Your event, on the other hand, is going to be gigantic," he informed Andy. "The talk of the town.

The ceremony of the century. A mind-blowing pain in the ass."

Lacy was baffled. Wasn't that a good thing for someone whose living was made off gigantic events?

"I know, Tim." The desperation in Andy's voice was at least half put on. "That's why I need you. I'm completely overwhelmed."

Lacy would have sworn he actually puffed up like a fancy bird.

He turned to pat her sister's hand. "I know, Andy. You do. You really do. Especially with this insane timeline you've given me. Less than four months to plan the kind of wedding you want? I'm the only one who could pull it off. Truly." Just as quickly, he dropped Andy's hand and swept his arm toward a tray holding two Bloody Marys, garnished with olives, limes, and beef jerky. "I made you drinks. You'll need them."

Lacy, who was bubbling with the urge to say a lot of things she shouldn't, grabbed one and took a large gulp. It was stronger than she'd anticipated, and spicier. She tried to disguise her cough with a moan of "yum," but Tim gave her a Look that said he knew what she was doing.

"Let's get to work, then, yeah?" Andy was stupid-perky. She took a small sip, which didn't seem to faze her.

"Have another," Tim said to Lacy when she'd finished her glass. She also thought she heard him mutter, "One more round ought to do it." It was hard to be sure since the first drink had been quite strong, and unless getting them drunk was the goal, another round was not a good idea.

He focused his attention on Andy. "We'll start small. Your event is going to be big news around here, so it should be equal parts traditional and progressive. Have you chosen a dress?" He looked like he'd not only swallowed a lemon, but could possibly be growing a lemon tree in his mouth at the thought.

"No, I thought Lace and I could do that together"

Tim looked both mollified and suspicious, if such a combination were possible.

"Fine. We'll go first thing tomorrow. Try to be sober." He sent sharp glances at the drinks he had just given them.

"You're going to come with us to pick out a dress?" Andy asked. Lacy wasn't sure if she sounded worried or hopeful at the prospect.

"Of course I am, gorgeous. You think I'd let you choose something so important on your own? Never. You could end up looking like a giant peacock." His eyes lit up as though he'd suddenly had a brilliant idea. "Unless you like peacocks . . ."

Lacy couldn't let that go without chiming in. "No, she doesn't like peacocks."

"I don't?" Andy asked, unsure.

Lacy shot her a glance that she hoped said, Who are you and what have you done with my usually self-assured older sister?

"I mean, I don't." Not quite as confident as Andy usually was, but it would do.

"Ah, pity. Moving on. Do we have a theme in mind? Say no."

"Um, no?" Andy smiled. "Tim, I'm relying on you here."

"Flowers," he stated. "I'm seeing lots of flowers. A December wedding means it'll be tricky, but we'll fly things in. Did you have a preference?"

"Either roses or lilies, whichever is more fashionable right now," Andy replied, clearly happy to have an answer.

"Roses!" Tim sputtered. "Lilies! No, no, no! I . . . I don't even have words . . ."

Lacy took several more gulps of her drink to cover her desire to break into laughter. She knew she probably should speak up and defend her sister's flower choices, but she'd done her duty when she'd nixed the peacocks. Now it was more fun to be a bystander.

Andy spoke tentatively over her glass. "So, roses and lilies are not available?"

"Availability is never an issue with Boston Brides," Tim practically screeched. "No one, and I mean no one, is using roses or lilies anymore. Are you under the impression that we are having an eighties' flashback wedding? If so you need to be looking elsewhere for your planner. Do you need to be looking elsewhere?"

"No!" Andy exclaimed, shaking her head emphatically at exactly the same time that Lacy's inner voice shouted, *Hell yes, find another planner! This one is cray!*

Tim let out a dramatic huff of air. "I don't even know why I ask for opinions. I should just do everything, like I always do. Anything you choose will be less than acceptable. The flowers will be tulips. Red ones to fit the season. Thousands of them, like the Dutch craze is happening all over again. You'll start a new trend in Boston. Stocks will soar. Fortunes will be made and lost over your wedding. Doesn't that make you feel amazing . . . powerful?"

Lacy could tell that Andy was purposely avoiding her eyes. That was good, because even with the drink held in front of her face, she wasn't sure she was going to be able to hide her hilarity much longer.

"I would say that makes me feel . . . some kind of way." Andy bolstered her statement with a smile.

Lacy choked a little. Andy was better than she'd given her sister credit for.

Tim gave her a tight smile. "Now. Venue. The Museum of Science's Blue Wing is available so I booked it. Imagine— dinosaurs, stars, a million volts of lightning. The wine glasses will be charmed with the planets of the solar system. And don't think I'm ignoring the Christmas Eve holiday. We'll thread lighted boughs of evergreen up and down the aisles and have the wait staff dressed as angels. This is going to be the wedding of the century in New England. You're welcome." He topped up their glasses again and sighed heavily. The girls looked at each other as they drained their glasses.

An hour later, they were holding each other upright, and trying to walk it off as they slowly meandered back toward their brownstone.

"Okay, okay, I admit that he's a little intimidating." At least he'd kept Lacy from thinking about her own abandoned wedding dreams.

"I told you so! Shit, Lacy, higeonpol—pigeonholing people is what I do for a living. But no, don't take my word for it. God, he loved you."

"He hated me, what are you talking about?" Lacy bumped into a building, and ricocheted back to Andy's side.

"Nah. He's extra mean to the people he likes."

She would have said there was no way that Andy could possibly know that, except that her sister had a certain gift for understanding people with very little interaction. "Do you think getting us drunk before noon was his plan all along? Keeping us pliable, so he'd get his way about everything?"

"Absolutely. How do you think he got me to hire him in the first place?" Andy giggled. "I was deeply impressed by his tactics. I'm going to borrow them at the office holiday party this year."

"I have to admit, I dig his vision. It's kind of bizarre, but you'll certainly have a memorable big day. Wait, where are we?" They looked around for thirty seconds before realizing they'd been heading in the wrong direction for the past ten minutes.

"I'm gonna call Blake. He'll send a car or something."

Andy fumbled around in her purse, her cell phone continually eluding her clumsy fingers.

"What? No. You can't call Blake. He'll blame me for getting you wasted before lunch." Lacy liked her sister's fiancé, but he was pretty straitlaced. Surely he'd be pissed.

"Are you kidding? He's about to get laid so good. He'll probably send you flowers and a thank-you card. Get my phone, will you?" She thrust her bag at Lacy and wandered into the café they found themselves beside. "We need lots of coffee, and very little judgment, please," she told the waitress as Lacy dissolved into laughter.

Later, as she watched her sister stumble into the passenger side of her fiancé's car, the fuzzy edges wore off. "Want me to drop you off at your place?" Blake sounded slightly irritated, but she guessed it was because he wasn't tipsy along with them and not because he was actually mad.

"Nah," Lacy said. "I'll catch the train." While the happy couple never shut her out on purpose, it was hard to not feel like a third wheel in their presence. And they deserved their time alone.

Lacy plugged her headphones into her iPhone and pushed play on the Blue Hills album she'd downloaded the night before. As the lead singer's voice filled her ears, it was the banjo player who came to mind—his nimble fingers, his penetrating gaze, his soul-filled eyes. She headed toward the nearest Charlie stop, humming along to the music, feeling considerably less lonely than she had only minutes before.

Chapter Five

"Hey, man, I wanna change the chorus on 'Godric's Hollow.'" Jax bounced from foot to foot and stared over at Eli.

Eli stared back at his lead singer. "What do you mean,' change the chorus'? We've been rehearsing it this way for two months. It's a really good song." This was so typical of Jax, just making a pronouncement like that in the middle of practice. Admittedly, it had been Jax's out-of-the-box way of thinking that had made Eli want to play music with him in the first place. And it was his unique style that had bonded them as friends. But lately, out-of-the-box was more like out-of-the-galaxy.

And it seemed Eli was the only one who had the guts to challenge him.

The other guys groaned and dispersed, used to these all-too-common breaks where the two strong-heads would duke out some decision.

"I don't know, man, I was up there last night and really feeling a connection with the crowd and all, and I suddenly got the idea."

"We didn't even do 'Godric.'" They'd done a pre-tour

gig the night before. A chance to test their chops before the real thing, but they'd performed only their older material. The tour would debut their new stuff, which was why these rehearsals were so important.

Also, he noted, his last sentence would have been a good line for someone to follow with *That's what she said.* How was he the only one who ever heard the innuendo in time to land a joke like that? Okay, maybe he was twelve.

"Right, but I had an inspiration about it during the show. It came clear as a vision, 'We should be singing the "Godric" chorus together.'" Jax smiled, nodding at his own wisdom.

Well, that suggestion wasn't *that* bad. "Yeah, we could sing it together. Some harmonies there might punch it up a little. That's actually a good idea." Eli started humming, already planning how to best complement the existing structure.

"Oh, no, you don't understand. Me and the *audience*, man. I want it to be *us*. So like, where right now the chorus is four lines, I just wanna change it to me singing 'yeah,' and then I hold out the mike and the crowd sings it back. It will make the fans crazy."

"So you mean cut the chorus. And replace it with 'yeahs' sung by you and the audience?" There was no way he'd kept his disgust hidden. Since when was fan engagement more important than the music?

"Yep." Jax nodded as if he believed Eli was completely with him. "Wouldn't that be amazing?"

No. No it would not be. It would be pretentious and oversimplify the whole song. Plus, that chorus was amazing. The word "yeah" is not.

But he wasn't going to waste his breath. At one time, these kinds of decisions had been made together. A collaborative effort. But then the band had grown more successful and Jax . . . well, he'd struggled. Without discussing it, the others seemed to agree that letting Jax have more creative control was a way to boost his spirits. But then he began to take advantage, standing firm on decisions even when the others objected. Now, if Eli put his foot down at changing the chorus, Jax would ignore him and 'yeah' through it anyway.

Honestly, maybe it didn't even matter. The Blue Hills were finally taking off. They'd had a few albums with mediocre response, but the last one had hit in the underground scene and now they had a pretty decent tour booked with the promise of more to come. This was everything Eli had dreamed of coming to fruition.

So why did it feel like more chaos than it was worth?

Eli already knew the answer. He could state it in one word—Jax.

While Jax was definitely the charisma of the band, he was also the drama. He turned their art into a statement. Perhaps it was the reason for their success. But sometimes Eli wondered if they'd done so well *despite* Jax, not because of him.

He'd always thought he was a musician who worked better in a group, but since the last album, Eli had wondered if maybe that wasn't true. A hundred times, he'd thought about branching off on his own. He had the talent. He wrote almost every song the band ended up using. He played enough instruments to be able to handle a solo album at a reasonable cost.

What he didn't have was the guts. Right now, if something the Blue Hills did failed, he could blame someone else. James's bass line. Wes's overlay on the drums. Jax. Going solo would mean all the risk would be Eli's and his alone. It wasn't just scary, it was petrifying.

So Eli stayed with the band.

Besides, he didn't want to push Jax. Not after what Jax had gone through in the last year. Jax needed Eli, whether he knew it or not, and Eli felt obliged to that. Especially because, despite all the trouble, Jax was very much like a brother.

A spoiled brother who always got his way.

"Whatever, man. If that's what you really want." Eli caught Wes's eye over the drum set and made a tiny face. Wes gave him a sympathetic shrug and twirled a stick. Turning back to his singer, Eli sighed. "Then I guess we can do that. Should we take it from the top?"

"You'll see, Eli. This is going to become our signature moment. I can feel it, right here." Jax gestured to himself in a manner that could have suggested either his gut or his crotch. Considering this was undoubtedly a strategy to collect more starry-eyed groupies, he really could have meant either one. When Jax talked about connecting with his audience, he invariably meant eye-fucking the front-row chicks.

Regardless of the origins of Jax's mysterious intuition, Eli was forced to accept that yet another of his songs had just gotten dumbed down and mangled, and also that the audience would unfailingly respond to it. It was undeniable, the magnetism Jax exuded onstage. If he'd sing the songs the way they were intended, he'd nail them. And they'd be good. But he had his own style and adapted all of Eli's work to fit it at one point or another. It was probably a miracle this song had lasted two months already.

With another deep breath, Eli picked up his instrument and signaled to the guys. The rest of practice passed in a blur of the usual. Long rehearsals were fairly routine this close to a tour, and with long rehearsals came tension. It was unavoidable. Musicians weren't meant to be locked up in a studio, listening to themselves play. It was fun for a while, but just like sex, it was better with a partner. In this instance, the partner being the audience.

But rehearsal was necessary. Mostly it was making sure the newer songs were tight, but also making sure everyone remembered how to do the older ones. It was always a little surprising how songs they'd written themselves, played a hundred times, and perfected could somehow grow fuzzy in their memories after a year's absence.

When it was over, Eli packed up as quickly as he could. His banjo and mandolin went in the passenger seat, and he went back to help Wes pack up the van. He rushed, glancing at his phone every three seconds to check the time. Practice had gone late, and he had a date.

Well, date-ish.

Well, a regular thing.

Well, he had a *thing*, anyway.

Okay fine, he was supposed to be online. This was exactly why he hadn't told anyone about his friendship with LoveCoda, because there was no real way to explain it. He was the first person to get judgey when his friends signed up for online dating. He'd grown up with the Internet, but even as a preteen, AOL chat rooms had held no appeal for him.

All those people misrepresenting themselves, even more than they did in person? No thank you. *Give me an evening of beer and board games any day, and I'll tell you who someone really is.*

But the Internet had proven a useful networking tool, and when he'd discovered the SoWriAn forum, he was instantly smitten. A thousand people, just like him, writing down their feelings in a form that rhymed. No one was concerned with what they looked like, or how old the person they critiqued was—and not just because that information wasn't allowed to be disclosed. It was just artistry in its purest form.

He'd be embarrassed to admit to his real-life friends how many online friends he now had. And yet, these were people who understood him in ways the guys he'd gone to school with never would. Who better to discuss the impulse to write that pulled him out of a dream at four in the morning and sent him to his notebook? No one else would *get* hiding in a bathroom at a party because something a drunk girl said sparked a chorus that had to be captured before it was forgotten.

Writers were a different breed, and no one would ever get it except other writers.

On SoWriAn, Eli could talk about the chaos that came with reaching a certain level of success. He could bitch about the time and energy it took to chase a dream without seeming ungrateful. It was also the only place he could vent about Jax and share his dreams of going solo. Eli vented and shared there often. Well, he vented and shared with one person there—LoveCoda.

LoveCoda and he had been spending basically every night talking music since they'd met almost ten months ago on the Write or Die boards. It had been casual at first, talking to each other only in group forums. Then it was an occasional note sent with a question, maybe, or a recommendation of a new album to check out. Over time, they'd gotten closer, and now they private messaged each other every day.

Truth be told, if Eli ever got the balls to cut a solo album, it would be because of LoveCoda. She encouraged him and supported him. She also seemed to accept his reasons for staying with the band, even though he'd never told her all of it.

In return, Eli had been strength for LoveCoda through her writer's block. Just because he didn't know the source of it, man did he know the feel of it. The few occasions in his life he'd been blocked he felt like a fish out of water, just gasping for the life force that normally surrounded him.

But, though the heart of their talk centered on their music issues, they had a connection that went far beyond. At least, Eli thought they did. Their conversations were the highlight of his days. Things she said online, comments she made clung to him through the rest of his life.

Tonight, they were trying something new. They were going to watch a movie "together" while messaging. They both had Netflix. They just had to choose something from their library and push play at the same time. Like a weird, postmodern blind date. Through the Internet.

Woot. Next level shit, right here.

But even as he ridiculed himself in his head, he was superexcited. This chick—even if it wasn't obvious from her profile, she'd made it clear she was of the female gender on many occasions—was so intelligent that he knew she'd have tons to say about whatever they chose.

So maybe it wasn't exactly a date. It was songwriting related, after all. The idea was to watch each other's favorites, and write songs about them. It was a plan he'd devised to help her with her block, but he was actually really looking forward to the creative possibilities it opened for him as well.

The songs Eli wrote for his band had a certain style, a brand even. It had been ages since he'd written a song for himself, something that was just his, the way the poems he'd jotted down as a teenager had been special and private. Those should clearly never see the light of day, but it was the *feeling* he wanted to recapture, that of something rare and precious nailed down like an Amazon explorer discovering a new butterfly. It belonged to its environment, and yet the display made people gasp in recognition of beauty.

So with his innate talent for capturing emotion and nailing its wings down—to continue the disgusting metaphor—he figured this would be the best writing exercise he'd had since college. He was supposed to choose first, and he'd been thinking about it all day, but still hadn't narrowed anything down.

For an artist, no matter the genre, it was always going to be difficult to pinpoint a favorite movie. As a songwriter, he was kind of obsessed with *Once*. As a psych major, it was *Memento*. As a dude, *The Dark Knight*. As a childhood remnant, he still found *Return to Oz* terrifying and inspirational.

But were any of those choices inspiring to *her*? Would they be enough to spark the perfect words in her brain, the plot and characters enough to rattle her block out of place?

Anything it takes, he had said, but what exactly would it take? He was afraid it might take a lot. The boards were meant to be entirely anonymous, and they really were, but he did know this about LoveCoda—she had suffered a loss. A deep loss. And that was the cause of her block.

The other thing he knew about her was that she was insanely talented. Most people wouldn't get how he could know that when he hadn't read anything she'd written recently, but she'd shared a few older pieces, and they were good. Damn good. Make-him-want-to-pick-up-his-mandolin-and-add-a-line kind of good.

Even if someone else could dismiss LoveCoda as just a hack, though, as someone who wrote a couple of ditties in high school and that was the extent of her songwriting repertoire, Eli knew better. He'd sent her tabs and lyrics on about fifteen of his own songs and she'd sent them back with the most incredible feedback. A hack couldn't do that. From advice on single notes to the absolutely brilliant one-word changes that made his songs almost sing themselves, he knew this girl had It. The elusive *It* that everyone was after.

At eleven thirty-one—a minute past their intended meeting time—Eli pulled up both browsers on his laptop, with SoWriAn on one and the movie rental site on the other.

Hey, you. It was his standard greeting, but it never failed to make him a little nervous. So stupid, this face-less, nameless girl giving him butterflies. But yet.

Hey yourself. How was practice? The standard non-greeting, that still gave him that excited feeling in his stomach.

Meh. Changed a song I was really happy with. Less happy now, but what can you do? Well, he could do plenty, but not if he wanted to stay in the band. And the band had been the best thing Eli had going for years now.

What?! Which one? Anything I know?

Godric's Hollow.

Shut. Up. That song was brilliant. Tell me it's just pitch changes. He smiled big at the screen. That song he'd workshopped with LoveCoda until it was one of the best he'd ever written. She had a vested interest in it.

I wish. The band thought the chorus should go. "The band" wasn't exactly the truth, but the band wasn't about to cross Jax, so it was still mostly the truth. Also, it was kind of embarrassing to admit how much he rolled over for his singer. He had a feeling that even if he explained his reasons—very valid reasons—it would come out lame. And it was heavy conversation for a girl you were trying to impress. Or—not impress, maybe, but inspire. Yeah. In-spire.

Uhhhh . . . Go? Like . . . what do you do instead of a chorus? It's called a chorus because it is a chorus. I'm utterly lost. She understood the pain of having someone else screw around with your emotions.

I completely agree. And I thought the chorus was the thing that made the song, but we're moving it to a call-and-response type thing instead. We'll see how people like it. If it sucks, I'll get to change it back. If it works, it works, yeah?

If it sucks, how do you know they won't want to cut the song altogether? Good question. Sometimes, honesty sucked.

I guess I don't know that. But we've played it a number of times in rehearsal and it felt good, so I assume we can go back to that.

Oh, God, I don't mean to make you feel insecure! I just worry about you.

Eli grinned at the monitor again. She was absolutely right the first time. If the "yeah yeahs" didn't work, Jax would likely eighty-six the entire number from their shows.

She was so easy to talk to that he could go on about his own troubles for hours. He even bet that she'd understand about Jax if he ever got the nerve to explain. And he would. One day. Just not tonight.

He poised his fingers over his keyboard and typed. *Let's not even worry about that. If I recall correctly, we're having a moment about YOU right now. Ready to start watching? There are new songs to be written.*

I was hoping you'd forget. ☺ Not really. I'm just nervous. This is a really good idea, but I might not be able to—what if I mess it up?

Shut up. How would you mess it up? He was the one who should be nervous. What if *he* mucked it up by choosing a movie that didn't hit her at all creatively?

I feel like the only songs I can write right now are silly. Remember Glen Hansard's Broken Hearted Hoover Fixer Sucker Guy? Yeah. Me.

You shut up. That song is kind of brilliant. It expresses every single thing he's feeling, in an unconventional way. And you know the movie Once. And that makes me so happy. Maybe this was a sign that it was the flick to choose.

One of my favorites. Doi.

Yeah, LoveCoda was pretty much perfect.

And he suddenly changed his mind about what they should watch together. He was surprised he hadn't thought of it earlier—a sappy classic bound to inspire anyone. Plus it had a songwriting B character that he just knew Love-Coda had to admire.

So tell me, Love, how long has it been since you've seen Say Anything? He held his breath while he waited for her answer. It would be fine if she said she'd never seen it, but what if she hated it? That would put a dent in the image he'd created regarding this mysterious stranger.

It's been ages. There was a pause before her next words appeared. *But it's definitely a favorite. So are we watching?*

He was wrong. LoveCoda wasn't *pretty much* perfect. She was *completely* perfect. He was grinning as he typed his response.

Already got it cued.

Chapter Six

"*I wrote . . .*" Lacy sang a capella before tearing into the guitar, "*sixty-three songs about you. I'm gonna play them, whoa, all tonight.*" *Nope.*

That wasn't even lyrics. That was just taking lines directly from a movie and attempting to put them to the most generic chord pattern possible. Blocked or not, she was better than this.

She moved on to "Take Nineteen," though she was pretty sure she'd hit "Take Nineteen" several times over now. "*It's all working out like we planned, it was all working out like we planned, until it stopped working, and now, hey isn't life grand.*"

Double nope.

Maybe she needed to retune. She adjusted her G string before trying something else. "*A little ditty, bout Lloyd and Diane . . .*"

Hopeless.

It had been a great idea, and an even greater night. Watching *Say Anything* with Folx had been fun and maybe even a touch romantic. She'd completely forgotten about her childhood crush on Lloyd Dobbler. The movie was, at its heart, as Folx reminded her, about honesty, about letting go. Two qualities he clearly noticed she was lacking in her songwriting.

And that was exactly her hang-up here too. How could she write a song about honesty? About letting go? She'd been so tightlipped about Lance and his death that she hadn't even shared the story with Folx. *But it's not because I'm holding onto anything.* There was just no reason to jump into that drama.

Which was fine for her to understand, but it didn't get her anywhere with a freaking song.

She set her guitar down.

Then she picked it up again. She wasn't going to let Folx down. Or herself. "*I'm afraid to fly, I'm afraid. I'm afraid to die, on a plane.*"

Blech.

It just wasn't coming to her. She stopped trying for lyrics, and started playing Peter Gabriel's "In Your Eyes" on Lucky instead. One riff led to another, and next thing she knew, she was just jamming out. *At least I can still play.*

Playing wasn't enough, though, and it wasn't the point of the exercise. Her fingers weren't blocked, after all. Blowing out a deep breath, she tried again. And again. Nothing was coming.

Maybe if I watched it again.

She cued up the movie, and sat in front of it with her guitar. As the familiar scenes played out, she strummed along, here a major, here a minor. Ninety minutes later, she had half a dozen viable chord progressions.

Not a lyric in sight.

Again. She restarted the film, this time with a notebook to copy down her favorite lines. Halfway through, the movie was starting to seem as trite and boring as the stray couplets she'd managed to scribble down here and there.

Also, half the day was gone, and she hadn't even eaten. She tossed her notebook aside and wandered out to find her sister.

Andy was lounging on the couch with a book in her hand. "There's leftovers in the fridge. I had Chinese with Blake earlier." Lacy padded over to inspect the contents. *Sesame chicken, score. No crab Rangoon, crap. Crab, crap. Crab crap. Five times fast. Could that be a song?*

Stop thinking and eat; you're delirious.

"I'm a little surprised you aren't with him, actually. Isn't Sunday normally your lazy day together?" Lacy stuck the box in the microwave and stared at it rotating through the little window, as if that would speed up the timer.

"Yeah, but I wanted to finish this book. It's better than I thought it would be." She vaguely gestured to the copy of *A Woman's Education* next to her on the cushion.

"Noah's book!" Their downstairs neighbor, Noah, was an in-the-closet erotic romance writer. Lacy had read his book as well, which often made it hard to make eye contact with him in the corridor. "It really is good. Why can't you read during Lazy Sunday?"

Deciding she didn't care about heat so much as just shoving something in her mouth, Lacy pulled the box out early and snagged a pair of chopsticks from the silverware drawer.

"It just seems rude." Andy patted the couch beside her for Lacy to join.

Lacy didn't get it. When Lance was alive, they spent plenty of time together not focused on the same thing. She plopped down. "You guys are engaged."

"Yeah?"

"That means you're getting married." Lacy couriered a bite to her lips, which burned, even as the inside turned to cold mush in her mouth. *Dammit. There are no shortcuts. Back to the microwave.*

"I know."

Really, sometimes Andy was such a dunce. "So, when the portentous event occurs, and you're living together, what are you going to do then if you want to pick up a book?"

"I know, I know. But somehow when you're living together, it doesn't seem weird to be in the same space but doing different things. Now, when I go over there, it's like there's some invisible pressure that I feel to do what he's doing. I mean, it's not like he picks all the things, but you know what I mean. We watch movies, or play pinball, or walk Puppy. It seems not cool to show up at his house, and then be like, 'Oh hey, I'll just be over here while you do that.'"

Lacy rolled her eyes at her sister from the kitchen, where she was once again staring down the small carton on its revolving trip. "Okay. I guess I get what you're saying. But it's still weird."

"I've always been weird, Lace. Get used to it."

"True that," Lacy muttered under her breath. Though, maybe Andy did have a point. Lacy and Lance had lived together during their engagement, while Andy was still living with her. Perhaps that made it different. Or maybe just relationships were different in general.

She wondered what she'd be like with Folx. Would she feel obligated to do what he was doing just because they were in the same room?

And what a stupid thing to be wondering because she and Folx had never been in the same room together, and at this rate, they never would be. The truth of that hit Lacy like bad crab Rangoon—she would never be in a room with Folx. Never see him in person. Never know if the feelings that she was currently nursing could grow into anything more.

Lots of "nevers" with no hope of becoming "somedays."

Not unless one of them got the balls to move their on-line relationship forward. And if she was waiting for that to be Folx . . . why?

Well, holy Chinese-food-inspired epiphany.

She could just as easily ask the questions that pressed at her whenever she thought about him. *Could they be something more than friends? Were they already? Would he be willing to find out? Did she want to?*

The microwave buzzed, shaking Lacy from her contemplation. It was certainly an idea to think further on. She didn't have to conjure up the guts to go forward with it right at that moment.

"Hey, it sounded like you were really on a roll in there," Andy called from the other room. "Wanna play me anything?"

Lacy was pulling out the carton with two fingers, getting burned, blowing on them, and repeating the process. The universal Dance of Nuking. Luckily, that gave her time to get a hold of her answer.

"Nah, I need to step away for a little while, get fresh before I finish that one." It was getting easier and easier to tell this particular lie. The one where she had been writing the whole time. The one where she wasn't a pathetic hack.

"No worries. I'm just curious to hear the new stuff."

She hadn't even told Andy about the change in her studio schedule because she knew she'd press Lacy to play her album list. Then she'd have to confess.

God, when had she become such a wimp? She'd always thought of herself as a strong person.

That was it. She couldn't live with herself if she was afraid of everything. Old Lacy would kick New Lacy's ass over this stuff. Though she wasn't ready to admit she was blocked in the songwriting department, she could at least get up the nerve to ask Folx about their relationship.

Next time they talked, she promised herself, she'd be brave. She'd be bold.

Lacy returned to the sofa and sat so her feet were on Andy's lap.

"Do you wanna hear the text Tim sent me at five in the morning today?"

Lacy smiled at her sister. "Obviously. Five in the morning on a Sunday? Does he sleep?" At least her evasion had gone well. Better than usual. And with her decision made about Folx, she felt slightly less pathetic than she had a minute before.

Eli was cracking up.

Tonight he'd agreed to give LoveCoda a rest on the songwriting help—he could practically hear the frustration through the instant messenger when she told him she'd watched the movie three more times with no success. Now they were doing what they did best—goofing off. She'd once told him that *Pitch Perfect* was her go-to Happy Place, but he hadn't seen it. So now, instead of watching a movie and hoping to derive Meaning and Inspiration, they were watching and deriving pleasure.

He probably shouldn't be online at all. It was after midnight, and he had a bus to catch in the morning. Tour time, which should make him excited. And he was. He loved performing his material in front of a live audience. Just . . . the whole band experience was beginning to seem old. But he felt so protective of Jax. Responsible. He couldn't think about leaving. Not now.

So he was going on tour in the morning. He should be focusing on that instead of laughing at the ins and outs of a capella. Though, what else did he need to do to get ready? Minus the mandolin sitting at his feet, he was already packed. And he could sleep on the drive.

He kept *Pitch Perfect* on.

The current scene featured the characters at a party after they had been initiated into their singing groups. Something about it nagged that little spot in his mind where the words lived. There was a song there, he was sure. Something about that almost psychic connection with someone else, where even in a gigantic party, you are somehow always aware of where they are relative to you. Something about the way the ambient noise fades and all you can hear is the melody of their voice. Something about how he was suddenly positive that he'd know LoveCoda even in the biggest crowd. A memory of the Blue Hills' last show sparked and flickered at the edge of his perception but faded as a tune flared up and eclipsed it.

He grabbed his mandolin and started to pick out the notes that were now surging through him. LoveCoda was repeating—typeating?—her favorite lines from the movie now with long strings of *ahahahaha*'s. It was so cute to see her happy—a genuine happiness that transferred through the machines and wires and satellite dishes that separated them.

He started jotting down lyrics.

Wake up to the buzz of progress
Another day, lightning striking
Life happening, high-speed passing
Everything around me
Chaos
In motion
And then you . . .
I hear you in the noise
I hear you in the noise

This disarray was unexpected
Advancing, closing in around me
But years I've waited for this take off

Breath held and I'm
Soaring
In motion
And then you . . .
I hear you in the noise
I hear you in the noise

Then there's stillness
Silence
Peace of mind
I hear you in the noise
And I remember
What I'm fighting for

I hear you in the noise

He half paid attention to the movie and her responses to it for the duration of the time it took to write down his song. The first song he'd really written for *her*. Jesus. Eli had to admit it—this girl, this anonymous girl, was so much realer to him than anyone he'd met in person.

He looked back up, finally, to see the main character surrounded by DVDs in her bed, *Say Anything* being the closest to her. Eli wasn't normally a man of faith, but this had the "coincidence" of a Higher Power written all over it. Love was commenting on it as well in the browser. He set his instrument aside and wrote back.

See, it really is one of the best music movies ever.

He smiled to see the little line turn into dots, indicating she was writing back. The dots disappeared then reappeared a bunch of times. So that struck a chord. Figuratively. Or literally. Who could tell the difference these days between those words?

Crybaby.

Ah, another music movie. Point to Love. That one was amazing.

Beyond the Valley of the Dolls.

He gave himself a point. The Carrie Nations was his favorite fictional band. Plus that movie was so bizarre, every time he watched it he was startled all over again.

Her next response came quickly. ***Spiceworld.***

What is wrong with you? He didn't really mean it, but kind of he did.

No one has answered that question yet.

And he hoped no one ever would. This chick was into John Waters, Glen Hansard, *and* the Spice Girls? She was probably the biggest genius he'd never met.

The Punk Singer.

Her dotted line was absent for five minutes after that. Had he said the wrong thing? That documentary was the most glorious celebration of women in music he had ever seen. He assumed Love would feel the same? Maybe he should have typed *Searching for Sugar Man*, another brilliant doc, less edgy.

This time when he picked up his mando, it was for comfort. Something had gone wrong somewhere in the conversation. Then the dots picked up again.

You're hot.

He laughed out loud. So it *was* the right answer. ***You are.***

He thrilled a little bit. Or a lot. They were nearly flirting. It was . . . nice.

Not for the first time, or fifteenth, he wondered what she looked like. There was an image in his head, but who could say if it was accurate? When he imagined LoveCoda, he pictured someone beautiful and capable. Tall-ish. Intense. Her eyes would be captivating. Beyond that, though, things got fuzzy. Blonde or brunette? Redhead, even? No idea.

He hummed a few bars of the song he'd just written for her. Wow. Of all the songs he'd worked on in their partnership, this was the first one directly inspired by her. It was also one of his best.

This was so stupid, this charade they were keeping up. He wanted to play her this song. His fingers hovered over the keys, trying to figure out how to ask her—what, exactly? He let his fingers drop. He didn't even know what he wanted, except that she be involved in whatever it was.

But then she was writing back: *Folx? I know I'm not supposed to ask . . .*

His heart rate quickened. Could she really be so in tune with him that she was thinking the same thing? *Go ahead . . .*

He hit return and tried not to be hopeful. She probably just wanted to find out the name of his band, or something like that.

Do you have a girlfriend? Or a boyfriend? It's the twenty-first century, I shouldn't assume.

He felt like pumping his fist in the air, but, even though they were in different spaces, he was afraid the movement would shatter the fragile moment that he so wanted to cling to. So instead, he scooted his chair closer to his desk, zoning everything out but the screen and her words and his answer. *I don't have either. And if I did, it would be a girlfriend.*

He paused long enough to get the courage to ask the inevitable return question. *How about you?*

Time stood still as he waited.

Neither. And if I did, it would be a boyfriend.

Eli let out the breath he didn't know he'd been holding, and he grinned. Ear-to-ear grinned. *That makes me happier than it probably should.*

Same here. Can we be totally honest? All cards on the table and all that?

Yes. Hell, yes. He'd tell her anything. Confess anything. Commit to anything. Just as long as the conversation kept going in this direction.

I think about you.

Eli read that line again. Then once more before going on to the rest.

I know, it's crazy because I've never met you in real life. I don't even know how old you are or if you're interested in that kind of relationship with someone you met online.

He'd never even thought about her age. What if she were fifty? Or worse, sixteen? Probably not, though, because no sixteen-year-old he knew was into the Spice Girls.

Never mind that he didn't know any sixteen-year-olds. It was just an educated guess.

When it came down to it, though, he didn't care how old she was. He didn't even care what she looked like. Okay, he cared, but he didn't think her looks mattered as much as they might have had he not already learned how kickass she was.

He liked what he had with LoveCoda. He liked it enough to want more. He showed his cards. *I'm thirty-one. And I'm interested.*

In case he hadn't been clear enough he added, *I'm interested in you.*

He imagined her breath catching. Even though he didn't know her in real life, didn't know her gestures or her mannerisms, he imagined her breath catching because that was the response he hoped she had. If he were not so intent on holding on to his manhood, his breath would have caught. Many times over at this point.

So now what?

He wasn't ready for that. He wanted to hear her say it back—see her type it back. *Well, first, I think, you should clarify if you feel the same. If you have the same interest.*

I do. Of course, I do. I'm the one who brought it up.

Had she been the one? He'd forgotten already, feeling as though he'd been the one. It had been his intention. He just hadn't figured out how to ask.

Also, I'm twenty-six.

You're a baby. He was teasing. He had no problems with her age. Not one.

Also, holy hell, he hoped the moderators weren't watching this. He could live with being kicked off the forum—as long as he got LoveCoda's info first—but he didn't want a lawsuit on his hands. He'd just tossed all the rules out the window.

Shut up. The dots of typing appeared and stopped. Appeared and stopped. Appeared again. She was trying to decide what to say next. Finally, she repeated her last question. *So now what?*

Good question.

He didn't even know where she lived. She could be across the country. Outside the country, even. Honestly, it didn't matter. He'd go wherever she was just to be able to meet her.

Only, he couldn't right now. He had the damn tour. Trying not to regret his obligations, he answered. *We should meet. But I have commitments right now. And so do you—you have that album.*

If I met you in person, maybe I could find my inspiration. She added both a smiley face and a heart at the end of her sentence. It was all he could do not to kiss the screen.

I wish. God, did he wish. *But I'm booked. How about this—we set a date for the future. And we meet.*

Several seconds passed, and Eli wondered if he'd misread her. Or if the admins of the site had found them out and cut their communication. Maybe that was overly paranoid. But then why wasn't she saying anything?

Then she typed. And her response appeared. *Like*

Sleepless in Seattle? Meet on New Year's on top of the Empire State Building? But not on the Empire cuz I'm afraid of heights.

Sleepless in Seattle. No band reference, but a great soundtrack. And I know about the heights. See? This wasn't ridiculous. They'd already shared enough details for him to know these random things about her. *And not New Year's—that's too far away.* His tour lasted only two months, but he didn't want to get in the way of her recording. When had she said that was happening? *Ten weeks.* He'd add a month to his own commitment to cover hers. *Christmas Eve. Three months from now.*

I have a thing on Christmas Eve. There was a pause in her typing. *But if you would want to come as my date. . . . It's formal and would require a tux so I'd understand if that doesn't work.*

I'll rent a tux. A formal first date would give him extra points with her, and he wanted all the points he could get. Besides, it would be easier to get away from his mom and her sisters and their total holiday extravaganza if he had an official type of place to be.

Cool. It's a date. I'll give you more details when we're closer. In the meantime?

In the meantime he'd keep holding onto her like he had been. How long had it been since he'd looked at another woman? How long since he'd shared a meaningful glance? Except for the chick in the crowd at the show the other night, it had been a while. Because he already thought of himself as weirdly "with" LoveCoda.

He couldn't quite say, *I think of you as my kind-of girlfriend.* He didn't want to scare her off, after all.

He thought carefully before entering his response. *We meet here online. Like we do. No commitment. Just friends with the promise of a possible more.*

Ha. A possible more. There's a song in that . . .

WRITE IT.

So Love might be blocked, but she still saw music in her surroundings. Saw music in their relationship. As if she were meant for him, sight unseen.

His screen was quiet for long moments. Eli began to wonder if Love really had gone off to spin a lyric. Or maybe she'd gone to the bathroom or to get a snack. Or the moderators had cut her account, which was unlikely since her icon was still lit up.

Or, maybe things were going to be awkward between them now. God, please don't let that be the case. He couldn't allow that to happen. He poised his hands above the keys to say something—*anything*—to reestablish their natural repartee.

But before he could think of something witty yet light, he saw the dots indicating she was typing.

How did we not even include Spinal Tap? We have failed.

And his worrying was over.

Chapter Seven

Lacy side-eyed the calendar as she signed off on her time card and didn't know whether to frown or smile. Each day that passed was one day closer to Andy's wedding, which meant one day closer to her date with Folx. Perhaps it had been an odd day to choose to meet him, but he'd chosen Christmas Eve first. When he'd said it—typed it—it felt right. She had a feeling she'd prefer having a date among all the Andy/Blake love, so why not with Folx?

Of course she hadn't explained to him that it was a wedding. She didn't want the mods to see, for one, but also, she was afraid the word might sound scary. Weddings as dates were for serious relationships. Somehow, though, she didn't think he would be scared by it so much as she was scared to say it. Anyway, he'd find out soon enough.

But also, each day that passed was another day closer to her studio session. Another day without a song written. She had only nine weeks left to pull this record out of thin air. At what point should she admit it to Darrin so he could book the studio time with another, paying, customer?

Not yet, she told herself. But really the words were

Folx's. She knew it was what he'd tell her. *Not yet. Don't give up yet.*

For that matter, Lance would have said the same thing. He'd never failed to be supportive and not in the "little gestures" way, but in the big ways. He was the guy who lugged all her equipment from gig to gig and hand-sold copies of her first CD to everyone he knew. He knew when she had a good song before she did, and he'd make sure she finished it. His faith in her was endless.

God, Lance . . . I feel like I'm cheating on you. But you left. You left me.

Sometimes she missed him so *so* much.

But now there was Folx, singing the same sentiments Lance would have. He made her truly believe he wouldn't give up on her either.

Still, it was with a heavy heart that she hefted the strap of her guitar case on her shoulder and turned to leave the studio.

"Oh, my God, Lacy! You're still here!"

Kat's shrill voice cut into Lacy's backside from down the hall. She closed her eyes momentarily, praying for the strength to turn around and face her sometimes friend with a smile. Her prayers were half answered—she found the energy to turn around, but she couldn't manage anything more than a tight line of her lips. At least she wasn't scowling.

Lacy didn't even have to say anything. Kat closed the distance between them in five bouncy steps, sort of like a real-life Tigger, and threw her arms around Lacy.

Crap, Lacy thought through an inhale of patchouli. *Now what?*

Kat leaned back, her hands still on Lacy's shoulders. "Guess what. You'll never guess though, so I'm just telling you. OMG you won't believe it. And you're going to love me so hard. Ah! I can't believe this is happening!"

"What, Kat? Just spit it out." She was not in the mood

for exuberance. Did her coworker just land another gig she'd wanted?

"Remember the Blue Hills? Remember Wes, the drummer?"

Lacy could honestly say she didn't remember the drummer, but she certainly remembered the Blue Hills. "Of course. They were hot. I mean, their music was hot."

"Well, they just left on a two-month tour of the Northeast, and their opening act had to cancel because he had a twerking incident. That look you're giving me is exactly the expression I had too. But we've all seen those YouTube vids, and this guy is apparently almost sixty but wanted to be cool and tried it at a show, which is weirdest because his music is ultra folk and doesn't lend itself to twerking at all, but anyway he injured his back. Both his disc—and his pants—slipped, ensuring the end of his music career for the time being at least, and hopefully the end of his twerking career forever.

"Anyway, again. That means no opening act and they're looking for someone last minute, and a few weeks ago I gave Wes your CD that you burned last year and he gave it to his manager and Wes just called me and they want you and that's so amazing that I can hardly contain myself so congratulations and you're welcome!"

Lacy was pretty sure that Kat hadn't breathed once during her monologue. For that matter, neither had she. Did Kat just say she'd gotten her a two-month gig? "Um, what?"

"I booked you a tour. If you want it. With the Blue Hills." Thank God, Kat slowed her speech this time.

"Oh, my God." Lacy was shaking. "Oh, my God, oh, my God." And she was talking like Kat and now she was even hugging Kat, patchouli and all. Lacy pushed aside her guilt at being so resentful, promised herself she'd stop being pissy that Kat had never suffered like she had. The girl had just given her the greatest gift ever.

"Can you be ready by one tomorrow? Wes said they'd send a car to take you to Worchester to meet them, but I told them not to bother. I'll totally take you. They'll reimburse me, of course. Sound check is at three. You'd go on tomorrow night."

"Oh, my God." Lacy took a deep breath. She'd been lacking in words lately, but she certainly could do better than repeating the same trite phrase over and over. After one more calming inhale and exhale, she opened her mouth to say yes.

Then she remembered her responsibilities.

But before she could bring them up, Kat said, "Don't worry about the studio. I can cover all your shifts."

"Are you sure?" Because that would be . . . awesome.

"Am I sure?" Kat's eyes went wide with unbelief. "Yes, I'm sure. It's not like we're getting that many hours anyway. Win-win situation here."

"Wow. Just . . . wow." Lacy's mind raced. Could she really do this? On such short notice? She had a couple of gigs scattered through the next month but nothing she couldn't easily cancel. This was a once-in-a-lifetime opportunity, after all. Touring with a band as up-and-coming as the Blue Hills could make her own career. And living and breathing music again—gah, she needed that like peanut butter needed jelly. Really, there was almost nothing that would be worth her *not* taking the job.

Except.

Dammit.

Andy.

Andy had made it clear that Lacy was the only thing getting her through the wedding plans. Of course she didn't really need Lacy, but she wasn't so sure her sister realized that. And if she didn't, and Lacy left, then Andy would be pissed and her whole wedding would be ruined.

Or maybe Lacy was just used to feeling like Andy

needed her. But did she really? There had been a time when she had. When she was out of a job and out of a home. But now she had an amazing job and a man she loved and, actually, Andy was doing just fine.

And if anyone would understand that this tour was an amazing opportunity, it would be Andy. She had been Lacy's biggest fan since her first ukulele at age three, rocking out to "Twinkle Twinkle Little Star."

"Well?" Kat prodded. "Don't leave me hanging!"

"Yes," Lacy said with as much excitement and thrill and trepidation as when she'd said the same word to Lance. "I'll do it. Thank you, Kat!"

After a phone call with the Blue Hills' manager to work out details and another twenty minutes of squealing and celebrating with Kat, Lacy left for home to pack. She was so excited that she almost splurged and took a cab. Then she remembered that would only get her to her apartment sooner . . . and to Andy. So she decided to take the train.

She needed time to decide how to break the news.

"No way," Andy said from the doorway, her worried look overtaking her features. "No. You're not going. You aren't ready."

"What, are you my mother?" After a half bottle of wine and three of her favorite truffles, Lacy had thought Andy would be more amiable to the idea of her going on tour. Her old tricks had seemingly lost their effect. Damn Tim and his strong-arm (strong-drink?) ways. He'd ruined all other methods of persuasion.

So there would be no persuasion. She understood. It hadn't been that long since Andy had been able to stop reminding Lacy to do basic things, like shower.

So she'd just have to show her.

A ping from her open Internet browser distracted her and she stopped there on her way to her closet, hoping it was Folx It was nearly midnight, but he'd told her he would be on later than usual for the next while. She knew he was touring. It felt right that they were both touring at the same time.

Hey, you.

It was him. With an uncontainable smile, Lacy typed, *Hey! I have good news!*

"No, I'm not your mother," Andy said, coming into the bedroom. "But apparently I'm the voice of reason at the moment."

The smile disappeared from Lacy's face. How could she convince her sister that a hint of Old Lacy was finally pushing through, when she'd been so poorly pretending the same for so long?

Another ping. *News? What kind of news?*

God, she wanted to tell him. Tell him all of it. Especially with Andy being so overprotective. Lacy needed Folx's support. But the silly site rules said she couldn't. They'd already crossed the line when he admitted to being on tour. Then a million more lines when they disclosed their ages and agreed to hook up in the future. She needed a contingency plan for that. Later.

Love?

He was still waiting for her response. She decided to be vague. *I booked a gig. Like, a big gig. Like, a career-changing gig.*

!!!! I'm so excited for you that I can't convey it in simple text. Congrats, Love. You deserve this.

"Are you even listening to me? This is not a good idea."

Lacy stood up from her computer screen and faced her sister, hands on her hips. Her sister-thing was kicking in, and even though she completely understood why Andy was opposed, she felt like a little kid getting a talking-to. "Why? What's not a good idea about this? Tell me."

"Everything! It's last minute. You've never been on tour. How can you possibly be ready? You don't even know these people. A band full of men? No women? What if one of them tries to . . . I dunno, have his way with you? You know what they say about those rock star types."

"Jesus, are you for real? *Raped?*" Lacy was beginning to think the wine had been a bad idea. Instead of calming her sister, it had only made her more creative with her reasoning.

She bent to type a quick response to Folx. *Thank you. I knew you'd be happy for me. You can't know how much that means to me.*

Then Lacy crossed to her dresser. "And they aren't rock stars. They're alternative folk musicians. Like myself. Which doesn't make any difference, really, because I'm not going to get forced into anything."

Lacy pulled a stack of T-shirts from a drawer, her eye catching on her very neglected vibrator buried underneath. "Besides, at this point, I'm not likely to say no to hot band-sex. If you haven't noticed, it's been a while." Honestly, the thought had only just now crossed her mind. Likely because she was talking to Folx. Also she had those . . . urges . . . the last time she'd seen the Blue Hills. So what if something happened with one of those fine musicians? There'd be no complaints from her. She had three months before she met Folx.

Lacy threw the pile of shirts in her suitcase and brushed past Andy to head toward her jeans drawer.

"Come on, you don't mean that. If you're ready to date again . . ."

The irony of her sister's statement was so hilarious, Lacy almost laughed. "Yeah, you cannot lecture me on that, Miss I Banged My Boss." It had been only the beginning of the summer when Lacy had a similar conversation with Andy, but their roles had been reversed. Andy hadn't listened to a word, obviously. So why should Lacy listen now?

Lacy chose three pairs of jeans, all tight and ripped up like she liked them, and also a couple of skirts before heading back to the suitcase. "And I said nothing about dating. I was talking sex. Release."

"I'll set you up with someone just to . . . you know." Andy's last job had been as a matchmaker, and apparently she thought she was still in the business. "What about the erotic writer guy? Noah. He's cute."

"Noah's with Jaylene, you know, our neighbor! Do you not pay attention to anything that goes on around here?" She knew Andy was distracted, but really. They'd had Jaylene over for drinks and heard all the yummy details.

Andy rubbed her fingers across her forehead. "Of course I do. I knew that. I simply had a momentary lapse in memory." Or she'd been desperate and reaching. "There's probably someone at Donovan Industries who'd be appropriate."

Of course I'm happy for you! Who wouldn't be? Maybe this is just the inspiration you need, Folx sent.

"Andy . . . please."

Who wouldn't be? Her own flesh and blood, that's who.

No, that wasn't fair. Andy was freaked that her little sis was overestimating what she was ready for. Lacy didn't want to talk about Andy with Folx though. *My thoughts exactly.*

"We're dancing around the point, anyway. Can we get back on topic? It's a great testament to your talent to book a tour from just your CD. I'm sure you're flattered and so you aren't thinking clearly. But trust me, this isn't what you need. You need to stay here and work on your next album."

Lacy turned to her underwear drawer then, so that Andy wouldn't see how irritated she was with her sister's condescension. "Not true. I can work on my album on the road like every other touring musician does. You're the one who needs me here. And you don't really need me."

"I do need you." Her sister's voice was somewhat desperate. "But that's not why I'm against this. It's bad timing. It's not safe. I haven't even met any of these men."

"Oh, hell, Andy. Would you just stop?"

"I will not stop. You are my sister. My baby sister. I know how much you still hurt, every single day, even though you pretend you're okay. You aren't okay. Not yet. You will be, but this is too soon. You're still too fragile."

"I'm not fragile, Andy. Not in the least. Why would you even think that? Because my fiancé offed himself a year ago? Because he left me alone to deal with his body and his belongings and this emotional baggage? Yeah, that sucked. But I'm fine. I've been fine. In fact, the only thing that has been *not fine* is all the people who treat me with kid gloves trying to protect me or coddle me. I need to move on. I need to spread wings and all that. This is my chance. Why would you not want that for me?" As soon as it was out, Lacy knew she'd maybe been too harsh.

Andy stared at her for a moment before bursting into tears. She threw herself down on the half of Lacy's bed the suitcase wasn't occupying.

"I'm sorry. I'm just—sorry. I'm scared."

Lacy shot a longing look at her laptop before snapping it shut and attending to Andy. Perching on the edge of the bed, she rubbed her big sister's back. This was the way it always seemed to end up with the two of them, with Lacy offering comfort instead of the other way around.

"Hey. I know. I remember, remember? Wedding planning is terrifying. Like Tim." That got a little grin out of Andy.

"I know you remember But I'm not afraid of the wedding planning. I'm not even afraid of crazy Tim. I'm afraid of losing you. If you're away from me, and off with a bunch of people—guys, no less—that you don't even know, how will I know you're okay? You barely talk to me about your feelings as is. Who will you talk to on the road?" She sniffled.

"I don't talk because I don't have anything to say right now. But when I do, you'll be the first to hear it. And you won't lose me. I'll call you every day and you can catch me up on the latest plans. This really is going to be good for me, you know. And good for you too."

"How is this supposed to be good for me? These are the last months of my single life. The last days we get to be together." And there it was. The truth. The real reason Andy had been pulling her to wedding planning meetings and going ballistic about a once-in-a-lifetime career opportunity.

The revelation pulled at Lacy's chest. Made her feel closer to Andy than she had in a while. Which was a nice feeling since she hadn't felt close to anyone lately.

Nice feeling or not, it left her a little speechless. "I didn't know you felt that way."

"Yeah. I do." Andy reached for a tissue, though her arm wasn't quite long enough. She wormed her way forward and stretched again. Lacy considered helping, but decided watching was more fun. On the fourth wiggle, she managed to grab one, though the box went toppling to the floor.

Lacy bit back a laugh. Then she reached a hand out to muss her sister's hair. "I'm glad you want to spend time with me. I kind of like you too." She winked. "But trust me—we'll still get time together after you're married. It's not like Blake's planning on chaining you up in the mansion and never letting you have visitors." She paused. "Except he is kind of caveman."

"He's not a caveman," Andy said with a scowl. "Well, mostly he's not a caveman."

Lacy smiled. "He's a little bit caveman, and he's perfect for you. But it doesn't mean he'll take you away from me. You were mine first."

"Actually, you were *mine* first."

Usually Lacy hated it when Andy pulled the big-sister card, but this time she let it slide. She let the smile fade from her face and put on her serious expression. The one that was hard to show even to herself. "I know I haven't been one hundred percent. And I'm really lucky that you've been here to help me through that. But I'm better now. I'm getting better, anyway. This tour is the next step. I promise I'll be okay. Okay?"

Andy nodded reluctantly. "Okay."

She blew her nose loudly and slid off the bed. "I'm still going to miss you though. You have to pinkie swear to call every day. And text sometimes." She held her fist out, pinkie extended.

"How about text everyday and call sometimes?"

"Fine. That."

Lacy interlocked her pinkie with her sister's, and they both kissed their thumbs. "So sworn. Now pick up my tissues, and don't you dare leave that nasty one lying on the bed. I'm not too mature to give you a wedgie."

Her sister managed a weak smile. "You're really going to do it, huh? Take off to find your fortune and leave me all alone with no one for solace."

This time Lacy let her laugh go. "You have Blake, silly. Remember him? Your husband-to-be?"

"Yes, yes. Of course. Blake. I love Blake. But he's not a replacement for my sister." She looked like she might cry again, but then she shook it off. "And he's not any help when it comes to Tim. Honestly? He came to the initial consult and walked out after five minutes. I found him in the bathroom, cry-laughing afterward. Weirdly, he adores that guy, but he can't keep a straight face around him. Anyway, I'll miss you. So don't wash your blankets so I can come in here and smell them when I get lonely. I'll cuddle up with them and cry. So when you think of me, just picture me lying on your bed. Throwing all the nasty tissues I want around."

"Ew. You're so gross."

Speaking of lying on my bed . . .

Lacy carefully removed Lance's pillow from his side of the bed and set it gently in her suitcase. It had remained there, unwashed and untouched, since the day of his suicide. She still felt him next to her at night with his pillow. If she was going to be staying the night away from their home for the first time since his death, that pillow was damn well coming with her. And away from those snotty tissues.

"You know who would just about shit and fall back in it if you invited her to help you plan? Kat. I can leave you her number."

Andy looked a little horrified. "Kat? She sets off my cray-dar, big-time. I don't know if I want her thinking we're friends."

"She does? I thought you liked her. Remember when we all used to go out? You always seemed to enjoy chatting. Kat's not all bad. And honestly, Andy, it's not like you have so many other friends there's no room for her." Lacy sat on her suitcase and started zipping.

"I was nice to her because I thought *you* liked her. Dammit. Without you around, maybe I *will* be forced to call her. Hey, how do you avoid that *perfume* she wears? Vicks VapoRub beneath your nostrils? I think cops do that in the morgue."

For all her faults, Lacy's big sister could be a real genius sometimes. She went to the bathroom and returned with the Vicks stowed safely in her purse for later.

Chapter Eight

The next day was a blur of preparation and excitement. Luckily, Andy had gone to work after breakfast so Lacy could focus. Their good-bye was tearful and sweet, and Lacy was forced to promise several times that she'd come home if it was terrible and talk to Andy every single day at least by text. It was emotional and draining and best to be done with early.

The rest of the morning, Lacy finished packing and worked on a few songs for the show. Kat arrived before noon so they had plenty of time to pack the car up and grab lunch before hitting the road. Lacy didn't even mind that they'd have an hour-long drive because it gave her someone to help plan her set list.

"You really didn't have to do this, Kat. I could have taken their car."

Kat made a pfft noise. "You think I'd let you play your first show on tour without someone you know in the audience? Hell, no. Darrin's got tonight covered in the studio, and I'll just drive back tomorrow." Lance had always said she was sugar beneath her patchouli. He was right.

"Besides, I'm hoping for a repeat with Wes. Did I mention how good he is with, um, tempos?"

"Please, don't," Lacy groaned. "He's my coworker now. I don't need to be thinking those kinds of thoughts about him." *Tempos*. If it were the banjo player, however, or even that too-pretty-to-touch lead singer . . .

There was an inner voice that wanted to tell Lacy to stop that line of thinking, but another voice said, *Hey, what happens, happens*. It was Lance's voice. She knew he'd want her to move on with her life, and that made it easy for her to think about being with another man guilt free. That asshole. How he could he be so selfish and leave her and still be the best man she'd ever known was irreconcilable sometimes. Now if only her muse would feel as generous and strike her with some damn songwriting inspiration.

Sigh.

But today wasn't for worrying about new material. It was for focusing on her current repertoire and making it sparkle. And focus on that she did. By the time they arrived in Worchester, she'd settled on a thirty-minute set of her best stuff and even had a couple of options for an encore if the opportunity so arose.

Lou, the Blue Hills' manager, was there to meet her when she arrived at the venue. He was bald and plump and talked faster than the most blue-blooded Bostonian, saying things like "kid" and "sweetheart." The perfect stereotype.

"Hey doll," he said when Lacy offered her hand. "Nah, that's not going to cut it." He pulled her into a hug that was professional, if hugs could be classified as such, and not skeevy at all. "After listening to your tracks I feel like I know you. We're on embracing terms."

Immediately, Lacy decided she'd like him.

"Your sound check's in fifteen. You got thirty minutes. Think you can handle that?"

"Yeah, sure. Where's the band?"

"They get the later sound check. Right before doors open. Privileges of being the headliner. Sorry, kid, you'll have to do the two trips to the venue thing each night."

"I'm cool with that." She was cool with anything at this point. Maybe she'd get a little more diva after a few tours under her belt, but right now she was all freshman and wide-eyed. "But I'd like to meet them at some point."

"Of course you do. And you will. Probably after the show. I'll do all the intros then and I'm sure they'll even take a pic or two with you for your social media if you ask nicely."

Oh. She hadn't realized there would be that type of segregation. Her face must have shown it.

"Don't worry, sweetheart. The boys are totally down-to-earth for the most part. And you'll all get bonding time on the bus. Just after the shows there's the fans and the pretty girls and . . . well, you know how it goes." He winked, and Lacy suddenly understood. The "boys" would want to mingle, so to say.

That was fine. She'd meet them tonight and chat with them tomorrow on the bus. Now that was really what she was looking forward to—hours spent with such inspiring musicians. Some of their creativity had to rub off on her. Didn't it?

Another cool part of being on an official tour was there were roadies. Well, roadie. Sammy. Sammy was short haired and butch enough to require several glances before Lacy was certain she was indeed a woman.

Not the only woman after all, Lacy thought to herself.

Between Kat, Sammy, and Lacy, her equipment was unloaded from the car in one trip and she was set up for her sound check with minutes to spare.

"Just mark your stuff with this," Sammy said, handing Lacy a roll of green electrical tape, "and I'll make sure it gets on the bus after the show each night and set up like this at the venues. Anything without the tape is your own responsibility."

"Great. Thanks." It took five pieces of tape and exactly three minutes to have all of Lacy's things marked. Then it was time for sound check, which went smoothly, and she got to run most of her songs.

"You sounded incredible, kid," Lou said patting her back as he escorted her off the stage. "Now get yourself settled in the hotel and be back here at six thirty. And don't forget to eat something. Don't look at me like I'm being a nag; I know how you folky hipsters get. 'I can't eat before a show if I want to fit in my skinny jeans.' Or, 'I use my hunger to reinforce the socially conscious vibe of my artistry!' Next thing I know you're passed out onstage and Sammy's the opening act for two nights while you're checked into the ER getting fluids and a lecture about eating regular meals. So promise me you'll be smart."

"All right," Lacy said with a chuckle. And, nervous as she was, she intended to keep her promise. Although she couldn't help but wonder what sort of an opener Sammy would make. Simon & Garfunkel covers? Stand-up? Either way, she wore a skirt, not skinny jeans, and her social conscience remained internal and unrepresented, so it was off for a burger with Kat.

As soon as the lights went down, Eli headed offstage to grab a bottle of water from the cooler and a towel from Sammy. He wiped the sweat from his brow and tossed it in the laundry bucket before heading to the green room. Mingling after shows wasn't usually his thing—he preferred getting back to his hotel room and online to talk to LoveCoda—but tonight was different. There had been a new opening act, and Eli was dying to meet her. He'd snuck out to watch from the back of the venue since all they could hear backstage was muffled sound, and he was curious. While he'd meant to stay only a few minutes, he found himself glued to her set. That voice, those words—he'd actually sent Lou to go get the other guys, knowing they'd appreciate her as much as he did.

She was waiting for the band with Lou and some other girl that Eli thought he'd seen with Wes on occasion. This was confirmed when Wes walked immediately up to the girl and open-mouth kissed her like he hadn't seen a woman in weeks.

"Get a room," Jax said, coming in behind Eli.

As if Jax was one to talk. He'd be out in the bar exactly five minutes after he showered trying to pick up a piece of something for himself. It wouldn't take that long. All the girls loved him. Eli had razzed Jax about it once and was met with, "Isn't that the role of a lead singer? To charm the pants off the women? It's good for the band. It gets us devoted fans. You should be thanking me."

Right. More like it lost them fans when Jax never returned phone calls and didn't bother to remember names the next time they were in town. Sometimes, when Eli had his head about him, he'd realize that Jax should be thanking *him*. Sure it had been Jax who had wanted to form a band in the first place but since then, Eli had done all the real work. Eli was the one who'd found them a manager. Eli was the one writing all the new material. Eli was the one who'd held the group together when Jax decided to slit his wrists one night after drinking a bottle of Smirnoff.

"It was art," Jax had insisted in his hospital room. "Jesus, I wasn't trying to kill myself. I did it for the scars."

And maybe Jax was just emo enough that he really had just been trying to decorate his body with "pain." But Eli didn't believe that, and, really, could he take that chance? So instead, he treated Jax with kid gloves, afraid to push him, always ready to kiss his ass. It was a detriment to Eli's own artistry—and hence the reason he'd joined SoWriAn—but it was necessary for the band. And wasn't that what mattered most—keeping the band on their track to stardom?

"And Eli Frank is that loser over there in la-la land. He plays banjo and mandolin and sometimes even hops on the piano."

At the sound of Lou saying his name, Eli snapped to attention. Apparently his manager was introducing everyone to the new girl. And he'd been too wrapped up in his own thoughts to have heard her name.

He stepped forward and held his hand out. "Sorry about that. Good to meet you. But I didn't catch your name?" He'd seen her before, he realized, at a previous show. That explained how familiar she'd seemed when he saw her on-stage earlier.

"Lacy Dawson." She took his hand and a shock ran up his spine. Not like the kind from an electricity transfer, but the kind that sparked from an attractive girl. A girl with pouty lips and dark blonde hair that fell in waves around her face. A girl with curves to match the sexy tone that came out of her mouth when she opened it to sing. Her smile was dazzling, her eyes hypnotic, and she smelled like something flowery with a faint hint of patchouli. Which was odd, but added to her mystique.

"It's really great to meet you," Eli said, his gaze still locked on hers. "Your set was good." *Not good. That was a lame adjective.* "Really good." *Yeah, much better wordsmith.* "Fantastic, actually." And he was still holding her hand. God, when had he turned into such a moron around pretty talented women?

Lacy—a much classier person than he was, Eli decided—slipped her hand from his gracefully and brought it to her chest in surprise. "You liked my set?"

"I did." Unlike the other guys who generally liked to hang out and shoot the shit in the green room before a show, Eli preferred a more meditative method of preparation. Often he'd sit with his headphones in a dark corner. He would have done that tonight if he hadn't been so wrapped up in the new girl's performance. Her music was at once interesting and intriguing. The chords she played were simple but she patterned them in her own style. Her voice was pure and unadorned with an occasional edge that hit the listener unexpectedly.

And her lyrics . . .

They were clever and poignant. He'd love to talk to her more about them, but her focus had switched now to Jax. In fact, it appeared as if Lacy Dawson, artist extraordinaire, was now getting acquainted with the Blue Hills' lead singer's infamous charm. And it didn't seem like she minded. Typical. And disappointing. He'd hoped her music proved a better indication of her taste.

Oh, well. He had LoveCoda. Why did he care about catching the eye of anyone else? Though he still felt a pinch of letdown as Jax perched on the arm of the couch next to where she was sitting, and she shifted to give all her attention to him.

Eli took the cushion on the other side of her—because it was the only seat left, not because he was trying to stay close or compete or anything—and listened to Jax tell his usual band stories, laughing on cue like the good friend he was. When Jax picked up James' guitar and strummed the opening chords to one of the only three songs he could play on the thing, Eli decided that further Jax kiss-up required beer.

He crossed to the mini-fridge across the room and grabbed a hard cider. As he turned back, he caught Lacy's eye. "Can I get you something?"

She paused, during which Jax's phone buzzed. He

stopped his performance and glanced at the screen. "Excuse me, I gotta take this. Be right back, sweetheart." He patted Lacy's arm before taking his call to a quiet corner.

Calling her "*sweetheart.*" Personal touching. Serenading. Yeah, Jax had already put Lacy on his list of possible conquests. Too bad. But, hey, if that's what she was into, he supposed it shouldn't be any of his concern.

Lacy pulled her gaze from Jax back to Eli, who was still waiting for her answer. "Yes, please. Same thing."

He grabbed a second bottle and returned to her, taking off the cap before handing it to her. "I didn't take you for a cider girl."

She chortled in a way that shouldn't be sexy, yet somehow was. "Uh, you don't even know me. So I'm more than intrigued to hear what you *did* take me for with such little to go on."

"After that song of yours midway in your set, I'd take you as a wine lover. You know, the one where you specifically referenced a bottle of red." He took a long pull from his drink.

"Oh that." Her eyes looked away self-consciously. It was understandable. Many artists were uncomfortable talking about their songs. It was funny how many nonmusicians didn't understand that. How it was easier to stand in front of an audience of hundreds and sing out your soul than it was to have a conversation with even one other person about the same things you sang about. He got that.

Still, he wanted to keep talking to her. And he was more than intrigued with her work. "What was that anyway? Ode to Chianti?"

"Congratulations. You correctly guessed the title of the song." She lifted her bottle in mock acclaim.

"I did?"

"No. I was teasing." Her lips curved into a radiant smile that made Eli want to be teased more. Then she pulled it in and he nearly sighed at its loss. "Actually," she said, not meeting his eyes, "it's not even a song about wine."

Eli frowned as he remembered the lyric from earlier.

The slope of your curve
Round bottom fiasco,
I go to you when I'm aching, aching
The sweet taste of you, Sangiovese
Buzzing through my veins
Your sugar running through my, ah, ah, body

The fiasco bottle and the Sangiovese grapes—definitely Chianti references. "Well, it's a metaphor then, right? For a relationship you turn to when you're in need?"

She took a swallow from her cider, then said bluntly, "It's a metaphor for masturbation."

"Oh." Then, since he didn't know what else to say, he added, "Ah." And, when his mind had wandered where it shouldn't—to imagining the song in action, Lacy's face flushed and her breath short—he said, "Hmm."

There may have been just a little too much moan in that "hmm," but it wasn't like he could take it back after it was out there. So he simply smiled.

"I mean, it's really old. I wrote it a long time ago. Not recently." Lacy seemed to have misinterpreted his "hmm" as judgment.

She paused for a second, her brow knit in thought. "I don't know why I told you that. As if it matters if I wrote it recently or not. Like the fact that it's old means that I don't do that *now*. Because obviously it doesn't mean that at all. I could totally still do it now. Which I don't. I mean . . ." Her cheeks reddened. "I'm not against it or anything. It's great and . . ." She brought her hand to her face and covered her eyes, her cheeks reddening. "I'm making this worse than it needs to be, aren't I?"

"I don't know. I'm enjoying it." He knocked his shoulder playfully against hers.

And there it was again—her smile. Coyer this time, but still as radiant. "Obviously I'm still working on discussing the stories behind my lyrics without being worried about what people think of me." She shaped her fingers on her thigh as she spoke, a nervous tic Eli supposed, and he recognized she was playing guitar chords. He wondered if she even knew. Probably not. Music was just *in* her. Like it was in him.

"It's not easy. For any of us."

She lifted her eyes to his. "Lyrics are too personal. Like journal entries."

He held her gaze as he thought about that. Maybe that was part of the reason he let Jax take the credit for the songs. People usually assumed that since he was the lead singer, and since he was so good at connecting with the songs emotionally, that Jax had written them. Eli rarely bothered to correct them. Was this why? Because they were too personal?

Or was he just an easy-to-walk-over chickenshit?

Whichever it was, he hoped he wasn't blowing smoke up her ass when he said, "You'll get more comfortable with it. Give yourself time."

"Thanks. Because it's really so hard."

He couldn't help himself. "That's what she said."

Her eyes widened, and Eli suddenly felt like the biggest twelve-year-old in the world. "I'm sorry. That was lame. Office joke."

But she was laughing. "No, it was funny. And I got the reference. Just unexpected."

Her expression was so sincere, her blue-grey eyes so pure, her smile so brilliant. She'd laughed at his dorky humor. And her music . . . God, her music was so charming and her lyrics so fresh that he opened his mouth to invite her out for drinks.

But before he could ask, Jax had returned. "Sorry about that interruption, babe."

"No problem!" She didn't give her whole attention to Jax, shifting so she included him as well. Maybe Eli could have a chance with her after all.

If it weren't for LoveCoda, he might have even been interested in trying.

"I'm gonna call it a night, though," Jax said, stretching.

Ha, more like the phone call he'd received had been a booty arrangement.

"Yeah, sure." Lacy turned to Eli, and he thought she might be getting ready to invite him to talk longer. But then she looked at the clock on the wall and exclaimed, "Oh! It's nearly midnight! I should call it a night too." She glanced over at the girl still making out with Wes on the other sofa. "Uh, Kat? Will you be all right?"

There was a sound from the lip-locked couple that might have been an "uh huh." Or it might have just been a groan of pleasure. Either way, Lacy seemed to think her friend was fine.

"Perfect," Eli said though he wasn't sure anyone was listening to him anymore. "I'm going to head to my room as well."

He didn't mean to sound quite so disappointed about the evening ending. He really wasn't upset in the least. It was almost midnight, after all, and he had his date with Love-Coda. At the very thought, he wondered if he should feel guilty about being so immediately attracted to Lacy.

Chapter Nine

Eli leaned back in the bus and stretched his long legs out as far as he could. It was his least favorite part of touring—the actual traveling. Maybe it would be different if the Blue Hills were a bigger band with a real tour bus instead of a mini-coach, half of which had been gutted to store the instruments that couldn't fit in the underneath storage. If he had a table even, or room to strum his banjo. Even room for his legs to not get cramped up would be an improvement.

Thankfully, most of the trips were short. Today's drive from Philly to Baltimore was less than two hours. Then they'd have three nights in the same place. Thank God—a break from the damn bus. They'd been in seven cities since Worchester in just as many days. Time on tour was never marked by days though—it was marked by venues, by audiences, by good shows. They'd had seven good shows in a row, some of the best receptions they'd had in years, and Eli had to think it was partly due to their new opening act. She knew how to warm up a crowd, that was for sure. Every time he heard her sing he fell more into her sound.

More than once he'd wanted to talk to her about her art, but after each show he'd found Jax hovering over her, and he wasn't interested in fighting for attention.

Too bad, he thought for the millionth time about Lacy Dawson. Too damn bad.

He closed his eyes and let his mind wander. As they usually did, his thoughts soon settled on LoveCoda. And as they had every time he thought about her lately, he found himself picturing blue-grey eyes, full pouty lips, and legs that went on for miles. In other words, he kept picturing Lacy. He'd fought against it, tried to shake the merging of the two in his brain, but that was the thing about subconscious thoughts—they generally refused to be controlled by the conscious.

The problem was that he knew LoveCoda's insides. And he was attracted to Lacy Dawson's outsides. He obviously couldn't ask Love to share a picture of herself. Not if they wanted to still be a part of the forum.

Maybe he needed to spend some more time with the woman on tour with him. If he got to know Lacy better, he'd be able to establish her as her own person. The merging would therefore end.

It wasn't a bad idea. Okay, maybe it was just an excuse to spend more time with a hot girl, but he couldn't find any argument against that.

Well, that wasn't exactly true. He could argue that it wasn't really fair to LoveCoda—more accurately, how he felt about her. Although they'd both agreed to just be friends until they met in person, his feelings went deeper than that, and he couldn't postpone those no matter what they'd decided.

So maybe he'd not *plan* to spend more time with Lacy. But if it happened, he wouldn't fight it. He'd just play it by ear. Let whatever happened happen.

After so much time thinking about Lacy, Eli had the

impulse to look at her. He stretched his arms over his head
in order to steal a glance. She was curled up in two seats
a couple of rows behind him across the aisle, writing something in a notebook. He casually looked around the rest of
the coach—Wes and the other two members of the Blue
Hills were planning how to fill their days in Baltimore. Lou
was absorbed in his phone. Sammy was watching something on her iPad with her headphones on—something
funny, apparently, since she kept chortling out of thin air.
Jax, of course, was sprawled across the backseat, asleep,
as always.

And on the seat directly behind Lacy was the cooler
that Lou packed every day before they left the hotel. If he
wanted to get, say, an apple, he'd have to walk right past
Lacy to get to that cooler.

Suddenly he really wanted an apple.

He stood up and headed to the cooler, feeling obvious,
as if everyone knew he didn't really want an apple. No one
said anything though. No one even looked at him. At the
cooler, he found his ruse had hit a wall—there were no
apples. He panicked a bit, then settled on a bottle of water.
Which was stupid since he already had a bottle of water at
his seat. He shook his head at himself.

Then, because he might as well finish out his play, he
searched for something to say to Lacy. Lacy, who still had
her head bent over her notebook. Now that he was standing behind her, he could see it wasn't a notebook, it was a
staff pad. A melody was sketched in across the lines, guitar chords written above each measure. She'd scratched out
a couple of the chords, substituting another in their place.
Question marks were written lightly by a few of them.

Eli cocked his head and studied the progression. The
song unfolded in his head. It was good. Plain, but good.
He watched as she tapped her pencil by a particular chord
marking. She seemed stuck on that one.

Suddenly he could hear it, could hear how the song *could* be and he knew what would take the song from plain to remarkable. "If you inverted the G chord so that it had a D base, that progression would have an entirely different feel."

Lacy looked up, her eyes blinking, surprised to see him. "Hmm, what was that?"

She hadn't realized he was standing there. Eli took the opportunity to start over. His approach *had* been a little brash. She hadn't invited him to critique her work, after all. He nodded toward her paper. "Are you working on something new?"

"I wish," she mumbled. Louder, she said, "Arranging one of my oldies."

"Something you've been singing on tour?" He already knew it wasn't. He didn't recognize it, and he would have since he'd watched every one of her performances.

"Nah. Though if I could figure out what's wrong with the arrangement, I might. I want it to sound more ethereal. Right now it's too . . . rooted. If that makes any sense."

He resisted the urge to tie "rooted" into a that's-what-she-said joke. "It makes perfect sense." He leaned on the back of the seat next to her. "Which is why I think you should invert the G chord so it has a D base."

She furrowed her brow skeptically. But then she looked at her paper, bobbing her head to an internal refrain. "Huh. Actually, I like that. It changes the whole thing."

"Doesn't it?" Eli slipped around to sit in the seat beside her, noticing the smell of patchouli was absent from her floral scent—*what flower was that, anyway*? "And if you put a seven on that C chord—or even a thirteen—can you play a thirteen chord?"

She scowled as if he'd been patronizing. "Yes, I can play a thirteen chord."

Eli put his hands up in a surrender position. "Hey, I wasn't trying to be snooty. Some guitar players never add anything past a seven to their repertoire of chords."

Lacy eyed him, studying his sincerity. Finally, she sighed. "You aren't wrong about that. And, honestly, I don't even use sevenths as often as I could. But anyway, I'm having trouble hearing that C-thirteen."

"It's subtle. Almost has the flavor of a C-augmented. Like"—he paused, trying to figure out how to describe the chord without an instrument—"like, C chord sounds like this." He hummed the three notes of the chord. "Now just add this." He hummed the six. "But imagine that an octave higher."

Lacy bit her lip as she closed her eyes, seeming to be listening to the change in her head. After a minute, she turned her head and faced Eli. "That's . . . incredible. It's exactly what it needed. Oh, my God. Thank you."

Eli was still thinking about her teeth wrapped around her bottom lip. She'd likely done it subconsciously, which was half the reason it looked so damn sexy. He wondered how it would feel to have her teeth rake against his own lip, against his tongue.

Stop it. Stop it. They were practically coworkers. He shouldn't be thinking about her in any way other than artistically.

The less-conscious-of-propriety-in-the-workplace side of him didn't fail to notice that his guilt had almost nothing to do with LoveCoda. Maybe he could postpone his feelings for her after all. He wasn't sure if he liked that about himself or not, but he did like the way Lacy got his blood flowing.

The bus turned into the parking lot of the hotel then, throwing Lacy against his side. His body tingled and sparked from the contact, leaving him warmer than he'd been just a second before.

She giggled. "Whoops. Sorry."

Were giggles supposed to be so adorable? He couldn't remember ever thinking so before, but there was no denying that Lacy's giggle was downright captivating.

"I'm happy to break your fall anytime you need it." God, he was an idiot with his words sometimes. He blamed it on her giggle. And the heat she'd ignited from her touch. And thoughts of her sultry little nip. He was sure it was those things that led him to say, "I could stick around after the show if you want help working it."

The part of him that worried about missing LoveCoda online regretted his offer, but his pragmatic side reminded him he was interested in Lacy's music too. Really interested. Besides, it wasn't good to focus all his attention on just one person—just friends or not.

Though maybe it had been too forward from an artist's point of view. Or even just a woman's point of view. So he added, "You know, if you want to."

She considered. "Yeah, I might take you up on that. Thanks again, Eli." She flashed him that gorgeous smile of hers.

It was a good thing they were unloading soon. Eli didn't know how much longer he could sit next to the pretty-smelling songstress without his thoughts straying inappropriately. Another minute and he'd talk himself out of why inappropriate thoughts were so bad anyway.

Lacy brushed her hair off her face and sighed as her eyes followed Jax out of the green room and down the corridor until he was out of sight. He was so damn good-looking. How had she gotten so lucky to be on tour with such eye candy? Between Jax and Eli her hormones were on constant overdrive. And both were such great musicians. She'd been too nervous to sneak out and watch any of their sets—afraid of confronting the audience after her own performance—but she remembered the show she'd seen before the tour. She'd love to talk to them about their music, find out their inspirations, discover who wrote what. But the only time it seemed appropriate was after their shows and she was too focused then on getting back to her room to talk to Folx.

The situation shouldn't bother her, and it didn't really. It was a comfortable routine, and she'd grown even closer to Folx online. She'd even felt the stirrings of a lyric or two after their conversations. Nothing that turned into anything, but it was a start.

Yet, even with their relationship going as well as it was, she found she was eager to connect with someone in person. Wanted to talk in an environment that didn't prevent secrets from being shared. Wanted to be able to read the subtext from a person's expression that she couldn't get from text on a screen. Wanted someone to exchange glances with, like the ones she occasionally exchanged with Eli. It was probably why she'd been picturing Eli recently whenever she thought about Folx. Which was a little weird on the surface but likely explained with some psychobabble term like "transference" or "substitution." Or plain old "wishful thinking."

She sighed again and absentmindedly reached for the staff pad she'd left on the green room table. She jolted as her fingers touched, not her pad, but other fingers. Lacy turned to find Eli had been reaching at the same time.

"Sorry," he said, his hand lingering on hers. "I was going to pass it to you. It looked like you were getting ready to leave and I thought you might have forgotten it."

"Oh. Thank you. I guess I wasn't really paying attention." Warmth shot up her arm from his simple touch. It was . . . nice.

But it also made her feel weird, like she shouldn't be touching him. Whether it was because of Folx or because of a lingering responsibility to Lance, she wasn't sure. She hadn't really been with a man since Lance. Well, there had been the rugby player from Australia that she'd made out with for two hours after a show a couple of months back. Honestly, she'd done it because she wanted to prove to herself that her feminine interests hadn't dried up like her lyrics. The encounter had been successful—she'd certainly been aroused, so to say, but she hadn't felt the shock of electricity like she did now at the touch of Eli's skin against hers. So what did this mean?

It was too big of a question to answer right there. She drew her hand away from his and decided to think about it more, later. Or not at all, if that worked out better.

"So. Is that what you were working on earlier?" Eli folded his arms across his chest, and Lacy wondered if he'd felt cold from the absence of her touch as she felt from the absence of his.

Which was ridiculous. Of course he didn't feel that. She was being crazy.

She mirrored his posture—because she *did* feel cold— hugging her staff pad to her chest. "Yeah. I played through the chords you suggested earlier. It really does sound so much better. Now I'm trying to match the verses to the chorus. But when I added thirteens there it seemed like overkill. So I don't know what I'm doing." She was never this forward about her process. It was too personal, too *hers*.

Though, that wasn't true. She'd been this forward with Folx.

But that had been online. There was certainly something different about discussing it in person. Especially with a guy who was part of a band that she admired so much. Especially with a guy as hot as Eli.

Strike that—his attractiveness had no bearing on whether she decided to talk more with Eli about her art or not. She wouldn't let it. Hotness aside, sharing made her more vulnerable. It was scary, no doubt. But it also made it easier to brainstorm ideas. Made it easier to say try this, and then they could listen to it together, knowing they were hearing the same thing.

Maybe she should take Eli up on his earlier offer to help.

As if he were reading her mind, Eli raised an inviting brow and said, "If you'd like me to take a listen, I'm here."

"Okay." It was out of her mouth before she could second-guess it. "Like when? Now?" Why on earth had she said that? She had a date with Folx. It was just that she was so excited about the progress she'd made so far on her piece that she was eager to dive in. And, if she skipped her nightly shower, she could still work with Eli for half an hour and make it online in time.

Eli hesitated, though. Maybe he hadn't really meant it when he offered. Then he said, "Uh, yeah. Now's good."

"Awesome. I'll just grab my guitar." Lacy went to her case, which was leaning against the sofa. Sammy had several times offered to pack it with the rest of her equipment, but no. Lucky was her baby. Lucky stayed with her.

Just as Lacy started to pull Lucky out, Lou bustled in. He seemed startled to see them there. "Hey kids," he said. "It's great that you want to stay up all night and keep the music alive. I'm all for it. Only you can't do it here. Our contract says we have to clear the green room by eleven. There's another band coming in after us."

"Oh. Well." Lacy looked to Eli for a suggestion. Part of her thought that maybe Lou's pronouncement was a sign—a sign that she should forget the whole workshopping thing and get back to her room to wait for Folx like a good online girlfriend. Not that "girlfriend" was what she was. But.

Another part of her, the part that was itching for inspiration, was aching to still feel creatively relevant—that part of her wanted to continue transforming her song with Eli's help.

Each half of her warred so equally, she left the decision up to Eli.

"We could move this to your hotel room, I suppose," he said. "Or mine."

"Yours."

She ignored the butterflies spinning in her stomach at the idea of being alone with Eli and the fear that she was doing something she probably shouldn't. Both fear and butterflies were good for inspiration, after all. The more the better.

They packed up and were headed out within five minutes.

Sometimes the venue they performed in wouldn't be near the hotel, and the bus would take everyone there after the show. This time, the hotel was next door to the theater they'd played, and as Eli carried her guitar and his banjo across the parking lot—he really was a gentleman—Lacy didn't wonder even once if going to his room was inappropriate because of Folx and all.

Okay, maybe once, but the thought was fleeting.

As they walked in the doors of the Marriott Express, she checked her phone to make sure that her sound was on, then put it in her pocket and promised herself she wouldn't look at it again unless it notified her.

Chapter Ten

Two hours later, Lacy's phone hadn't done a thing, and she didn't care in the least.

Spread out across the floor of Eli's room, the two had completely reworked her song, plus they'd fiddled around with another one. Now she had two pieces to add to her set list. It was the next best thing to writing something new, and it made her feel a little more legit. Like she actually belonged in this songwriter biz after all.

It wasn't long before they'd gotten hungry, so they'd ordered pizza from the Italian joint next door, which they paired with sodas from the hotel vending machine. Between the two of them, they downed forty-eight ounces of caffeinated sugar and a medium supreme hold the mushrooms.

Lacy took one more nibble of her slice before she threw the crust into the box and shut the lid. With an exaggerated sigh, she fell back against the leg of the loveseat, hands on her belly. "I'm so stuffed, I may need to be rolled out of here."

Leaning against the bed across from her, Eli shrugged. "Or you could just stay."

She froze. What did that mean? Was it a come-on? Or was she misreading? Did she want it to be a come-on? Was she too full to be sexy? Maybe she *did* want it to be a come-on. Her stomach flipped at the idea. And not exactly an uncomfortable flip. More like a somersault—an easy roll that quietly set all her nerves on alert.

Before she had to think about it too long, Eli added, "We can talk a bit while the food settles."

"Okay. Sure. I'm good with that." Then not a come-on. She was almost disappointed. "Go ahead. Talk."

He laughed as he scratched the back of his neck. "Well. Tell me about yourself."

She practically rolled her eyes. Trite, wasn't that? But she played along. "Like what?"

"Like anything. Come on, this is good. But nothing musical. Nothing work related."

Nothing musical. That took out pretty much her whole life. What did she have left after that? "Um, let's see. I have a sister. Andy. She's my best friend."

Maybe this could be fun. It was exactly the opposite from talking to Folx. There, the only thing they could talk about was their art. It had been so long since she'd talked to anyone about the basics, after all. Maybe she was overdue.

"A sister." Eli nodded. "Okay, we're getting somewhere. Older or younger?"

"Older." Lacy thought about her sibling and their roles for a moment. "But a lot of the time she acts younger."

"In what way?" He was probably being polite, but he actually sounded like he was interested.

"She's just . . . not very nurturing." That probably wasn't fair to Andy. Still, it was the truth.

Eli tilted his head. "Hmm. Do you expect that from her?"

"Not necessarily." Lacy scooted back so she was sitting more upright. "But she wants to be nurturing. Our parents died when I was in high school, so I think she thinks she's supposed to be a substitute parent. Only most of the time, it's me doing the parenting." They'd been that way as long as she could remember—Andy impulsive and indulgent, Lacy quiet and low-maintenance. It wasn't fair that their parents' deaths had forced Andy to try to fit a role she'd never been made for. A role Lacy had never expected her to take.

Hmm. Maybe she should tell that to her some time.

"Man, that sucks. Car accident?" Eli picked the meat off a slice of pizza, but kept his eyes on hers.

Lacy was used to the charity looks she got from mentioning her childhood heartache. She was also used to topic changes or avoidance tactics. Eli's encouragement to say more along with his focused gaze—that was new. That threw her off guard.

She stumbled a bit over her next words. "Um. Cancer. Ovarian. Mom, anyway. Dad followed a year later with a heart attack."

"God, that's shitty. Really shitty." He took a deep breath, as if taking in the magnitude of her pain. As if attempting to share it with her for the briefest of seconds. When he let it out, he shoved his hand through his hair and offered a kind expression blessedly empty of pity. "I'm sorry, Lacy. No wonder you write."

"Gotta capture the pain, right?" She forced a laugh that did nothing to lessen the gravity of the conversation. Surprisingly, the depth of the topic didn't bother her as much as she would have thought. But it did feel rather one-sided. "Your turn. Siblings?"

Eli shaped his hand to make a zero. "Nada."

"You're an only child?" This was unexpected. Most of the only children that Lacy had met were self-centered, obnoxious know-it-alls. Huge generalization, but it was quite often a shoe that fit.

"Lonely only. That's me." Eli elongated the vowel in *lonely* and *only* in a way that made him appear younger and probably worked to bleed the hearts of many a woman.

Lacy wouldn't let him get away with that. She'd had real heartache—she wasn't going to give him credit for a pretend one. She put on her best snark. "Ah, no wonder you write. No one else to talk to, huh?"

"Whatever. I had friends." His smile faded. "And a dad. Who liked to hit."

And she'd misjudged him again. "Not good. You win. Child abuse trumps dead parents." Not that it was a contest. It was simply her way of saying she acknowledged his pain even though she couldn't identify with it.

Eli shrugged. "It wasn't abuse. It was 'tough love.' I honestly didn't have it as rough as some kids. I simply found life was better if I stayed out of his way."

Then he wasn't seeking pity at all. He was just sharing. Lacy really needed to work on her communication skills. If she learned that she misread everyone as often as she had tonight, she might find she liked people better in general. How was it she was related to Miss-Intuition-Andy.

But beyond her minor epiphany, she wondered at Eli's ability to talk about the worst parts of his life, to share them without any embarrassment or show. There was talent in that. Perhaps she could learn from him.

Unusually eager to hear more about him, she pushed him. "Pop wasn't a musician?"

"Nope. It was a talent I got from Mom." His eyes narrowed as he pointed a long finger at Lacy. "And we're not supposed to be talking about music. What else about you?"

Eli put his hands over his head, fingers laced, and stretched.

God, he had nice biceps. And triceps. All his 'ceps were good.

"I don't know. Um." It was suddenly hard to think. It was also warmer than it had been only a minute ago. She took a sip of soda to focus her or cool her off or buy her time. A refreshing swallow later, she said, "Andy's getting married in a couple months. She lives with me now, but, obviously, she'll move out."

"Then what?"

Lacy put her hands up in a shrug. "She'll probably get pregnant and have three kids and a nanny. Blake's rich." Thank God for that too, because Lacy couldn't imagine her sister being a parent without any guidance. Though, to her credit, Andy would make an awfully doting mother. Which might be nice. If you were a kid that liked doting.

Eli frowned. "Not 'then what' *her*, 'then what' *you*?"

"Oh." Lacy frowned too. She hadn't really thought about it. How would her life change when Andy moved out? Well, the house would be quiet. That thought saddened her a little. She'd have to handle the rent on her own, which was going to be hard on her current income. "I don't really know, actually. I guess if I don't get enough gigs, I may have to go back to waiting tables."

"You don't make a living on your music?" He seemed genuinely surprised.

She liked that. "I was starting to. I've been doing studio work to supplement what I get from playing live, but my hours got cut recently."

"You need to do another album."

"I have one booked. Already paid for too." That was the great thing about working in the studio. Darrin took a part of each paycheck and held it toward her scheduled sessions. Of course, without any new songs, a new album wouldn't be happening. But that wasn't something she wanted to bring up with Eli. He looked at her like she was a real artist, and it made her feel good. She didn't want him to see her for the fake she really was.

"Great! A new album of your stuff will book you gigs easy. No waiting tables for you. Hell. You're way too good for that." Eli seemed so confident. It almost made it easy for her to believe it as well.

It was her turn to ask him something personal, but she was too wrapped up in her last thought, and he beat her to the punch. "What about a significant other for you?"

And what a punch it was.

"What—do you mean do I have a man?" She knew exactly what he meant though. She was stalling.

He shrugged. "Or a woman."

She shook her head, briefly thinking of Folx and when she'd asked him the question in very nearly the same way. "I have neither."

"No one?" Eli poked at her shin with his toe. "There has to be someone. Pretty girl like you."

Ah, he was flirting. A little bit anyway.

"Nope. No one . . . at this moment." She was enjoying the flirting. Really enjoying the flirting.

"Huh. That's surprising." He grinned.

She loved the way his smile lit every part of his face. "There was someone. A fiancé, actually. But . . ."

Her voice trailed off as she tried to picture Lance's face. She could only conjure up his eyes. How quickly the dead disappeared. She'd lost her parents . . . she should know this, shouldn't she? Somehow, she'd thought that Lance would be different. That she'd always carry him with her, even if she didn't try. But his fading scent on his pillow was the realest he'd been to her in months.

"But . . . ?" Eli prodded.

Lacy looked up, having forgotten for a second that she'd

been speaking out loud, and forgetting for another two seconds what it was she'd even said.

Then she remembered. *Ah, but . . .*

She wasn't sure she should talk about Lance. Wasn't sure she *could* talk about him. Mostly because she hadn't talked about him at all since his death. Not to anyone. Even Andy. Part of her said that she was saving it all for the songs that were buried within her. Another part of her knew the truth—she was chickenshit.

But she didn't feel so chickenshit at the moment. Not with Eli's kind eyes and seemingly genuine interest. His room felt like a safe place. She decided to test the waters, try out the words she'd been holding onto. What did she have to lose?

Letting out a deep breath, she said, "But he died. A year ago. Overdose."

"Jesus," Eli muttered, surprised. "Accidental?"

Lacy flicked her gaze from the carpet pattern she was studying up to Eli's face, gauging his reaction. His expression was sympathetic, for sure, but not full of pity like she'd expected. Like the looks she'd received from so many other people. It gave her strength to go on. "No. It was on purpose."

"My God. I don't know what to say. What happened?"

"Honestly? I don't know. I mean, I do know some things. He'd had an injury on his knee—Lance was a runner— and he was prescribed some pain pills for that. And one day, he just took the whole bottle."

"Was he in that much pain?"

"Not physically. But I guess he was emotionally. Lance was probably the happiest person I'd ever met. He was funny and lighthearted and optimistic. About everything. He could make cockroaches seem necessary. There was always a silver lining and he never failed to see it.

"Except, then he was dead on our bathroom floor. And

I realized all that other stuff was just . . . talk." She considered for a moment.

"No, I don't mean that. It wasn't talk. It was sincere. He really made life better with his attitude. For me, anyway. And other people around him. My guess is he gave away so much . . . that he didn't have any left for himself." It was the most heartbreaking thing about the whole situation, knowing how often she'd lain in his arms and soaked up all his optimism about their future, never giving anything back to him to hold onto in his own moments of uncertainty.

When Eli moved closer and put his arm around her, she knew for sure it wasn't a come-on. It was a comfort. "Wow. I'm . . . I have no words."

Funny, neither did she. "I don't expect you to have any. It's what it is."

"Did he leave a note?"

She leaned back into him a little. Was she that lonely for touch? Or was it just the quiet strength she was drawing from him that let her open up like this? "Yeah. It was short. Said he'd been sad and fighting depression for a decade. Said he couldn't do it any longer." She smiled at the irony of the next bit. "Said he knew I'd be just fine without him."

"Are you?" Eli pulled back a little so he could look her directly in the eyes.

"Yeah. I really am. More fine than I should be, probably. I promised myself that I wasn't going to let his brightness die with him, so I've focused on the things that he did and believed in that made life nice. You know?" She smiled.

He nodded, and she wasn't sure if he was honestly agreeing with her or if he was quietly disagreeing.

Maybe her answer had seemed a bit far-fetched. She clarified. "Of course, I have regrets. Who doesn't? I regret that I didn't know. How did I not know? I mean, we lived with each other. I was planning on marrying this guy. How did I not see that he was in such horrid pain? Doesn't that make me the shittiest of all girlfriends?"

"Uh, no. Not in the least." He shifted, letting his arm fall, and she immediately missed it. But she was too enrapt in his words and the way his gaze was piercing into hers, warming her in ways his touch hadn't. "Actually, it kind of makes him the shittiest of all boyfriends, if you ask me."

Well, maybe she didn't like his words quite as much as she thought she did.

Eli shook his head. "I'm sorry, and not to speak ill of the dead, but isn't a relationship about letting each other in? Letting one another know all the good and the bad and the ugly and the bullshit? That's what love is in *my* book. And that's fabulous that he wanted your life to be all roses and rainbows and unicorns, but that's not real. It's not fair. And it's particularly not fair that he instructed you to have those things even knowing that you were going to be the one to find—sorry. I'm totally out of line."

"You're not." These were things she'd thought herself, often enough. And she'd opened the door for him to speak, so what did she expect? It didn't mean she was totally comfortable hearing it. That was why she usually closed that door in her own mind.

But Eli wasn't being mean. And he had no loyalty to Lance's memory like she did. And maybe, just maybe, it was okay to let someone tell her that he had been a selfish prick to do what he did.

She softened her expression, and Eli took that opportunity to say more. "It just seems like, yeah, you're doing fine. But maybe you could be doing more than fine. If you forgave yourself for something that wasn't even your fault in the first place."

Her breath tripped. He'd nailed something there. Hit it square on the head.

Eli gave a no-more gesture with his hand. "That's it. I'm done. Like I said, I'm out of line and I'm done now."

"It's fine. And maybe it's spot-on. I have to mull it over a bit." *Or a lot. Or not at all, maybe.* Some piece of her broken heart had fallen back into place at Eli's words, recognizing their truth.

He squeezed her thigh, another compassionate gesture. But with it came the itch of awareness that crawled up her skin, sending her hair to stand and goose bumps to form.

God, where on earth had she taken this conversation? Hadn't they been flirting earlier? How did she get back to *that*? "Hey, thank you by the way."

"For completely telling you your life even though I just met you?" His hand dropped from her thigh and all she could think was *put it back, put it back*.

But she tried to remain cool as a cucumber. "Well, for listening and feeling comfortable enough to speak your mind. And for not being all 'poor Lacy' about it. I am sick to death of that shtick."

"Oh, no. I don't do 'poor me.' You want pity, call . . . I don't know. " He chuckled. "Call someone else."

"Call my sister." Lacy giggled. Andy would be beside herself right now, knowing that one of the potential bad boys she was on tour with had become her new confidante.

"Yeah, call her. But don't call her right now. I'm enjoying your company too much at the moment." He pulled her a little closer, and she wasn't so sure anymore if it was comfort or come-on.

She sort of wanted it to be the latter. "And I'm enjoying yours." Tentatively she laid her head on his shoulder. He didn't pull away. "Or I was before it got all heavy."

"Then let's lighten it." And the moment turned into something else.

Eli moved away to pick up his banjo. "Shall we?"

Lacy hesitated for only a second before reaching for Lucky. Though the mood had gotten weighty, as she'd said, she felt surprisingly lighter. Looser. Unbound. It was . . . nice, actually. More than fine.

She crossed her legs, her skirt settling around her as she set her guitar in her lap and tuned. "What are we playing, boss?"

"Anything we want."

They spent the next hour or more—Lacy wasn't exactly sure about the time at this point—playing through songs they liked and admired, jamming between swigs of 7Up.

"Minor, minor!" Eli shouted as they played through a rendition of Fleetwood Mac's *Go Your Own Way*. "Play it slow and in minor."

Lacy laughed as she slowed her tempo and changed her G chord to an E minor. The song was suddenly sad and mournful. "Oh, God. That's so depressing."

"Then, then!" Eli sat up excitedly and leaned across the pizza box to press a string on the neck of her guitar. "Add the nine. See? See?!"

"It's not even the same song anymore," she said laughing so hard she could barely get her words out. He was about the cutest thing she'd ever seen. How come more musicians didn't express their joy in the process? It was like there was an unwritten law that said everyone had to pretend art was hard and miserable.

"Isn't it? You only changed the atmosphere of it. The basics are still there. It's called a fresh arrangement, Songbird." His tone was teasing, not condescending.

"Songbird?" she asked as she continued to move through the refrain, playing the changes he'd suggested.

"Yeah, that's what I'm calling you. Go with it." He adjusted her hand to take over the chord he'd shown her, his touch once again sending a spark of electricity straight to a spot between her thighs. "Keep going from there. I'm just going to . . ." He took his hand off of hers and began to pluck at her strings as she strummed, creating a counter melody.

They played like that through the rest of the song— Lacy strumming, Eli's fingers dancing around her hand as it changed from chord to chord, their eyes locked as they sang in harmony. It was both the sweetest and strangest of Fleetwood Mac arrangements she'd ever played, let alone heard. The sound moved her, each new measure filling her creative well. Maybe it wasn't A Best Day Ever, but it was A Most Inspiring Day Ever.

Whether it was the inspiration or the unbinding from Lance or the brush of Eli's hand against hers or the intense way he looked at her as though he could see *into* her, Lacy couldn't say, but regardless of what struck the mood, it was there, sweeping her away.

So when they'd finished their song, Lacy waited exactly two seconds before she set Lucky to the side and rose up to her knees. She wrapped her hands around Eli's neck and kissed him.

Then, because the first taste of his lips was so pleasant, she did it again.

And again.

And then she realized Eli was kissing her back. Like, really kissing her back. His tongue stroked across the bottom of hers, teasing her mouth open wider, and she was happy to comply. Her hands tightened at his neck, and he wrapped his arms around her waist, pulling her body flush against his.

My, oh, my . . .

If Lacy had any doubt before whether or not Eli had been *inspired* by their evening as she was, she didn't anymore. Because suddenly "inspiration" was poking her in the belly. She quit being tentative about her kisses then, if she'd even been tentative before, and let herself give in to the mood completely.

Eli was right with her. His mouth grew frantic on hers and his hands traveled down to caress her ass through her skirt. It was Lacy who took things further. Her fingers crawled beneath his shirt and up until her palms were spread along the taut muscles of his chest. Man, she hadn't realized that Eli was so fit. With Lance, she'd been used to long, lean runner's muscles. These were bulkier. Solid. She wondered how the soft of her breasts would feel against the hard of him.

Only one way to find out.

Lacy pulled away long enough to remove her shirt. She tossed it aside and noted Eli's smile before she pushed him down to the ground.

And onto the pizza.

At least the box was closed. "Sorry! Sorry." She laughed.

Eli laughed with her as he shoved the box aside. Then he pulled her down on top of him, his lips on her neck, and there were other sounds to make. Like "oohs" and "ahs" and "yes, right there."

Eli licked and nipped down along her collarbone, and then lower. Over her bra. He tugged at her nipple through her bra until it stood tall while he tweaked its twin with his hand. Damn. She'd forgotten how good it felt just to have her breasts played with. Especially like this—a little rough and a whole lot new.

Lacy sat up, straddling Eli, to remove her bra.

"Wow, Songbird," Eli said, his voice choked with awe. "You've been hiding."

She blushed at his compliment, but she didn't let herself get shy. As he palmed her bare breasts, she arched into his touch, enjoying it. Reveling in it.

Still, she wanted to feel her nipples against the skin of his chest. She tugged at his T-shirt, hinting.

"Yep," he said, as if she'd spoken her request. "It's going now." He sat up and crossed his arms to pull it off.

And jabbed Lacy in the jaw with his elbow as he did so.

"Oh, shit! God, I'm sorry! Lacy, are you okay?" He cradled her chin with his hand then kissed it softly.

"I'm totally fine." And she was. Especially now, because she had his bare chest in front of her to explore. Her fingertips traced the ink embedded in his skin. A raven, over his heart, held a tattered heart in its beak. The branch it was perched on scattered tiny leaves that turned into baby ravens as they flew across his torso. Her hands explored their path.

Then, what she'd been aching for, she wrapped her arms around his neck and pressed her breasts to his skin. The sensation of her soft breasts and pebbled nipples brushing against his rock-hard pecs sent shockwaves to her nether regions. Her mouth reclaimed his and they danced like that—their upper bodies melded together, their tongues tangled. Twisting and moving to a beat that was unheard, but felt by both of them.

Eli's hands swept up and down along her bare back. Beneath her, his erection strained against her crotch. He leaned into each grind of her hips—and there were many. She couldn't help herself. She was like a woman possessed, rubbing against his length in an attempt to ease the ache at her very core.

There was an easier way about this, she knew. But could they do that? Could she let him do that to her without being labeled as a tour-slut?

And did she really care?

Hell, she didn't know. What she did know was that she was wet and yearning. Seriously, she was about to burst. And when Eli's hands moved under her skirt and up her thighs, sliding slowly higher like a question, Lacy gave an answer. "Touch me."

That's all he needed. Eli's fingers slipped up and past the elastic band at the leg hole of her panties, landing on her clit with firm, sure pressure. His stroke was confident and sincere as he circled her nub, setting her in flames.

"God, yes, yes," she moaned against his lips. She bucked into his touch, wanting, needing more. Her fingernails dug into his back as her vision began to cloud and the muscles in her legs clenched.

"Fuck, Lacy, you're killing me." Eli slid a finger lower to circle the rim of her hole. "I want you so bad. Do you want me to make you come?"

"Yes, please!" She'd never begged for an orgasm, but she'd never wanted one so desperately as she did right now. Yet, she was also afraid—afraid that once she got the release she was aching for and her mind began to clear, she would rethink this whole adventure and want to leave. Afraid because that wouldn't exactly be fair to Eli, who was so obviously wanting a release as well.

So she amended her plea. "But not like this. I want you inside me."

His cock leapt against her and his eyes widened. "Are you . . ." his voice trailed off as if he couldn't bear to ask if she were sure, in case she said no.

They were both half naked and, at least he, visibly aroused. Wasn't it a little late to be asking? Lacy didn't bother to point that out, however, saying simply, "If you have a condom, I'm more than sure."

Eli chuckled. "Are you kidding? I'm a musician on tour. Of course I have a condom . . . even if I haven't used one in a while." He moved her off of him so he could scramble out of his jeans.

She giggled at his comment, especially because she was pretty certain Eli wasn't the type to go cruising, but she was done by the time he'd finished flipping through his wallet to find a foil packet. Then she grew completely serious because Eli had pulled down his boxers and released the thing that had been teasing her for the better part of their make-out session.

And, wow, oh, wow.

Either she'd forgotten exactly what a cock looked like in the flesh or Eli was what they called "hung." She bet it was probably a combination of both. Either way, it was impressive and her insides quivered with anticipation as Eli ripped the packet open and unrolled the condom along his thick length.

A shiver slid down her spine. This was happening—totally unforeseen and unplanned—and she was one hundred percent certain it was exactly what she wanted.

Which meant she should probably lose her own panties. Like now.

With another half giggle, Lacy stood and pushed her skirt and underwear down together. Eli watched her as she undressed, and her skin pinked from head to toe. It wasn't that she was self-conscious about her body, but the way he was looking at her—it was so appreciative. So filled with awe. As if he found the sight of her naked self extraordinary in some way.

It made her dizzy and giddy. It made her feel beautiful. It also made her even more eager to not only have him but to give herself to him.

She stepped one foot over him and lowered to her knees, once again straddling him as she hovered over his cock.

The melody that had been hiding just beneath her perception swelled within her as they moved together to join their bodies. The feel of him filling her set off sparklers in her nerve endings she had forgotten existed, if she'd ever known.

She kept her eyes open, kept her focus pinned on him as he moved inside her. All her senses were ignited. Her vision was drunk with the sight of his face, her body on fire everywhere they touched. The smell of his sweat mingled with hers. The salty taste of his skin lingered on her tongue.

And the music . . .

In her head spun fragments of a song. Words and phrases that hadn't settled to make any sense but whirred around, dizzying her with their potential melody. It was there, ready to pluck from the air like ripe fruit on a low branch. In pieces, maybe, but a song nonetheless.

Eli quickened his pace, thrusting in and out of her now with abandon. Her nails dug into his shoulders, clutching to the song in her mind as she clutched to him. She could feel herself tightening and Eli's drives slowed some as he pushed through.

When they came together, the notes in her head coalesced at the same time she fell apart. Gasping for air, they held each other while their heartbeats slowly returned to normal.

And once that happened, Lacy's head was suddenly on straight. Her heart rate might be normal, but there would be nothing normal about this tour again.

They were quiet as Lacy gathered her clothes. She slipped on her blouse and skirt, and stuffed her panties and bra into her guitar case alongside Lucky. When she turned back to Eli, he'd pulled on his jeans, the button still undone at his waist. She didn't look him in the eye. She couldn't. She kept her focus on her feet as she slipped on her sandals then on her case as she flung it over her shoulder.

Then she headed for the door. Eli followed after her.

She paused, her hand on the knob, and cleared her throat. "Well, uh, thanks for . . ." For what, exactly? The music? The pizza? The quickie on the carpet? All of it, really, but saying any of it sounded silly.

"Hey," Eli said, tilting her chin up with two fingers

until she had no choice but to meet his gaze. "Let's not do that awkward thing, okay? Not tonight. I had a good time."

"I did too."

"Then let's focus on that." He kissed her—slowly, sweetly—his thumb caressing her skin as he cradled her cheek. When he pulled away, he said. "We'll deal with awkward tomorrow. Okay, Songbird?"

"Deal." God, he was great. But her focus was already beyond him and on the song dancing in her head.

Lacy went to her room and crawled into her bed. Sleeping while a song brewed had always proved a good tactic. She'd wake up and have words and melody created in her dreams. She plugged in her phone next to her and set the alarm, not bothering to check if she'd missed any notifications from Folx. Reading a message from him now would be awkward. And she wasn't dealing with awkward until tomorrow.

Chapter Eleven

Sometimes on tour, Eli woke up confused, a few seconds passing before he remembered where he was and why. It was the side effect of every day a different city, every night another bed. Similar was the stress of remembering his room number. Was he in three-twelve or was that the last hotel? More than once he'd stuck his key card in the wrong door, unsure when it didn't work if he'd accidentally swiped it against something magnetic or if he'd gotten the wrong room. Again.

This morning he had no such confusion. Last night's indiscretion crashed over him before he was even conscious of having woken. He was even pretty sure he'd been dreaming about Lacy—her mouth on his, her nipples rubbing against his skin. His dick was awake and at attention even before he opened his eyes.

He groaned.

He felt like an absolute shit.

Not surprising since that's what he was—an absolute piece of shit. The list of reasons was unfurling like silk scarves from a magician's sleeve—they just kept coming.

Lacy, a woman he worked with, had opened up to him emotionally, and he'd gotten a hard-on. He'd missed his date with LoveCoda to bang a chick who'd cried on his shoulder. He'd disrespected not one, but two women with one sexual encounter. What kind of person was he?

He pulled his pillow over his head and screamed into it.

After a trip to the bathroom—not an easy task with his insistent morning wood—and a splash of cold water on his face, he returned to his room and looked around. Remnants of the night before lay all around him. Empty pop cans. His banjo abandoned on the floor. The smooshed pizza box. With another groan, he slumped on the couch and attempted to put some organization to his guilt.

Lacy Dawson wanted center stage in his thoughts. He was still half hard, and her presence was still alive in the room. The image of her sweet smile and warm touch tried to press in and remind him of how good she'd felt in his arms, but he shoved it away and focused on the heart of his regret instead—he'd cheated on Love.

He squeezed his eyes shut as he ran his fingers across his lids to pinch the bridge of his nose. His father had been that kind of asshole. The one who not only yelled and hit but had a woman on the side most of the time. Eli hated to have anything in common with his dad, and for the most part he succeeded. Until now, when he'd broken a vow he'd made to one woman for the silky heat of another.

So maybe the vow didn't really count since he'd never said it—typed it—to LoveCoda, but it felt like it should. Because he'd made the vow in his heart. Was it any less to break a promise to himself than to someone else? And he'd wanted to keep this promise. It wasn't like he'd cheated on his New Year's resolutions that he really couldn't give a flying fig about three weeks into the year. He'd broken a vow he'd *wanted* to be true to.

Yep. An absolute shit.

Then there wasn't just the fact that he'd cheated on his girlfriend-who-didn't-even-know-she-was-his-girlfriend. He'd also blown off their standing date. God, he hoped she wasn't pissed. Or worried, more like it. She was the kind of girl who would be concerned over his well-being, rather than angry about a missed chat. She was officially too good for him.

Needing to toss something, he threw the couch pillow across the room and blew out a stream of curse words that would make his mother scold him.

Well, it wasn't like he was going to tell her why he'd missed their date. He reached for his tablet and pulled up the chat.

Hey, you. I feel like a total asshole. Sorry I missed last night. Something came up, a friend needed help. I ended up falling asleep. Hope you slept well. Wow, he was really bad at this. Only one lie was needed. He deleted some words and rearranged some others. Then he added some xx's at the end. He felt good about the x's. Sending hugs was always a good thing. Or were the x's kisses and the o's hugs? He never could figure that out.

Whether kisses or hugs, it was appropriate. Probably. He pushed enter, and waited to feel marginally better.

It didn't happen.

Something was nagging at him. Something more than the guilty voices shouting in his head.

He blinked at his screen. LoveCoda hadn't written to him, either. He wasn't the only one who missed the date. Strangely, this also failed to make him feel better. Now *he* was worried about *her*. Some irrational fear that she somehow *knew* what he had done pricked at him. What if she never logged on again? She might avoid him forever. She might even leave SoWriAn or adopt a new screen name just so she wouldn't have to face him again. If she'd found another guy, he'd do the same thing.

God, he was an idiot.

He wouldn't do the same thing. He'd stick it out and try to mend their relationship. He was a total romantic.

He was an idiot again, because she didn't *know*. She couldn't. And it didn't really matter if she did, because the two of them were not dating. Not really. It just felt like it.

He threw himself back onto the bed again with a dramatic flair that Jax would have been proud of. If somehow Love *did* know—which she couldn't, but *if*—then he was sure she'd judge him harshly.

Okay, that was idiotic too since she'd never given any indication of being any type of a judger.

Which only made him feel worse. She *should* judge him. She should decorate him with a scarlet A for "Asshole."

What had he been thinking?

He could make up excuses. He'd just been going with the motion, for example. She was the one who'd chosen his bedroom. It wasn't his fault she'd had those sad eyes and pouty lips.

The truth was Lacy Dawson was the coolest girl he'd met in ages. Playing music with her felt as natural as playing with his own band. That said something, since the Blue Hills had been together in various incarnations since sophomore year of high school. So he played with her, insisted they talk, pried into her personal life, passed harsh judgment on her dead fiancé, and then fucked her when she was most vulnerable.

And, man, had it been amazing. As in A.Maz.Ing.

Really, he should be castrated. That was the only fitting punishment at this point.

He glanced at the bedside clock and realized it was past time for him to get up. Sammy would be pounding on his door any minute. The days they weren't traveling belonged to the band to do with as they pleased for the most part. Today they had a load in at the new venue later that morning, followed by sound check, and then they were free until the show. Lou, though, was a stickler for breakfasts. More specifically, he was a stickler for free breakfasts, and he encouraged his boys to take advantage when they were offered.

Eli pulled a worn tee and jeans on as slowly as he could, dreading the moment when he'd head down to the lobby and see Lacy. He'd told her last night they'd deal with awkward today. He was regretting that now that today was right this minute. She probably hated his guts now that she'd had a chance to think about it, although no one could possibly hate him more than he hated himself.

The part he hated most was how he was still fighting down the erection that had threatened him from the moment his eyes opened and he recalled the sight and feel and scent of her body on his. Though they hadn't had a drop to drink, he had been dizzy as he inhaled that soft floral scent from the hollow of her neck. Even if they'd gone no further, he'd felt drunk on her kisses. He glanced down. Well, everyone would notice *that*.

On the way to the lobby, Eli forced himself to think of nothing but baseball until he'd gotten himself under control. Then he planned for the moment to come. The real problem was going to be what Lacy thought of him, not what he was thinking about. Last night he may have been the kind of man he didn't want to be, but this morning was his chance to prove to her that he wasn't a horrible person. This was his chance to be the man he thought of himself as, the kind who owned up to his mistakes, the kind who apologized and promised to never let his mistake happen again.

He'd started to feel better about the whole thing. Or at

least as though he might be able to get through the day.
Except then he got to the lobby where breakfast was laid
out, found the table where the guys were sitting, and realized that Lacy wasn't with them.

Eli rubbed at his scruff, suddenly worried about what
her absence meant. Was she too embarrassed to face him?

He should ask about her. Unless that seemed weird.
Lacy always ate with them, so curiosity about her whereabouts should be normal.

"What's your deal, a-hole?" It was a standard greeting
from Jax, and pretty reasonable since Eli had been standing in one place looking like an idiot since he'd arrived.

He lied, of course. "I'm trying to decide if I want pan-
cakes or waffles." Then he felt bad about lying. Probably
because he felt bad in general. He tapped Sammy on the
shoulder. "Hey, where's Lacy?"

"Dawson? I don't know. Do I look like her mother?"
Sammy eyed him.

He pressed her further. "You usually wake us up. Didn't
you go to her room?"

Sammy laughed around a mouthful of eggs. "I don't
wake up Dawson." Well, that was certainly news. "Lou
says women are smart enough to not need to be reminded
to eat breakfast. Though he does seem to nag at her about
dinners, so I'm not sure his reasoning there."

Somehow it didn't surprise Eli that Lou didn't wake
Lacy for breakfast. Eli had often believed the routine for
the boys was only to make sure they didn't stay up all night
partying. It made sense, considering Jax was in the band.
At the moment it was unfortunate, though, since that left
Eli in a state of concern. Maybe he should go to Lacy's
room and check on her himself. But if she were avoiding
him, then that really would be awkward.

He searched for a reason to send Sammy. "But don't you
need her for load in at the next venue?"

"That's not until eleven." Sammy wiped her mouth with the back of her hand. "If she doesn't make it to the bus on time, I'll go after her then. Stop your worrying, nerd. You got a thing for her or something?" He could feel himself blushing as he tried to make appropriately horrified faces.

Eleven. That was two whole hours away. He should probably go and talk to Lacy before that. Make his apology. Promise to behave in the future.

However, thinking of talking to her alone in her hotel room didn't seem wise at the moment. Not when memories of the night before were still strongly singed in his mind and in his pants. And come to think of it, he didn't even know what room number was hers. Sure, he could ask, but that would be really obvious. So he decided to just play it the way he had been and let whatever happened happen.

Yeah, because that was working out for him well so far.

The sun streamed through the hotel window, hitting Lacy smack in the face and waking her earlier than she'd wanted. Dammit. She'd forgotten to close the blackout curtains. A glance at the alarm clock said that it wasn't even nine. As a musician who worked and thrived at night, she hadn't seen before nine in eons. God, it sucked.

She stretched her arms over her head and her toes toward the bottom of the bed. Man, was she stiff. Her thigh muscles were singing and stinging like she'd been in a rodeo. What was up with that?

Then it hit her. Memories flashed before her like a pornographic slideshow. Eli. Eli naked. *Her* naked. Their naked parts together.

Then another thought—Folx.

Aw, crap.

She couldn't remember the last time she'd missed a date with Folx. And that she missed it because she'd been with Eli. Intimately . . .

She felt like a sack of the brown stuff.

Funny, though. Her phone hadn't buzzed with any incoming messages the night before. Maybe something was wrong with her cell. She scrambled out of bed to use the bathroom. On the way back, she grabbed her laptop and climbed back under the covers. She logged in to SoWriAn. There it was—a single message in her queue left less than half an hour before.

Hey, I feel like a total asshole. I fell asleep and missed you last night. Hope you slept well. xx

He'd sent kisses. That was new. And sweet.

Lacy threw herself back on her bed with a sigh. The whole message sent a burst of warmth through her body. Followed by a shower of ice-cold regret. She felt so much for him—*so much*—and she'd cheated on him.

Okay, technically, she hadn't cheated on him. They'd both agreed to put anything they had together on hold. But how could she do that, really? Just pause her emotions like a button on Spotify. It wasn't that easy.

Or was it? Because, if she was honest—and hell, this was all in her head so what was the harm in a little truth—she'd had a pretty excellent evening with Eli. Not just the sex, but the sharing. The connecting. Finally unloading about Lance.

And, yes, the sex.

All of it was incredible. So if it really wasn't cheating—and it really wasn't—then maybe she could embrace it for what it was. Something good and beautiful and very much needed. Like hearing an unexpectedly brilliant song in the middle of a lousy playlist.

Oh, my God!

Lacy bolted upright. There had been words! A phrase. Lyrics swarming in her head. She searched her memory to see if she could recall them, which was a bit tricky in between all the particularly pleasant thoughts of Eli kissing her, touching her, moving inside her. Eli certainly was a good lover. The kind of lover she wouldn't mind a repeat tryst with if she was—

Her train of thought derailed. Because, there they were. The words.

Pieces of me.
You're just pieces of me.

She shot out of bed to grab her guitar and her notepad. The second her hands struck the first chord, the melody came, clinging to the lyrics in her head as if they'd been born together. A whole refrain came out within minutes.

There's pieces of me
Where you live
Like you never went away
And there's pieces of me
That can't focus off your face
And there's times I believe, I'll move on,
That I'll be whole and healed someday

But I'm busted and broken
And there's just pieces of me

She played it over and over, the weight of the song on her tongue comforting and electric and new. Like a comet streaking through her with its light and its fire, the darkness on her writing had been lifted.

She nearly wept from the exhilarating release.

Then she reached the verse, got one line in, and the block was back. There was nothing. No more words. Nada. Zilch. A big fat absence of lyric.

Lacy spun Lucky and shook its neck as if she were throttling the instrument. "Gahhhh!"

Immediately she felt sorry. It wasn't Lucky's fault she was a worthless songwriter. What had she expected anyway? Nearly a year of nothing, no matter how hard she'd tried, and now she thought she'd be able to write a whole piece like she'd never been blocked? Maybe it was unreasonable.

Or . . .

Maybe she just needed to figure out what it was that had struck the inspiration in the first place. There were a number of factors at work, of course, the most obvious that she'd been with Eli. They'd been talking music. They'd been jamming. But she'd jammed at the studio and onstage. She'd talked music with lots of people. And she'd had just as many deep conversations with Folx and hadn't been able to open up.

Which meant it had to be the sex.

Oh, my God.

She sat up as the realization dawned on her. *I need orgasms to write songs!*

Could that actually be the issue? All this time it wasn't Lance's death that had left her dry, but a lack of sex?

No way. That was just absurd.

Come to think of it, though, she'd only written sparse poetry before she lost her virginity at fifteen. Yes, she'd been an early bloomer. Songwriting had come soon after that. She'd been sexually active with one boyfriend or another from then on. Of course she'd written more when she was in love—that was pretty standard—but she'd never connected that her inspiration might be the sex.

She burst into laughter. There was no other possible response. She'd always considered her lyrics her superpower. Now she found it might be triggered by O's. It was rather hilarious.

It was also problematic. She had a whole album scheduled to record in a couple months time and only half a song written. And except for the one encounter the night before, she wasn't getting any. If her theory about the sex and the inspiration was correct, then she was screwed.

Screwed by being not screwed.

She let out another *ha* at that. Well, what else was she supposed to do?

Actually, what she had to do was test her theory out. She needed to have sex again and see if more lyrics came. Her true love interest only knew her online. Maybe she could suggest an earlier meetup with Folx. Except she was on tour and he was on tour, and even when they did meet it didn't mean there'd be sex. At least, not right away.

That left Eli.

She'd have to have sex with Eli again. The event had gone well enough. There was no reason to think he wouldn't be interested in a second round. Yes, that was what she needed to do—hunt him down and attack.

Lacy showered quickly then threw on some cut-off shorts and a tank top intending to head straight to Eli's room. While she searched for her key card, though, there was a knock on her door. Maybe it was Eli coming for her. Wouldn't that make things easy?

She put on her sexiest smile and opened the door wide.

Sammy stood there with a rather intimidating scowl on her face. "It's eleven oh three. We were supposed to leave for the venue three minutes ago. You're late."

Already eleven? Man, she'd forgotten how time got away from her when she was in the creative zone. "Gosh, I'm sorry, Sammy. I lost track of the hour. Let me just grab my things."

This was fine, too, Lacy decided as she flung her bag and her guitar over her shoulder. She'd get her sound check over with and then she'd have all afternoon to bang Eli and bang out some words.

Chapter Twelve

Lacy skipped to keep up with Sammy as she followed her down to the bus. With each step, she grew a little less excited and a little more nervous about seeing Eli again.

What she was, really, was a girl on a morning-after high. A girl who wanted to repeat the night before, but for convoluted reasons. It was perfectly natural to feel a little anxious.

She kept her eyes down as she climbed onto the bus and deposited her guitar in its storage rack. Not only because of her anxiety but because Sammy was currently embarrassing her with an announcement to the others.

"I got her. Obviously. Miss Thang seems to have 'lost track of the hour.'" Sammy turned back to her victim. "Don't let it happen again."

Lacy couldn't stop herself from spitting out a "Yes, ma'am." Which earned her a scowl. It was undeserved, in Lacy's opinion. Her ma'am-ing was only fifty percent sarcastic.

"Next time, the bus leaves you."

This time, Lacy bit back any response fighting for release. It seemed best to let Sammy have the last word.

Sammy headed back toward her usual seat, and Lacy finally braved a glance up at the others. Immediately her eyes found Eli's. Her body thrummed like a tuning fork to his perfect note, her skin beading in goose bumps, her nipples pebbling under her tank. His expression was serious, so he was difficult to read. At least he wasn't avoiding her. She was instantly more confident in the likelihood of their repeat sexing. Excited about it even, the nervousness and anxiety ebbing.

She smiled at him and went on to take the empty seat in the next aisle. Before she sat, though, she shot a smile to the rest of the bus, an apology for her tardiness. It was then she noticed that Jax, sitting in his typical backseat location, wasn't in his typical prone posture. And he wasn't—as he typically was—alone. There was a girl next to him. Not just any girl—Kat.

Kat? Really?

Lacy huffed to herself as she slunk into her spot. One of the plusses about taking the tour had been the prospect of not seeing the endlessly optimistic, always-got-it-together Kat. And yet, she kept seeing Kat. And wasn't she supposed to be covering Lacy's shifts at the studio? She must have hopped a train that morning. It was sure convenient how she'd somehow managed now to weasel her way onto three stops of the circuit under the auspices of "gaining roadie experience," as if Kat was about to embark on a tour. She didn't even have a band. But banging the drummer did seem to give her a few perks.

Did one of those perks have to be infringing on Lacy's personal space?

Whatever. It was fine. Kat *got* her this tour, she had no room to exclude her.

The bus lurched into motion and Lacy centered herself,

practicing meditation from her yoga days. *This is a beautiful day. I'm in a beautiful space. I'm on tour making beautiful music. I had xxx's from Folx. Eli's still making eye contact.*

And I wrote a song! An actual song. Not a jingle. A song.

Part of a song, but still, a major thing to be happy about.

Also on her list, *I got laid.* But she felt a little weird about celebrating that when she and Eli hadn't made it through the awkward stage yet, which was a very real part of the getting laid. So it counted, but she pretended it didn't. Fortunately she was well practiced at self-delusion.

After coming to terms with her just-got-laid status, Lacy found she couldn't think of a good reason to let anything bring her down today. She concentrated on letting potential negative energy go, and by the time they pulled into the venue parking lot, her chakras were charged and her atman was at peace.

She felt so good as she stepped off the bus that she couldn't keep from giggling out loud. The tang of the Baltimore harbor wafted over her with all the promise it held of adventure and good food. The sun poured down like glory. And she'd written (part of) a song for the first time in a year.

She threw her arms out and spun in place like she was in her own personal *Sound of Music.* It was going to be A Best Day Ever; she could just feel it.

Oh, no. That was Wes's nose that she felt. With her elbow.

"Calm down, there, Lacypants. The hills may be alive, but Wes won't be if you keep that up," Jax muttered as he shoved past her fumbling apologies, followed by James and Eli and the other band member whose name Lacy couldn't seem to remember. And Kat.

Sammy, obviously over her earlier irritation, smiled. "I'll get your shit, kid. If we get right in there, we should be able to knock out your sound check before the boys are even loaded in."

Getting her sound check done early? Definitely the beginnings of A Best Day Ever.

Thirty minutes later, Lacy's sound check was in the bag, and the boys were onstage for theirs. Her afternoon was free and clear, and since the only thing she had on her agenda was jumping Eli, she decided to stick around and listen to the band.

She found a seat in the middle of the venue and, because of her earlier banishment of bad energy, wasn't even irritated when Kat took a seat next to her. Even though there was a whole auditorium of other places where she could have sat.

"They're so good," Kat said while the band was still tuning. "This has to be the greatest gig in the world. Listening to them every night. Hanging out with those beautiful men every day." She sighed.

"I actually haven't really listened to them until today," Lacy admitted, glowing because *she* was the one with the greatest gig in the world and not Kat. "And usually we don't do much hanging during the day." That was about to change, if Lacy had anything to do with it. Though it wouldn't be *those beautiful men* she'd be hanging with, but *that beautiful Eli*. And "hanging" wasn't exactly what she had planned, though it did rhyme with it.

"You haven't? Some of us were planning to see some of the town after this. Join us!"

"Uh." It depended on whether "some of us" included Eli. Lacy really was dying to see Baltimore. It was high on her to-do list, right under "write beautiful lyrics" and "get it on with beautiful guy." She said, "That might be something I could do." She was proud of that answer. Not a yes, not a no. She could decide for sure when she found out what Eli's plans were.

After a few minutes of individual mike and instrument testing, the band launched into a song. Just like it had been at the show she'd seen previously, their synchronicity was amazing. Lacy decided they must have worked together for a long time now. How else were they reading each other's minds like that? A look between Jax and Eli somehow translated to the drummer, Wes, and they extended a jam before returning to the main riff. Jax swayed like a hypnotized snake, and she could imagine how it would draw all eyes to him when the place was filled. How he'd woo the women before he even opened his mouth.

"He's like sex on legs," Kat purred. "I want to lick him from head to toe."

Lacy made an "mm" in agreement, though she didn't mean it about Jax. Kat could have the lead singer, for all she cared. Or the drummer if that was still going on. Both of them, even.

Because it was Eli who was the cause of Lacy's hum.

He fascinated her with his subtle, perfect artistry. With the easiness with which he played. With the way his hands moved up and down his instrument, his long fingers spreading nimbly across the strings. God, those hands . . . those fingers . . .

She crossed her legs as a warm flush of memories from the night before poured through her like a shot of whiskey. Warm and sweet and delicious.

And he played good music to boot.

Yes, this was the greatest gig in the world.

The instrumental prelude gave way to another song and, though her eyes never left Eli, she was aware of Jax belting out a verse in that gorgeously raspy voice. He was like a scoop of cream on top of her Eli sundae. She was so lost

in the heaven of the moment, it took her several lines before she really heard the words of the lyric.

With a sweep of your hand and a curse
You've ravaged my world.
Destroyed all I cared for and then
You leave me to live

She uncrossed her legs and sat up straighter in her seat.
They weren't just good lyrics. They were exquisite lyrics.
But that wasn't what had the hair standing up on the back
of her neck and goose bumps racing down her arms.

"What is it?"

Ignoring Kat's question, Lacy's asked one of her own.
"They didn't do this song the night we saw them, did
they?"

"At Tigerstripes? I don't think so. Wes said they saved
all their new material for the actual tour. Why?"

Lacy's heart was pounding and her hands were sweaty
as she turned her attention back to Jax. *Because I know
this one.*

Out loud she said, "It's good. I was sure I'd remember
it if I'd heard it before." She hadn't actually *heard* it before. She'd only seen the words. She'd workshopped those
words. "Godric's Hollow." It was a genius of a song, comparing the pain of a destructive relationship to the worst
night in Harry Potter's life. Before she ever even heard the
music that accompanied it, she'd already loved this song.

But of course she'd love it. Because this was Folx's song.

And that meant . . .

No way.

It couldn't be possible. It was too much of a coincidence.
Wasn't it? Could Folx really be a member of the Blue Hills?
And if so, which one?

She meant to scan her eyes over all of the boys, but she

didn't get past Jax. He was front and center, singing in a grit-filled voice, delivering the lyric with such conviction. Watching him perform this song was like looking into something personal, something private. He sang it like he owned it. It was *his* song.

And if Jax was singing it, then it had to mean that Jax . . . was Folx.

Her breath caught at the full implications of her realization. So many warring thoughts ran through her head— excitement, nervousness. Stone cold fear. Jubilation. What were the odds? That they were both from Boston, that they were on tour together. How had she looked when he'd first met her? Not as good as she'd planned to look, that was for sure. At the wedding in her formal dress and makeup, she'd be looking, well, better than she had any day on the tour.

But enough about how she looked. On to how *he* looked. Because oh, my god, Jax was Folx, and Jax was hot, but wow. This was not what she was expecting. She'd imagined him plenty of times, of course. In her head he'd been darker, less pretty, more gruff. Attractive like . . . well, like Eli.

She swallowed back the strange taste of disappointment. This would take an adjustment, that's all. But she could get used to it. She'd thought he was attractive from the first minute she'd met him. Though the zing he'd initially sent to her girl parts had dulled, it was still there. Probably. She eyed up and down his lean form in those tight jeans and plaid shirt. Oh yeah, he would work.

And ohmygod, he was Folx!

She knew him. He knew her. They were bonded. Joined at the soul. The song he was singing? It was, in a way, theirs.

"Unfuckingbelievable," she said with a laugh.

Kat glanced at her, but seemed to think she was talking

about how amazing the song was. And that just made Lacy laugh more. Then the band was at the chorus, which was another point of amusement. It was the part that Folx, uh, Jax had said the band cut. Sure enough, he was singing a line of "yeahs" then holding his mike out to the audience—which at the moment consisted of two. Good old Kat echoed him back in her screechy, though perfectly pitched, soprano.

Lacy refrained from joining in, too stunned. Too awestruck. Too devoted to the original architecture of the song. Though she'd never heard the melody of the chorus, she remembered the words and could feel how they would have fit in harmony with the mandolin line. She sang them in her head.

> *You break me, you make me*
> *You take me, you wake me*
> *You set me to fire and I burn*

They would have been incredible. Much better than this commercial gimmick that Jax was leading. The audience probably loved it, but musically . . .

Well, it was a shameful loss. But who the hell cared— she was listening to Folx sing for the very first time!

For the very first time since she knew he was Folx, anyway. And like a true performer, Jax was making it work, despite the flawed arrangement, playing the part with enthusiasm and soul. It was impressive. And bewildering. She'd had no idea from his online conversations that he was so charismatic. So commanding of the stage.

It bothered her just a little. As if she'd somehow hoped his charm was meant only for her. The way that Eli's charm always seemed meant for her.

Oh, shit.

Eli.

Sweet, incredible, the guy-she'd-banged-the-night-before Eli.

Well, this was awkward. And not in the way that she'd thought the day after was going to be. She turned her focus back to him and found he was watching her. As soon as their eyes met, he smiled, and the sincerity of it made her legs feel like jelly even though she was sitting down. Before she knew it, she was smiling back.

But, wait. Should she be smiling at him now? Now that Folx wasn't just a person-she'd-meet-in-the-future person, but a real-life flesh-and-blood person she already knew.

She didn't know. There wasn't protocol for this. And she didn't want to stop, uh, *smiling* at him. Because Eli did things to her . . . amazing things . . . wonderful things. And he'd inspired words.

But he wasn't her soul mate. He wasn't The One. He wasn't Folx.

She looked back at Jax-who-*was*-Folx, and the minute she did, he threw his gaze directly at her—or, maybe at Kat—and winked.

Ah, Folx.

I mean, Jax.

It was a Plot Twist Moment. Something else Lance used to like to celebrate. Those moments that changed everything. Where nothing could be the same after. *This* was one of those moments.

Because this couldn't just be a coincidence. Folx—the man she'd been dreaming about, the man who'd been with her through the worst of it, the man she'd been falling for little by little for the better part of a year—was on the very same tour she was on. That had to be kismet. That had to be A Sign.

Also, Plot Twist.

And one she never saw coming.

Now she just had to figure out what to do next. Should

she tell Jax who she was or not? She should. Of course she should.

Just then, Jax growled into the microphone, as if concurring with her decision.

"Damn," Kat said. "Just . . . damn."

Now that Lacy knew who Jax was, she wasn't so comfortable with Kat's adoration. "Uh, aren't you and Wes still a thing?" Surely, they were and Kat was just expressing the general reaction of all women when they encountered Jax.

"We're a thing," Kat confirmed. But then she added, "Just not a monogamous thing. And I'm thinking it might be time for another thing." The sultry narrowing of her eyes as she looked toward the lead singer made it apparent that the other *thing* she was referring to was a thing that involved Jax.

An alarm went off in Lacy's head. "Is Jax going with you to see the town?"

"Yeah. Pretty sure."

And that was a reason Lacy should tell Jax she was LoveCoda. Because she couldn't possibly let him hook up with someone like Kat, even for just a night. The thought of Folx hooking up with anyone who wasn't her was bothersome, actually. Even when they hadn't made promises, Folx was hers. Not Kat's.

Er, *Jax* was hers. Jax/Folx. Except, she wasn't as bothered by the idea of a Jax and Kat hookup as she was a Folx and Kat hookup. Weird. But explainable. She wasn't used to Jax and Folx being the same person—that was all.

Really, it wasn't fair that she be bothered by any of it because she'd hooked up with Eli.

Eli. Her stomach fluttered when she thought of him. It was silly post-sex body reactions. Yes, that. Eli had conditioned her hormonal response. Nothing serious. She'd be over it as soon as she moved on to someone new. To

Folx—correction, Jax. Which she'd do as soon as sound check was over.

Probably.

No reason to even hesitate.

Though . . . Folx had been the one to pick Christmas Eve as a date to meet. Maybe he'd made it so far out because of the tour. But that wrapped up in November. Which meant that he must need the extra time for some other reason. Maybe he wanted to get settled back at home first. Or had some other obligation she wasn't aware of. Lacy didn't want to push their relationship to happen before it was time.

So she wouldn't tell him. She'd keep the status quo and maybe try to get to know him more in person. Give him the space he needed before the big reveal, though not so much space that he'd jump into bed with Kat. He'd probably appreciate that later.

Yes. It was decided. She'd keep the secret until Christmas Eve. For him.

Certainly not because *she* wanted more time.

And, even more certainly, not because there was anyone else she wanted more time *with* before she committed completely to Folx.

Though, after sound check was done and the band was let loose for the afternoon, it sure was a whole lot easier to decide to join Kat and Jax on the town when Eli said he'd come too.

Chapter Thirteen

"So what are we doing, LacyP?" Jax asked, when the four-some stepped out of the dark venue and into the sunshine.

She hadn't said a word while the plans were made to explore together. There was still the awkwardness with Eli and now that she knew Jax's true identity, she felt strange around him as well. Nervous in a way that was new. Starstruck, almost. Now when she looked at him, she remembered words he'd said online, jokes he'd made. The sweet, tender gestures that had made her fall for him. But since he was still in the dark about her identity, it was as if he were a celebrity and she was a fan. She knew every-thing about him, and he knew nothing about her. It was hard to know how to talk to him, so she'd hung back and let the others do the talking.

But now he'd initiated the conversation, and not only was he putting her in charge—*take that Kat*—but he'd given her a nickname to boot. Giddiness swept through her along with the overwhelming feeling that everything was right with the world. "Boats! Food! Is it dangerous to go explore where they filmed *The Wire*? But first, food. All we eat today is crab."

"Eh, I don't really like seafood," Kat moaned as she threw an arm around Jax and another around Eli.

"Then order off the goddamn kids menu," Lacy snapped. "We're in Baltimore! We eat crab." With that, she stalked off, toward the harbor, letting out a breath of frustrated air.

"Do you know where you're going?" Eli asked, catching up.

"I haven't the slightest. But I had to leave on a high note." She kept walking though her insides tightened at his nearness in a way that gave new meaning to the term "muscle memory." She was a little worried how Jax had taken her explosion, though.

Then Eli leaned in close, and the hairs on the back of her neck stood up in awareness and she forgot all about Kat alone with Jax behind her. "If you take a left at the next corner, you'll be headed the right way."

This was their first conversation since *it* happened, and they were talking about something as commonplace as directions. And . . . it didn't feel awkward. It felt easy. More, she was grateful he'd helped her with her awkward exit.

Lacy flashed him a smile. "I don't know why she grates on me at times. It's really shitty of me." Nope, not admitting why to him. Not admitting she was jealous. She wondered if Jax was following. Was that weird to care when Eli was there?

Yes, it was weird. The whole thing was weird. But that didn't stop the impulse to glance over her shoulder to see.

Jax *was* following. As was Kat. They were no longer touching, though, and they seemed to be walking in silence, which added a boost to Lacy's step.

"Really? I actually thought you guys were friends." Eli drew her attention back to him. "I think she's a bit much, but I was being nice cause I thought you liked her." He slipped a pair of aviators on and dimpled up at her. The hot day was only getting hotter, between the two frontmen of the Blue Hills. That was cool, right? To be totally into both of them for such different reasons?

She was confused. That's what she was. Really confused.

Also, she was perturbed to have to share the outing with Kat. "Well, I think Wes likes her, so you should probably still be nice." She brightened as she said this, realizing that Jax wouldn't hit on Kat because it would be rude to Wes. Folx was the type of guy who put his band members ahead of his music. Of course he wouldn't try to steal one of the others' girls.

It didn't mean Kat was as decent, however. Lacy scowled. "I have to work with her, so I have no choice either."

Maybe that was a little harsh. Or a lot harsh. Okay, really unfairly harsh.

She softened. "Plus, she's really generous. She basically got me on this tour. I owe her big." Lacy took the recommended left and pulled her oversized shades off her head and onto her nose, hoping the dark lenses covered the guilt welling up inside. "In fact, I should be nicer."

"Oh, I don't have to be nice just because she's sleeping with Wes. We have a groupie clause. No false politeness required, and we can even share." He winced as if realizing that might be inappropriate considering their recent activities.

Lacy, however, was grateful for the information. Hopefully that meant no hard feelings between the boys when she finally got together with Folx. Uh, Jax. Not that she was a groupie. And . . .

Wait a minute . . .

She peeked again over her shoulder at the two stragglers. They were chatting now, Kat smiling more than Lacy thought was reasonable, but otherwise a pretty innocent scene. *Hmm.* The band's groupie clause might encourage a fling between Jax and Kat, after all.

Maybe she should be walking with them and not with Eli. Maybe Jax even thought Lacy was into Eli. Shit! She was, of course, but . . . dammit!

This needed to be a group adventure and not a double date if she was going to keep her bizarre new relationships on track.

She slowed her pace, hoping Jax and Kat would catch up quickly.

"You know though"—again Eli drew her attention back to him—"if Kat's responsible for getting you here, I guess I owe her a beer." He slid his shades down and winked. It sent a little shiver down her spine. He wanted her here.

Maybe the alone time with him was just fine after all.

"Hey, it's a Crab Cakery!" Lacy exclaimed, both to break the delicious tension and also because *crab.* She led the way through the door. "Bet you could even buy that beer here," she teased, as they took off their glasses to adjust to the lighting inside the crab shack. It smelled like heaven, if heaven were a divey seafood bar. Which, if you asked Lacy, it had to be. Why else would people look forward to the hereafter, if lobster rolls and whiskey weren't on offer?

"Sweet Jesus. It smells like heaven," pronounced Jax, from behind.

Thank God he feels the same. She turned in time to see him run a hand through his shaggy blonde hair and inhale again appreciatively. So did Lacy, as she watched his eyes close in pleasure. She attempted to put the image to memory. She needed to draw this image of Folx when she fantasized about him in the future and not the old Eli-like image she had of him.

"I hope they have chicken tenders," whined Kat. Or not really whined, but Lacy thought it was near enough to call it that.

Eli patted her on the shoulder. "You can drink your lunch, if you want. I'm buying."

Kat grinned toothily at Eli, not even questioning why he'd offer.

That was a good solution—Eli and Kat should pair up.

Except that didn't feel right either. Not at all. And not just because she needed him for lyric-inducing orgasms. Wait a minute. Would it be wrong to continue to get it on with Eli now that Jax was Folx?

In her gut, she was pretty sure sleeping with one while planning to be with the other wasn't the most couth of plans. She didn't want to earn the same groupie reputation that Kat boasted. But she'd already been with Eli, so it probably changed nothing to do it again. As long as she cut that off before sleeping with Jax, she should be good. Once more was all she needed to confirm the lyrics-orgasm connection anyway.

Probably.

Or maybe not. The sweet thing Eli had said about her only a few minutes before was still fresh in her head, and she realized she felt truly torn between the two men. Like, maybe she might want to consider Eli as more than just a source for song material. Both men drew her to them physically—she'd known that since the first night she'd seen them onstage.

But then she remembered everything else Jax was when he was his Folx persona and the dilemma seemed moot. Her heart belonged to Folx. Every time.

Besides, Eli buying Kat's lunch was sweet, not romantic. She'd try to remember that the gesture was about her and not anything about Kat.

"That's so nice of you to buy," Kat said, sidling up to Eli. Lacy scowled.

Jax's brows shot up. "You're buying?"

Lacy was pretty sure Eli had just meant he was buying Kat that beer, but suddenly it looked like a Blue Hills party in the making. They slid into a booth and ordered crab cakes, beer, and shots.

Lucky thing about crab and alcohol—it rebalanced Lacy's positive energy, subduing her confusion about the men and her irritation with Kat. "You guys, I am so happy about today. I have been watching John Waters movies since I was a kid, but I have never been to Baltimore. To the Best Day Ever!" Lacy clinked her bottle of Natty Boh against the others.

"You're a J–Dub fan? Me too! You know, I was gonna go to school for photography after I saw *Pecker*. But, you know, couldn't let the guys down." Jax leaned into Lacy. She thought she saw Eli frown a bit across the booth, but she couldn't be sure. Could have just been the spicy aioli that accompanied the fried crab patties.

"Is that like a porn thing? Oh my God, I thought about doing that too! But I didn't know there was a school. Where is the school? In Baltimore? They say you learn something new every day, and I think they were right." Kat downed a shot, and smiled lovingly at them all.

Eli opened his mouth to explain that *Pecker* was a comedy and not a skin flick, but Lacy kicked him. It was too funny to fix. Even Jax was smirking. But then, Jax was usually smirking.

"Hey, I heard you can visit some of the old sets from *Hairspray*. Wanna try?" Jax downed the rest of his beer and glanced around.

"I don't even like John Travolta," Kat groaned.

This time Jax was definitely smirking at her. The other two, again, didn't bother to correct her.

"Thanks for buying, bro," Jax said when they'd finished their meal, patting Eli on the back as he stretched.

Lacy was going to let him know that Eli was only buying Kat a beer, but the strip of golden skin visible between his jeans and the riding-up hem of his button-down was far too distracting to allow words to come out. She wasn't the only one who noticed, either. Kat admired him openly. Her whole face retained the appraisal as they walked back out into the jarring sunlight.

It's not mutual appraisal, Lacy told herself, trying like hell to hold onto her happy place.

"So what's the deal with this John Rivers guy, anyway?" Kat asked, taking Jax by the arm.

Lacy shot daggers at the girl, which seemingly went unnoticed.

"Waters, man," Jax corrected Kat. "He's an iconic movie director, although a lot of his movies haven't been, like, super-commercial. And they all take place in Baltimore. Have you ever seen *Serial Mom*? That was one of his." His smirk was fading into something just as sexy— passion. His whole face lit up like Christmas while he discussed his favorite movies.

This, Lacy realized, *this* was the Folx she knew online, silly and serious all at once. She could feel her face softening as she watched him gesture. Could feel her connection with him sparking like it had so many times during their late-night conversations. Or could feel it about to spark. The actual electricity between them hadn't quite ignited yet. Which was probably just because she was so distracted with being irritated with Kat.

"He's something else, huh." Eli's voice was quiet. In fact, the more Jax talked, the quieter Eli became. Lacy hadn't put it together before, but thinking back, it was a pattern. She guessed that was why Eli wasn't the lead singer. Though he *could* be—she had no doubt in either his talent or his magnetism. He simply seemed to pale when Jax was around.

It was a shame he didn't fight more for himself. It definitely couldn't be Eli who was changing all of Folx's songs since he was so deferential. Maybe it was Wes. Or Other Guy.

"He is, yeah. It's cute to see a grown man so excited." As she noticed Kat was feeling it too, finding excuses to touch Jax. Seriously, couldn't she keep her hormones in check?

Lacy squashed the momentary thought that someone could say the exact same thing about her.

"It is. It's good to see him like this." Eli looked so serious. Lacy knew there had to be more to the story.

She looked expectantly toward him, wanting to hear more about Jax. Wanting to learn the personal side of Folx she'd never gotten the opportunity to learn. Also wanting to hear Eli say more just because she liked the sound of his voice.

He paused, seeming to consider what or if he wanted to share. Finally, Eli said, "He's had some rough times. I think this tour is doing him a lot of good."

"Not just him." She squeezed Eli's shoulder, and something passed between them, something like an understanding. And maybe something else, something more charged and confusing.

But this was a happy day, and not time to dwell. Later, she'd spend more time with Eli. Alone, where she could appreciate him—and, yes, use him—in ways that were too complicated in the company of others.

Now, though, was her chance to get to spend time with the man who hid her Folx within him. It was also her chance to make sure that Kat didn't have more of his attention than Lacy felt was appropriate. So she skipped ahead and landed in between Kat and Jax, slinging an arm around each of them, leaving Eli behind.

Trailing Jax was a position Eli seemed to find himself in more and more these past few years, but he didn't have to like it. Especially now that Jax assumed many of Eli's thoughts and ideas as his own. It hadn't always been that way between them. When they'd first met in college, Jax had been innovative and daring. He'd written half of the songs on their first album and had been the one to get the guys together in the first place.

Now . . . well, now Jax was still innovative and daring, but also less interested in the *music* than the *show*. It was as if somewhere along the way he'd decided that image was more important than the craft. He let everyone else deal with the actual art, and then he came in and made it all *performance ready*. The last album had been ninety percent Eli's songs, but Jax changed them, morphed them *just enough* to feel like it was acceptable to call them his own. Eli had the credit on the liner notes, of course. But how many people read those? Many fans assumed they'd been written by Jax, and he never bothered to correct them.

Lately, it wasn't just the songs, but Eli's ideas that Jax had "borrowed." Even the things Eli liked. It was Eli who had introduced Jax to John Waters. Sure Jax had come to love the director too, but certainly not more than Eli did. And who the hell didn't want to become a photographer after watching *Pecker*? The strip-club scene had surely spoken to every teenage boy who'd seen it.

Honestly, sometimes Eli wasn't sure why he put up with the guy anymore. Except, that was a lie. He put up with him because he still remembered the guy who'd overheard him singing in the shower and convinced him to join a band. He put up with him because Jax made him feel like he belonged when Eli was a lonely kid. He put up with him because he worried about the Jax of today. And with Jax's recent past, it was only natural that Eli worried.

Which was why he was already feeling shitty about his bitter thoughts. Besides, he knew the reason that he was irritated with Jax had nothing to do with John Waters—it had to do with Lacy Dawson.

The thing with Lacy—it was weird and guilt laden, but that was his. Something Jax couldn't take and twist and make his own. Even so, watching the three of them up ahead, there was more than a hint of jealousy rising in his gut.

Eli kicked at a pebble on the sidewalk in front of him and laughed inwardly. Why on earth he was jealous was beyond him. Jax, actually, was a very good solution to his whole Lacy problem. If she had another guy to lean on, Eli could feel less guilty about telling her that what happened last night—incredible as it was—couldn't happen again. And wouldn't it be good for Jax to find someone as amazing as Lacy?

Somehow, his reasoning didn't do anything to ease the tight ball of envy. Perhaps it wasn't even Jax he was jealous of, but Lacy. It had been a long while since Jax and Eli had just hung out like the brothers they once were. Today would have been a perfect day to reconnect, to see what kind of friends they could be after all the bullshit that had gone down.

Unfortunately, Eli had been the last one to notice this impromptu gathering was even happening. He glanced at his watch. They didn't have to be back at the venue for another four hours. Four more hours of watching the girls fawn all over Jax while he tagged along like the designated driver. Eli sighed. When had he become such a bystander in his own life?

"Are you coming, or what?" Lacy's eyes were sparkling as she called back to him from the vintage record store Kat was pulling them into.

He snapped himself out of his stupor in time to respond, "That's what she said." But, even though Lacy gave him a genuine laugh, he still felt glum.

Snap out of it, doof. What was wrong with him, anyway? Besides his tormented friendship with Jax, his regretful affair with Lacy, and his overall lack of cojones, life was great. It was a beautiful afternoon and he was in one of his favorite cities. And he had Love.

Well, he had Love virtually, and that was really what was wrong with him.

Eli wanted to spend a beautiful afternoon in one of his favorite cities with LoveCoda, not with his tourmates. He wanted to take the Poe tour with her, to grab drinks in his favorite dive bar, to catch a show by local musicians. His problem wasn't the band or Jax or even Lacy, it was that nothing in his life was going to be as colorful now that he and Love had set a tentative date. It was like all the hue in his world had gathered and ran ahead to settle on Christmas Eve leaving him with dull watered-down grays.

He meandered through the record store, picking up vinyls then setting them down without even reading the titles. He passed by Lacy, and she winked at him. His stomach dropped.

All right, he'd been lying to himself. The problem wasn't the date. It wasn't even that he'd had Lacy's legs wrapped around him only the night before. It was that he couldn't stop picturing the online girl of his dreams with that face, that hair, and that salacious wink. He couldn't stop wishing that Lacy was LoveCoda.

God, honesty sucked.

He had to put a stop to the thing between him and Lacy.

Had to cut things off with her with one clean slice. As soon as he could get her alone, he'd do it. He had to.

Now, he needed another drink. "You guys wanna go grab another beer? There's a place not far from here with crab mac and cheese that Lacy *has* to try." He waited a beat. "And I'm buying."

Suddenly, everyone was in agreement.

"So do you spend a lot of time here? You seem to know the city pretty well." Lacy linked her arm through his, sending a rush of electricity through him that was already making him rethink the clean slice idea.

A little friendly-friendly couldn't hurt, right? He relaxed into her grip. "I grew up here. Moved up north after middle school when my dad died, that's when I met the guys. But Baltimore is always going to feel like home to me. The bar we're headed to? I had my first beer there, just before I moved. Seven years later I hopped a train to go back, and have my first *legal* beer in the same place. It tasted better, the second one, probably because it wasn't the dregs of my friend's brothers', gulped down in the men's room." Eli suddenly realized he was rambling.

"Anyway, this bar has been here for two hundred something years. It served Poe his last drink. I think everyone who comes here should put it on their must-do list." He fell silent, a little embarrassed, a little unsure what the hell he was doing talking to her so openly.

But Lacy was looking at him with that piercing stare she sometimes got. "So why have we been following Jax around? You should be playing tour guide."

He stared back at her, not really sure what to say. No one had called him out on bowing to Jax before. Probably because everyone else knew why he did it. "Eh, he likes to be in charge. It's no biggie."

She started to press him, but he pointed ahead to the wooden sign swinging outside the tavern. "There we go."

"The Horse You Came in On," she read aloud. "Well that's about the best bar name ever. It would be a good song title too. Dibs." They strolled in and found a table. This time Kat managed to shove her way in next to Jax, leaving Eli and Lacy to slide in on the other side. He noticed Lacy's frown, but tried to pretend it meant nothing. As her bare thigh grazed his, he had to admit he, for one, wasn't altogether upset about the seating arrangement. He decided that while he was in his favorite bar, he wasn't going to think about Jax's history with him or his own missing balls or the strange dichotomy of being so incredibly turned on by the girl next to him while his heart belonged to a girl in a chat room.

"Crab dip! Crab cheesesteak! I'm getting both," Lacy informed the table, daring them to judge her. Or maybe daring them to try and sample her precious, it was hard to say. Either way, Eli was not happy. Because it was adorable, and his heart was getting tugged again.

Some Best Day Ever.

Chapter Fourteen

After the Poe bar and a bit more city traipsing, the four-some headed back to the hotel with a couple of hours left before their call time. Though the afternoon had been a nice variance to their routine, Eli was grateful for it to be over. He needed space away from Lacy and the war she started inside his mind and body.

But first, he had to give her the talk he'd been putting off all day. Well, not exactly putting off—he hadn't gotten a real moment alone with her. Certainly not enough time to tell her what he needed to say. He'd thought he could catch her alone at some point, but then she'd been glued to Kat and Jax all afternoon. Which had bothered him.

God, he just needed to get this over with. Hopefully when the words were out, he'd be able to put the stupid attraction behind him.

He trailed behind Lacy in the hotel as she headed toward her room. Ahead of her was Jax, whose room was at the other end of the hall. Eli watched Lacy stop at her own door and her eyes follow longingly after Jax before opening it and disappearing into her room.

Jesus, if she wanted the guy as badly as it seemed she did, why didn't she just follow him to his room? Jax wouldn't turn her down. He never turned any chick down.

With that thought came an intense pang in his chest. A pang that had to be removed once and for all.

He crossed to her door and held his fist up, ready to knock. Then he paused. He had to make sure he knew what he was going to say. Dammit, why hadn't he thought about this earlier? He practiced the speech in his head now. *Lacy, last night was great.*

It had been fabulous, actually. Really fabulous. Even just the thought of how snugly she'd fit around him, and he was half hard.

Shit. That wasn't how the conversation was supposed to go. He tried again. *Last night was great, but it can't happen again. There's someone else.*

Someone else whom he felt committed to. Someone who didn't flirt with another man in front of him. Someone he hadn't even ever seen a picture of.

Was this idiotic? Giving up a real-life person for someone he'd bonded with online?

And was Lacy even his to give up? The way she'd eyed Jax this afternoon, was this conversation even necessary?

Actually, it probably wasn't. Which was a relief.

But was also kind of sad.

He'd wanted their night together to have been special enough for at least a word of closure, but, hell, it really wasn't. It was his artsy sensitive side pretending it had been more than it was. It wasn't the first time this had happened. He imagined it wouldn't be the last, either.

If there's nothing between us, why am I even doing this? If he was doing it only for himself, well, that seemed a waste of time. He had better things to do than construct a not-even-necessary breakup. Like go apologize more to LoveCoda.

He began to turn away when the door flung open unexpectedly.

"Oh! You're here." Lacy's smile brightened her whole face. Almost like she was glad to see him.

"Uh, yeah." Now that he'd changed his mind about talking to her, he was caught off guard. Might as well stick with his original plan, then. He ran a hand through his hair, composing himself. "I thought we should . . . talk."

He would have sworn her gaze darted down to his lips before returning to his eyes. "We should. I was just coming to your room, in fact."

"You were?" He almost got excited before he remembered he was ending things, not starting them up again. Besides, she'd likely prepared a similar speech. Yeah, that had to be why she'd been on her way to see him. At least she'd also thought something needed to be said after their time together.

He wondered why that disappointed him as much as it did. There was that irritating pang again. It was probably the spicy aioli.

"Yeah. I was. Wanna come in?" She stepped aside to let him past her.

He walked in, stopping just inside the door. No reason to get too far into the room. Otherwise he'd see her bed. Then it would be so much harder to say the things he needed to say because he'd be picturing her laid out on top of the bedspread. Naked. Spread. Wanting him.

What was he thinking? He didn't even need the bed to be picturing that. Just the sight of her and he wanted to spend an hour making her come.

Fuck. He had to get this over with.

He waited while Lacy closed the door, his mouth open to speak.

But when she turned around—before he could get any words out—she pounced.

Literally, pounced.

One minute she was at the door, the next she was in his arms, her legs wrapped around his waist and her tongue thrust between his lips.

Well, damn. He wasn't expecting that.

Which made it nearly impossible to form a reaction. Except to just give in and kiss her back.

So kiss her back he did. He met her with equal fervor, his mouth sucking and sliding with hers, his teeth nipping into her upper lip as he tangled his hands in her long hair.

Lacy responded by bucking her hips up and into his pelvis. *Christ.* His semi was instantly a full-on erection. She thrust again, and the way her center stroked across his cock was both exquisite and painful. He had to touch her. Had to have her hands on him. Now.

Without breaking their kiss, he shifted to brace her against the wall. He pinned her with his hips, so his hands were now free for other things. Like removing his shirt. Then removing *her* shirt. Then her bra. Then, for caressing her gorgeous breasts.

And, God, did Lacy Dawson have nice tits. Firm and round. Not too big, but large enough to fill his palms. Perfect strawberry-tipped nipples stood at attention under his stare. A sprinkling of light freckles dusted her skin, giving her bosom a charming character. Yeah, they were damn nice breasts. He could write a song about them. Maybe two.

Lacy pushed his head down to her chest, knocking him free from his stupor. Yes, she was right. Her breasts deserved more than his eyes. He took her tip into his mouth, alternately sucking and tugging at her nipple until it was fat and swollen. After, he repeated his ardor on the other side until Lacy was writhing and moaning.

Then, he was so aroused that he was aching. And she still had shorts on. They suddenly seemed like such an enormous barrier. If it weren't impossible, he'd rip them off of her with his bare hands. The longer they stayed on her, the more he began to think maybe it wasn't so impossible. Surely, where there was a will there was a way.

Fortunately, Lacy recognized the obstacle as well, and took care of it in a more sensible way. She let her feet slide to the floor and pulled her shorts and panties down in one swift movement. Then she began fumbling with his pants, undoing his belt and then his fly. As she nipped along his shoulder blade, she slid her hand inside his boxer-briefs and stroked his cock. Her palm slid across his crown, nearly buckling his knees.

Fuck.

He couldn't wait any longer. She was ready for him too. The sweet scent of her wafted up to his nose, filling him with an urgency that bordered on craziness. He pulled a condom out of his back pocket—okay, he'd started the day hopeful—and pushed his boxers down just far enough to release his cock. Exercising his inner caveman, he ripped it open with his teeth, and threw the packet on the floor.

Lacy seemed just as impatient. She'd already hooked her knee around him and was already climbing back up as he slid the condom down his length. He laughed. "Hold on, hold on. Almost there."

Then he was sheathed. He put his hands under her tight ass and lifted her up against the wall until she was at the right height. Though it killed him, he paused at her entrance. This was fast, frantic. Though he wasn't against mindless sex, it somehow felt wrong with Lacy. She deserved more. Some sort of connection.

Her eyes closed, she wiggled, trying to get his cock where she wanted it most. He was tempted to slide in.

It took all of his strength to resist, but he did. "Lacy? Lacy, look at me."

She moved her head higher to kiss along his jaw now. Her breathing was wild and erratic, like an untamed horse.

Or a bird about to be caged. A wild songbird. Her eyes, though, she kept shut tight, as though she knew she were going to be reined in and she didn't want to acknowledge her captor.

"Lacy!"

His sharp tone reached through to her. She stilled, her lids popping open. Her eyes found his, and there it was. The connection. He needed this. She, he suspected, needed it too.

With their gaze locked, he pressed into her wet core. Ah, she was tight and warm. Her heat radiated in him—through him—until it was everywhere. Until his whole body was on fire. So hot, like he'd melt into her. It was amazing. Electrifying. Perfect.

Lacy ground her hips against him, urging him to move as she reached her hand down to rub her clit. Now that was even hotter. Her finger flicking across her most sensitive spot—part symbol of her independence, part statement of willingness to contribute toward the outcome they were both seeking. Yeah, totally sexy.

But then he pushed in deeper, and her lids flickered. "Don't do that," he scolded. "Keep your eyes on me." He wasn't going to let her disappear from this moment. Whether they meant anything to each other outside of this or not, they would at least be together now.

She obeyed his command, and, hell, if that didn't turn him on more. He pulled out and thrust in again. And again, quickly returning to the frenzy they'd had just minutes before. All the while his eyes never left hers, their connection never broken.

Eli gripped his fingers into her hips and tilted her legs up further around him. Holy mother . . . this angle was amazing. The friction was . . . oh, God. He hit against her in so many places, he couldn't even tell where he ended and she began anymore. Lacy was feeling it too. Her moans came faster and breathier. Her face contorted and scrunched up with the pleasure. Her lids struggled to remain open. But she managed. Until suddenly she cried out, her entire body tensing as her legs shook around him.

Sexy. As. Hell.

Eli pumped through her contractions around his cock. Once, twice, three times, and, then he was seized by his own release. It ripped through him like a shooting star, lightning his nerves as it surged up and out, leaving spots of light in his vision. Incredible.

Lacy fell limp against his chest, and somehow that was incredible too. Barely able to stand any longer himself, he hobbled with her to the couch, his pants at his ankles preventing him from walking normally. Then he sat with her still wrapped around him. His hands stroked leisurely up and down the bare skin of her back. He felt good with her here like this. Maybe they could have something more together, something like a relationship. That would be nice. Very nice.

Except, he'd have to end things with Love. That idea made his heart sink. Almost as much as breaking things off with Lacy.

Problem was, he was spun up in both of them—Lacy *and* LoveCoda. Two women feeding different parts of his soul—one physical, one emotional. He'd have to choose between them. Somehow. Eventually.

There was probably a song waiting to be written in that too.

Lacy kept her eyes closed tight and let the post-sex haze take her away. Were there words here? She searched for inspiration as her breathing regulated and her body grew lax, throwing her into a meditative state. A phrase flitted through her mind that she tried to catch to no avail. There was something in her way. Something preventing her from capturing her song. What was it?

Eli.

It was Eli.

Her head lay against his chest and she could hear his heartbeat settling underneath her. An erratic rhythm easing into sweet and steady. Then there were his breaths coming in and out at regular intervals. He was fascinating—music in his own right. And while there could be a lyric wandering around in her head, it didn't seem nearly as captivating as this. As just being in the moment. Being in the arms of someone who seemed to care about being in the moment with her. So she ignored the words and held onto the man.

"Well, that was unexpected." Eli's ragged voice cut into her reverie.

"Hmm?" Her voice hummed against his body, reverberating back into her.

Eli swept her hair aside and kissed her forehead. "Not unwelcome. Just unexpected."

She pushed up to a sitting position and stretched, her breasts popping forward as she did.

Eli lifted up to lick at one of her still-erect nipples. "Now you're taunting me. I should have spent more time on these." He sucked her peak into his mouth, his thumb flicking across its twin.

"Stop," she said without much conviction.

He pulled back to meet her eyes, kneading her breasts with his hands. "Do you really want me to?"

"No. But it's getting late. And we have a show to get ready for." She stood and crossed to the closet to grab her robe. Not that she minded being naked in front of Eli, but she seemed to be distracting the man. Sure enough, his eyes were pinned to her body until she wrapped it up.

With his distraction out of the way, Eli's attention turned to himself. He rose to his feet and pulled up his jeans. "My performance is going to be on fire tonight, Songbird. After that. Thank you for the inspiration."

At the word "inspiration," Lacy's thoughts returned to the lyrics that her orgasm was supposed to have elicited. It was the reason she'd jumped him after all. The words were there, she felt it, waiting for her to conquer them with her pen. She glanced at the alarm clock on the nightstand and calculated her time. If she sped through her cleanup, she should have time to jot some things down before her set.

As long as Eli left, that was.

And she wasn't entirely sure she wanted Eli to leave. She had a ridiculous urge to tell him to push his pants back down and join her in the shower. Now he was reaching for his shirt. She'd better say something soon.

But the words . . .

She was torn.

Eli caught her watching him and paused, his arms poised to put on his tee. "You keep biting your lip and looking at me like that, I might have to make you late for your show."

"Make me late? I don't think that's necessary." The scenario she had in mind wouldn't take long—just her on her knees and hot water falling on her back. Oh, and her mouth. But she could be awfully quick with her mouth.

Eli dropped his shirt to the floor. In two steps he had her in his arms. His lips pressed against hers, his tongue teasing inside to slide along hers. "You sure are full of surprises, Lacy Dawson."

Lacy tugged at his fly, noting that his cock was already thickening again under the zipper. That was the second time he'd made such a statement. Had she been too forward?

As if reading her mind, Eli expounded. "Today you

seemed to only have eyes for Jax." He swept her hair off her shoulder and nibbled on her ear.

"Oh. Jax." *Folx*.

Well, shit. Wasn't that a mood killer?

Lacy pulled out of Eli's arms and busied herself with gathering her clothes into a pile. What could she say about Jax? He'd been there online for her when no one else had been. Sure, he didn't realize it, but he deserved a chance with her for what he'd been to her.

Yet here she was selfishly jumping Eli for her own artistic gain. And also because she couldn't stop thinking about him. She had to at least be honest. "Well. I like Jax, too."

"You *like Jax*, too." Eli repeated her words. Slowly.

She forced herself to stop straightening and face the man who'd only moments before been inside her. "Yeah. I like him too."

Eli's jaw tightened. He crossed his arms over his chest. "What does that mean exactly?"

Lacy pried her eyes from how yummy Eli's biceps looked in that position. What had she been saying?

Jax. She'd been talking about Jax. "It means I want to spend time with him. Want to get to know him."

"And . . . ?"

Wasn't that the million-dollar question. If Jax let himself be Folx, if he let himself be the man he was online, then, yeah, Lacy would be interested in that "and." "And maybe more. I don't know yet."

She found her panties on the lampshade and threw them on her dirty clothes pile. Seriously, that Eli had quite an arm.

An arm that now pounded a fist against the wall behind him, startling her enough to make her jump. "What the fuck, Lacy?"

Admittedly, it sounded a little bit . . . well, bad. It

sounded bad. Still. She hadn't made anyone any promises. "I don't understand the big deal here, Eli. We aren't a thing. We slept together a couple times. And it's been good. But we're not exclusive or anything."

"No. But . . ."

"But what? It's not like I'm sleeping with him."

"You're not ruling it out, though."

Lacy took a deep breath. Then she blew it out. "No. I'm not."

She brushed past him to the bathroom vanity to search for a hair tie. She didn't have time to wash her hair so it needed to be pinned up in the shower. Or at least it was something to keep her from having to look at the hurt in Eli's eyes.

"Ah. I get it." Eli moved behind her to lean in the bathroom doorway, angling himself over her shoulder so that he could see her in the mirror. "I'm just a placeholder then, am I? On your way up the band ladder. If you can get the lead singer, then who needs the other guy. He's only backup, after all."

She spun toward him. "No! That's not it at all. Is that really what you think of me?" Even as she uttered the words, she realized she didn't have much to back them up with. She'd acted exactly like that on their outing, choosing Jax's attention over Eli's.

He shrugged. "Should I be thinking something else? You're not giving me a lot to go on."

"This has nothing to do with your place in the band. It's just . . ." She closed her eyes and scratched at her brow. How had she planned to finish that statement? *It's just that Jax and I are practically in love online. But he doesn't know it.*

Um, yeah. That wouldn't cut it.

She opened her eyes again. "Look, Jax and I have something else. I can't explain it. And if I have a chance to see it through, then I have to." There. That was the best she could do. Eli would have to accept it or not.

"As I said, I'm a placeholder. I'm the groupie clause." His voice all but trembled.

Shit. "No. I'm . . ." Her fingers curled around the tie of her robe as she searched for the thing to say to make it right. "Look, I'm trying to be honest here. I like you. I like this." She gestured between the two of them. "I'm happy with our situation." Though if things changed between her and Jax . . . "I'm happy right now, anyway. Today. Can't we just take it like that? One day at a time? Let whatever happens happen?"

"Sure thing, Lacy. Let's do that." Eli's voice was thick with sarcasm and resentment. "How about you let this happen—I'm leaving."

Panic coursed through her like ice in her veins. "Eli, wait!"

He turned back, his expression impatient but obviously willing to hear her out.

Except, she didn't have anything else to say. Nothing to make it better. The truth was, he really wasn't more than a placeholder. Their first night together had come about organically and unplanned. And she'd enjoyed it more than she'd thought possible. But was one night of good sex enough to make it worth throwing away a whole seven plus months with someone else?

No. It wasn't. She was holding out for Jax, and her tryst with Eli today had only been an experiment in stimulating her creative juices.

God, who was this person she had become?

Eli was still waiting for her to speak. Lacy met his eyes and said the only words she could. "I'm sorry."

If the hotel didn't have those mechanisms on the doors to make them close slowly, she was certain hers would have slammed behind Eli as he left.

Numb, she stripped and climbed in the shower. Any words that had been floating inside had left with Eli. She leaned her head against the tile and let the water pour down on her. Even though it was steaming hot, she still felt cold.

Chapter Fifteen

Lacy paced the green room waiting for the Blue Hills to finish their last song and meet back there as always. It had been only twenty-four hours since she'd been there last, and so much had happened. Her night with Eli, her day in Baltimore. Her afternoon with Eli that ended in her saying all the wrong things.

Or all the true things, anyway. Funny how true things often felt like wrong things when said out loud.

The memory of how she and Eli had left things made her stomach tighten and twist—and not in that fabulously delicious way he'd made it twist the night before. He probably hated her. And he should. She'd used him. Worse, was what she'd done to Folx. Her heart belonged to him, which in turn meant it belonged to Jax, and she'd been caught up in a silly physical connection that somehow seemed to spark her creative inspiration.

She felt terrible. Truly, truly terrible. She had to find a way to apologize to Eli. Then she needed to cut things off with him for good and focus on Jax. If she could just get him alone long enough to have a meaningful conversation, she was sure their online sizzle would translate to real life. At least, she hoped it would.

First, though . . . Eli. She had to deal with this if she was going to sleep tonight.

The door burst open, and Lacy spun around to face the band. Wes led the way, followed by James and Other Guy, the guitar players. Then Jax arrived. The door closed behind him.

She waited for a few seconds for Eli to show, but the door stayed shut. "Uh, where's Eli?"

"He went straight to the hotel," James said standing in front of the portable fan in the corner of the room. "Goddamn, that feels good. It was hot out there tonight. Did the AC break or something?"

"We were just on fire," Jax said. "The audience loved me."

"What they loved was Eli." Wes dropped onto the couch, a cold beer bottle pressed against his face. "He nailed every single riff. Killed it."

Lacy bit her lip remembering how Eli said she'd inspired him for the show. She didn't know if she should feel guilty or flattered. Maybe she should stop by his room . . .

"He might have played great, but his mood sucked ass." Jax wiped the sweat from his brow with a towel. "He seriously needs an attitude check. Thank God he went to bed instead of grumping on all of us for the next half hour."

Maybe she wouldn't stop by then.

"Hey, Lacypants, would you mind dropping this in the basket over there?" Jax threw Lacy his towel, not waiting for a response.

She caught it easily, trying not to cringe at the source of its dampness. "Sure thing." *It's a step in the right direction*, Lacy told herself. Sharing sweat was intimate. Right? Although she could do without the patronizing nickname now. What seemed cute on the streets today was a lot less cute when she was playing den mother.

He winked as he grabbed himself a beer from the cooler. "Thanks, baby."

Now he'd called her *baby*. That was definitely an improvement, a good sign.

And if Eli was gone for the night, then perhaps she should skip her amends and work on Jax. "Hey, so . . . Jax . . ." Why was it so much easier to talk to him online than in person? After the day they'd spent together, this shouldn't be so awkward.

He hadn't heard her anyway. Too busy giving Wes a high-five about something or other. She took the opportunity to swipe a beer for herself. After wrestling with the cap, she tipped back a swig. Or several, rather. Nothing wrong with liquid courage. She'd learned that from her big sis. And had it reinforced it by her wedding planner. God, she missed Andy.

Lacy knew the alcohol wouldn't do anything that fast, but she convinced herself she felt braver anyway. Then she stepped up to join the conversation. Perfect timing too, since Wes and James were discussing their plans for the rest of the night.

"They have pool next door," James said. "I owe you for that slaughter last week."

Wes smirked. "You mean you're ready for another ass kicking? I could go for that."

"I'm in." Other Guy stood—what the hell was his name?—and stretched. "I'll hit the shower and meet you guys over there in twenty?"

The guys nodded and dispersed. Jax, however, was still there, scrolling through his phone.

"How about you, Jax? Are you joining the others for pool?"

"Huh?" He looked up as if just realizing everyone had

left. "Oh, nah. I've got—" His phone chirped, interrupting him. Whatever the message was, it made him smile. She wondered if her messages made him smile like that. She hoped so.

The thought of it gave her a burst of fearlessness. "Because, if you aren't hanging with them, I thought maybe we could grab a drink or something?"

Jax typed something into his cell, then stood and pocketed his phone. "Actually, I have, uh, something I have to do. Someone I'm meeting."

"Like a date?" She was sure he meant LoveCoda. Maybe he'd admit it.

"Sorta like that." He gave her his best panty-melting smile. "Rain check?" He waited for her nod before shooting her a wink and leaving.

I'm holding you to it, she said to herself as a sudden sweep of loneliness fell over her. Oddly, it was Eli whom she imagined comforting her, not Jax. Surely that was only because she felt so embarrassed about how she'd acted. That had to be it.

So she'd go back to her room then. Alone. But not for long. Folx/Jax would ping her later, and she'd forget all about Eli. She hoped.

When Lacy entered the hotel lobby, however, an unexpected sight met her. Eli at the front desk. With her sister.

"Andy?"

"Ah, there you are, thank God." Andy gave a dramatic sigh of relief that may have only been half exaggerated. "I tried to explain to the desk clerk that I was your sister, but he refused to give me any information about you. Wouldn't even tell me what room you were in. I don't know. Must be a HIPAA compliance thing or something."

"HIPAA is for doctors, not hotels. What are you even—I can't believe you're here!" But as she questioned her sister, Lacy kept her eyes on Eli. He refused to meet her gaze, and that stung. More than she wanted to admit.

Andy waved her hand dismissively. "Then the National Security Act. I always get the two mixed up. Ruined my surprise." She glared at the hapless desk clerk. "Anyway, get over here and hug me." Andy pulled Lacy into her embrace, and the feeling of *home* was overwhelming.

Eli cleared his throat. "You've found her now. I'll be going. Nice to meet you, Andy."

Andy shoved Lacy away in order to give Eli a proper wave. "You too, Eli. Thanks for the help. Hopefully we'll see each other again." Then she pulled Lacy closer. "God, he's delicious. Please tell me that you're, you know, getting with him. Because, clearly, I'm off the table."

Thankfully, Eli was well out of earshot at this point.

"Why were you even talking to him?" That probably shouldn't have been her first question. Lacy corrected her mistake. "Why are you here?"

"Eli heard me telling the clerk your name, and he stopped to help me out. I wouldn't have even known I was in the right hotel if he hadn't confirmed it. Nice guy, that one." Andy sighed as if remembering the extent of Eli's deliciousness.

Which bothered Lacy. She never lusted after Blake. Because, for one, *ew*. But, for two, not appropriate. Not that Eli was comparable to Blake in terms of their relationships. Just . . . it was weird.

"And I'm here because I missed you! Blake sensed my misery. I wasn't exactly subtle, though. Anyway he sensed it and offered me a surprise trip to visit you."

If she were a crier, Lacy was sure this was one of those moments that might have made her teary. An impromptu visit from her sister was exactly what the doctor ordered. "You know what, Andy? I've never been fonder of your fiancé."

"I knew you'd warm up to him eventually." Andy threw an arm around Lacy's and tugged at her rolling luggage with her other hand. "Show me to our room. I brought wine."

Thirty minutes later, their wine had been uncorked and their second glasses half-consumed.

"I have a confession," Andy said, drawing Lacy's eyes up from her phone.

Lacy was sure Folx would ping her any moment now, and she didn't want to miss it. But Andy's serious tone warranted attention. "What's that?"

"I didn't just come because I missed you. I have another meeting with my wedding planner, and, well, I just couldn't do it without you."

"So you flew to Baltimore? What, did you bring him with you? Is Tim hiding in your suitcase?" Frankly, it wouldn't totally surprise her if he were. Tim was nothing if not committed.

"Ha ha, funny." Andy watched her thumb trace along the rim of her glass. Was she avoiding Lacy's eyes or just suddenly interested in hotel tumblers? "No, my appointment's via FaceTime. I thought maybe we could talk to him together."

"Okay." And there was the real purpose of Andy's visit. But Lacy didn't mind. She was happy to have her sister around, wedding freak-outs or surprise wine party or whatever. Unless it was just an excuse for Andy to check up on her. Her heart swelled a little. "When's the call? I'm free all day tomorrow until six. Except for a load in at two. That will only take half an hour or so though."

Andy finished off her glass and poured another before responding. "Actually, our appointment's now. Well, in three minutes. At midnight."

"At midnight? Who makes appointments at midnight?"

"He's a night owl. He said he prefers the way the full moon inspires him, or something goofy like that. As if he wasn't inspired in the daylight when we saw him last. Oh, God." Andy took another gulp from her glass.

Lacy grabbed the glass from her sister's hand. Then swiped the bottle away when Andy tried to drink directly from that. "Why the hell are you drinking? This is your chance to face him sober."

"You know I'm terrified of him. I thought the wine would settle my nerves."

"Jesus, Andy. Get a grip. He's *your* employee. You aren't scared of *him*, you're scared of planning this huge public wedding." Lacy's phone buzzed with an incoming message. She glanced down to confirm it was indeed Folx. Dammit.

Obviously, Folx would have to wait. She entered a quick message. *Family emergency. I'll catch you tomorrow?* This would be two nights they'd missed each other. But it couldn't be helped.

His response came back quick and made her smile. *I'll be here, Love.*

Now. Back to Andy. "So it's midnight now. Do we need to log in or something?"

"He's calling my iPad." As if on cue, Andy's bag began ringing. "That's him. You answer!" Lacy would have protested, but her sister had flung the tablet into the air, and she had to dive to catch it.

"Hello, Tim," she tried to be cool, as if she hadn't just accidentally hit the connect button at the same time she'd connected with the floor.

"Oh God, it's you again." His scowling face filled the screen. "I thought I only had one opinion to override."

"No such luck, Timmy. I'm sort of part of the Andy deal." She could practically see the steam curling from his ears at the unwanted nickname. Now this could be fun. Without him personally there to cow her, she could mess with the guy a little.

"Hi, Tim!" Andy yelled from over Lacy's shoulder. His eyes were darting back and forth between them.

"Are you . . . ? Have you . . . ? Why don't you two just grab a drink and set me on the desk so we can talk." He was making a visible effort to take back control of the situation.

"Oh, we aren't drinking tonight." Lacy nudged Andy to slide the bottle of wine away as she set the iPad up on the desk as requested. His sharp intake of breath almost made her lose her poker face.

"What do you mean you aren't drinking? Just one, then, to be polite."

"Nah, we're fine. You wanted to talk catering tonight, right?" Andy smiled innocently at him.

"Yeah, catering. I had some thoughts, but I was hoping to share them over a beverage . . ."

"We didn't even consider that, Tim. Sorry. Go ahead with your thoughts, though." The girls sat and waited. He adjusted his collar. Then adjusted his glasses.

"French food, in small plates. We'll serve it in courses, with wine pairings. Are you certain you don't need some wine to have this meeting?"

"Nope. Tell me more about the food. I'm not really sure . . ." Lacy leaned out of the frame to hide her grin. She knew perfectly well that Andy adored French food, possibly more than most French people. Who knew it was so easy to get Tim's goat? The man was actually beginning to perspire.

"Soup in shot glasses. Something light, maybe leek or asparagus. Beef tartare, and a beet version for the vegetarians. Those—*people* always want something. Sherbet after that course, made with champagne. No one leaves a Boston Bride's wedding sober." He smiled at the thought.

"Yeah, I was thinking something a bit more avant-garde. I hear in Japan the new thing is McDonald's weddings. My fiancé does tons of business in Japan, so it would look good for us to incorporate some of that stuff into our special day." The fact that Andy was saying this with a straight face deeply impressed Lacy, who was all but hyperventilating at this point.

Tim, to his credit, didn't crack. "Where are you girls?"

"A hotel outside of Baltimore. What do you think about the burger buffet?"

"Which hotel, Andrea Dawson? I refuse to discuss this any further with you sober."

"Oh, I don't know, Tim. A Marriott or a Wyndham maybe. I wasn't paying much attention. You know, I think it's a good thing for me to have more input into this wedding."

"Is it the Marriott Express near the convention center?" On the screen, Tim was typing away on his phone.

"Perhaps. What are you doing, Tim?" He looked up, eyes blazing.

"What am I doing? I am attempting to find you and order room service for you. Somewhere in Baltimore there is a bottle of rum with the Dawson sisters' name on it, and I will not rest until it is drained! The only thing worse than working with opinionated brides is working with sober brides. Brides with opinions! You are going to *ruin* this wedding, and I will not stand idly by!" His voice was nearing an actual shriek, the pitch almost matching the laughter neither girl could hold in any more.

They finished the meeting and a second bottle of wine in fear of Tim's retaliation. They had been sternly informed that no further input from Andy was needed on her own wedding. Lacy's head was spinning from both the booze and the rapid-fire decisions that had been made.

When they'd finally hung up, Andy tossed her iPad to the floor and lay back into the comforter. "God, that was fun." She turned to her side and propped her head up with her hand. "See? I wouldn't have handled that alone."

Lacy tsked. "You would have. Well, maybe that wasn't true. And you definitely wouldn't have punk'd him on your own. But I'm happy to have helped. You know, though, if you really felt like you needed someone to meet with you, you could have asked Blake."

"That would never have worked out. Tim would have fired Blake on day one."

Lacy laughed. "That's probably true." Blake had a fairly domineering personality at first meeting. He'd loosened up since he'd gotten with Andy, but he still could be awfully abrasive.

"God, I love him though." Andy's grin was the kind that took over her whole face, sparking her eyes and flushing her skin.

Lacy smiled too, letting herself remember for half a moment what that was like—loving someone like *that*. With her heart and soul and body. Not meaning to, her eye flickered to Lance's pillow. Even though she wasn't even on the bed, she could feel its presence. It had its own warmth and character, a fragment of the person it once belonged to.

God, Lacy had loved him. She still did, only it didn't come with the sharp pain anymore. Watching her sister plan this wedding to the love of her life should have been debilitating. Yet, she wasn't feeling the anticipated jealousy. Maybe she had started to heal. Or maybe she'd just stopped paying attention to the wound.

"Hey." Andy knocked her knee against Lacy's, pulling her from her daze. "You okay?"

"Why wouldn't I be?" Lacy sounded snippier than she'd meant to. She softened her tone. "I'm fine. Really. Do I seem . . . not . . . fine?"

"No. You seem fine." Andy cocked her head, studying her. "You also seem a bit . . . I don't know . . . quiet."

Next to Andy, everyone seemed quiet. Lacy decided to go with honesty. Semi-honesty. "I'm working through some things, I suppose. Touring is new. I'm still adjusting."

Andy waggled her eyebrows, something she really didn't do very well. Particularly when inebriated. "You should adjust with that Eli. I can't say what it is, but he's got something."

"That something is he's hot." Lacy wondered if she should say more and decided she probably should. Andy was her sister, her best friend. They used to share everything. Well, Andy still did, it was only Lacy who'd pulled back. "And I have adjusted with him."

"Yes. He's hot. That's what . . ." Andy trailed off. "Wait. What did you say? You've adjusted with him? Does that mean you've"—she lowered her voice even though they were the only two people in the room—"slept with him?"

Andy had this adorable inability to say words that related to sex without getting totally embarrassed. Which, of course, Lacy took advantage of as often as possible. "No, I have not slept with him. But I did bang him. Twice."

Andy's hands flew to her mouth. "Oh, my God! You *didn't sleep* with him!"

Yes, that was fun.

But now that the admission was out and the shock expressed from Andy, Lacy had to admit the rest. "It's not anything though. We're not anything. It's done."

Andy pursed her lips as if trying to bite back whatever it was that she really wanted to say. Finally she settled with, "Is that what *you* want? Or what he wants?"

"It's what I wanted." Lacy frowned at her past tense choice of verb. "I mean, it's what I *want*." Wasn't it?

"Do you want to talk about this?"

"Not really. Will you let me get away with that?"

Andy considered for a few heavy seconds. "Yeah. If you don't want to talk, you don't have to." She patted Lacy's thigh. "Put it in a song, and I'll hear about it all later."

Yeah. *Put it in a song.* If only it were that easy.

Except there was a niggle somewhere in her chest. An itching that radiated outward through her limbs. As if something were brewing. Maybe she did have a song rumbling around inside. She needed some time by herself with her thoughts to find out. Which was going to be hard to find with company and conversation.

Perhaps, after Andy fell asleep . . .

The hotel did have a secluded lounge. She could sneak down there for a couple of hours with her guitar and staff pad. See what transpired.

With that plan in mind, Lacy curled up next to Andy to watch some late, late talk show, and waited for the sound of her sister's snores.

Chapter Sixteen

It was less than thirty minutes later that Lacy found herself in the hotel lobby, her guitar case over her shoulder, staff pad tucked under her arm. She even brought her laptop to record what she worked on. Except for the night clerk, the place was empty. She found a nook out of sight of both the front doors and the front desk and settled in.

Before even attempting any new words, Lacy played through the refrain she'd composed that morning, changing a few of the chords and tightening the melody. She opened her laptop and laid a rough track so she wouldn't forget it, then turned to her staff pad. Once upon a time, a blank sheet looked like a red cape to her bullheaded approach to life. It taunted her, teased her, begged her to make something of it.

Tonight the empty page stared at her like a dead end street.

Somehow, she had to recapture the emotions she'd had that afternoon with Eli.

She leaned back into the leather upholstery of the wing-back chair and closed her eyes. It had been ages since she'd actually gone to a yoga class, but she used to love the meditative nature of the art. Maybe it would help now. Taking a deep breath in and then out, she concentrated on the feeling of her orgasm. The tightness of it followed by the much-needed release.

She'd barely conjured up the memory when a ping from her computer interrupted her thoughts. Glancing down at the screen, she found a message from Folx.

I know you're not around tonight, but I just wanted to say good night one more time. Thinking of you.

Lacy sat up, retrieving her laptop form the side table. *I'm here! Family emergency over. I thought you'd be asleep by now.* Sure she was supposed to be writing, but chatting with Folx was always preferred.

I couldn't sleep. I've missed you.

Same here. And, man, had she. Even just one day without talking to him and her world had turned topsy-turvy. *I'm really glad you couldn't sleep.*

Me too. How about you? How are you doing? Why aren't you sleeping?

Lacy hit her head against the chair several times before responding. The answers to his question were wrapped up in Eli. It took a moment to pick apart the sections of the last two days that didn't include him. Finally, she typed, *I was attempting to get some words down. I actually wrote a refrain today!*

Yes!! I'm grinning like a mad man. What caused the breakthrough?

I'm not sure, exactly. She paused, wondering how much she could say without explaining her tryst with Eli. Of course, she could leave it vague, but she hated that. She didn't like walls between her and Folx. More, she wanted to share her theory with him. He'd been her primary confidant in her blockage crisis and she couldn't imagine shutting him out now. *But I think I have an idea what might help the rest of the block.*

What's that?

The last time I wrote anything—never mind that it was just that morning—*I'd been inspired by sex. So I'm thinking . . . what if orgasms inspire me?*

Man, did that sound lame. Thank God for the anonymity of her username. Otherwise she was sure she'd be dying of humiliation at the moment.

Wait a minute, wait a minute . . . Folx said nothing more for several seconds and she was afraid maybe he'd put two and two together—if she'd written that day and this was her theory, then shouldn't it follow that she'd had sex with someone?

But Folx's next words went another direction entirely. *If you think that sex might be the missing ingredient to your songwriting, and you haven't been able to write in almost a year, does that mean that it's . . . been that long?*

Well, wasn't that just as humiliating? She almost wished she could tell him about her recent escapade—*escapades*, she'd almost forgotten it was plural now—just so she didn't have to confess the truth of her pre–last night sexual status.

No, she didn't want him to know about Eli. Even if he understood now, when he realized who she was, he'd certainly be upset that she'd slept with his bandmate. His bandmate, of all people!

More guilt. More ignoring. She took a deep breath and typed. *I haven't been with anyone in a while.* She added a winky face to make the admission less painful.

I didn't realize how long a while was.

God, now he probably thought she was ugly or that there was something wrong with her. Actually, it might not be far off from the truth.

He typed again before she could think of anything to say. *But not even, you know, manually? You've been orgasm free?*

Until last night . . . *Not even manually.* If she hadn't been blushing before, she certainly was now.

Wow. I mean, really. Wow. You have to know this is turning my thoughts dirty.

She had to read that twice. *Dirty? Why? Because my lack of orgasms in all forms gets you off somehow?* Though, now that she let herself think about it, underneath the humiliation the talk was kind of arousing. She crossed her legs to ease the pulse that had taken up between her thighs.

Because now I'm thinking about how I can help you test out your theory. But, I must admit, online sex is new to me.

Oh. The pulsing turned to throbbing as heat bloomed inside her. Online sex with Folx. That was totally next level. The idea had her squirming and intrigued. And really freaking turned on.

She paused for a moment before responding further, about the moderators of the forum—did talking sexy count as personal information exchange?

But then she remembered the entire chat room on SoWriAn dedicated specifically to this sort of stimulating conversation. The foreword had read, *"Since inspiration is sometimes best found in the erotic . . ."* and then followed with a reiteration of the necessity of assumed identities.

After she took a peek inside, she had a better understanding of said "necessity." The filthy chats there made *Fifty Shades of Grey* seem like a Disney cartoon. She could just imagine the media backlash that might occur if one of those naughty songwriters turned out to be, well, anyone.

Point being—if the mods let that kinky porn happen, then she and Folx could certainly indulge in a round of sex-chat.

Then she remembered where she was. In a public place. Her disappointment was immeasurable as she typed, *I can't.*

Oh, ok. Sorry to cross the line.

Cross the line. That's what Eli had said when he'd spoken out about Lance. It was a popular expression, but she hated the way she kept thinking back to Eli. It was distracting and made her slow in her response. *Wait, no! Not because of that. Please don't think that. I'd love to. Really, I would. I'm just not exactly alone at the moment. Rain check?*

Now *she* was planting connections in *his* head. Jax had offered her one earlier that night. She wondered if he remembered that as he read it on his screen now. If he thought of Lacy Dawson and began to pair her with the girl he knew as LoveCoda.

That is a rain check that I will definitely take you up on.

It was silly how twisted up and excited that simple statement made her. In many ways, it was a reassurance. It was a confirmation that she'd chosen right when she'd decided to commit herself to a man she'd never met in real life.

It was a reminder that she'd mucked it all up when she'd sexed up Eli. Twice.

Good thing she'd made the mistake before she actually made a verbal commitment to Folx. Now it was out of the way and she could move on. No more trysts with Eli. No more trysts with anyone. She was saving herself for Folx. For Jax.

She needed to hear he was in the same place she was. Careful to make sure her wording wouldn't alert the mod-

erators, she typed, *Hey, Folx, Christmas Eve is still on,*
right?

I'm more on than I've ever been.

A wave of relief washed through her. Still, she wanted
him to say more. Needed to hear more. *What's that mean*
exactly?

She drummed her fingers across her knee as she
watched the dots on the screen that indicated he was
typing.

It means I think about it all the time. I think about
you all the time. If I didn't have commitments right now,
I'd beg for your address and show up on your doorstep
tomorrow, forum moderators be damned. What about
you?

Until that moment, Lacy had loved the tour and the opportunity it gave her. Now she wished with all her heart
that neither of them had any obligations. Wished that she
could wrap herself up in a world filled only with Folx and
her and their music. It wouldn't last—she knew that—but
that didn't matter since it was only a fantasy anyway.

In this space, in this forum, she could let that fantasy
live. She was filled with such conviction that she didn't
even care if the moderators slapped her with a warning
when she typed her next entry. *To say I think about you*
all the time is an understatement. As soon as you ask,
my address is yours. Just send an email to the other ad-
dress, no begging necessary.

Thank God. Begging is so unmanly.

She giggled. She also disagreed. She'd seen the puppy
dog eyes that Jax used in performance. *I don't know. I bet*
you could pull it off without losing any man points.

I'll let you keep thinking that. In the meantime, I'm
still stuck in the dirty thoughts from earlier. I should get
off-line. Very bad pun intended.

You do that. And she'd be a good girl and try not to

think about exactly what it was he was doing. Though she wouldn't try that hard. *Goodnight, Folx.*

Goodnight, Love.

Honestly, Lacy was still feeling a bit horny herself, though she wasn't sure if it was from the flirting or the memories of Eli she'd focused on earlier. Whatever the source, she was aroused. And she still hadn't gotten a chance to test her orgasm-equals-lyrics theory. She debated going back to her room and sneaking into the shower for alone time. Except, if inspiration struck, it would be a bitch to write anything down in the steamy bathroom and she really didn't want to wake Andy. What other options did she have?

Lacy looked around the lounge. She'd told Folx she wasn't alone, but in truth there was no one in sight. The desk clerk was out of her line of vision and no one had been by the entire time she'd been there.

No, no, no. You need to stop thinking what you're thinking right this minute, Lacy Rae Dawson.

Except, she didn't stop. What would it really hurt? She could be quiet. And she'd keep all her clothes on. So why not?

Her hand had already slipped past the drawstring of her night shorts and inside the elastic band of her panties. She was even slick with arousal when her finger settled on her clit. A quiet sigh escaped her mouth as she began to circle her nub. Eyes closed, she hummed the tune of the song she'd started writing as she focused on the flirty words delivered by Folx. Then she tried to imagine him—Jax— above her, on her. Inside her. But she couldn't hold his face in her fantasy.

Her thoughts flew naturally to Eli instead. Earlier that afternoon. The way he'd been with her. How charged their connection had been. His hands on her. His mouth on her nipple. His eyes piercing into hers while his expression showed the effort he exerted. She hummed her tune louder. Then sang it, using whatever came out as a placeholder for lyrics.

"Eli, Eli, Eeeeliii," she crooned, as the memory overtook her. It was so real she could practically feel his cock thrusting inside her. Could very nearly see his face in front of hers. Could almost hear him calling her name . . .

Actually, she could clearly hear him calling her name. As if he were standing right there with her. She peeked out of her clenched lids.

And then she wanted to die.

"Lacy?" After he got her name out, Eli was speechless. He was shocked he'd managed even that. The sight of her there . . . like that . . . was . . . *whoa.*

Hand down her pants, her face flushed, her breathing heavy as she sang an unfamiliar melody—and was that his name she was singing? It was a miracle he didn't take her right there. Not surprising, he had an instant hard-on that was unmistakable beneath his sweatpants.

"Oh, my God!" Lacy's face reddened as she jumped up from the chair she'd been, uh, lounging in. Her hand flew from her shorts to cover her mouth. Then, realizing where her hand had just been, she gasped again and hid it behind her back. "It's not . . . I'm not . . . this isn't what it looks like."

"Huh. I'd love to hear what it really is." Actually, he really shouldn't hear it. He'd only come downstairs after his talk with LoveCoda because he'd been so worked up about her that he couldn't sleep. The idea of her pleasuring herself to his comments made him hot and anxious. How ironic to walk in on another woman doing exactly what he'd been trying to get away from picturing.

How ironic that Lacy was the face he often gave LoveCoda, especially when he pictured her in any sexual way.

Of course, Love was exactly the opposite of Lacy—
Love hadn't gotten any action in almost a year, and Lacy
was obviously a sex addict. Too bad.

Also, was it a problem that at the moment he couldn't
think of any reason that sex addiction was a bad thing?

Yes, it was a bad thing. A very bad thing. He'd just committed himself to Love. Again. This thing with Lacy had
to end.

"It's . . . I'm . . ." Lacy was still trying to come up with
an excuse for her actions. "You know what? This doesn't
really need explaining." She crossed her arms over her
chest—but not before he noticed her nipples were beaded
under her tank top. "What the hell are you doing here
anyway?"

"In the hotel? Or in this lobby?" So being horny made
him a little bit of a dick. Could anyone really blame him?

Lacy rolled her eyes. "In this lobby."

He couldn't keep the smile off his lips. She was adorable when she was frustrated. "That's the only vending
machine that has corn nuts," he said nodding toward the
vending machine tucked in the corner behind her.

She followed his nod, her brows knit in confusion or
maybe agitation. "Corn nuts?"

"I was feeling a bit hungry and I like corn nuts. Though
I seemed to have lost my appetite. For food anyway."
Watch it, horndog. "Now back to you—what the hell are
you doing here?"

She tightened her jaw and raised a challenging brow.
"In this hotel or in this lobby?"

"Funny." It really was kind of funny. He had to hand it
to her.

Lacy kept her lips pursed for another beat. Then she
sighed. "I don't know. I wasn't ready to sleep. And my
sister's passed out in my room. I came down here so I
wouldn't disturb her."

"I see how you think your actions might have been disturbing. They'd be disturbing to me. In a good way, of course." *What the hell are you doing? Stop flirting!*

"Just . . ." She covered her face with her hands and shook her head. When she lowered them, he could see her cheeks had brightened again. "Can we just forget this ever happened?"

He laughed. "I don't think I can ever forget this, Lacy Dawson." Not in a hundred million years. "But I can try to pretend if you'd like me to." Because they did have to work together, and that wasn't really nice to keep hanging the situation over her head.

"I would like you to. Very, very much."

Eli had never thought of himself as one of those alpha types. He was all man, yeah, but more the artsy sensitive type. It worked for him. No woman had ever complained. But, hell, if he didn't like the sound of Lacy's pleading. It crossed to a beg and suddenly he began to see the appeal of a submissive chick.

Or maybe he just liked messing with this one.

"Can I just add one more remark first?" Nice or not, he had to get at least another word in on the subject before he left it alone.

"Do I have a choice?" she asked through clenched teeth.

"You know where my room is. You could have just knocked." He winked and hated himself even as he did it. This was wrong. So wrong. Only five minutes ago he'd been about to talk dirty to LoveCoda, and now he was down here propositioning Lacy. He was seriously an asshole.

An asshole who couldn't help himself. Despite his hasty exit after their last tryst. "Standing offer. Right here."

Lacy studied the carpet, her mood suddenly somber. "About that . . ."

Yeah, about that. What the hell, Eli? Even if Love wasn't around, this girl wants Jax.

"We should talk." They said it together, which made them both chuckle in that weird, awkward, we're-expected-to-laugh-now way.

"Anyway." Lacy took a breath then gestured to the chair next to hers. "Have a seat?"

His chest tightened as he sat down. It was a necessary conversation, but this type of talk was never fun. At least that's the reason he told himself that he was dreading her words.

They could be *his* words, he told himself. He could take the lead and be the one to say what needed to be said. That was a helluva lot easier than hearing it.

That it was the harder part to listen was what made him let Lacy speak. Sometimes he wasn't an asshole.

"So." She cleared her throat. "I wanted to say I was sorry for earlier. I realize that I wasn't fair to you. I used you—"

"It was kind of my pleasure." He didn't know if he cut her off because he hated where she was going or if it was because he needed her to know that he'd had a good time. Maybe a bit of both.

"Well. Thank you. It was my pleasure too." She tucked a stray hair behind her ear, but it immediately fell right down again.

His fingers itched to push it back. Then to circle his touch back around her lobe and down across her jaw. "But . . ."

"But. I, uh." She bit her lip, and the memory of the nip of her teeth on his skin burned like a splash of hot oil. "I still want to get to know Jax. There's a connection I have with him that I don't know how to explain to you."

That statement burned even more. He lowered his eyes to study a callous on his fingertip as she went on.

"Even if there's nothing there. Not because he's the singer in the band—"

"I know." This time he cut her off because he didn't need to hear that from her. "That was shitty of me to accuse you of that. I know that's not why you're into him." Women were just into Jax. *People* were into Jax. He was *that* guy. The one you wanted to hang with. The one you wanted to be friends with. The one you wanted to be important to. He'd felt the same way when he'd met the guy too.

It certainly wasn't a flaw of Lacy's to notice Jax's magnetic awesomeness.

She smiled, and Eli suspected she'd gotten out the worst of her speech. "Thank you. I know I'm being sort of cryptic, and it might seem really ridiculous to you, but we sort of—"

"You really don't need to explain." He might understand her attraction, but he didn't have to hear her break it down for him. Besides, he had his own special connection. With someone who deserved a lot more of his faithfulness. "The truth is, Lacy, I sort of have someone else too." Eli cringed at his need to say *sort of*. But at least he'd gotten it out there.

Lacy sat up slightly. "Someone back home?"

It made him happier than it should to detect the jealousy in her tone.

"Yeah. Yeah, back home." In many ways, LoveCoda was his home. And it was easier than explaining the whole thing.

She nodded slowly, and he wondered if she thought he was making it up. Or if she was disappointed. Then he realized she was probably just judging him. "I mean, it's not a committed relationship—I don't want you to think I'm an out-and-out cheater or anything." Why her opinion mattered that much, he didn't know. "But I think about her a lot. And I feel pretty lousy about us. About what you and I did. It's not just unfair to her but to you as well."

She nodded again, and this time he sensed it was a nod

of understanding. She confirmed it with her next words. "So we're both in the same situation, it seems."

"Seems so." This was good. Really good. Damn if it didn't feel more like really not that good.

They sat silently for a few seconds. Right as it bordered on becoming uncomfortable, Eli stood and held out his hand. "Friends?"

Lacy took his hand, her warm fingers wrapping around his before she pulled up to a standing position. She held it for a moment before agreeing. "Friends."

"Come on. We can at least be friends who hug." He tugged her into him before she could argue. He needed this. Needed a final embrace. Needed the closure. And the artsy sensitive Eli was back.

Lacy let him hold her, turning her face to lie on his shoulder as she moved more fully against him.

And more fully against his hard-on.

She pulled away instantly. "Friends don't usually have that, though." Her eyes shifted down to his crotch then back to his eyes.

"That's still from earlier." The attention she was giving it didn't make him any softer, however. "A guy walks in on a girl with her hand in her pants and that's what happens."

Her eyes widened in dismay. "We said we were going to forget that."

"We said we were going to *pretend* to forget that."

"Jerk." But she was smiling, so he knew things were good between them.

"On that note"—it was his turn for his eyes to fall to her crotch—"I'll let you get back to what you were doing."

"Stop it!" Her expression softened. "And thank you. Seriously, thank you. And good night!"

"Good night, Songbird." His chest ached as he walked across the lounge, away from her. Hurt more than he thought it should over a girl he barely knew. Against his better judgment, he turned back to say one last thing. "I have to admit, Lacy, that it's easy to forget about her when I'm near you. I don't know what it is, but you really get me going."

He liked the way her mouth parted in surprise. Liked it too much. Which was his cue to turn away from her once and for all.

Chapter Seventeen

Lacy finished setting up the stand for Eli's banjo and started on one for his mandolin. She was grateful that they could be easy like this after, well, after everything that happened before. Or at least it was easy with everyone else around. Andy's presence might also be a contributor to the lack of intensity between them. She was admittedly a nice buffer.

Lacy was glad that her sister was at today's load in, not just because of her buffer attribute, but also because she got to see the tour environment firsthand. It felt like ages since Lacy had shared music with Andy. SoWriAn, was a secret of course. And the whole writer's block thing. Which made the things that Lacy *could* share even more special.

"Just set it down anywhere over there," Sammy pointed and instructed to Andy, who had just carried a bag of microphones in from the bus.

Andy set her haul down then sat on Wes's drum stool. She wiped at her brow with exaggeration. "You have to do this at every new venue?"

"Uh-huh." What Lacy really wanted to say was, *The microphones aren't even that heavy.*

"And you're basically at a new venue every day?" Andy fanned herself with her hand, then checked for newly sprouted muscles.

"Yep." Lacy grinned at her sister's overdramatization. "Sometimes we have to unload after the show too, though Sammy usually feels bad for us and does it for us or finds some locals to help her with it in exchange for a beer."

"Hmm. I had no idea being a musician required so much physical exertion."

Lacy finished with her stand then turned to stare Andy in the face. "Are you complaining or complimenting?"

"A little bit of both? Oh, come on. You know you make me proud." Andy pushed the pedal for the kick drum. Once, twice. Three times. "God. It takes energy to do even this."

Lacy shook her head. What did her sister think she'd been *doing* all this time? But then, she normally showed at the venue just in time to grab some wine before the show. They'd never done a setup together.

Eli finished tuning James's bass and set it on its stand. "Oh, this isn't that bad. We pre-work off our post-show beers. We're lucky we don't have a big set with our show. But Kat should be here helping us out, if you ask me."

"I really don't mind that she's not," Lacy muttered under her breath. She was still unreasonably annoyed that pretty, flirty, talented Kat had decided to spend as much time on the tour as she had. "Anyone know where she is, anyway?" She hoped she didn't sound like she cared that much. Honestly, she didn't. She mostly just wanted to know where she'd spent the night before.

"She took off in the middle of last night's show," Jax said, changing the height of his microphone for the sixth time. "Said she had to be back for an early recording session."

Lacy tried not to mind that Jax knew Kat's whereabouts and focused instead on the joy of knowing that wherever she had slept, it hadn't been with him. "Yeah, she's covering all of my shifts so I can be on this tour. She's been genuinely sweet." It was easier to admit Kat's generosity when she wasn't overwhelmed by the other girl's physical presence.

"Are we about done here?" Jax rocked on the balls of his feet, obviously ready to be on his way.

Eli scratched the back of his neck and scanned the stage. "I think so. I have to tune my mando but it can wait until sound check. It will just need to be tuned again then anyway."

Lacy looked around the stage as well, mostly so she could avoid the weird tingle in her stomach at the sight of Eli's flexed bicep. "I'm not sure where Sammy went. Should we wait for her to say we're good to go?"

"We can, I guess. I'm going to check out the green room." Jax stepped across an instrument case at Lacy's feet before turning back to her. "Wanna come with?"

"Sure." Her heart flipped. Jax had never invited her to do anything with him. So this was only a trip to the green room, but, hey, it was something.

He held his hand out to her, lifting her off her spot on the floor. He was strong—strong like Eli—and his hands were warm. There wasn't any spark of electricity like when Eli touched her, but that didn't mean anything. Maybe Eli was just a better conduit or Jax wore thicker socks.

And why was she comparing the two men, anyway?

He let go of her hand when she was upright and headed offstage left. "I don't know where it is. This side proba- bly." Lacy followed after him. Just beyond the curtains, he stopped suddenly. "Oh, cool. There's a catwalk." He nodded to the metal ladder bolted into the cement wall. "I love this shit. My high school had one in their auditorium. I used to sneak up there with the girls."

She cocked her head hoping she looked flirty. " 'Girls'? As in plural?"

"Plural as in multi trips up the catwalk. Not like multi girls at once." He paused. "Well. Okay. *Usually* not multi girls at once."

Lacy was surprised. Her impression of Folx had always been that he'd been shy in high school. "Jax, I had no idea you used to be such a ladies man."

"*Used to be*? There's no used to be about it." He winked at her before putting two hands on one of the ladder rungs and pulling himself up.

Lacy felt a rush of panic. "Where are you going?"

"Up."

"Right now?"

"Yep." Jax was already at the top of the ladder, hoisting himself up to the metal bridge.

Great. Well, Lacy wasn't going up there. No way. No how. Heights were not her friend. She preferred to be on solid ground.

"What's up there, anyway?" Andy asked from behind her.

"A bridge so the techies can adjust the lights without having to bring the whole electric grid down."

"Can you just go up there?"

Lacy shrugged. "He did."

"Cool." Andy started to climb up.

"You're going too?" Lacy couldn't hide the irritation from her voice. Andy knew that Lacy didn't do bridges. Or ladders.

"Sure. Why not?"

Because that left her alone down at the bottom, that's why. Left her alone with Eli.

As if summoned by her thoughts, Eli came up along-side her. "Hey, a catwalk. I love these." And then he was climbing.

"You too?" Jesus, was everyone leaving her? Just what she needed—to feel like a losery loser while everyone else went exploring.

Eli paused to call over his shoulder, "Join us."

"I can't." She hesitated at his questioning look. What-ever, it wasn't that humiliating. Not like being a songwriter unable to write songs or being walked in on while mas-turbating in a hotel lobby. "I'm afraid of heights."

"Really? Huh." Eli let go of the rung he was on, letting himself fall to the ground. He stared at her, a moment too long for comfort. "I know another girl who's afraid of heights."

"Eh. It's not really an uncommon fear." She was sure, however, that it wasn't that common to look so good jump-ing off a ladder.

He wiped his sweaty hands along his jeans. "I guess not."

Now she truly was alone with Eli. And that whole *I'm glad things are easy between us* vibe she'd had earlier seemed to be fading away. Maybe she'd rather be alone without Eli. "You don't have to not go up because of me."

He cocked his head, a gleam appearing in his eye. "I know. And I don't plan to not go up. But I want you to come with."

"Eli, I'm not kidding. I'm not good with heights." Terrified, more like. "I quit gymnastics as a kid the min-ute I stepped up on the balance beam. And playground slides? The only times I made it to the top was when Andy climbed behind me and held me tight on the way down."

"And you loved it, right? 'Cause I can tell from your

expression that you wish you weren't afraid now. You want to be up there."

Lacy bit her lip. "Maybe." But that was just because everyone else was up there. "No." Except she did kind of want to see what it was like. "I don't know. Maybe."

Eli chuckled. "So let's do this. You go ahead of me and I'll follow behind you like your sister did when you were kids. You don't have to worry about falling, because if you slip, I'll catch you."

He'd said something like that before. On the bus, when she'd crashed into him as they took a turn. He'd said he was happy to break her fall. That stirred something in her now, not just because he was saying it again, but because it felt like it meant so much more than just a physical, literal thing.

She was being ridiculous, though. He had someone. What else would he mean by it? Though there did seem to be some lyrics buried in there somewhere.

Lacy looked up the ladder and considered. She could hear Andy and Jax up above her, laughing about something. She wanted to go . . . but . . . "I'm not just afraid of falling. There's the whole looking down and getting dizzy thing."

"Then don't look down. At least not while you're climbing. When we get to the top, if you want to look down, I'll hold you while you look. Then if you get dizzy, you'll have someone to lean on." Eli grinned then, that wickedly bright grin that made her knees knock.

This probably wasn't a good idea.

"I don't know." She shook her head.

"Never mind then. See you when we get down." Eli grabbed onto a rung.

"No. Wait!" She couldn't stand it. Couldn't stand to see him climbing up without her. Couldn't stand to keep on living her life in fear of what was next. "I'll go."

"Awesome." Eli waited while she got her grip, then helped her get her footing. "That's it. One rung at a time. Just keep looking forward."

She moved one foot and one hand up. Then the other hand and the other foot. As Eli had suggested, she kept looking forward, her eyes glued to the bridge above. She felt him below her, and though she wouldn't glance down, she knew he was watching her. Protecting her.

Near the top, the metal wrapped around the top of the ladder, encasing the climber so that if she leaned back she would fall against the enclosure instead of down to the ground. That added to her confidence. She came out from it and found Jax at the top to give her a hand up to the bridge.

"Glad you could make it," he said as he pulled her to him. Their bodies were flush against each other and she thought she saw a hint of interest in the way he looked down at her. Still, something was wrong. Probably the fact that she was standing on a bridge way too high above the ground. Humans were not meant to do this.

Oh, God, what had she been thinking!

"Can you make a guy a little room?" Eli was stopped at the top of the ladder, Jax and Lacy blocking him from coming all the way up.

She giggled stupid nervous giggles that were definitely because of the height and not because she was smack between two gorgeous guys. "Of course. Come on up." Lacy pushed against Jax to make space.

Jax took her hand as he led her further out on the bridge. "Are you nervous about heights or something?"

Not wanting to seem like a total scaredy-cat to Jax, she underplayed her fear. "A bit. But it helps to have something solid to hold onto." Her free hand quickly found the side railing. It was cold steel in her hand and nothing had ever felt better.

"That's what she said." Eli came behind her as she gave a shaky chuckle. He put his hand on her elbow. "You okay?"

Well, maybe she'd been exaggerating about nothing feeling better than the steel because his touch felt pretty good right now too. "Yeah. I'm pretty okay."

Andy stood ahead of them at the center of the bridge examining the lights on the grid above. As the threesome neared her, she turned toward them. "Lacy! You climbed up here?"

It was encouraging to have her sister witness her bravery. But she played it down. "Well, don't be too impressed. I haven't looked down yet, and I just realized I'll probably have to do that on the way back down the ladder."

"You haven't looked down?" Jax seemed flabbergasted. "There's no point in being up here if you don't look out at the view. It's awesome. You never get to look at the audience from this viewpoint—above the lights so you can actually see them."

Eli's hand fell from Lacy's elbow, but he still stood near. "You do realize there's no audience out there right now, right?"

Jax smirked at his bandmate. "Shut up. Imagine it. The sea of faces. That's how many seats they'd fill." He dropped her hand and gestured out in front of him. Toward the audience, Lacy guessed—she still didn't dare to look anywhere but at the people around her.

He sat down on the bridge and let his feet dangle off the side.

Even though there were three sets of safety bars, Lacy was not doing that.

"It is a pretty cool view," Andy admitted. "But not because of the imaginary sea of faces. It's cool because it's just something you don't usually see."

"All right. I'm going to look." Lacy took a deep breath.

Then another. Then a third. Gripping the steel with both hands, she looked out.

And saw nothing but the back of the curtain. "You can't even see the audience. The masking's in the way."

"That's why you sit, Lacypants. Try it." Jax extended his hand out to her. "Come on. I'll help you down."

Ah, dammit. "Uh, okay. Oh, my God. I can't believe I'm—" She broke off in a chain of swear words that lasted until her butt met the metal of the bridge. She crossed her legs Indian style. "Okay. I'm here."

And wow. The view really was . . . cool.

Eli sat on the other side of her, mirroring Jax. "Now dangle your feet over the side."

"Are you freaking kidding me?" Her heart rate picked up just at the thought.

Eli put his hand at the small of her back. "There are bars. You're going nowhere. And I'm here." He cleared his throat. "All of us, I mean. All of us are here."

Man, she must have taken a crazy pill that morning, because she was about to do it. She held both hands on the lowest bar and threw first one leg, then the other, over the edge.

Something about the new position made her feel looser, more like she was free in the air. Sort of more like flying. But because she had the bars and a strong man on either side of her, plus her sister nearby, she also felt really safe.

"Lacy, this is really amazing," Andy said standing above her. "Look at you! Does this mean you'll finally join me at the top of the Prudential Tower?"

"Uh, yeah, no." *Hell no.* "That's like seven hundred fifty feet high. This is, what? Fifteen feet? Eighteen?"

"Twenty-six feet," Jax said.

"Holy sh—" Lacy swallowed. That was more than four Eli's stacked on top of each other. And just one Eli was pretty tall. She took another yoga-deep breath. "Fine. I'm fine. It's all fine. How's everybody else?"

Andy took a seat on the other side of Eli. "I'm doing great."

"Me too," Eli said, his hand still pressed to the small of Lacy's back.

She glanced down at his arm, not sure if she really wanted him to remove it but knowing that it would be best for both of them if he did.

Perhaps unfortunately, he caught her meaning. "Oh, sorry," he said quietly, letting his hand drift to the metal bridge.

And now Lacy wasn't afraid of the height at all because all she could think about was missing the warmth of Eli's touch.

Jax leaned forward, his hands clasped on the lowest supporting rod as he surveyed the space in front of him. "I love it up here, man." His voice was wistful—dreamy, even. "Sometimes I wonder if this would have been the better career. A behind-the-scenes guy. They can come up here and enjoy the crowd without having to deal with any of the pressure of being the talent. They can just, like, enjoy the music. You know?"

Lacy patted his thigh. "I do." She *did* know. Even though she didn't have pressure from fans like she was sure that Jax did, she did have pressure. Pressure to record her next album. Pressure to write her next song. Making music was a job—she'd never expected it to be anything different—but that knowledge didn't make it any easier to stay current and relevant when her creative muse had gone MIA.

It was that type of pressure that made her do crazy things. Like jump unassuming nice guys just to get a few words written down.

Yeah, she understood Jax. She understood big time.

But on the other hand, wasn't the pressure what made it worth it? Right now, the fear of being so high in the air was what made the view worth it. A view that was really nothing but an aerial of an empty theater was suddenly special.

She opened her mouth to say just that when she was interrupted from a voice below. "Okay, kids. I'm locking up now. Time to go." It was Sammy.

Jax put a finger to his mouth. "Shh. This will be fun," he whispered.

Lacy stifled a giggle that was just as much a release of the nervous energy she'd kept bottled the last twenty minutes with the guys as it was from the game they were playing on Sammy.

"Did you guys sneak out already?" Sammy called. "Dawson? Babyface?"

Lacy's eyes widened as the urge to laugh grew more insistent. "*Babyface?*" she mouthed.

"She's not talking about me," Eli whispered, pointing to Jax.

Of course it was Jax Sammy was talking about. Even under the hipster-required facial hair, he had those soft features that would probably age gracefully—almost *too* gracefully—while Eli's face was all man, complete with laugh lines and the wrinkles at his eyes that said he smiled often. They were both so breathtaking in such different ways.

Jax shot daggers at his bandmate. "Shut up, Grandpa."

"You know, I can hear you." Sammy was underneath them now, looking out around the empty seats as if the foursome might be hiding out there.

"Now you've done it," Eli said, not bothering to hush his voice.

"Maybe we should go down. She's a bit scary."

Sammy's head shot up toward the ceiling, her hand over

her eyes to block out the lights. "Aha! I see you up there.
Do you think I'm an idiot? Bunch of hanging feet in the
air . . ." Her voice trailed off as she muttered to herself.

Now all four of them were laughing. The kind of laughing that made Lacy's belly ache and tears gather in her
eyes.

Sammy shouted again. "If I lock up and you're still in
here, then you'll be stuck until sound check."

That was all the encouragement they needed. "Coming," Eli called down as Jax helped Lacy up from her sitting position.

Andy was already on her way to the ladder. "I'm not
getting locked in here on my one day in Baltimore with
my sis. We have plans."

It was the first Lacy had heard of plans. She suspected
that meant the afternoon would be free of the men, but
perhaps it was good to have a break from the conflicting
emotions that both sparked in her. "Conflicting desires"
may actually be the more appropriate term. Time with
both hotties had stirred her feminine hormones into a
storm. Was this what The Weather Girls meant by "It's
Raining Men"? If so, she wasn't singing, *Hallelujah*. She
was praying, *Help me, Lord*.

Partly, though, she was praying because she was now
about to head back down the ladder.

"You really don't have to look down." Eli's voice was
encouraging behind her. "Go slow. Keep your focus on
your hands. On the next rung down. Your feet will find
their own way."

There's definitely a song in this experience.

"And I'm going before you," Jax said, "So if you fall,
you'll hurt me. So you won't fall."

"Not helping!" Lacy said. "How are none of you even
a little bit frightened of being so . . . up?"

"What are you talking about? Of course we're scared,

Lacy. Maybe not of being up, but of something. Not a one of us has our shit together no matter what it seems." Eli brushed a hair off her cheek. "Everybody's faking it."

She liked that. Liked it a lot. It spoke to her in ways deeper than the moment. Even after Jax ruined it with "That's what she said," which was actually sort of funny, but also a mood killer.

Everybody's faking it. She repeated the phrase silently over and over as she took Eli's advice and kept her eyes on her hands while she went down. Sure enough, her feet found their own way and soon she was on solid ground.

She broke into a giant grin.

"Happy you did that?" Andy asked. "I'm definitely proud!"

Lacy nodded. Because she was happy, but even more she'd realized something else too. If she could face her fear of heights and climb more than four Eli's above the ground, then she could face her empty staff pad. She just had to stop looking down on the whole thing. Focus on her hands as they strummed on her instrument. The words would follow.

And while she waited for the rest to come down, it felt comforting to know that she wasn't the only person faking it. Which it begged the question—what was Eli faking?

Chapter Eighteen

Lacy pulled her sunglasses from her purse as she and Andy exited the theater into the bright sunlight. She couldn't stand not knowing any longer—she had to ask first thing when the two were finally alone. "So. What did you think?"

They'd left the guys behind with Sammy so the girls could pursue whatever Andy had planned for the afternoon. Lacy followed her sister as she led the way to the curb.

"I think it's amazing." Andy grinned at her. "A real band load in with a roadie? You're on your way, girl. I'm proud of you. And of me! I called it a load in! Look how jargony I am."

Though the praise was nice, it wasn't what Lacy had been referring to. "It really is crazy. But that's not what I meant."

Andy held her hand out, easily flagging a cab. Really, she was excellent at that. Lacy had never mastered the art of cabbing in the same way her sister had.

"Are you coming with?" Andy asked.

Lacy was so busy admiring her sister's talent, in fact,

that Andy had already given directions to the driver and climbed in before Lacy had a chance to process it all.

Of course she was coming with. Even though she had no idea where "with" was. She slid into the backseat and shut the door. Honestly, she didn't care where they were going. She wanted Andy's opinion on The Guy. "Back to before," she nudged with her elbow. "What did you think about *him*?"

"Oh! Him. Sorry, I don't know where my priorities were." Andy crossed one leg over the other. "Well. He's amazing too. Really amazing. There's a depth to him I didn't notice at first. He's strong *and* a caretaker. It's a sexy combination, and he'd be good for you."

"Thank God you think so." Muscles that Lacy didn't realize had been tensed relaxed with Andy's proclamation. There was always something so reassuring about the acceptance of your chosen man by the women you cared about. By your family. "Gah, I'm so glad you like Jax. I was worried that you wouldn't 'get' him."

"I do get"—Andy paused, her nose wrinkling up—"Wait a minute—Jax? I was talking about Eli. Isn't Eli the one you, you know, got it on with?"

"No!" Except Lacy was *no*-ing the idea of Eli being her man and not what Andy had actually asked. "I mean, yes, but I told you that was over. It was only a one-time thing. Or a two-time thing. Whatever. He's not the guy. The guy is Jax. What did you think about Jax?"

"Huh. Jax." Andy traced her brow with her finger over and over though it did nothing to relax her confused crinkle. "You really like Jax? What's wrong with Eli?"

The question irritated Lacy, and she didn't keep it from her tone. "There's nothing wrong with Eli. He's just not The Guy. And yes, I really like Jax. Do you not?"

Andy shook her head. "No, I like Jax fine. He's just not for you."

"What's that supposed to mean?" Lacy's volume rose, earning a glance in the rearview mirror from the cabbie. The volume was necessary though. It expressed her sincere distress at the situation. Couldn't Andy just be happy for her? Happy she was moving on finally, even though it wasn't with her preferred candidate?

Andy sighed, somewhat overdramatically if anyone asked Lacy. "Jax is . . . well, he's still finding himself. And looking everywhere but inside. That's not what you need. You need softer. More compassionate. Wiser."

Lacy gripped her fingers into the edge of her seat. This was so typical. Andy thinking she knew everything about everyone on first glance. So what if she was right ninety-nine percent of the time? This was clearly the one percent.

"I do enjoy his *Lacypants* nickname," Andy added, as if Lacy wasn't at all about ready to blow. "I'm keeping that."

"You're *not* keeping that." *No way.* Lacy liked that it was Jax's name for her, sometimes, but there would be plenty of time for him to find a better one. One like Songbird. But more importantly right now, "And how do you know what I need?"

"I'm your sister. Duh." Andy turned to Lacy, eyebrows raised as if she was the one offended. "And do I need to remind you that I did this for a living?" She leaned forward toward the voice opening in the partition between the front and the back of the car and added for the driver's sake, "I was a matchmaker."

This was almost laughable. "You matched one guy. *One guy*, Andy. With everyone *but* the right one. Remember the whole Jane situation?"

Andy clasped her hands around her knee. "Low blow, girl. Although, for your information, I still regularly think angry thoughts at Jane. But may I remind you that you were the one who pushed me into that career in the first place?"

Lacy rubbed at her neck, which was hot and red from frustration. "Only because we were desperate for money. It wasn't a career—it was something to get by. Remember? You did it for me."

Andy opened her mouth to speak, but then closed it again. She cocked her head and studied Lacy. "This isn't really about me, although of course you know I would do anything for you. Why are you being so weird about all of this? You used to value my opinions."

Lacy threw her head against the seat back and sighed. "Because I really like Jax. Like, really really like him." Well, she really really liked his alter ego, anyway. "Andy, you don't get it. He's different with me. When we're . . ."— she was not about to admit online, so she said—"alone, he's sensitive and supportive and all about me. What you saw today is only one side of him."

"I'm sure I don't see all of him," Andy conceded. "Just like I'm sure you don't see what I see in Blake. But when I'm in a room full of people, I still recognize the same inner qualities that I see in Blake when we're alone. They may be hidden or obscured, but they're still there. So, while I can't be the judge of Jax, you have to ask yourself—is he the same guy? Because if he's a chameleon, if he changes his colors, then my next question for you is, who is he really?"

Lacy turned away and bit her tongue. She didn't want to say what she was really feeling, which was, *leave me alone*. She also didn't want to admit that there was a lot of valid wisdom in Andy's words. Lacy liked Jax. He was a good enough guy. Why was he so different when they were face-to-face than he was when he was online as Folx?

She hoped that as soon as he realized she was Love-Coda that he'd show her more of his other side. She *hoped*.

But what if she was wrong? What if Folx was just an aspect of him, and not his true self?

She didn't want to think about that right now. She definitely didn't want to discuss it anymore with her psychologist sister who had the man of her dreams waiting for her at home. And she didn't want to be fighting, either. Not on the one afternoon she got with Andy in town.

Lacy took a deep breath and turned back to face her older-but-not-necessarily-wiser sister. "You have a point, Andy. I appreciate your insight. But let's not spend anymore time talking about boys on girl's day." She plastered on a smile. "Did you say earlier that we had plans?"

"We have the most serious of plans." Andy bit her lip as if the news she was about to deliver wouldn't be taken well. "You need a maid of honor dress. I've already made a list of local boutiques to hit. We're on our way to number one now. If you can do this, I will buy the Best Bloody Marys Ever."

Though fancy clothes weren't really Lacy's game, dress shopping was a helluva lot better than debating the merits of men she didn't totally understand in the first place. "Well, okay then."

Andy put up a hand as if in protest. "I know you said we'd have time to get it later, but you don't know how hard it is to find something perfect. And there could be alterations and that can take a few weeks. We have to do it now."

"Fine. I'm in."

"We won't spend—" Andy halted. She narrowed her eyes suspiciously. "You mean you're not arguing with me?"

"No, I'm not. Sheesh, Andy, I don't *always* argue with you." So maybe she mostly did. That's what younger sisters were for.

For the second time that cab ride, Andy opened her mouth and closed it again before speaking. "No. You don't. In fact, there's a whole lot of times I imagine you swallow what you really want to tell me. Have I told you lately how much I love you?"

"Not nearly as recently as you should have."

Andy patted Lacy's thigh as the cab pulled up to their destination. "I love you, Lacypants. Now let's go find a dress."

Lacy smiled as her sister paid the driver. This was fine. Andy would learn to love Jax the same way Lacy had learned—er, was learning—to love Blake. Which reminded her—"What if we find the perfect dress? Won't Tim be upset that he didn't have a say in our choice?" At least picking out a dress in Baltimore instead of Boston kept her from having to deal with the man's histrionics.

"Oh, no worries there. I, uh"—Andy kept her eyes at her feet—"brought my iPad. Okay, then, let's go!" She headed toward the store entrance.

"Andy!" It was funnier than she'd ever admit to see her strong, bullheaded sister so cowed. Still better the iPad than having the man in person to cow her too. "Okay"— Lacy trotted to catch up—"but lunch is on you. And it's going to be crab. I know a cool bar."

Sammy pulled on the door of the back entrance, making sure it was secure. "Okay, I think we got all the doors locked. I had to move the bus from the loading zone so it's across the street in the public parking lot. Follow me."

The roadie took off at a surprisingly fast pace for someone with such short legs. Eli looked at Jax, who just shrugged. "Guess we're following her."

"Guess so." Jax started after her.

Eli matched his leisurely pace. He so rarely got to hang with his friend these days. Maybe they could spend the afternoon together. Do lunch. Catch an afternoon show. Spend a little time remembering all the reasons they were friends, and not just bandmates.

Eli was just about to suggest it when Jax stopped walking and glanced behind them. "What happened to the girls?"

"You mean Lacy and Andy?" They'd left the minute they'd come down from the catwalk, nearly half an hour ago now. Jax could be so clueless. "They had some other plans in town, I guess."

At the mention of them, Eli wondered what they were doing. Wondered if Lacy was forcing her sister into a crab shack or if she had taken him up on the idea of exploring the Poe House.

He hoped it wasn't the latter. He wanted to show her that himself.

And when would he do that? On their next trip to Baltimore? No, there was no *their*. God, why was that so hard to remember?

Jax stepped off the curb and into the crosswalk. "Too bad. She's kinda adorable."

Eli was glad his sunglasses hid his eye roll. "She's engaged."

"Lacypants is engaged?"

"No. I thought you meant her sister." Actually, he *wished* that Jax meant Andy. He didn't like the idea that other people realized the awesomeness of Lacy like he did, unfair and unreasonable as that idea was.

"Nah, the sister's not my type. But Lacy . . ." Jax trailed off, his eyes dreamy as his mind drifted with the thought. "She's got a great ass too. Had a great view as she was coming down that ladder. Nice."

Guess Jax didn't miss much after all.

"Yeah, she's something." Because what else could he say? The adjectives he could use to describe their newest tour member would fill at least a page of his spiral-bound notebook. Maybe even the whole notebook, if he let his mind get carried away. And *great ass* would not be anywhere on the first page. Though it would probably be in the first five.

Lacy *did* have a great ass.

They'd reached the other side of the street by the time Jax spoke again. "Hey, you're not interested in her, are you? Because if not . . ."

Eli couldn't bring himself to say he wasn't interested. He was very interested. He just wasn't allowed to be interested. Their decision to be friends prevented that. And Lacy had her own interest—namely Jax.

And since he knew that Lacy was into Jax, he had to encourage the relationship. It was the honorable thing to do, no matter how much it pained him. He loved his friend, annoyed as he could get, and Lacy—well, she deserved more than his two-timing heart. It was only right to allow them to be happy together. "If you like her, you should go for it."

Eli wasn't honorable enough, though, to not qualify his statement. Or maybe he was exactly that honorable. "Just don't be a dick about it, Jax. Lacy's not the kind of girl you can fuck and forget." He happened to know this from experience.

Jax eyed his friend. "You're talking like you're into her, bro. Say the word and I'll keep my hands off. Though, you know, the Groupie Clause says sharing's acceptable."

Eli's hand clenched instinctively into a fist at his side. Not that he'd ever actually punch Jax, but it felt good to pretend he might. "She's not a groupie, ass. She's a co-worker. And because of that you need to show her a little respect. While we're on this tour, she's practically a member of the band."

"Good point. Maybe I'll wait until after the tour to hit that, then."

"Sometimes you're such an asshole." Suddenly Eli wasn't interested in lunching with his old friend, with reconnecting. He wasn't even sure he wanted to ride with him back to the hotel.

Jax climbed the steps of the bus then turned back. Spreading his arms in a this-is-who-I-am stance, he said, "It's called charisma, Eli. You don't recognize it because you don't see it when you look in the mirror."

"Full of yourself much?" Now Eli was sure he didn't want to ride with Jax. The hotel was only five minutes away—he could walk it. It probably took longer in traffic than on foot. But that would be out and out rude at this point, so he followed up into the vehicle.

Then, when Jax ignored his usual backseat sprawl to sit by the others, Eli felt obliged to take the spot in front of him. At least Jax was trying to be social. The two hadn't had a conversation that didn't revolve around a song or the tour for months. The least Eli could do was meet him halfway.

But he wouldn't connect by talking about Lacy anymore. He waited until the bus had lurched out of the parking lot and was on the road. "Can I ask you something, Jax?"

"Dude, it's big. That's all I'm going to tell you."

"What? Are you twelve?" Eli groaned. "I don't want to know about your dick."

Jax laughed. "My dick? I was talking about my vocal range. Where's your mind?"

"Ass." Eli shook his head. He deserved it, though, since he'd fallen for Jax's setup.

"Anyway"—Jax angled himself so his back was to the window—"what did you want to ask?"

Eli bit back his irritation and asked the question that had been itching at his mind since the beginning of the tour. "Where do you go every night after the show?"

Jax's jaw tightened. "Why do you want to know?"

"Just curious." Even more curious now that Jax seemed

so opposed to answering. They used to tell each other everything. He wasn't even sure who'd stopped first.

"Where do *you* go every night? Like clockwork you head out of the green room thirty minutes after curtain." It wasn't unusual for Jax to turn the tables.

Eli was prepared for that. He got that he often had to give in order to get with Jax. He also knew the art of disclosing only enough information to seem like he was being fully open. "I have an online thing I've gotten into."

"Like a hookup site?"

"Something like that." Eli cleared his throat. "Your turn. You used to always mingle with the fans. Have a drink"—*or seven*—"at the venue bar. Now you disappear. Where do you go?"

Jax pinned his gaze out the window across the aisle. "Nowhere, really. I have some girls I know in some towns and I hook up with them. Mostly, I wander. Sometimes I check out another bar. Sometimes I just end up walking."

There was nothing wrong with Jax's answer. Nothing that would seem out of place with any typical artist-type. But the lead singer of the Blue Hills was not a typical artist. He was more spotlight and less streetlight. And what was with his monologue on the catwalk about wanting to be a backstage type rather than a performer? That had seemed rather out of character.

Eli suddenly felt cold worry along the back of his neck. "Are you okay, Jax?"

"I'm fine." It was obvious he didn't want Eli to pry.

But the last time Jax hadn't wanted people to pry, Eli hadn't. And he'd regretted it. He'd never stop regretting it. So now he was prying whether Jax wanted it or not. "That's not like you, dude. You love hanging out with the crowd. You thrive on their energy." There was no way Jax wasn't into that anymore. "Are you sure you're all right?"

"I said I'm fine," Jax snapped. He turned to sit forward

in his seat. "You know what you do, Eli? You put me in a box. You think you know who I am or what I want. You don't have a fucking clue."

Before Eli could say anything in response, Jax stood and moved to the back of the bus.

Eli didn't go after him. He didn't even look back. There wasn't anything to be said, really. And if Jax wanted to be alone, then so be it.

Wasn't that how it always went anyway? Jax getting exactly what he wanted?

Or maybe he was just being pissy so he could avoid recognizing that the people he put in boxes included himself.

Chapter Nineteen

"They encored me! Can you even? I can't even. This is A Best Night Ever!"

Darrin's delighted laughter on the other end of the phone warmed Lacy even more. Hearing his voice almost overwhelmed her with homesickness, but the elation she felt from this show kept her from examining that too closely.

"I'm stoked for you, Lace, but I can't say I'm surprised. About time more people started noticing you. Soon you won't even remember me anymore."

"Are you pouting, D?" She grinned into the phone and flopped on the couch in the makeshift green room. Good thing they hadn't kept looking for it earlier. She and Jax never would have found the part-closet, part-bathroom with a curtain, part-lounge tucked beneath—not behind—the stage.

"I'm pouting."

"I'll be back before you know it, and you'll wish I was gone again." She kicked her feet in the air. Too much energy for the couch, she hopped up. She could faintly hear the Blue Hills launching into "Godric's Hollow," and started to dance a little.

"Never. But while you are on tour, are you using the crowds to get reactions to your new material? God, I wish I could be there to catch some debuts." This was exactly why she hadn't been calling Darrin, giving herself a brief respite from the weight of her lies. But right now, she could be completely honest. For once. She gave an extra little shimmy-shake.

"I debuted a new one tonight. It's what got the encore," she said proudly as she continued to sway to the music. Wow, that felt good. Honesty only sucked when you didn't like what you had to say. Of course, she wasn't going to mention that this was the first new one she'd played on tour. Nor was she going to mention that it wasn't even finished—she simply repeated the one verse and chorus and added an instrumental bridge to make the song feel complete. Still, lies of omission were almost no big deal at all compared to the whoppers she'd *been* telling.

"I'm so proud of you, sweetheart. Go celebrate. But when you come home, don't think you're getting out of a champagne party with me." Although that opened up a little can of worms as to why she'd confided in a stranger instead of him. For the first time, Lacy considered that maybe this whole thing wouldn't have spiraled as it had if she'd only been honest with her boss from the get-go.

"I've told you, D, adding Sprite to your boxed wine does not equal champagne. But I'll still take you up on it. Love you!" They hung up and she twirled around the room, blessedly not smacking anyone this time.

This was the most amazing feeling. Perfect strangers had liked her music enough to ask for more. Not her old fans, or people she knew. Total strangers. This was the whole reason she'd started writing music, started performing. The only problem with this perfect moment was that now she was off the phone, there really wasn't anyone to share it with.

Andy had to leave the minute Lacy's set was over, catching a red-eye back to Boston. Jax/Folx was onstage right now, and from the sounds of the audience, killing it himself tonight. Sammy had given her a noogie and gone back to watching *Orange Is the New Black* on her iPad while waiting for tear down. Lou was off wooing a potential new client, some kid he'd seen on YouTube. It was weird to be lonely, surrounded by so many people. She flopped down on the sofa again, suddenly less ecstatic than she'd been earlier.

But—it was the special-est of occasions. So she allowed herself to do the thing that if Andy had been here, would get her pulled from the tour.

Pulling her cell from the inner pocket of her guitar case, she took a deep breath. And called the number she'd always know by heart. The number she'd called so many times this year. The number her sister had once found her redialing over and over, sobbing herself hoarse on the same bathroom floor she'd found him on.

Lance's voicemail came on and her eyes filled with tears as the familiar sound of him came on the line. Something was different this time as she hung up, though. The tears weren't so much about missing him as they were about missing her old self, the self that had left a hundred messages for the man she thought she knew. Lacy blew her nose and tuned back in to the sounds floating down from the stage.

She was still in that pensive mood when the boys came offstage. Jax threw himself down next to her. Eli sent her a smile before Lou dragged him off to talk to the new protégé. The other guys headed to their usual beer and argument over who was better that night.

Her spirits sunk further as she realized that the people

who would care about her accomplishment had just walked out the door. Or, person, rather—Eli. She was a little surprised that he was the one she had first thought of squealing to when it happened.

He was the first person she thought about a lot though lately, if she were honest. But she'd had enough honesty tonight and didn't want to think about things that were going to dampen her mood even more.

Jax ruffled her hair. "Encore tonight, Lacypants!"

The feelings swelled in her chest again at the acknowledgment. She should have known he'd notice. Well, actually, there was no way she could have known since he'd never said anything about her sets before, but she should have guessed. Folx would never miss acknowledging a friend's triumph.

"I'm so excited, I can hardly stand it. Did you feel this way, the first time?" She smoothed her mussed curls back into place.

"Honestly? I still feel that way every time. It's a drug, being loved. I'm addicted."

It was a complete contradiction to his words earlier on the catwalk and she wondered if he was being sincere.

He smiled, though, and the corners of his eyes crinkled just a bit, enough for her to know he meant it. "Come on, we should celebrate. I'm calling in that rain check on the drink. If we hurry we can sneak out the back before any of the fans catch us." He held out a hand, and pulled her to her feet.

His hand was warm, and strong, and she told herself that was just as exciting as the electricity she never stopped hoping would suddenly show up when they touched. Probably it was just the edge of disappointment at not doing a meet-and-greet on her biggest night yet. Because this *was* exciting. Jax was finally giving her some of what she had always known he was capable of. Folx and Love were going to go have a drink, and really get to know each other. She wondered if he suspected her true identity. Funny that she should think of her pen name as her true identity, but in so many ways it was.

Jax offered her his arm, and together they stepped out of The Dog House and into the humid Baltimore night. This was comfortable. This was nice. He didn't say anything, and neither did she. Lacy had assumed they'd stop in the first place they saw, but Jax seemed content to ramble past all the lit neons, crossing streets seemingly at random, occasionally checking his phone or typing things in. Texting someone, perhaps. Or tweeting. She was curious, but let him have his space.

This introspective side of him was new, at least new in person. Selfishly, she wondered if he was thinking about LoveCoda and regretting coming out with Lacy. She wondered if she should casually mention something about the forum, just to bait him a little. See if he brought her up in conversation.

At the thought of SoWriAn, though, she suddenly wondered if Jax would message her to say he couldn't meet tonight, and if so, what his excuse would be. As if on cue, her phone pinged. She glanced at it.

Sorry to cancel. Have to meet with another singer tonight.

It was true she supposed, though she didn't like the "have to" connotation. And why had it taken her so long to get the message? Jax had been on his phone but it had been several minutes ago now. Huh. Maybe the forum had a delay. She didn't know how apps worked, anyway. Magic, as most technology seemed to be.

She shrugged and stuffed her phone in her purse, trying not to dwell on the Jax she knew online and instead focus on the Jax she was with. Finally, after several blocks of roaming, a set of stairs leading down to a basement-level dive bar caught his eye, and he held the heavy metal door open for her.

He ordered for them, a vodka rocks for himself and a G&T for Lacy. She was touched that he'd memorized her drink order from their day out on the town. She didn't think he was paying that much attention. Which was good, since he wasn't supposed to be paying attention to anyone but Love. She made a conscious effort not to consider Kat and the Groupie Clause.

Although Kat and the Groupie Clause would make an excellent band name.

"So. Me and you, alone at last," Jax drawled, and took a large swallow from his drink. He winced a little as he swallowed. "First sip's always a little rough. Mind if I?" Without waiting for an answer, he reached over and plucked the lime from her drink and added it to his own.

Actually, she did mind, but it was no big deal to reach across the bar and spear another wedge with a toothpick. Something he could have done himself. She squelched her irritation. Jax was the lead singer of a very popular band. It was probably second nature for him to expect people to bend over backward for him. It sure looked like his whole band did, anyway. A picture of Eli floated across her vision, and she waved it away.

"What are you waving at?"

"Oh. Just a gnat that flew by my face." Lacy took a sip of her gin. "So, yeah, me and you. Are you happy with the tour so far?" His smile faltered just a little.

"Yeah, man. I'm pretty happy with the tour. The fans can be sweet. They can also be obnoxious. I like the pics and the free drinks, but enough with the autographs. I need my hand to be uncramped for performances."

Though it wasn't like he played an instrument onstage. So did it really matter if his hand cramped the night before? But she just smiled and nodded.

The nod encouraged Jax to say more. "We just keep getting bigger. That's pretty cool. I mean, I always knew we were awesome, but now other people know we're awesome too. You know?" He smiled again, and downed the rest of his drink.

As he signaled the waitress behind the bar to get him another, Lacy stared at him. She wondered if he was nervous. He had to be. Nervous to be alone with her like this. Because even though they were together, and guards should be down, he was still lapsing into Jax-mode, that rock-star act. That thing where he didn't come off as the thoughtful intelligent guy she knew him to be.

Or . . . maybe he wasn't the guy she thought he was at all. She'd decided he was Folx because she'd heard him singing Folx's song. But that didn't necessarily mean Jax had written it, even if he sang it like he did.

For the first time, it occurred to her to ask. "Jax, the songs you play—did you write them?"

"The band's songs?" His eyes flicked around the bar. "Yeah. Totally."

"Like, 'Godric's Hollow'? That's yours?" She had to be certain.

He met her eyes, grinning with self-assurance. "I'm responsible for everything you hear, baby."

Of course he was. He was Folx, like she'd thought. He just was also *not* Folx. Not on the outside, and she wasn't sure how to change that.

She needed a plan to get him to loosen up a little. Or a lot. How did people usually get her to lower her defenses? Besides Folx and Eli, she could only think of one person who had really gotten to her recently.

Wedding planner Tim.

"Let's do shots," Lacy proposed. *Lots and lots of shots. I'll hold back on the insults, though.*

Jax grinned at her, and called the girl back over. "What are we doing?" he asked Lacy.

"Have you ever had a Christmas Wisemen?" He shook his head. "Jager, Rumple, and Hot Damn."

"Sounds potent! I'm impressed. You aren't who I thought you were." His smile faded into a more intense look.

"And who did you think I was?" Lacy felt her heart rate speed up.

"Oh, I don't know. No one, really." He held up his shot and winked at her. "To new friends."

"To new friends." *No one? He thought I was no one? Sheesh kabobs.* Her thoughts overrode the burn of the liquor, and the liquor overrode the burn of the comment. Drinking was great.

Jax shook his head vigorously at the aftertaste. "Damn! Another, please, darlin'."

The bartender winked at him and lined up a shot for herself as well. No one was immune to that man's charms. Really, it didn't bother her like it might have. Maybe she understood that Jax was a man to be shared.

Or maybe she was just numb from the liquor. Cause he wasn't like a Groupie Clause. Haha. The third shot spread fuzzy warmth out from Lacy's throat to her arms, and she grinned at Jax.

"I really like your music," she told him, perfectly aware that she was only a couple of drinks away from telling him that "music" was code for "hot body."

"Hey, thanks. I like yours too. I don't normally dig chick singers, but you've got a whole thing going on that's pretty cool. With all the, uh, hair, and guitar . . ."

She narrowed her eyes. "You've barely listened to my music, huh."

He collapsed into giggles and signaled for another round.

"I watched you the first night, and I was impressed. Really. It's just that I have my pre-show ritual, so I do that while you're doing your set, you know?"

It occurred to her to be offended. But she let the idea pass. This was part of getting to know someone—working out the kinks, finding common ground. Music was totally their common ground. Jax just didn't know it yet. And she had a pre-show ritual too. "*Red leather yellow leather.*" So much in common.

He slid one of the tiny chilled glasses toward her and raised it. "To your music."

"To my goddamn music. It *is* good." Lacy was growing in confidence with every tipsy moment. "What's your pre-show ritual? I'm always curious how other singers warm up."

"Oh, I don't really warm up. I just get ready to be seen. So first I exfoliate. That's really important. You know, you should probably be doing it too. Let's see, I use lotion after that, it has a little bit of shimmer in it in case I take off my shirt onstage. Not, like, *glitter*, it's a manly sort of shimmer. My hair only takes a few minutes, just a little product. Then I pretty much just spend some time with the mirror, stretching, a little yoga, some affirmations. Do you do affirmations? You should. I'll give you some, and some scrub. I'm going to help you, Lacy. You could be really big."

Lacy stared at him.

This time, it was she who flagged the bartender for more. God, Folx never talked like this. But then, when did they ever talk about the performance? They talked process, writing, the quiet private moments. Was this really what he needed to take him from that time to the public arena of the stage? Was it okay for such a smart guy to be so shallow?

And was her skin dull and really in need of a scrub?

"Thanks, Jax. I really appreciate your advice. But I'll admit, I'm more interested in the process of actually making the music." *Okay, if he figures out who I am, he figures it out. But I'm drunk already, and I don't know how else to pull him out of his shell.*

"For me, making music is kind of a collaboration." *Finally!*

"I always thought of it as pretty intensely personal, but I'm starting to understand the collaboration thing." She winked at him. Well, she tried to wink, but both eyes closed, so really what she did was blink very hard at him.

"It's like that feeling, when you know you've just nailed it?"

She nodded and smiled. Nodded because she did understand that feeling. Smiled because it would be a perfect time for one of Eli's that's-what-she-said jokes.

"God, I live for that feeling." Jax leaned forward, clearly feeling as drunk as she was. "Do you know what I mean?" He put his hand on her thigh and squeezed. He used it to push himself back onto his own barstool before she had a chance to react.

There was some lingering warmth where his fingers had rested, but nothing that made her need to excuse herself for some alone time. Probably that was the alcohol numbing her nerve endings. She gave her arm an experimental pinch. It didn't hurt. Definitely the booze.

"I do know what you mean. It's like that song had always existed, and was just waiting for you to uncover it." He stared at her like he hadn't really seen her until just then.

"Damn, Lacypants. That's really profound. For me, it's like I just know—just *know* when it's right, right here." He gestured to himself.

"I literally cannot tell if you mean your gut or your crotch right now." Lacy giggled. "Crotch" was a funny word.

"It's a little bit of both. It's just—*here*." He gestured again, more expansively this time. The leather cuffs he always had on his wrists beneath the tattoos had slipped down a little, and Lacy's breath stopped cold.

Because beneath the rock-star cuff on his right wrist was the unmistakable scar of a suicide attempt.

He was still talking, but she wasn't listening. After a second, he followed her wide-eyed gaze. She had never seen Jax blush before, but he did as he straightened the strip of material. Her head was whirling, and it actually wasn't the copious amounts of liquor. Folx had battled depression. This was why he understood her so well. This, *this* was the source of the disconnect between his anonymous self and his in-person personality. Suddenly all the pieces were clicking into place, showing her the picture of a much more complicated man than she'd even guessed.

"Jax—" she started.

"Lace—" he said at the same time.

"Jinx," they said simultaneously, and the giggles broke some of the tension of the moment. That and the drink refills Lacy couldn't remember either of them ordering. She took a fortifying sip. "You first."

"I don't really know what to say. I don't talk about it with most people, they wouldn't understand. The band sure never did, even though I tried to tell them . . ." He trailed off. It looked like he was having a hard time making eye contact, and she totally understood that. It had to be embarrassing and painful to relive.

"You don't have to talk about it. But I understand. Really. My fiancé—he was like you. But he didn't have music. You have *music*. Doesn't that change everything?"

She knew there were better ways to explain herself, but she couldn't Word after this much to drink.

"It does. God, you really *get* me." He pulled her into a hug that left her gasping for air, but also feeling profoundly grateful. She'd finally broken through. She finally understood what made FolxNotDead27 the man he was.

And more importantly, she understood her draw to him. Something—a higher power or the universe or whatever—had brought her to this man so she could fix him in the ways she couldn't fix Lance. Jax was her do-over.

Challenge accepted. She'd notice this time. She'd recognize his sad. She'd make sure it didn't leave him so empty that he felt the need to leave this world. So maybe he wasn't quite who she'd imagined he'd be in real life. She was still right for him. More than right. It was a twist of fate that could be described as a Plot Twist.

Man, that revelation felt good.

"Wanna dance?" she asked as he broke their embrace. The exhilaration of everything that had happened in this perfect, perfect night made it impossible to stay still. Also, assuming she stayed vertical, sweating out some of the alcohol would make for a better morning.

Instead of answering, Jax ambled over to the jukebox and started inputting a playlist. Perfect night, perfect man. Any echoes of Eli that resulted from that thought could just go take a hike.

As the opening notes of a Sleigh Bells song blared out of the speaker, she got up, and left all of her doubt sitting on the chair. There was dancing to do. And from the looks of Jax's moves, if she didn't get over there soon, someone else would. Drunk or not, that guy could *dance*. For the umpteenth time, the realization of what a fantastic lead singer he was came over her.

And the realization of how lucky *she* was came close

on its heels. Lacy had never considered herself much of a stereotypical girl, but the utter smugness she felt at knowing every girl (and a few of the guys) in the room was looking at the one she came with—well, she had no guilt.

She did have a fleeting thought that being the envy of the town—the world even, if the Blue Hills continued their rise to fame—shouldn't be her foremost reason for being with a guy. But it wasn't the foremost reason she was with Jax. She was with him because, in his words, she got him. Eventually he'd get her too. Probably.

They closed the bar down dancing with only a couple of more supplementary drinks. By the time they stumbled back out into the heat of the night, Lacy needed more than wanted Jax's arm.

But that wasn't it—what was it she wanted to ask him? Oh yeah.

"Where even are we?" she asked, looking around. Not that looking around meant much. Things were a little blurry, and she wasn't familiar with the city anyway.

"Oh, who knows. We'll figure it out." Jax had a lazy smile on his face that was at odds with the slight amount of panic Lacy was starting to feel.

"We will? Will we? I haven't the first clue where to go." Thank God she wasn't wearing heels. She had to look down at her feet to make sure she was still wearing shoes at all.

"Of course we will. I do this, like, every night." He strode confidently down the sidewalk and hit the button at the stoplight.

Lacy hurried to catch up with him. *Every night?* She imagined him messaging her on his phone for their dates on SoWriAn as he wandered the town. And what about the nights he'd missed their dates altogether? Shit, was he drinking this much solo? *He must be more troubled than I realized.* She resolved to pay a little more attention to what he was doing after the shows.

Ten blocks later, she was sobering up, but not lightening up. She wished she had a jacket as the chill cut through the leftover warmth from the liquor. Her feet were aching, even without heels, and all she wanted was a bottle of water and a place to sit.

She was also pretty sure Jax had no idea where they were, but he still looked happy, and she wasn't going to start stressing him out. A drop hit her head, and then another, and then the rain started coming in earnest. He threw his arms out and laughed.

Well, hell. Three-thirty in the morning or not, her Best Night Ever wasn't over, and damned if Jax was going to have all the fun.

She grabbed his hand and tossed her head back. They danced together on the street corner and caught raindrops on their tongues. It was the perfect ending to a perfect night. She looked at Jax, laughing, but it died on her lips as he started to lean in, close enough to catch that sexy, raw scent of his. It didn't grab her the way she thought it would. But she was probably just overanalyzing or judging too soon.

Because this was Folx—the man she'd been dying to kiss for so long. She closed her eyes, anticipating the moment when her lips would meet his for the first time.

Instead, the play of blue and red lights on her closed lids caused her to open her eyes, finding Jax staring at the cop car that had pulled up to the curb.

The officer was clearly not amused, or impressed with the cute romantic moment they were having. "You wouldn't be Jax and Lacy, would you?"

Her stomach dropped. Being picked up by the police

was never a good sign. "Oh, no." Was someone hurt? Was
it Andy?

"You're not?" The cop narrowed his eyes.

"No, I mean, yes. We are Jax and Lacy. I meant, oh, no
what's happened?"

"Someone named Sammy is pretty pissed at you right
now. Get in and I'll take you to your hotel."

Lacy and Jax exchanged looks that were equally cha-
grined and terrified. Though relieved to know nothing
bad had happened to anyone she cared about, Lacy knew
Sammy had to be super worried to have called the cops.
She pulled her phone out of her pants pocket—dead.

Jax held up his own blacked-out device as well. "Oops."

She leaned her head onto his shoulder for the rest of the
ride, but the moment of their near kiss had disappeared,
washed away with the rain, if the moment had even really
existed in the first place.

Eli stopped his pacing of the hotel lobby as soon as he saw
the police car pull up. He waited until he saw both Jax and
Lacy get out of the backseat before announcing, "They're
here."

Sammy jerked up from where she'd been half asleep on
an armchair. Eli stood back out of the way as Sammy met
the truants, one hand balled in a fist at her hip like a concerned mother.

Well, not quite a mother—Sammy's expression could
never be called loving even though her heart might actually be made of gold.

Jax, apparently, didn't see any of the gold in Sammy. He
stumbled toward her, obviously pissed as well as inebriated.
"Do we suddenly have a curfew I don't know about?"

Sammy met his irritation without batting an eye. "If we
have a problem with irresponsible band members, then

maybe we'll have to establish one. You didn't answer your phones."

Jax took an aggressive step toward their roadie. "So you called the cops? I had no idea that a dead battery was a crime."

Lacy stepped up behind Jax as if aligning herself with him. Or like she was with him in general. It made Eli's eye twitch.

Sammy shrugged. "Hey, I only did the dialing. The order didn't come from me. Though I agreed with it."

"Who then? Lou?" The look on Jax's face said he was already ripping apart their manager in his mind. Probably firing him as well.

Good thing for Lou it hadn't been him who'd woken Sammy from a dead slumber and persuaded her to call 911.

Sammy didn't answer Jax. Instead, she looked over her shoulder, making eye contact with Eli.

Jax followed her gaze, his eyes landing heavily on their destination. "Jesus, I should have guessed." If he hadn't been completely pissed before, he was now. "What the fuck, Eli?"

Eli glanced over at the desk clerk who was watching the entire scene with rapt attention. "How about we not talk about this in the lobby?"

Jax pointed an accusing finger at his friend. "How about you stay out of my fucking business?"

"Jax." Eli layered his voice with a warning he didn't usually use with his lead singer. It seemed to work. Jax's shoulders didn't relax, but his chest seemed to deflate the tiniest bit.

"I think you got this handled," Sammy said, already shuffling back toward her room. "I'll see y'all in the morning. Be up for breakfast."

Eli shifted his gaze to Lacy. She was still in the dress

she'd performed in, the thin white material wet from the rain and nearly transparent. It clung to her long legs and outlined her breasts. His jeans suddenly felt uncomfortably tight. He needed her out of there, out of his sight.

He moved his focus back to Jax. "Let's get Lacy to her room, and then we can talk."

"What? Am I some child that can't hear the grown-ups talk?" She crossed her arms over her chest, which did nothing to ease Eli's arousal. If anything, her new posture made her sexier. Especially as she jutted her chin out and said, "This involves me too. Whatever reason you felt like you needed to play protective Dad, you can tell it to my face."

Eli opened his mouth to speak. Then he hesitated. It wasn't exactly that he felt uncomfortable discussing his reasons with her, but he had a feeling Jax wouldn't be so pretty in his end of the argument. She might have some sort of a "connection" with Jax, but he'd bet she didn't know all of the ugly mess that had gone down last time.

Jax seemed to agree the conversation should be private. "It's got nothing to do with you, Lacypants. This is between me and fucktard here." The look he gave Eli burned straight through his skin and into his blood. He was prepared for a fight.

Fine. Just fine. Eli felt his own fight-or-flight instincts kick in. Usually he kowtowed. Not this time.

Lacy seemed unconvinced. Her eyes darted from Jax to Eli and back to Jax. "Am I missing something I should know about? Does this have anything to do with the Groupie Clause?"

Jax shook his head, a superficial smile flickering across his lips. "Nah. Nothing like that. It's band stuff. I'll walk you to your room." Jax took Lacy's hand and led her down the hall toward her room.

Eli waited half a beat before following. Partly to calm himself down and partly because he didn't want to watch

Jax and Lacy say good night. It wasn't his business, he told himself. Though he did feel somewhat gratified knowing that Jax wouldn't be staying in Lacy's room.

He could still meet up with her later.

Eli tried not to think about that possibility. He took another deep breath and ran his hands through his hair. Then he headed after the couple. He cringed internally at the idea of Jax and Lacy as a couple, but he wouldn't let himself call them anything else. Even in his head, he had to get used to the idea that they could be together. Had to remember it had nothing to do with him. He'd given his blessing. He couldn't take it back.

Fortunately Eli dragged his feet long enough to only catch Lacy's door shutting, leaving Jax in the hallway. The singer turned to face him. "My room."

Then Jax turned and walked three doors down the hall.

Eli trudged after, biting his words until he was alone with Jax. Then he was sure to speak first. "Where the hell were you? I called and called—"

Eli had been prepared for Jax to blow up. To yell like he usually did. Instead, he sat on the bed, leaned back on his elbows and cocked his head at Eli. "Why?"

"What do you mean 'why'? I called because I was trying to find you." The irritation in Eli's voice was thick, and he didn't care that Jax heard it.

"But why?" Again, Jax was nonchalant.

And it was pissing Eli off. "Because you left. You disappeared without a word to anyone. You can't do shit like that when you have a history. For all we—*I* knew you could be out trying to kill yourself like last time."

Admittedly, Eli may have only gone there because he wanted a rise out of Jax.

It worked.

Jax shot up from the bed, his face filled with rage. "First of all, that wasn't *last time*. It was months ago. I've been out every single night of this tour and this is the first time you've given an ounce of shit."

"Great phrasing."

Jax ignored him. "Second of all, I never fucking tried to kill myself. How many times do I have to explain that to you before you get it through your thick skull?"

Eli rolled his eyes. Over and over, he'd heard Jax's excuse for the slits he'd put in his arms. It didn't change how ridiculous it sounded. "Right, right, right. You were never suicidal. You were just a cutter. Doesn't really change my impression of your mental health status."

"Not a cutter, man. It's art! It's a statement!"

"A statement that you keep covered up. That sure speaks, doesn't it?"

"I keep it covered up because all of you are too dense to get it. I'm surrounded by ignorance." Jax waved his hands around, demonstrating the extent of ignorance that surrounded him.

"Yep. That's it." Eli couldn't contain the sarcasm in his voice. "Surrounded by ignorance."

Jax looked as though he might hit something. But when he spoke, his words were calmer. Measured. "Don't patronize me, Eli Frank. I see right through you."

Eli let out a sharp laugh. "Oh, you do. Tell me, what exactly do you see?" As if Jax saw anything. He was so self-absorbed, so lost in his own gut-crotch awareness that he never saw anything around him.

But his friend surprised him. "Like, for instance, I see that you calling the cops tonight had nothing to do with me. It was who I was with."

Eli's jaw twitched. "Bullshit."

"Not bullshit. You were worried about the chick." Jax seemed even more convinced of his theory with each word. "You were worried about the chick being with me."

The statement felt like a punch to the gut. Which was

weird. It wasn't true. It hadn't been the reason he'd been worried about Jax. Well, not the only reason.

He shook his head a little too defensively. "You don't know what you're talking about."

Jax hooked each of his thumbs in a belt loop on his jeans and rocked back on his heels. "I hope for your sake that that's true. Because I connected with Lacy tonight. She gets me in the way that none of you ever have. And I intend to spend more time with her. Whatcha gonna do about *that*? Call the goddamn cops?"

Eli shrugged, but there was no confidence in it. "I don't care. It's not my business who you spend your time with. And if she's fooled by your charm, well, that's too bad."

Too bad. How many times had he said that in reference to Lacy's infatuation with Jax? How many times had he said it about Lacy in general?

How many more times would he have to say it before he was as disinterested as the words were meant to make him appear?

"Yeah, too bad. Too bad you don't know how to stop lying to yourself."

"You know what? I don't have the energy for this. I came in here to explain why I called the police. I called because you left without a trace and none of us could get ahold of you. You were distant today. I was concerned. I'm sorry that I ruined your date with our opening act. I'm not sorry that I cared about your whereabouts. I'm not sorry that I cared enough to go there, because I fucking care about you!" Even to Eli's ears, it sounded like he was trying to convince himself more than Jax.

"Uh-huh." Jax pressed his lips together tight, clearly skeptical. "Well, you explained it. If you don't have anything else, you can go now."

"Don't *you* have anything else? An explanation? An apology?"

Jax shook his head. "Nope. Got nothing to explain that's any of your business. Got nothing that I'm sorry for."

"Jackass." Eli didn't even bother to mutter it under his breath. He threw one more sharp glare at Jax, then turned and left.

He stopped in the hall outside the door though. He leaned his back against the wall and let out a string of quiet curse words. When the hell had he and Jax grown so far apart? He knew they'd been strained for a while—since the cutting/suicide incident. Before that, even. But he'd always thought the gap between them could be closed again. Now . . . he wasn't so sure.

But it wasn't the relationship with his friend that had him riled up the most—it was the truth in his accusations. He hadn't cared where Jax was on other occasions. Tonight, though, when Eli had seen him leave with Lacy, when hours had passed without their return, when neither of them would answer their phone—Eli panicked.

And it wasn't because he thought that Lacy was in any danger with Jax.

It wasn't because he thought that they'd get in any trouble.

It was because the thought of her . . . alone . . . with him . . . did something to Eli's insides. Tore him up. Made it hard to catch his breath.

Why couldn't he just let this girl go?

He had an answer. It wasn't one he wanted to think about, but it sat in his belly like a boulder that refused to move.

He slid down the wall and sat on the floor. Now what the hell was he going to do?

Chapter Twenty

Lacy woke up to loud pounding on her door.

Dammit. She'd forgotten to put the Do Not Disturb sign up. It was probably housekeeping. Her head throbbing, she dragged herself out of bed and over to the door. Luckily she was still wearing last night's clothes so she didn't have to grab a robe.

She leaned her face against the cool metal frame. *Oh, that feels good.* "I'm still in here. Come back later."

"Lacy?"

Not housekeeping then. Though she didn't recognize the voice, she opened the door and peeked out. "Sammy? It didn't sound like you."

"I was trying to be quiet in case you had a hangover." The roadie's tone was soft and gentle, barely above a whisper—a complete contrast to her usual tough demeanor.

"That was nice." Lacy opened the door to let her guest in. She hadn't forgotten Sammy's role the evening before, however, and so her voice held remnants of irritation. "Then why did you knock so loud?"

Sammy stepped in. "I didn't."

Ah. So she *did* have a hangover. Well, that explained the throbbing in her head.

"Hold out your hand," Sammy whispered. She placed two pills in Lacy's hand then handed her a bottle of water. "For your head."

"Thank you, thank you." Lacy's gratitude was genuine. She threw back the pills with a long gulp. Then held the cold bottle to her face. "And really, you don't have to whisper."

"Ah, fine then." Although no longer whispering, Sammy still kept her voice hushed. "I'll grab your luggage for you later if you want, too."

Lacy ran a hand over her face. "That's right. We leave today. What time is it now?"

"Eight-thirty. You still have two hours."

"Thank the Lord." Lacy couldn't believe they'd been in Baltimore only three days. Had it already been two days since Eli had had her against that very wall?

Thinking about Eli, like that, caused a blush to creep up her face. She turned away and busied herself with gathering her personal items strewn all over the room so that Sammy wouldn't see her flushed. "I can get my own luggage. Though I appreciate the offer."

"No problem. It's my way of apologizing. For the cops. I'm sure that wasn't exactly a great way to end an evening."

Lacy waved it off. "It's fine. Really. I hadn't realized anyone would worry." Actually she was embarrassed about the whole thing. She'd rather never have to talk about it again.

But Sammy, it appeared, wasn't ready to let it go. "Of course we worry. But I also realize we may have overstepped our bounds."

There was no "may have," in Lacy's book. They *had* overstepped bounds. It wasn't anyone else's business where or how she spent her nights. It wasn't like she was a little girl out in a strange city. No one had worried about her the night she'd spent with Eli.

Her face heated again at that thought, but now it was more from irritation. "I'm not mad at you, Sammy. Really. Though I'm a little upset with Eli." Or a lot upset.

Or maybe that was just an excuse to have emotions toward him without feeling guilty.

Sammy nodded sympathetically. "I get it. I really do. But don't be too hard on him. He has his reasons for worrying about Jax."

Lacy stopped her gathering and poised herself to argue when she remembered the things she'd found out about Jax the night before. He'd attempted suicide, and her impression was that it had been fairly recent. That was a cause to worry about someone. "I think I understand," she conceded. "I mean, the reasons weren't about me, were they?"

Sammy scratched the back of her head. "Maybe. But if they were, they were also about Jax."

"I see." Of course Eli's reasons were primarily about Jax. She didn't know why she'd think they would be about her. Had they been about her, she didn't know if that would have made it worse or better.

"I hope none of it ruined any of your plans . . ." The way Sammy trailed off, it was evident she was fishing for information.

Lacy chuckled to herself. She had no idea Sammy was into tour gossip. "No. You didn't ruin any plans." Okay, she'd ruined a kiss, but Lacy wasn't as disappointed about that as she thought she would be.

"You got along with Jax then?"

Lacy smiled. "Yeah. I did. He seemed to need a friend. And, actually, I kind of did too. Then we made a connection. So."

Sammy considered, seeming surprised by Lacy's answer. "Hmm. Good to hear. Anyway. I promise not to call the cops again."

"I'm going to hold you to that." Before closing the door after Sammy, Lacy called out, "Thanks again for the Advil."

Alone and already feeling less like death warmed over, Lacy considered packing her bags. Except, there was a phrase wiggling around in her head that she should probably get down. She hummed as she looked for a pen and sat down at the desk to jot notes on the hotel stationary.

Hmm, that melody is good too. If only she hadn't left her guitar for Sammy to load in last night. Oh, well. She could compose without it.

The thought stopped her in her tracks.

She could compose . . .

But she hadn't composed anything in months. Not without sex to inspire it. And here she was with words lining up inside her mind, ready to be written down and manipulated and twisted into lyrics.

Halle-freaking-lujah, her block was over! She was writing a song.

Though she wanted to think about it more, analyze the whys and hows and causes of her inspiration, she first had to get it out, before she lost it. Having finally located a pen, she let the words flow freely.

You're standing ahead of me,
Standing just out of reach
And any step that I take gets me nowhere
Never moving ahead, like in one of those dreams
I'm trying to keep you mine
Running around this wheel
And though you're never out of my sight
I'm so afraid that you're already gone

So if it's going to happen anyway
I'm going to make it happen
in my way

I'm going to lose you
Lose you inside of me
I'm going to break you
Remake you as part of me

You're talking around the truth,
Still I hear what you really mean
I want to say the words you need
But I'm not sure what they are and they come out
*   wrong*
I'm trying to keep you here
Circling around our fate
And though you're never out of my heart
I'm so afraid that you're already gone

So if it's going to happen anyway
I'm going to make it happen
in my way

I'm going to lose you
Lose you inside of me
I'm going to break you
Remake you as part of me

I'm going to lose . . .
I'm going to break . . .
You're always going to be
Somewhere inside of me

When she'd finished with the words, she pulled out her
iPad and plucked out the melody on her keyboard app,

matching it with the correct chords so she could play it later on Lucky. By the time she was done, she had an entire song. It was complete and whole and incredible.

She'd done it. Finally.

She stood up and twirled around. She might have even let out a little *squee*.

Again she wondered what had been the change that had finally let her muse break through.

Then she realized—it was Jax. Not sex, *Jax*. The words were totally about him. He'd let her see a glimpse of his pain—pain that had led to a suicide attempt—and now that she knew about it, she could help make sure he stayed safe. Her song was about that. Probably.

No, for sure. That's exactly what it was about.

She twirled one more time, her face beaming. Then her eyes landed on the nightstand clock. It was ten-fifteen. Shit! She had to get moving or she'd be late for departure.

She changed quickly, then ran to the bathroom to scoop up her toiletries and threw them and her clothes in her case. While she gathered her things, she mentally made plans to sit with Jax on the bus. They hadn't talked much about music the night before. She could play him some of her favorite songs on her iPad. Or listen to his favorites. Maybe she'd even show him the song she'd written. Later. When she had Lucky, maybe.

As she pulled her bag down the hall, an unexplainable melancholy overcame her. Maybe she felt bad about leaving Baltimore behind. So much had happened there. She'd found her inspiration, she'd connected with Folx, she'd gotten her first encore.

And there had been Eli. She didn't want to forget him on her list.

Though she had a feeling forgetting Eli would never be a possibility.

*   *   *

Eli leaned back in his seat and did his best to keep his focus forward as the bus pulled onto I-95 on the way to DC. He felt a mixture of emotions, as he always did when he left his hometown. Though he loved Baltimore, the driving away always made him feel like he was moving on and moving up. It was a sign of progress, even if it meant leaving behind sights and sounds and smells that were as much a part of him as his music.

This time, the departure had an added component of separation. Baltimore was the city of Lacy. It was the place where he'd given in to his inexplicably overwhelming attraction to her. Instead of fixating on what his tryst with Lacy meant to his relationship with LoveCoda, he decided to accept it as an incredible experience that now he'd put behind him. He'd move on and up from Lacy just like he'd left Baltimore so many times now. It was the only way to look at it and not be overwhelmed with guilt. The only way to not taint the whole thing.

The only way to not find himself standing in front of her door asking for more.

This was the truest test of his character that he had ever faced. He couldn't say for sure what he felt for LoveCoda—he knew he had to spend some real time with her first. But he respected her enough to give her that chance. Because he might not be able to name what he had there, but it was important and meaningful. Even when he *could* name the feelings he had for Lacy. Like admiration, companionship, adoration.

And yes, love.

He loved Lacy Dawson. It was the truth that had crushed through him as he'd stood in Jax's hall the night before. He was in love with Lacy.

But he couldn't be. For so many reasons. Number one being that Lacy was obviously not in love with him. And then there was LoveCoda—a woman he probably *could* love. *Should* love, if he hadn't put so many barriers up on-line.

And there was Jax.

Too many obstacles stood between him and anything more with Lacy.

So he'd love her in Baltimore. And that's all.

Against his better judgment, Eli threw a glance toward the back of the bus where Lacy sat with Jax. She'd left her things at her usual seat and joined him about thirty seconds after they'd pulled away from their hotel, as though she couldn't wait to talk with him. Even though they'd been connected at the hip all through breakfast. Now, they were listening to something on her iPad, her earbuds split so one was in his ear and one in hers. How high school.

How Eli wished he were in Jax's place.

No, he didn't. That was his Baltimore self talking. Now he was past that. Moving on.

Kind of moving on. He turned around from looking at the two, and jumped a mile as he came nearly nose to nose with Sammy.

"Did I scare you?" She looked positively gleeful at the thought.

"You know you did," he muttered. He really was not in the mood to banter.

"I'm sorry about last night, kid." Her expression grew serious. "I know how that feels."

"Know how *what* feels? Worried sick about your friend, wondering if he's in a hospital or a gutter somewhere?" The bitterness in his voice surprised even him.

"That, too. Come on, I'm a roadie. I've pulled more of my friends out of gutters than not. No, I mean the girl." She gave a little eyebrow waggle.

The girl. That ache in his chest deepened at the mention of her. But of course, that wasn't what Sammy was referring to. "She was irresponsible. I thought she was better than that. I guess I didn't know her as well as I thought I did." That hurt too. Really hurt.

"I think you do. I talked to her this morning. She saw him hurting, wanted to keep him company. Something no one else on this bus has been doing." Sammy's tone made it clear she more than included him in that statement. "Anyway. She's a good kid, that one."

Eli didn't like the sincerity he saw in her eyes. "Are you trying to make me feel guilty for what I did? I get to be upset." Jax had called him out on his true motives for calling the cops, but it didn't mean he had to admit to them. Especially not to Sammy.

"You do get to be upset, but not because the two of them went out running around after the show. You get to be upset because you're into her, and she's looking quite struck by him." She turned and gave Lacy and Jax the once-over herself. "Sure not how I thought this was going to end up." With that, she heaved herself up and headed back to her usual seat.

"Yeah. Me either," Eli whispered to himself.

He turned back to glance out at the window. The trees lining the highway sailed by in a repeating pattern of sameness. There was a rhythm in it, and probably a metaphor for his life. Something about the comfort in consistency. Something about how he couldn't really be moving on if he was still trapped in the same bus, with the same view.

Something that turned into a lyric began weaving through his consciousness.

There's a path I've been taking
Leading me where I'm meant to go
But I keep coming back to
You
I'm only on loan here

I can't stay when I'm meant to fly
But I keep coming back to
You
To you

I won't let this hold me
And yet I can't let you go
There's words shared between us
And feelings I'll never show
But just so you know
Can't love you or leave you
So I'll love you and leave you
In Baltimore

Lacy's laugh pulled him from his composition. He refused to look back at her. Also, he didn't want to write this song anymore. He would eventually, because that's how songs worked.

But right now he couldn't bear to think about Lacy. Couldn't *let* himself.

He wanted to think about LoveCoda instead. She was his anchor. If only she were in his life for more than just an hour every night. He needed her as much during the daylight—more even. Especially after having missed their date the evening before because he'd been stuck with that stupid client of Lou's.

An idea struck him—one that should have seemed so obvious but had never occurred to him. Why did he have to wait until their date time to send her a message? He could send her one now just as easily. Though he'd always sent to her through the website, he knew that SoWriAn had a phone app. Maybe she had it. So maybe she wouldn't be available. She could respond later. At least it would make him feel more connected to her.

And he needed that right now. So needed that. Sammy

was wrong, this wasn't about Lacy and Jax. Scratch that. It *was* about Lacy and Jax. But it didn't need to be. Not outside of Baltimore. Not in the rest of the world where he spent most of his time. And that world he could fill with any girl. With LoveCoda. A girl who just happened to look like Lacy in his imagination.

He pulled out his phone and after a few minutes found the app and downloaded it. Another few minutes and he was logged into the site. Jesus, he was an idiot for never considering this before. Now to think of a message.

He typed and erased several before settling on *Thinking of you. As always.*

Feeling better already, he pushed send and smiled to himself.

Not even half a second later, he heard a ping coming from the seat where Lacy usually sat. He glanced over and saw her phone sitting there. Well, that was awfully coincidental— her phone pinging just as he'd sent his message.

It *was* a coincidence . . . right?

Of course it was. But just to totally drive the impossible idea out of his mind, he entered another message to LoveCoda. *I'd love to hear from you anytime.*

Again, Lacy's phone pinged.

Eli nearly dropped his own cell, catching it before it clamored to the floor. His pulse quickened, somewhat from the near drop, but mostly from the realization that was washing over him like a bucket of ice water.

No. Freaking. Way. I'm imagining this.

He looked back at Lacy's phone. Then back at the girl-who-just-might-but-couldn't-possibly-be-the-girl-of-his-dreams. She had her eyes closed now, her head swaying to the music only she—and Jax—heard. His stomach tightened. If Lacy really was LoveCoda, then what was the whole Jax thing about?

Nope, nope. He was jumping too far ahead. One step

at a time. It was ridiculous that the two pings could have been coincidental, but it was just as ridiculous that Lacy could be LoveCoda. He had to be sure.

He raked his teeth across this lower lip as he tried to come up with one more message to send Love. Finally he had one. *xxx*

Another ping from Lacy's phone.

Eli shot up from his seat. He had no plans for going anywhere—he hadn't even intended to stand. Just, his energy, his excitement, his pure and utter shock drove him up.

Lou peeked at him from underneath half-closed eyelids. "Problem, kid?"

"Uh, no. I just really wanted an apple." Eli headed straight to the cooler, kicking himself. Apple? Seriously? He already knew Lou didn't generally buy apples.

Eli was already at the cooler, so he didn't need the confirmation, but Lou gave it anyway. "I don't think I got any apples. Didn't know anyone wanted them. I can add them for next time, though."

"No problem," Eli said. "I'll take a string cheese." *And a peek at the phone on Lacy's seat.* He grabbed a plastic-encased piece of mozzarella and slowly ripped it open while simultaneously leaning forward to check out Lacy's cell.

Unfortunately, her cell was facedown. *Dammit.*

He snuck one more glance back at Lacy who had her eyes open now was talking with Jax who, appeared to be only half listening while he played around on his phone, and another at Lou, who had gone back to his dozing. Quick—he'd do it quick and no one would see. Eli bent down and snatched Lacy's phone. He turned it over and swiped his hand across the screen, praying it wasn't locked. It wasn't.

And there they were—three notifications from her SoWriAn app.

All from FolxNotDead27.

Holy hell.

Lacy was LoveCoda.

LoveCoda was Lacy.

The revelation sent sparks of fire to every nerve ending in Eli's body. There were things to process about this, definitely, but his initial reaction was ecstatic elation.

"Is that my phone?"

Funny thing about ecstatic elation—it made it easy to block out the surrounding environment. Eli hadn't heard Lacy coming back to her seat until she was standing there looking at him holding her cell with a look of wary confusion.

"Yeah, it is." *Tell her! You have to tell her!*

But he couldn't tell her. Not here. Not like this. "I think you got a message. I was just going to take it back to you."

"Oh." Her expression eased as she took the device from Eli's outstretched hand. "Thanks." She slid her finger across the screen then read her messages while she stood there. Her brow furrowed for a moment. She glanced back to Jax—Eli followed her gaze to find his bandmate still buried in his phone. Then he followed her gaze back to her phone. She read the screen again, and this time she smiled. Brightly.

She sat down in her seat and began typing something into her cell. Which was Eli's cue to return to his spot. As soon as he sat, his phone, which was on vibrate, buzzed. It was a reply from LoveCoda—from Lacy. *Thinking of you too.*

His heart somersaulted in his chest, something that Eli had always believed happened only to girls. His eyes shot once again to Lacy. Who was staring intently at Jax. Who was still buried in his phone with something or other.

What the ever-living hell?

Seriously, Eli was overwhelmed. And confused. And still ecstatic. He didn't even know where to begin with his jumble of thoughts. Because, holy shit, Lacy was Love-Coda.

Lacy is LoveCoda.

In his wildest fantasies, his online soul mate was also the cute singer who'd brightened the last few weeks of his life, but never in a million years did he actually believe there was any reality in it. This was like winning the lottery. Or getting a major recording deal.

No, this was even better than that. This was finding that the girl that he very nearly loved online was the woman that he totally loved in real life.

Yes, loved.

He could say it now that there wasn't the guilt involved.

Hey! No more guilt! And no more isolating his memories of Lacy to just Baltimore. He could love her everywhere now.

But . . . but . . . God, there were other parts of this that were more confusing. He wiped his hand over his face. For one, Lacy had jumped Eli while she had Folx waiting on the side. Did that bother him?

No, that was fine. Mostly it was fine because he'd been the one benefitting. He wasn't sure that he'd feel the same if she'd jumped someone else. And he'd done the same. They had too much of a natural connection. One they couldn't ignore. Though they'd both tried. He because he wanted to be faithful to LoveCoda, and her because she'd wanted . . .

Well, now here was the weird part. She said she'd wanted Jax. And she'd started spending all her time with him. Yet, online she'd been even more committed than ever. Was she two-timing? Or—

Another realization burst through. All of Lacy's stories belonged to Love and vice versa. Love had lost her fiancé. Lacy was blocked on her songwriting. Love had said she'd written something finally. And that she thought orgasms might help her writing. Jesus, that was after he'd had sex with Lacy. Had he inspired her?

He paused to let himself feel proud about that idea.

Then he was back to sorting out the facts. Such as, why hadn't Lacy recognized any Blue Hills songs? She'd work-shopped more than one of his lyrics. She knew the words inside and out. She'd never heard the melodies, though. Could she possibly have not listened during any of their performances? That didn't seem like her.

And how the hell did her fling with Jax fit into this whole thing?

Unless . . . unless she *did* recognize the Blue Hills songs. And, what if, like everyone else, she assumed they'd been written by Jax? Was that jumping to con-clusions?

He thought about how she'd said she had a connection with Jax that she couldn't explain. Yet, come to think of it, she hadn't really spent time with him at that point. Then he thought about how she looked at her messages just min-utes ago—Folx's messages—then how she'd glanced back toward Jax.

He wasn't jumping to conclusions. He was standing smack dab in the middle of the most likely possibility. Lacy thought Jax was Folx.

Oh, no, God.

He wanted to stand up again. Needed to pace. Needed to move over to Lacy's seat and say, *Here I am; it's me*. Wanted to take her in his arms and kiss her finally without the guilt and with all the emotion he'd been saving for LoveCoda. He wanted to make her his once and for all.

But all the buts . . .

But the bus wasn't a great place for a reveal. But they needed privacy. But what if she wasn't happy that he was Folx?

And what about Jax? Despite all his raging irritations, Jax was the only brother he had. The one he never had. The kind you didn't leave, regardless of whether they'd saved you or you'd saved them, because in the end it all tangled into a platonic love that wouldn't fade anyway.

Besides, the bus was pulling into their venue in DC. Which was good. Load in would settle some of his restless energy. And after that . . .

After that, he'd find Lacy and he'd tell her . . . everything.

Chapter Twenty-One

"I got the amps plugged in and the wireless mike is on the charger. Anything else?" Eli tapped his foot impatiently while he waited for Sammy's response. Load in had never taken so long. Every time he thought he was about finished, the roadie had another chore for him. Like she was looking for stuff for him to do. He knew it wasn't really the case, but it sure felt like it.

And where the hell was everybody else?

Or, more specifically, where were Lacy and Jax? Jax always bagged off early at load in. He wasn't fond of physical work. But Lacy usually stayed the course. He figured she was probably in the bathroom or something, but then he noticed her guitar was missing from its stand. So she was tuning it. Or running through a song or something somewhere.

Whatever she was doing, he wanted to be there.

Sammy finished surveying his work. "This looks good. I think Wes might need some help with the drums. Check with him."

God, he couldn't take this anymore. "Sure. I'll do that." He started toward the drummer's set, but kept his eye on Sammy. As soon as her back was turned, he darted off the stage—which was really just an unoccupied corner of The Night Owl—and slipped down the hallway to the back rooms. He found the restrooms, a supply closet, and the manager's office with no sign of Lacy. Opening another closed door, he found stairs to the roof. He began to shut it when he heard her.

Her voice floated down the stairwell like an angel. She was singing. Something beautiful. Something new— new to him anyway. He took the stairs two at a time and then paused to look out through the half-open door at the top. She was sitting on a rise just ahead of him, guitar in her lap. *Lucky*. LoveCoda always called her guitar Lucky. How surreal to realize the strums he heard every night came from that instrument he'd come to admire virtually.

How surreal that the woman he'd become so close to online was the woman he so adored.

He stayed at the door, listening to her song. Taking it in. Not wanting to interrupt. He savored each note that spun out of her mouth—was it a new song? She hadn't played it on tour, and it was too good to have not been included in her set. Which meant she'd written something new. She'd broken through her block and this time finished a whole piece. He didn't think he could be more filled before that moment, but he was, pride layering onto the incredible wealth of emotions bursting through him.

The chorus came around again, and he moved with the melody, burned with the words.

I'm going to lose you
Lose you inside of me
I'm going to break you
Remake you as part of me

It was incredible how it spoke exactly to the way he felt about her. He'd been so struck by this woman—so hit over the head with love. There were so many pieces of her he'd already accepted as part of himself. Things LoveCoda said, the way she encouraged him and bolstered him, the connection he saw in Lacy's eyes, the way she clung to him when he buried himself inside of her. Both sides of the woman that he knew were completely inside of him. The song was perfect.

She was perfect.

When she finished, he let the last notes settle around him. Then he began to push the door open.

He was stopped by the sound of clapping.

Jax moved into his line of vision. "That was incredible, Lacypants. You were right—your music *is* good."

Eli's stomach dropped. *So she shared her song with him. It doesn't mean anything. She thinks he's you.*

Lacy met Jax's applause with genuine astonishment. "Really? You really liked it?"

"Liked it? I loved it. I have a couple suggestions, of course. Like, you could cut the leading bridges. They're kind of out of place. And then, you could layer the chorus with a choir."

Screw Jax with a bagpipe; he was so ridiculously full of himself. The bridges weren't out of place—they were a colorful contrast to the pattern of the verses. And the chorus was gorgeous in its starkness.

Eli would tell that to her as soon as he got a chance. Wouldn't let her change a single thing.

Thankfully Lacy seemed reluctant to accept the notes. "Yeah, yeah. Some good ideas. I'll keep them in mind." But then she said, "I'm so glad you liked it though. Because . . . because it's for you."

Now it was Eli's heart that dropped. Lacy had written a song . . . for Jax?

"For me?" Jax's surprise echoed Eli's.

But it was probably really for Folx. She wrote it for Folx whom she thought was Jax.

Except then Lacy lowered her gaze to her shoes, and said, "Yeah. I wrote it this morning. It's about you and me. It's about last night."

Eli's heart dropped further, if it were even possible. Last night—what had happened between them, exactly?

"I'm so glad last night meant as much to you as it did to me."

Was there more than their night out on the town? After Eli had left the hallway, had Jax gone to her room?

"Oh, it did."

They could have hooked up earlier even. Eli knew as well as anyone how unnecessary a bed was. How unnecessary night was.

"And that you inspired me . . . well, this is embarrassing, but I've been having trouble writing lately. But you've helped me break through that. In ways you can't even imagine."

That hurt Eli the worst. Because it didn't even matter if Jax and Lacy had done the deed. He obviously meant something to her—meant something big. He'd done for her what Eli hadn't been able to do. He'd inspired her. He'd helped her break free.

"I'm flattered. Thank you for letting me be your muse."

Jax's cockiness irked Eli to no end. But the emotional reaction it stirred in him was nothing compared to the one that followed when Jax took a step closer to the songbird, leaned down, and kissed her.

Eli immediately pulled the door back to its near closed position, unable to watch further, and leaned against the stairwell. He hadn't watched long enough to figure out what kind of kiss it was—a first kiss, a muse's kiss. A lover's kiss. He couldn't bear to see her lips pressed against another's. How had he ever thought he could walk away from her? For brief seconds he fought the impulse to walk out, to interrupt the embrace, but that would only stop the moment. It wouldn't stop the relationship.

There was one thing that *would* possibly stop the relationship—if he told Lacy that Jax wasn't Folxnotdead27. And Eli wanted to tell her. Wanted to tell her more than anything, especially now.

But he knew deep in his gut that he wouldn't. Even as he continued to debate it in his mind, his heart rate had already slowed to long mournful beats. She may have fallen for Jax believing he was the man she connected with online, but it was the man she'd spent last night with that had inspired her song. *That* was the man she needed. The man who made things happen. Not the one cowering in the sidelines. Not the one hiding in a stairwell.

Eli's steps were heavy as he descended back to the bar. He'd been on a mission when he went in search for Lacy only a quarter of an hour before. How quickly his plans had changed. He still had things he had to say to her, but now they were very different things. He had words to say to LoveCoda as well. Both could wait a few hours though. Long enough for him to find his voice. Long enough for him to figure out the words to let them both go.

Lacy was in her blanket fort when her phone dinged. She ignored it. The blanket fort was a sacred place of creativity. She retreated further inside the warm, dark cave of hotel comforters.

A few moments later it dinged again. Unacceptable. She extended an arm and groped for the offensive device. A flick of her finger turned the ringer off.

She pulled Lucky back onto her lap and resumed strumming. She pushed the pedal to start it looping with her left hand, and moved back to start some fingerpicking. Her eyes closed, and she sang a few bars. *No, it should go up at the end*. That sounded better.

It was absolutely amazing, how the words were flowing today. Not like a broken dam, just like a fast stream, clear enough to let her dip in and pull out just the right lyrics.

The bus ride to the hotel had been pretty solid too. Jax let her listen to a new singer-songwriter he'd discovered, and it had given her some cool ideas about how to arrange some of the lyrics she had dancing around in her head.

And best of all? Even though she was certain Jax had yet to make the connection between her and her alter ego, he'd sent her a message in the middle of the day. That was *not* the way they usually did it. Clearly, some of the darkness that had kept him wandering the streets instead of confiding in her online was dissipating. And it was her, Lacy Dawson, who had done it. Between the drinks, the dancing, and the unconditional understanding she'd offered him, she'd broken through. Things were going so well between them, she was tempted to reveal her true identity to him early.

Though that was equal reason *not* to tell him she was LoveCoda. She wouldn't want to ruin their budding relationship with unnecessary details. She'd wait until Christmas Eve as planned.

In the meantime, the overwhelming sexual feelings she had for Eli would die naturally. She hoped.

Anyway, it didn't really seem like Jax was lacking for orgasms. If he was occasionally guilty of dipping in the pool that was the Blue Hills groupies, he also certainly spent enough time alone and with his mirror. Lacy was pretty certain he spent more time satisfying himself than she did.

Then she'd sung him the song, the song she'd written after their connection. And she could see in his eyes that the connection was really mutual. She'd touched him in the same way he'd touched her. And remarkably, it was a pants-on type of touch, even though he'd ended it with a kiss. Who knew you could achieve that level of intimacy without fooling around?

She swapped the last two verses, and sang through the new song again. *Nailed it!* This time, it was a knock at the door that interrupted her.

"No!" she yelled at it. The knock came again. Dammit, probably Sammy needed to change call time or sometime. These tiny interruptions could completely derail an entire afternoon's worth of work, and nonwriters just didn't get that. She flung open the door in a huff, only to see Eli's shy smile instead of Sammy's goofy one.

"Oh. Hi. Sorry, I thought you were Sammy." She stared at him for a second. "Come in, I guess." Hopefully he got the picture that she was only offering out of politeness, and not because she really wanted to deal with him right then.

"Thanks. I, uh. I owe you an apology, Lacy. I had no right to treat you badly last night. You were helping a friend. Helping *my* friend. And I wasn't a very good friend to either of you about it. Can we still—do you hate me?" He looked so earnest, she sort of wanted to pinch his scruffy cheeks.

"Of course I don't hate you. But thank you. I was pretty pissed you were mad when I was just trying to break him out a little." She stepped away from the door so he could actually take her up on the offer to enter.

"Um, well, I guess that's all I had to say. The apology. But to prove it, I kind of felt like maybe you'd like to share some wine?" He looked positively terrified, which was kind of adorable. But then the surroundings caught his eye.

"Is that a *blanket fort*?" He looked equally incredulous and impressed.

"It is. Wanna check it out?"

"Obviously." He got down on the floor and crawled in, affording her a very nice rear view in those jeans. *Oh Em Eff Gee. STOP. Dying naturally. Let those sexy feelings die.* "Oh, hey, you've got your stuff set up in here!" he called. She dove in after him.

"I mean, everyone loves a good blanket fort, but I actually did this *so* I could set up in here. The acoustics are much better when you're letting the mattress and comforters absorb sound, rather than letting it bounce off these shitty hotel walls."

Eli was staring at her in a way she knew meant he was thinking about kissing her. Well. It was probably going to revolutionize the way he wrote songs on tour, so she probably deserved a kiss.

For Christ's sake, Lacy. You are terrible at ignoring this attraction. Like the worst. And she'd been kissing Jax—her true love—only that afternoon. Geez, what kind of a girl was she?

She should thank Eli for the wine and send him on his way. "Um, did you want to hear that song you had helped me on? I finished it."

So inviting him to stay and listen to her song was another way to deal with things.

He grinned, and leaned his elbow into her side gently. "I've already heard it. It got you an encore last night. I should have told you then how proud I was of you."

"You noticed?" she asked.

"Yeah, I always watch your set. I went and told the guys so they could come see too. We're all so happy you're on this tour, Songbird. It seems like the audience is pretty happy too." Lacy's spirits were dampened for a second at the realization that Jax hadn't been watching her to know. He'd kind of led her to believe that. Well, no, now that she thought about it. He had never said he was watching.

And if he *was* watching her every night, LoveCoda

would have to be a little concerned, wouldn't she? This was so freaking confusing.

"I really couldn't be happier to be touring with you guys, either," she said, and meant it.

"Hey, I have to admit, I had other intentions besides the wine. I know it's not right, but . . ." The fort was dark, but not too dark for her to see the flash in Eli's eyes as he leaned in. He also seemed strangely excited. He must be really sorry, and expecting a big apology make-out. His lips gently touched hers.

No, no no. Nope, n-okay. Just one kiss. Okay, just a few kisses. She wanted to hate herself for being so powerless to resist him, but the man kissed like no one she'd ever met. She could not be held responsible.

She expected his hands to start roving right away, because that was kind of their thing, that the kisses just led to *stuff.* But instead they just deepened, and grew. His tongue was gentle, not probing. He pulled her closer. *What is this? I feel like a teenager, making out under the covers.* It was kind of cute, and kind of hot. And most definitely the last time.

Once—*oh God, he just bit my lip*—this was done, she was going to have an actual breakup talk with him. She did a shit job of it last time, but this time she had the words. She had the words! Words were a thing. That she could do now. Finally.

But in the meantime, kissing was a thing she could also do, and his kisses were soft and meaningful. His tongue glanced around hers, and then moved deeper, but pulled back to trace her lips.

It struck her that the tone of this kiss was melancholy and somber. Like a last kiss. Was Eli telling her good-bye? Because if he was, well, that was good because of the whole *last-time* thing she'd just committed herself to. Again.

But also, the idea of a last kiss with Eli—a last kiss for real—made her sad.

So she changed the subject. "Okay, okay, okay. I have to ask your opinion on this one part of my new song. Scoot. You're too distracting this close."

He pulled back, reluctantly it seemed. She took a deep breath. Poor Lucky had gotten wedged half outside the fort, just next to—

"Is that a sippy cup?" Too late, Eli had spotted it.

"I don't want to take any risks around my equipment," Lacy said stiffly, knowing full well that her dignity had just abandoned her. With Lucky on her lap, she cleared her throat and started the loop and sang for Eli. Was it horrible that she was singing Jax's song to Eli? Not the time to think about it—it was time to do the chorus. She let the notes fade.

"Do you see what I mean? I'm just not sure I have the chord progressions right on the transitions." Eli had his eyes closed and was doing that cute little thing where he was humming to himself. He held out his arms for the guitar, and she passed it over. He started to experiment a little with music, and already she could tell that his ideas were much better than the whack suggestions Jax had given. Maybe he was the type who could only have vision on his own songs, though he wasn't like that online.

She flopped onto her tummy and automatically reached for Lance's pillow. *What was that?*

Something had fallen from the pillowcase, a little square of paper. She slowly unfolded it, her body shaking as she revealed familiar scribbly handwriting. Lance's handwriting. Words and lines had been scratched out and rewritten, and there were a couple goofy little doodles in the margins of bells and doves. The blood rushed through her ears as the sounds of her song drifted into dull background.

She was holding lost words from Lance. Her throat

grew dry. Her heart quaked in her chest. She couldn't read them.

But then again, she couldn't *not* read them. Her eyes were already floating across the lines, slowly, breathing each sentence into her body.

> *I promise you, Lacy, my love.*
> *I promise to be in the front row at all your shows.*
> *I promise to pour your wine in the evening, and*
>   *your coffee in the morning.*
> *I promise to let you win at Scrabble, but never at*
>   *cards.*
> *I promise to put you before me, every day, for the*
>   *rest of my life.*

Lacy hadn't registered the guitar stopping, or her own tears replacing the sound, but suddenly Eli was holding her hand.

"It's—he was writing his vows. Oh God, Eli. He must have hidden them in the pillow, and I never knew, and I'm sorry. Geez, I'm sorry. All I do is cry on you." Because she'd moved into him unconsciously, her damp cheek pressed against his chest. He stroked her hair, and shushed her.

For the rest of my life . . . he had done that. He had fulfilled all of his vows, for the rest of his life. He'd put her first, never telling her about the pain devouring him, until the last day of his life. He'd faked it.

She let the sobs rack her for a few moments, remembering how he'd always greeted her in the morning with a fresh mug of coffee. And Scrabble. . . . He'd always been atrocious at the game. He'd pretend to be holding back, even though they both knew she was the wordsmith of the two. He *owned* Texas hold 'em, though; she never stood a chance. "Losing at Cards" would be a good song title, by the way. Even Lance would think so. He always told her when she found a good one.

Dammit, how could she be thinking about song titles at a time like this?

Then . . .

Song title.

Songs.

Lance.

Suddenly, the realization came crashing down like a ton of bricks, shocking her right out of her cries. The paper fell from her grasp, unheeded.

That song hadn't really been for Jax. It was Lance that she lost inside herself. Lance that she remade as part of her. And her other song—the pieces of her—those were Lance too. The orgasms had never had anything to do with the songwriting. Or Eli. Or Folx or Jax. It was Lance, all along. It was talking about him, it was opening up to someone else. She'd known she was fine without him, but still, she'd never let herself truly grieve.

The songs were her grief.

And the words that came out, they were the ones she'd been hoping to write all along—they were about her first love.

"Are you all right?" Eli asked, and she remembered he couldn't hear her thoughts and had no idea what sort of epiphany she'd just had. She pulled him down with her to embrace on the nest of pillows.

"I'm going to be all right. I just realized that. I think I was faking it before."

He brushed her hair away from her face. "Everybody's faking it, remember?"

She chuckled softly. "I do." Then she grew serious again. "Will you just hold me?" Though she meant more than hold and her tone said that. "I really need to feel some love right now. I know we can't keep doing this. But just for now. Just be with me?"

"Just for now," he repeated, and she knew that he knew it was over too. Tonight, though, she needed someone.

No, not someone—she needed Eli. She was scared to be alone, with the weight of her newfound grief, but she was just as scared about being without Eli. About letting him go too, and she had to in the morning because even without Jax in the picture, Eli had his own somebody else, and she refused to stand in the way of his happiness. He deserved that.

But tonight she deserved Eli. She deserved some comfort while she finally let go of Lance. And wasn't one love lost enough for one day?

Lacy traced Eli's cheeks and met his eyes. "Just love me," she said, knowing she'd regret it later.

"I do," he said, and she knew he didn't mean it, even though it sounded sincere, but it counted. It was what she needed.

She tipped her face back up to his, and reinitiated the kiss from before. If anything, it was sweeter this time, if also a bit salty from her tears. Her hand strayed up to hold his face, her fingers carding through his hair. He tilted his head to rain kisses on her neck, and she pressed into him, relishing the feel of his strength against her softness. She was melting.

His hand ran up and down her side, until it gently pushed her down so he could move on top of her. He propped himself on his elbows, and kissed her as she slid her hands up his shirt and over the ridges of his abs. He scrambled to his knees and pulled it off as she struggled to remove her own tank. Eli stopped her, gently pulling it over her head for her. Her breasts ached for his attention, and received it as he licked and sucked on each one in turn.

He continued kissing further south, down her stomach, until he got to her skirt. He slid it down her hips, kissing each exposed inch until he got to the spot she wanted him at most. He blew gently, the cool air delicious on her warmth, before turning his head to the side and kissing the soft inside of her thigh. She moaned, wanting more, needing it.

His tongue slowly, softly traced up and then down her most sensitive spot as his callous-roughened fingertips pushed her legs further apart. He licked her like he needed her too, like the cries he was pulling from her nourished him, like this was all the inspiration he wanted. He licked her until she couldn't tell the difference between her wetness and his, until her need spilled over into a fountain of pleasure.

As she came down from the heights Eli sent her to, Lacy shivered and came back to herself. Her hand strummed through his dark waves. This guy. This guy was too good to her. Eli was the best man she'd ever known. And the sex was kind of the best ever, too. She knew, she *knew*, that it would get better with the right man, the man she was meant to be with, but for the life of her she couldn't say how. Because Eli? Eli played her like a mandolin.

Every touch left her humming, and depending how he did it, the pitch changed. Thank God they were in a tent of covers, because she did not want him to see the flush on her face, the ridiculous faces she was making at the things he was doing to her. He moved back up, covering her exposed body with his warmth.

She buried her head in his neck, riding the last of the wave and inhaling his familiar sandalwood scent. His arms slid up her arched back, and she realized he was picking her up. The fort collapsed around them as he brought her to the bed, briefly giving the impression Eli was wearing an enormous cape. A king. Her king. She liked that. For tonight.

She lay back on the nearly stripped bed and watched him slide his jeans down his legs, releasing his cock. She licked her lips, and moved forward to take him in her mouth.

"Not—not tonight. Tonight's just about you," he said, gently shoving her back down. She relaxed into his kiss until she felt the familiar need start to creep up again. Her leg hooked around his back as she drew him in. With one push, their bodies joined.

He stayed like that, inside her, until she caught her breath. When she had adjusted to his thickness, he started to move slowly.

"I didn't put on a condom," he said at the same time she realized it. "I didn't even bring one. I mean, this was completely not planned."

"It's okay, it's okay, birth control." Her words didn't make the most sense, but he knew what she meant, which was to keep going. She couldn't tell if he knew what she really meant, which was *I can't get enough of this feeling.* Which was *I don't want anything between us.* Which was *I trust you.*

The muscles of his back were tense beneath her hands as she tightened her grip. Every thrust made her cry out. Her head sought the comfort of his shoulder again, but he leaned back to stare into her eyes.

He spoke to her as he pounded into her. Words fell from his lips in broken poetry, half-cocked phrases and sentiments. "You're beautiful," he told her between raspy breaths. "Like something I can't hold. Wild. I'm inside you. In the deepest part of you. And I still can't get deep enough." His words sparked something in her, highlighted something.

One time, Lacy had run across the word *kintsukuroi*. Japanese in origin, it meant "to repair with gold." There was a style of clay pottery it referred to, cracked then crafted back together with pure shining gold. It was more beautiful for having been broken. Finally, a year after having been irrevocably shattered, Lacy finally felt beautiful, even at the broken spots.

She murmured "please" and he moved faster, but that wasn't what she wanted. She stilled him and flipped them over so she could show him the depths of her feelings. She moved over him slowly, savoring it, making it last longer than she thought she was capable of. And in those prolonged moments of ecstasy she realized that not only was she beautiful, but stronger for the broken spots that had been crafted back together. With gold. With love. With this king's love. If only for tonight.

As the orgasm built, first slowly and then suddenly, she stopped moving. Eli's hands gripped her hips and he set the pace, urgently sliding her over him, until he stopped with a cry. As he started to pull out, she bore down and rode out both of their orgasms until she collapsed into his arms, heart racing. He was still whispering to her, but she could no longer hear what he was saying. She closed her eyes to savor this incredible moment, and never noticed the moment when her reflection slipped into unconsciousness.

Eli stared at Lacy as she slept next to him, cheeks still flushed from their lovemaking. She looked more peaceful than he had ever seen her. The usual furrow in her brow was smooth. He stroked the curls away from her face and stared into it as long as he could without losing his nerve.

He hadn't planned this. Truly, he'd meant to come and kiss her good-bye. And then leave. But even if she hadn't been so sad, even if she hadn't begged him to stay, he'd wanted to be there. Wanted to adore her properly, before he didn't have the right to adore her at all.

Whatever he had planned and whatever he had actually done, there was something he had to do, now, before she woke. So he softly rolled her off his arm, gathered his things, and moved toward the door. First though, he stopped at the desk and tore off a piece of stationery, scribbled a few words. One more glance before he turned off the light switch and headed back to his room.

There, he opened his laptop and took a deep breath. Time to do what needed to be done. For the sake of every-one.

Chapter Twenty-Two

Lacy knew she was alone before she opened her eyes. The bed was too cold, the room too quiet. At the realization, she willed her heart to go cold and quiet as well. But it was no use—Eli was in her. Inked permanently to her insides like a tattoo.

She kept her lids shut tight. *I get to hold onto him for five more minutes. Then I'll open my eyes and be done.* Not that she could know exactly what five minutes was without looking at a clock. The total running time of "Godric's Hollow" was about five minutes. She let it play in the back of her mind as a timekeeper. Was it wrong that Jax's song was the soundtrack to her good-bye with Eli? It felt appropriate somehow. Not just the lyrics, but the sound of it, the mood—it fit Eli.

But here she was already at the first chorus, and she'd yet to think the thoughts she really wanted to think. Thoughts from the night before—Eli's mouth on her body, between her legs. Eli's soft words, the poetry he'd spoken to her both out loud and silently. How he'd listened to her and held her when she most needed comfort. The way he'd cherished her and adored her and moved her. He'd made her come physically, and he'd also made her come emotionally. Her feelings, the ones she kept so buried inside her, had come to the surface because of him. Had shaken her nerves and exploded through her just like her orgasms.

Was that what it felt like to fall in love? It had been so long since she'd fallen for anyone—so long since the beginning with Lance that it was hard to remember what falling felt like. She remembered the actual being in love. It was a feeling that didn't leave. It left scars.

It left tattoos.

God, she *was* in love with Eli, wasn't she? Not Jax. Eli.

And what an absolute horrid time to figure that out—when she'd so blatantly told him she was unavailable. She could change her mind, though, couldn't she? Tell him that it wasn't Jax anymore who interested her. Tell him that she'd been blind and ridiculous and that Eli had always been exactly who she'd needed.

Then she remembered why she'd told Eli she wanted Jax in the first place. Because of Folx.

Thinking of Folx made her heart squeeze and twist. He meant so much to her. He'd been so instrumental in her life. But honestly, he hadn't been what Eli had been. And maybe that wasn't fair to compare when one was online and one was standing in front of her, but that was just it— *one was standing in front of her.* Why would she turn down the man who would hold her in hopes of a man who only *might* hold her someday?

It hurt to think of letting Folx go. Yet wasn't that exactly what she was thinking? She wasn't sure she wanted to be thinking about it at all anymore. Not before coffee and a shower. Also, "Godric's Hollow" was over now. Time to stop thinking Eli thoughts.

And maybe all of this would feel different when she faced the light of day.

Lacy opened her eyes.

The room was still pretty dark, though, with the black-out curtains mostly shut. A sliver of sunshine poked through the open crack, enough light to see a piece of hotel stationery propped up on the bedside table. It stood next to the folded sheet with Lance's vows, and though she was somewhat afraid to read what Eli had written her, it couldn't possibly be as intense as the words she'd read from her dead fiancé.

Still, her hand trembled as she brought the note closer. She clicked on the table lamp and forced herself to read Eli's words.

Songbird,

I can't begin to express what I'm feeling right now. I'm honored to have been able to comfort you when you needed someone the most. And last night was beautiful—every second in your presence is like a melody that I want to play over and over. A beautiful song that I want in my head, in my body.

But we have to end things here. I have someone, and I have to be true to her. I have to give her what she needs.

And you have someone too.

So thank you for the song. I'm sorry it has to be a single instead of an album. I promise though, it's a greatest hit.

Eli

Well, dammit.

Eli's note made it harder to think that choosing him was even an option. And what was with the tears gathering in her eyes? One emotional breakdown and now she was going to be a regular waterworks? She sure hoped that wasn't the case.

She swiped her hand across her eyes before anything had a chance to spill and sat up, determined. So Eli's good-bye was an obstacle, but, hey—any good-bye could be erased with a good hello. She simply had to decide if she had a good enough hello. Or if she even wanted to say it in the first place.

Lacy groaned and got up to find her phone. She should at least check in with Folx even if she wasn't quite ready to deal with anything else. His message sent the day before had made her beam, but it also confused her. He'd said he was thinking of her—LoveCoda—and he'd sent it when he—Jax—had been hanging out with Lacy. It bothered her a little to have Jax thinking of anyone else while he was with her, even if the anyone else was herself. God, the whole thing was so confusing. Perhaps, though, Folx was as torn between the real-life love interest and the virtual one as she was.

She'd have to forgive him for that then.

Her phone turned up on the floor, hidden under her bra. And it was dead. She grabbed her robe and trudged over to the desk to boot up her laptop instead. She logged into SoWriAn and waited for a notification, hoping that Folx had missed their date the night before as well.

But there was a message waiting from him. So now she hoped he'd say something that would make it easier for her to choose to fight for Eli.

She didn't miss the fact that hoping those things at all indicated her choice had already been made. Still, she wasn't acknowledging that because then she'd have to figure out how to end things with the others—aka Jax and Folx—and she didn't want to deal with that yet.

So Lacy opened FolxNotDead24's message, and read it. And what it said changed everything.

She read it again.

This is one of the hardest messages I've ever written,

but it's been a long time coming. I should have told you sooner, but the truth is, I've met someone. I wasn't looking for her—I swear. She completely caught me off guard. Then she swept me away. Though I meant to meet you, I can't now. I also think it best that we end our dates and our conversations here. You've been a great friend so I know you'll understand. Good luck. I know you're going places.

Lacy shut her laptop, put her head on the desk and moaned.

Folx had met someone. Which meant Jax had met someone. And, considering that Jax had kissed her the very day he sent that message, she was pretty sure that someone was her.

Well. Her decision was made then. She'd be with Jax. And this really was the end of thinking about Eli. Really, she didn't know what was so sad about the idea. That had been her original plan. She'd been perfectly fine with it before last night. She could embrace it again.

Jax. She'd be with Jax.

She forced herself to smile about it. He really was a great guy. And if she could somehow get him to be his real self, his Folx self, then he'd be an even greater guy. It might be easier for him once he realized she was LoveCoda. She'd tell him, of course. Eventually.

But not now.

Now she needed time to mourn the loss of Eli before trying to connect like that again with someone else face-to-face. He'd released so many emotions in her that needed a chance to breathe before being reined in, transformed into feelings for someone new.

There were songs too. Now that her block was fully lifted, now that she had so much to say—there were many, many songs to write.

And tears, it seemed. Because her eyes weren't just

filling now, waterfalls were streaming down her face. She refused to let this be the new norm. She would not become a leaky faucet.

But Eli deserved tears. Deserved a good cry. Maybe even two.

The next two weeks blurred together as the tour turned back north, stopping at cities more inland. Hagerstown, Harrisburg, Allentown, Scranton. Eli didn't pay attention to where he was anymore—just where he wasn't. He wasn't in Baltimore. He wasn't in SoWriAn. In fact, he'd closed his account.

And he wasn't with Lacy.

He barely spoke to her, making sure he sat away from her at breakfast and that he didn't work next to her in load ins. He sat as close to the front of the bus as he could manage, though that wasn't really necessary since Lacy was always in the back with Jax.

He'd found that helping Sammy pack up after each show kept him occupied and out of the way from the rest of the tour members. Which was exactly what he needed. Because more than needing to not spend time with Lacy, he needed to not spend time with Lacy and Jax. Together. And Sammy's stupid pitiful glances weren't freaking helping.

It was what he wanted for her, of course. The night he'd gone to her room, it was so obvious. Jax was helping her. He'd been there in a moment of weakness, something he would never regret, but it wasn't him she'd needed that night. So yes. He'd meant for them to become a couple. But he didn't have to watch it enfold in detail. It hurt too much, and he wasn't a masochist.

He did allow himself one concession of pain, however. Every night, without fail, he watched her set. It seemed she added a new song to each show, each better than the last. With each unfamiliar note that rang out from her voice across a restless crowd, he fell more in love with her. Each word seemed to sing his own anguish. He felt them in that vague place Jax always gestured to—part groin, part heart. They wrapped around him and wrung his misery out of him so that his shows were also the best he'd ever performed. So many believed the theory that heartache bred art. He'd never realized how much that was true for him until now.

Along with his agony, though, Lacy's songs gave him validation. He'd done the right thing by letting her go. She'd been so desperate to tear down her block, and now, not only had she found her words but also she'd become prolific. It made him feel good about himself. Made him feel honorable despite the heavy ache he carried.

While avoiding Lacy, Eli also avoided Jax. It was pretty much impossible to see one without the other anymore, and though Eli recognized the strain his avoidance had put on the entire band, he wasn't sure how to remedy the situation. And that depressed him almost more than anything. Music was his fallback. It was where he lost himself when he most needed to be found. Though his performances were stellar on a nightly basis, the broken connection with the lead singer hurt their overall sound.

Eli still worried about Jax, too. He was so volatile, so fragile—it was another reason Eli felt miserably good about Jax and Lacy as a couple. Hopefully Lacy grounded the man, gave him strength. Lord knew she'd done that for Eli.

If she did do that for Jax, Eli couldn't be sure. There was too much tension between him and Jax to know anything going on personally. Unfortunately other people noticed too.

In Albany, Lou advised, "Whatever's up between you, kid, you need to fix it."

In Springfield, Wes got involved. "Dude, one of you

needs to suck it up, and we both know it isn't going to be Jax."

No, it would never be Jax. Quite the opposite, actually. In Hartford, Jax called another impromptu rehearsal before the show that night in order to "fix" a few of the songs. Eli suspected it was a power move rather than a true displeasure with the arrangements.

But whatever it was meant to be, it was also Eli's chance to repair things with Jax. So for the whole practice, Eli played nice. He complimented Jax's observations. Then he sucked it up, as Wes recommended, and conceded to every change Jax suggested. By the time the rehearsal was over, the strain among the group seemed to have lessened.

Too bad it made Eli feel so shitty about himself. Since when did being the better man require being such a pussy? It really blew. Not to mention the total suck of watching his art suffer for the sake of someone else's ego.

But since he'd already begun mending their friendship, he might as well see it all the way through. Reluctantly, while the rest of the guys cleaned up the area in prep for the show later that night, Eli took the moment alone to catch up with Jax in the green room.

"Great session, Jax." He was such a prick to his own art; dismissing the death of his songs for the sake of keeping the peace. "Good call to add that rehearsal." Jesus, he couldn't stop himself.

Jax's lip ticked up in pleased astonishment. "Glad you think so. I'm a little surprised you went along with my changes. Usually it takes you a while to see the vision."

"Guess I'm more in tune with you than usual." In tune with what Jax wanted to hear anyway. Which wasn't the point of the conversation at all. Instead of sucking up and blowing steam up his friend's ass, he meant to be fixing the things he really was sorry about.

Eli grounded himself, both feet flat on the ground.

"Hey, I never got a chance to apologize. For Baltimore."
He could still defend his position and reasonably convince
even himself, but the truth was that he'd intervened for the
wrong reasons. Reasons he needed to let go of now.

"For Baltimore?"

Lord, had Jax already forgotten the whole thing? "For
the argument after the calling-the-police thing."

Jax nodded as understanding spread across his features.
He fell into a ratty old armchair and kicked his feet up on
the empty keg cum coffee table. "Oh, no worries, man. I
get it. It had to be an icky situation for you. You were interested in the girl and she happened to like someone else
better. I should really be apologizing to you."

Eli debated between simply walking away and kicking
Jax where it hurt, in that vague region between his junk
and his stupidly toned abs. It would feel good to let his anger out in a physical altercation. It would also feel good to
leave the asshat to his narcissism and never look back.

He had to admit by now—Jax was no longer the guy
who'd pulled him from the shower to join a band, rescued
him from loneliness and given a brotherhood.

Eli was committed though—to the band anyway. That
made him committed to Jax. They had been best friends
once, he needed to remember that for the sake of the Blue
Hills. And for the good of Jax—and Lacy—he had to per-
petuate the story that he had a woman waiting for him
elsewhere.

Of course it had been the truth when he'd first said it.
He'd had LoveCoda waiting. Even then it had been hard
to say he wasn't interested in Lacy. Now, it practically devastated him.

Still, he managed to get the words out. "I told you I
wasn't into Lacy. I was worried about *you*." Then, to make
sure the lie was really out there, "I have someone else."
Eli kept eye contact through his blatant fabrication, which

made him feel more like a tumbling dickweed than he'd felt before. As if lying poorly would somehow make up for the fact that he was lying in the first place.

Jax narrowed his gaze. "Oh, yeah. From that hookup site?"

"Does it matter where from?" *See? There. I don't make up stories that well after all.*

"Just asking, dude. Thought we were having a bonding moment. Guess I read it wrong."

"Jax . . ." God, talking to him just wasn't going to be easy no matter what. It would be one thing if Jax really were trying to bond, but he wasn't. He was trying to poke fun at Eli and his attempt to reconnect.

Well fuck that. He needed to stick to the script. "So you accept my apology then? We're cool?"

"We're cool." Jax popped a peanut into his mouth from the jar that sat next to the chair. Then, with a sour look on his face, he proceeded to spit it out. Back into the jar, in fact, which he examined briefly before tossing it across the room into the garbage can with a dramatic swoosh of his hands. "Two points!"

Eli should have left it there. He meant to. He even turned to walk away. It was a good note to part on, after all—the *we're cool*, not the *two points* from tossing expired peanuts into the trash—and not as dangerous as the note floating around in his head, nearing his tongue, begging to be spoken. Not nearly as painful either.

But against his own better judgment, Eli turned back. "So things are good with you and Lacy?" Dammit, he'd asked. What the hell was wrong with him? It was as if he wanted to feel as bad as possible.

"Yeah, sure." Jax crossed his arms over his chest and smirked. "If you aren't interested in the girl, then why do you ask?"

Good question, Eli. Why the eff did you ask? "Just

because you'd said you were going for her." *Yes, that was believable.* "In fact, you made a big deal about it to me, and now you're spending lots of time together. It seems like it's working out for you. You don't get that way about chicks."

Jax shrugged. "It's fine. She's fine."

What the hell did that mean? Were they happy with each other or not? If they were, then fabulous. Well, not fabulous, but Eli could pretend.

The question nagged at him, so against his better judgment—again—Eli decided not to let the conversation lie. "That doesn't sound very fine."

"It's exactly fine. She's cool, I'm cool. Am I missing something?"

Eli's heart skipped a beat. Maybe they weren't together then. Which changed everything. But of course they were together. He'd seen them kissing. And Lacy was with him nonstop. "I think *I'm* missing something. Are you or are you not with Lacy?"

He practically held his breath while he waited for Jax's answer.

Jax shifted his hips up so he could pull his phone out of his back pocket. "We're friends. You know, we hang."

"And that's it?"

Jax held his phone up and looked toward the screen.

"Our relationship is evolving organically." Jax ran a hand through his hair before clicking the phone off and pocketing it again. "I can't predict where it's going to end up."

Eli wanted to be comforted by Jax's answer, but there was something stopping him. Namely, Lacy. She wanted a relationship with the guy, narcissistic prick that he was. She'd put herself out there for him, and he didn't seem to give a flying rat's ass. Despite all signs pointing to Jax evolving for Lacy, confiding in her, letting her be the new Eli. What if that had never been what was happening?

Suddenly Eli feared for Lacy's emotional well-being. "Shit, Jax. Are you kidding me? I mean, *evolving organically* is great and all, but does she know you're not actually together?"

Again, that carefree shrug. "I don't know. I guess so."

"You *guess* so? You do realize that most girls think there's a relationship when you have sex with them repeatedly." Because he was more than certain Jax and Lacy were having sex. "It's really not cool to string her along."

"Dude, calm down." Ironically, Jax's volume was louder than Eli's had been, which somehow made his words even more patronizing. He sat up and lowered his tone. "I'm not stringing her along. I haven't even fucked her."

"She's not someone you can just"—Eli halted as Jax's words hit him—"You haven't slept with her?" That was . . . weird.

And a relief.

A huge relief.

But again, weird. Jax wasn't the type to hang out with girls that he wasn't sticking it to.

Jax let out a breath, the hair across his forehead bouncing up with the force. "Nah. Like I said, we're evolving. Taking it slow."

Just like that, the relief that Eli felt evaporated.

If Jax was taking it slow, it meant Lacy was special to him. Jax never committed to women like that. This was different. Which was good. For Lacy. Still hurt like a bitch. "Then you really do like her."

Jax threw his hands up as he stood. "I barely even know her." He took a step toward Eli and put a hand on his shoulder as if confiding in him. "Look, here's the truth. She's a sweet girl with an even sweeter rack. She doesn't bug to hang out with. In fact, she's a really good listener. She's a good kisser too. To be honest, though, I was mostly interested in her in the first place simply because you liked her.

When she showed interest in me I saw the opportunity to show you that you can't get everything you want. Like you usually do."

"What the—" There were way too many things for Eli to react to, that he didn't know where to start. No, he knew where to start. He wanted Jax's hand off him. Eli brushed out of his grip. Then he picked one of the myriad crazy comments to address. "I don't get everything I want. That's you. You're the one who gets the girls and the attention. The one everyone concedes to."

Jax stepped back to lean/sit on the arm of the chair he'd previously occupied. "I have to work for that shit, man. You get it naturally. Without even trying, the songs just *come* to you. And the ideas. All the talent. And I promise you, if I sat quiet in a room, all the girls would flock to you. Even Lacy. Because you're the real art around here. You're the real showpiece. You don't have to worry about what you wear or practice a bunch of witty stories or need to slash your skin to feel like the real deal."

Eli drew in a sharp breath. Was that why Jax had cut himself? Because he didn't feel like he was really an artist? The idea spliced through him, a figurative knife cutting at his insides.

He started to say something, though he didn't know what. Anything to make it better.

Except he hesitated too long and Jax went on. "But guess what. Despite all that? Lacy liked *me*. Liked me when I didn't even try very hard, and that means enough for me to give her a shot. A shot at a night, anyway. Am I in love with her? No. Am I looking for a thing with her other than friendship? Yeah, I'm hoping for a chance to get in between her thighs, but that's all. Apparently, Lacy Dawson isn't the type to jump into bed with the first musician she meets, so it's going to be the slow seduction with her."

"Wait, wait, wait . . ." The sympathy Eli had felt only a

moment before was smothered under the irritation surging through his veins, but before he acted on it, he'd be cool
and get some clarification. "So you haven't slept with her
because *she* doesn't want to?"

"She doesn't want to *yet*." Jax pointed his finger at the
same time as he delivered his last word.

"Meanwhile you're biding your time." It wasn't a question. It was a stalling statement—one that might give Eli
enough time to cool down or perhaps redirect Jax into saying something that wasn't quite so maddening.

Better yet, Eli knew he should use the time to figure out
how to focus back on the remarks Jax had made earlier,
the ones about not being talented. The ones about cutting
himself for attention.

But then Jax said something else. "Yeah, since we're on
the road together, I figure hanging with her is something
to kill the boredom." *Or, maybe even more maddening.*
"Don't worry, I still have other girls. I'm not picking them
up from the crowd anymore—that would particularly be
poor taste in front of Lacypants—but I'm getting taken
care of. In fact"—he looked at the time on his cell phone—
"Chelle is meeting with me any minute now. You remember Chelle. From the last time we did Hartford?"

"Jax, you're an asshole, you know that?" Also, he didn't
remember Chelle, but who could keep up with all the girls
Jax had entertained on tours past? The war inside Eli had
reached its Gettysburg. Friendship and past with Jax was
battling empathy and future with Lacy, and the outcome
would be essential.

"Dude, what is your deal? This isn't anything new on
my part. You got a thing for Lacy, don't you? You said you
didn't, but you totally do." Jax jabbed a finger into Eli's
arm. "Admit it."

Eli took a step forward. "The thing I got for Lacy is
called respect. Something you've got zero of for anyone

including your bandmates. You walk all over everyone like our sole purpose is for your own convenience. Your own gain. Your own entertainment. Well, that's bullshit. I'm better than that. Lacy's better than that. This whole band is better than that. And I, for one, am done."

Jax scratched at his chin as he studied Eli. "Ah, I get it. You're pissed because I changed up 'Bruises.' You're so damn precious about your songs. What's with that? Don't you know I'm the one who makes them? They're nothing until I turn them into my own."

Eli let out an exasperated chortle. "You're delusional. You ruin those songs. Massacre them from what they're meant to be. But right now, I couldn't care less about what you do to my songs. What I care about is what you do to Lacy Dawson. She's an amazing, wonderful woman who you're charming simply so you can get in her pants? You deserve her less than you deserve my songs."

He paused only long enough to make sure his next statement was a declaration—firm and nondebatable. "From now on, my songs are mine. You'll never have another one to bastardize again. And as for Lacy, you keep your slimy hands off of her."

"*Your* songs?" The shock evident in the woman's tone behind him was only surpassed by Eli's shock at her arrival.

He turned to face her, aware from the tension that radiated from her body and from the order of the things he'd said that she'd heard enough. Heard too much to go back to the lies and the pretending and the distancing. He looked into her horrified face, at her beautiful heartbroken eyes.

He knew his next words would be the door that opened everything.

And still he said them. "Hello, Love."

Chapter Twenty-Three

Lacy's head was spinning, whirling with the conversation she'd just overheard. She'd heard a great deal of it, including the part where Jax was simply biding his time until she welcomed him into her bed. But the part that had really stopped her—the part that made her heart stop beating for a full second, causing the blood to rush through her ears when it finally picked up again—was the inference that Jax didn't write the Blue Hills songs. Those songs belonged to Eli.

Well, that was the part that had caught her until she was struck on the head with Eli's greeting. He'd called her Love.

She felt Jax's arm wrap around her waist. "Hey, baby doll," he said after kissing her cheek. "Eli and I are just having a little band disagreement."

"No." She'd heard the conversation. He'd said he had other girls. Like a woman named Chelle. She pushed out of his arms. "No!"

"Listen, Lacypants, whatever you heard . . . well, it was

taken out of context. Most likely. I never want you to infer I'm not interested in sleeping with you."

Jax was speaking to her but she had her eyes glued to Eli. "What did you mean by *your songs*?"

Eli sighed, which was definitely not a helpful answer. Lacy crossed her arms over her chest and turned to the other one. "What does he mean, Jax? Do you not write the band's songs?"

"You know how it is in a band. Lots of collaboration. They're *our* songs."

"Who writes the songs, Jax? Who?" It was a really roundabout way of finding out the answer to the question she really wanted cleared up. W*ho the hell is Folx?* Somehow it was more comforting this way. Because if she just came out and asked that one . . . and then if she got the response that she was beginning to think she was going to get . . .

She just wasn't sure she could take it. Yet.

Jax turned her toward him, one of his hands resting on each of her upper arms. "Come on, Lace. Does it really matter to you who writes the songs? Don't tell me you're one of those chicks who groupies over the behind-the-scenes guy instead of the front man."

Lacy stepped back and out of his grasp, her hand covering her mouth. "Oh, my God." She felt like she wanted to throw up. But sort of in a good way. Was that possible?

Jax continued to defend himself. "Plus, I contribute. They aren't all his words and notes. I'm the one who makes them hits. *Me*. Their soul—that's me. I give them the—"

His hand moved in front of him, but Lacy put up her own to stop him. "Please, don't. Not the gut/crotch clutch again. That's not a Thing, Jax!" Suddenly all of Jax's egotistical behavior was magnified in her mind. She'd put up with it simply because she knew who he was underneath,

but now she was finding out she didn't really know who
he was underneath at all.

And it wasn't really the revelations about who Jax was
or wasn't that had her stomach flip-flopping like a fish out
of water, but what they meant about Eli. She needed one
more confirmation. "Just tell me this, Jax—did you cut
the chorus of 'Godric's Hollow'?"

His proud smile gave him away before he even spoke.
"Yeah. I added the audience participation part. Brilliant,
right?"

"Oh, my God." Again, she covered her mouth. This
time she didn't want to throw up so much as squeal. Really a happy sort of squeal, though there would have been
some other complex emotions jumbled in as well and she
had a feeling she would have sounded more like a dying
pig, and that wasn't what she was going for.

She turned her attention to Eli—the man she should
have been looking toward all along. "It's you."

Eli's Adam's apple bobbed as he swallowed. "It's me."

Wow, it was . . . she was . . . wow.

Weeks of frustration melted off her like the sunlight finally hitting a patch of winter ice. She'd been trying so
hard to make things work with Jax. But the more time she
spent with him, the more she missed her online dates.

And Eli . . .

Oh, how she'd missed Eli. His touch, his smile. His
eyes, the way they raked her body as if he were already
undressing her. Mostly, though, she missed the way he
made her feel about herself. He made her seem important
and interesting and the main show, where with Jax she was
always only an opening act, a curtain jerker.

But Eli was Folx and everything made sense and none
of the rest mattered because she didn't have to deny the
feelings she had about him anymore. Talk about a Plot
Twist.

Except, wait . . . everything didn't make sense.

Like, why did Eli look so guilty? And why wasn't he as surprised by the revelation as she was?

She felt a punch to the chest as she realized why. "And you knew. All this time?"

Behind her, Lacy vaguely registered a female voice. "Hey, Jax. I've been waiting for you for almost ten minutes."

And then Jax's greeting. "Chelle. Glad you found me, babe."

But Lacy didn't turn her head. Her focus was pinned on Eli.

He kept his gaze on her as well. His head shook slightly. "Not all this time."

"Look, you two seem to be having a happy enough chat without me."

Jax seemed to be talking to her and Eli now, but she refused to acknowledge anything but the man in front of her who said, "I've only known for the last couple of weeks."

"And since I have other plans that start, like, right now. I'll just be going."

Seriously, Lacy wished Jax would stop talking. It took energy to block him, and she was beginning to realize she needed all her energy for her conversation with Eli. "Like since when exactly? Before you broke up with me online?"

"If you don't mind, man. Gir—woman. People. Peeps." Jax's voice droned on like a fly buzzing in the room, distracting and irritating as it tried to steal the attention. "Eli . . . ? Lacy . . . ?"

"Go!" Lacy said in unison with Eli.

"Awesome. Catch you two later." There was relief evident in Jax's voice as he shot out of the green room with his guest. As if he'd been let off the hook, and for half a second Lacy wondered if she should feel hurt by that.

But there wasn't any room for that offense in her well

of emotions. She was too hurt at the moment from Eli's
disclosure. Or Eli's potential disclosure because he hadn't
said it yet, but she felt the truth in her bones like she could
feel the change of weather from fall to winter.

Still, she pressed on, needing to hear it verbalized.
"Before you broke up with me online, Eli?"

His shoulders fell and his eyes lowered. "Yes. I figured
it out earlier that day. That morning."

She wanted to ask him how. It was a fairly interesting
question and her mouth opened to ask it, but no sound
came out. Her mind was already past that, already at the
what-he-did-with-the-information-when-he figured-it-out
part. She didn't have to try to remember the details of that
day—they were cut into her memory like etched glass.
He'd come to her room to apologize. Then they'd made
love. Not had tour-sex. Made love. And then he'd ended
things both in real life and online.

He'd figured out who she was and then he'd broken off
all intimacy.

Which meant . . . "Oh, God." She swallowed, hard,
but she couldn't swallow hard enough to push down the
truth—Lacy Dawson didn't live up to LoveCoda so Eli cut
his losses while he could.

"I'm such a fool." Such a ridiculous fool. Tears were
springing at her eyes, and the pain in her chest wrenched
and twisted. She didn't know she was still capable of
this much heartache. She thought living through the worst
would make her capable of living through everything
else. It turned out that "worst" was a category, not an
absolute.

Lacy needed space. Needed air. Needed to be anywhere
but where she was right then.

She turned and left.

"Lacy . . ."

She heard Eli call after her, but she couldn't acknowledge

him. How could she? She was utterly humiliated. Instead, she kept walking down the hall looking for the door to the parking lot. She'd come in this way only a few minutes before with Lou. He'd come over from the hotel to check on the guys at The Night Owl, the venue for the night, and she'd tagged along, hoping to catch a snippet of their rehearsal. While the manager talked with the band, she'd gone looking for the bathroom. Thankfully she'd found it before she'd overheard the loud voices coming from the green room, because she really couldn't have held it this long and there was no way she was looking for anything but the way out now.

The first knob she turned, however, led her not outside but to an office. And spread out across the desk in an intimate—and rather awkward—position were Jax and Chelle. Damn, they were fast.

They paused their foreplay to glance at their intruder.

"Seriously?" Lacy slammed the door shut before either of them could respond. *Not that one, then this one.* She turned the next knob and this time was met with sunshine. *Thank God.*

Lacy bent, her hands clutching her thighs for support as she took in large gulps of air. Her mind was dizzy with the revelations. There had been a moment earlier, when she'd realized that Eli was really FolxNotDead27, where she'd felt relief. Elation even. No more pretending that she and Jax would ever have more than an occasional passing in the drunken night. No more fighting what she wanted to freely shout out to the world—her love for Eli.

But that moment had scurried out faster than it came, and the joy that had flooded through her still lingered under the horrid layer of betrayal.

She heard the door swing open behind her alerting her to his presence long seconds before he spoke. It didn't do any good to run. Where would she go? Besides, she couldn't hide from horrible feelings anymore. She'd learned that from hiding from Lance.

It didn't mean she had to turn and face him, though. So she didn't.

Long seconds passed before he spoke. "Look, I know what you're thinking . . ." His voice trailed off, then she could swear she heard his head shaking. "Actually, I don't know what you're thinking. But I know none of this looks like what it really is."

Grief and rage balanced for a moment, and then rage tipped the scales. She couldn't help herself—she spun toward him. "And what is it really, Eli? Because let me tell you what it looks like. Like when you found out that I was really LoveCoda, you were disappointed. The girl you were holding out for really wasn't all that special in real life and so you found a way to kill two birds with one stone and ended it with both me and her." She crinkled her brow as she reevaluated her last words. "Me and me, I mean." Dang if two identities wasn't the most confusing thing ever.

Eli scratched at the back of his neck, and it gave Lacy a small bit of satisfaction to see that his expression seemed lost and desperate.

His jaw worked and his eyes grew dark. "I fell in love with you, Lacy."

A ball formed in her throat. Man, he did know how to get to her. She wanted to fall into his words, fall into his arms, but so much left unsaid held her back. And even when the words *were* said, she had to remember that he was a natural poet. A professional liar, like all writers.

Her guard remained up. "Yeah, sounds pretty plausible."

In contrast, Eli's hands fell to his side, leaving him open and vulnerable. "I did. I fell completely. I love music, you know that, and you make me feel like there's music everywhere. In crab shacks and blanket forts. And I'm not talking about the sound, but the feeling. Possibility hiding behind every moment. The feeling that music gives me—you give me that. You're my songbird."

Lacy's heart squeezed in a way that was simultaneously painful and paradise at once. The ball in her throat thickened. There were things she wanted to say, but she couldn't get them out if she tried. It was like all the months of writer's block had swum back up to strangle her.

Which was fine, it seemed, because Eli had more to say himself. "But I had a commitment to LoveCoda—to you—and when I realized . . . God, Lacy, when I realized you were her . . . I was thrilled. Ecstatic. Over the moon. It was the best moment of my life and I'm not even being a little bit dramatic about that."

It was too much—the emotion, the ache, the poetry. And none of it could possibly be true because he wouldn't have dumped her if it were.

She dug deep and found her voice, pulled it out through the block, choked though it may be. "Why are you doing this? Why would you say all of that stuff? Are you trying to be the biggest dick in my world? Because right now you don't really have to try."

"That's what sh—" He realized it wasn't the time for comedic relief when she met his eyes. "I'm saying this because it's the truth, Lacy." He took a tentative step forward, but stopped when she retreated. "Listen to me. You know me. I'm the guy you've been talking to for months. We've been through it all together. You've trusted me and I've never lied to you." His lids closed halfway as he realized that wasn't true. "Well, mostly never."

"Exactly." That was the point. She really couldn't trust him. Especially not with something as precious as her heart.

Except that she *wanted* to trust him. Which was why she hadn't walked away.

"I only lied that once, Lace. When I told you there was someone else." He ticked his head back and forth as he reconsidered that. "In a way that wasn't a lie though either because there *was* someone else—you. There was you."

"And you dumped that version of me too. After you made love to me like I actually meant something to you. Or did you forget that?"

"No. I'll never forget that." Eli's voice was soft. Sincere. "It was everything."

When he said things like that, she was crippled with doubt. She wanted to believe that her night with him—that every moment with him—had meant as much to him as they had to her. "Then why? Why would you dump me after?"

His lips parted to speak then closed, his chest falling with the release of air. These words were hard for him, she could tell. "Because you wanted Jax."

"I wanted Jax because I thought he was you. Because I thought he was Folx." For someone as brilliant as he was, it struck her that he was also the biggest dolt to not have figured that one out.

"I considered that. I did. And, at first, I'll be honest, whatever reason you liked Jax didn't matter. I wasn't going to let him stand in my way of getting you. For once, I wasn't going to back down." He paused. "But then your song . . ."

"What about my song? Which song?"

"The song you played for Jax. On the roof. You said it was for him. That you'd connected with him, and I realized that he'd helped you break through. Not me. Him."

Lacy frowned. "But that wasn't . . . I didn't . . ." Never mind that he'd just admitted to spying on a moment that she'd thought had been private. She was upset and distracting herself, but what he was saying was wrong.

Plus, Eli had yet to explain why any of that had even mattered.

As if reading her mind, he said, "He helped you do what I couldn't, Lacy. I'd tried and tried to help you with your writer's block. . . . Then Jax comes along, spends one night with you, and your block is over. He fixed you. He was the one who deserved you."

"He didn't . . ." She halted her explanation as the meaning of his words settled through her. "So you decided that since Jax cured me—which he didn't, by the way—that I shouldn't have the right to choose that I might want to be with someone else?"

"No, it wasn't like that."

The hurt and despair she'd felt only moments ago made way as anger again pushed forward. "You mean that you didn't completely pull the wool over my eyes then? How long do you think it would have worked with me and Jax before I realized that he wasn't what I thought he was? Don't you think we'd have talked about it eventually?"

"I guess I didn't really think about that."

She'd caught him off guard. Good. She wanted him to feel as unbalanced as she did.

Except then he regrouped. "But then would it even matter? If you were already into each other?"

"God, are you a matchmaker now? I have one of those already." A matchmaking sister who had said point-blank that Eli was the one for her, but that was beside the point. "And why did you make love to me if you were just planning to pair me up with Jax and break my heart?"

Aw, fudge nugget. She bit her lip hoping he hadn't realized she'd revealed as much as she had. The whole situation was messy enough without him knowing how messed up in love she was with him. *So much for being a professional liar myself.*

"I wasn't planning—" He stopped mid-sentence. "Wait, I broke your heart?"

Double fudge nugget. "Yes! Of course you did. I was

in love with you too." Crap, past tense wasn't truthful. "*Am* in love with you, I mean." Except she didn't really want him knowing that necessarily. "I mean . . ."

She met his eyes, found him smiling. Which pissed her off more because she was not through all her anger yet and because he'd tricked her into saying things she hadn't planned to say. Pissed her off most because his response was a triumphant smile, and not reciprocation. That pretty much proved it, right there. She was a conquest, not a love. "Are you happy now? I admitted it. There. Point is I was devastated when I found your shitty, arrogant note."

His smile faded. "And how was I supposed to know that? You asked for one night. Every time we were together you followed it up with 'we can't do this again.' You had me spinning in circles. I was trying to honor your wishes. And . . . I wanted the note to be sweet."

His chin nudged up, and she saw sparks of irritation in his eyes. "And, come to think of it, you thought Jax was Folx and you still kept jumping me. What was that about? At least I wasn't cheating on someone I'd actually met."

"Oh, don't try to make my actions any worse than yours." As if. "And we'd said just friends so neither of us was even cheating on anyone."

God, it really was a mess.

Eli nodded in a reluctant concession. "It felt a little like cheating, though."

"Yes. It really did." There was something soothing about that point of agreement, and she let herself take a brief moment to recognize that before heading back into the fight. "But sex with you wasn't about emotion. Not at first. That was about orgasms. For the songs."

"What?"

She flushed, not wanting or knowing how to explain that one. That she'd first thought orgasms led to lyrics was ridiculous in itself, and then that she'd put the time and energy into researching the theory was simply bat-ass crazy.

And then she realized she didn't need to explain any of it at all. "Actually, that's a lie. The sex wasn't for the songs. That was an excuse I told myself." As long as they were being honest and all. . . . "I was drawn to you, Eli. It didn't matter who I thought Jax was. I was pulled to you."

"Maybe that should have been a sign that you weren't supposed to be with him."

"And maybe I would have figured that out, but you didn't give me the chance when you chose for me."

They faced off for several seconds, the tension pulled taut. Lacy let her shoulders sag first. She shouldn't have said that last thing. They'd already been over that, and Eli's preceding statement would have been a perfect chance for her to say, *You're right. I shouldn't have been with Jax. I should have realized he was the wrong guy.* It was a flaw of hers that Andy often pointed out—not letting the argument die long after the rounds had all been fought.

Though the same could be said of Andy—more so even—so Lacy had never really counted it as a true flaw until that very moment.

Now she wished she'd let the argument die. Or, more, she wished she could find the words that could bring them together because they were so close. He'd admitted he loved her, she'd admitted she loved him—what else was left standing between them?

Eli apparently also wanted a truce. His head bowed as he ran his hand through his hair. When he brought his gaze back to hers, his expression was soft and regretful. "Look. I was wrong, okay? I made a mistake. I wasn't trying to make your choices for you. I was trying to be . . . I don't know . . . noble. I saw two people that I love—two people who haven't had the easiest time as of late—coming together, fixing each other, and I . . . shit, I didn't think I had the right to step in and mess that up."

He brought his hand up to his chest, clutching his fist almost in that weird way Jax always did except with actual meaning. "But please, please know that I wasn't pushing you away because I didn't want you. Even now I want to pull you into my arms and kiss all of this away. Letting go of you has been hell, Lacy. Pure hell."

Oh, how she wanted that too. To be in his arms, kissing away all the misunderstanding. "Then do it."

His brow furrowed while he seemed to try to remember what it was he'd said he'd wanted.

In that brief pause, Lacy realized what it was that was still standing between them. And it was too big not to address even if it meant she was dragging the argument out further. "See, *that's* the problem, Eli. You talk about love like it's supposed to make everything better with its magical properties, but that only happens in romance novels. Real life doesn't work like that. You can't fix someone else, no matter how much you want to. Believe me, I know that now. It was never your job to fix me. And you can't fix Jax." *Just like I couldn't fix Jax, even if he was Folx. Couldn't fix Lance. Can't fix anyone but me.* "That has nothing to do with how much you love someone."

Eli started to say something, but she stopped him with a single finger and continued. "But let me tell you what love really is. It's standing up for that person. Standing beside them. Having the courage to go after them. Not coddling them or giving them up in some patronizing show of nobility. When's the last time you fought for the people— the things—you loved? Fought for your songs or your career or for yourself even? You've mentioned concern for Jax, but when have you actually fought for him? Because letting him have his way isn't how that works. That's not how *any* of this works. Like me . . . you love me? That means you go after me. That means you stay. That means you don't say words that are flowery and beautiful and hope that's enough."

Lacy had a feeling she was talking as much about Lance now as she was Eli. It didn't matter—the same principles applied. "Love means you don't give it away; I don't care what the old *set it free* cliché tells you." It wasn't necessarily the best line to end with, but she didn't have anymore to say without repeating herself. Besides, she'd said a lot already, and Eli had listened to her patiently.

Now it was her turn to listen to whatever rebuttal he might have. But he simply said, "You're right." Then, after a beat, "So now what?"

They were the words she'd posed to him when they'd finally decided that they'd meet in person. What a different place they were in now. It was actually a very good question that exposed the problem with delivering fantastic words of advice—the words usually required some sort of follow-up. Follow-up that often demanded action on the part of those who offered the advice as well as those who received it.

It seemed, perhaps, a good time for her to leave—then hope that he might follow. She shifted, half turning to go before realizing she might want to communicate her plan. Just taking off after a question was asked was not only rude but also confusing, and there had been enough confusion between them already.

She cleared her throat and lifted her head. "Now I'm going to walk away. You have to decide what you're going to do about it." Then she walked to the edge of the building and turned the corner.

Once she was out of sight, it took everything not to stop and lean against the outside wall of The Night Owl. Her confrontation had taken a lot of strength, but she couldn't cop out now. Besides, Eli would follow. Of course he would.

Except that he didn't. Even after she slowed her steps, she still made it to the curb without him stopping her. Had she been too harsh with her words? Had he decided that she really wasn't worth fighting for after all? Or was he actually the coward she'd accused him of being?

She refused to go back. She'd been humiliated enough for one day. What could she do then but keep going?

A single tear slipped down her face, but she wiped it away and stuck out her hand to hail a cab.

Eli stood in one place for longer than he intended to, soaking in Lacy's words. They stung, made him feel less manly than he liked to feel. But what struck him most was their accuracy. He'd been dead-on when he said she knew him.

He also liked that she was willing to challenge him, because he needed that in his life more than he'd realized. She'd pushed him, then walked away—which was really in direct opposition to her speech about staying and fighting—but he could forgive her for that. It wasn't her that needed the testing; it was him.

So what was he going to do about it? He was going to go after her, of course.

He broke into a grin as he took his first steps in the direction she'd gone. His first steps toward being the man she deserved.

Before he'd gotten more than three steps toward his destiny, though, the back door of the theater opened and Lou stuck his head out. "Eli! Thank God. Come with me. I need you."

There was a note of panic in Lou's voice, yet Eli was focused on his mission. "Can it wait? I'm in the middle of—"

Lou cut him off. "It's Jax. He's hurt. The ambulance is on the way."

Eli's smile faltered as alarm spread through his body at lightning speed. He'd heard those words before—*he's hurt*. Last time, he'd arrived at the hospital and found slits in Jax's wrists.

Still, though he knew to take the message seriously, he paused now. There was a part of him—a really selfish asshole part of him—that wanted to ignore Lou and go after Lacy. He needed to prove himself to her, and abandoning her now was not the time.

But Eli didn't just love his songbird. He also loved Jax, current states of their friendship notwithstanding, and as Lacy had pointed out, he'd done a shit job of proving that as of late.

So right now he had to go fight for Jax. But after, he'd fight for Lacy too.

Chapter Twenty-Four

Eli paced the small area beside the hospital bed while the nurse added another dose of pain meds to the IV running in a long clear line into Jax's arm.

"This one should really make a difference with the pain," she said. She turned to the others in the room—Lou, Eli, and Wes who had arrived just a few minutes before. "You boys can stay until the surgical prep team gets in here which should be within the next half hour or so. After that, I'll show you to the waiting area."

"Thank you." Lou nodded in appreciation as the nurse slipped out of the emergency room.

It was the first time they'd been alone with Jax since arriving at the hospital almost two hours earlier. Well, the first time they'd been alone that he was actually calm. Before the first dose of pain meds kicked in, Jax had been screaming obscenities at the top of his lungs while the doctors examined his injury. Eli and Lou had been in the waiting room then and could hear him through the thick doors that separated them from the ER.

While they waited, Lou made all the phone calls. He

talked to Sammy and asked her to inform the rest of the tour members that the show was canceled for the night without giving any details. He called Wes to be another point of support. He called the manager at the venue and apologized for the inconvenience.

It was after he'd finished all his other calls that Lou got the text. "Dawson's going home until the tour resumes," he told Eli. "I guess that's best at this point."

For a moment, Eli felt his chest collapsing with disappointment. Then he realized Lou was right—it was best at this point. This didn't mean Eli and Lacy were done. Not if he had anything to say about it, and he intended to have a lot to say about it.

He knew he should call her, or text her at least, but he just . . . didn't. The things he wanted to say to her—and do to her—required them to be face-to-face. Besides, he had a few things he needed to get settled before he could really fight for her the way he wanted to.

Like Jax.

When Lou and Eli were finally allowed back to see Jax, they still didn't get a chance to really talk with him. His room had been a constant in and out of doctors and technicians and nurses. He'd been taken for an X-ray, and immediate surgery had been ordered. Then, another visit from the nurse as Jax's pain, and temper, flared up again.

Now—finally—he was calm.

In fact he was smiling a little like when he'd gotten drunk on Nyquil that one time in college.

"Feeling a bit better?" Lou asked. "Well, as better as you can feel considering?"

"Yeah, man. I really am."

Though they'd heard a few details of the story from the staff, Eli had to know. HIPAA had censored all the good bits. "So what exactly happened? Exactly . . ."

"Ah, you want the details."

"No, I don't. I really, really don't. I want a brief summary."

Wes leaned forward in his chair. "*I* want the details."

Jax beamed. "Well. Chelle and I were getting it on. Like, ah-ha-haaawn. We were on this big oak desk and I was under her while she was doing this reverse cowgirl thing." He started to buck his hips and describe shapes with his hands, boob and butt shapes, demonstrating.

"Should you be doing that?" Eli wasn't even sure *how* he was doing it with all the equipment he had connected to him. Or with all the drugs he had in him, although that explained the sudden drawl.

"I'm totally fine right now. The morphine has so kicked in. So-hooo kicked in. Anyway, then she did this backbend and kissed me. That's when I heard the crack."

All the men groaned in unison, and Eli shifted as nonchalantly as he could, his crotch suddenly feeling very vulnerable and unprotected.

"Oh, God, I can't . . ." Lou trailed off.

"It actually made a crack noise?" Wes asked in awe.

"Swear to God," Jax nodded. "Followed by immense, thought-I-was-dying pain. I'm pretty sure I passed out."

"You did," Lou confirmed. "That's when that chick of yours came to find me. You were just coming to when I got there."

Jesus, it sounded terrible.

Wes leaned forward in his chair. "A backbend, though. Dude!"

"I know, right?" Jax drug-hazed grin also showed a fair amount of pride. "Chelle's a gymnast."

"High-five, man."

God, they were ridiculously juvenile. High-fiving over broken equipment? Eli couldn't begin to understand. "And where is Chelle now? She didn't think she should see you to the hospital?"

"She offered, but I said hell no. I don't need to have any press leaks attaching me to a specific girl. Not good for my bachelor rep." Jax waggled his eyebrows around, held up a wavering hand for another high-five that nobody took.

"What press leaks? What rep? Do you have some secret celebrity identity that I'm unaware of?" Eli was genuinely confused.

"Damn, you have a stick up your ass today, don't you? Maybe if you're nice I'll share some of my meds with you later. It will chill you out." The hand was still just wobbling around in space. It was becoming distracting.

"I don't need meds and I don't need to chill," Eli tried to say in a placating voice. The guy had been through enough, but even he could hear the hard edge was still in his voice.

"Is this still about earlier? You'd think you'd give me a break considering my condition." The hand began a familiar vague gesture.

"Yes, this is about earlier. Not just earlier today, but even before that. And give you a break? That's exactly what I'm giving you. But I meant what I said this morning—I'm not giving you my songs anymore. And I'm not giving you my sympathy. I'm giving you notice. The Blue Hills are done. There's your break." So much for placation. The dude had broken his junk. May as well give him the broken-band news too. At least he had morphine.

Wes sat up, his eyes wide. "You're quitting the band?"

"Eli, he's about to go into surgery. Do you really think this is the time or the place for this conversation?" Lou's hands began to do wiggly things similar to Jax's, but his were born of horror, not forgetfulness.

"Probably not, Lou, but this can't wait. See, I think half the reason Jax keeps doing these stupid things"—no, he needed to direct this at the guilty party—"I think half

the reason *you* keep doing these stupid ass things is because you think you have to. You think you have to be an
ass to be a star. Or that you have to contribute to the songwriting to be part of the band. You don't think that what
you are is good enough. So you show up late and change
my songs and cut your wrists, all so you'll be noticed."

Jax lowered his head and studied his hospital gown. "It
was for art," he mumbled, though not with as much conviction as he usually did.

"Here's the thing, Jax. It backfired. You cried wolf and
instead of getting noticed, you made us—you made *me*—
want to ignore you. Or put up with you. But I'm not doing
that anymore. I'm not putting up with you. Because I notice
you. And I love you, Jax." Eli shot a glance at the drummer
in the corner. "I love you like a brother, J. You're a talented
son of a bitch. You used to believe that. You're the person
who first inspired me. You still inspire me and I want you
to be happy. And I don't think you're happy at all. I think
you're faking it."

Jax peeked up at Eli. "Everybody's faking it."

Eli couldn't help smiling. His own words thrown back
at him. Touché. "I do think everybody's faking most of life.
The I've-got-it-together part, anyway. But maybe happiness can be something we can have for real. At least, I
want to try. I hope you want to try too."

He'd been thinking about this for the last two hours, but
once he said it, it would be real. His next words would
change everything.

But they'd open all the right doors too. Clear the right
paths. Doors and paths that led back to a man who just
might be the one Lacy was looking for. Sure going solo
was scary. So what? He'd have to record an album as soon
as possible and set up gigs, if he wanted this to work.
Which meant it might be longer than he liked before he
got back to his Songbird. But she had an album to record

of her own, and he would never forgive himself if he stood in her way.

But he was getting ahead of himself. He had this next thing to do first. "So I'm not quitting the band, exactly. I'm proposing that the Blue Hills go on indefinite hiatus. It will give you a chance to get your head together and regroup. Rediscover your talent. Figure out what you really want out of this music thing. What you really want out of life. Help you realize who you are. And . . ."

He looked around at his other bandmates, guys he was bound to by music, if not by friendship. "I'm really sorry it happened like this. I hope you know how much all this has meant. And I want—God I want it to work out . . ." But that was all he could get out before he got choked up.

It was like all the words he knew he should say to make it right with the other guys, the guys who had nothing to do with Jax's problems, had gotten trapped somewhere under the lump in his throat. It was like he couldn't force them out. It was like he understood, for the first time, how Lacy must have felt.

Lacy huddled in her blanket fort and studied the way the light snuck through the thinner parts. She should grab the thick quilt from her closet to make a really good fort, but as much as she wanted the darkness, she didn't want to move from her spot. She'd done a lot of not moving from her spot since she got home from the tour. In fact, except for working her shifts at the studio and the rehearsals she'd scheduled for herself to get ready for her recording session, not moving from her spot was all she did.

Thirteen days. It had been thirteen days since she came home. Thirteen days since she'd last seen Eli outside The Night Owl. When he hadn't followed her, she'd gone back to her hotel room and tried not to fall apart. A half hour or so later, Sammy had texted to tell her that the show was canceled for some undisclosed reason. In fact, the whole tour was on hiatus until further notice. Since they already had the following day off, Lacy had bought a spur-of-the-moment train ticket home.

As she left, she told Sammy to call her when it was time to return, but not to contact her otherwise.

Thirteen days later, she hadn't heard from Sammy or Eli. But she had heard from Lou. That very morning, in fact. She wasn't sure how she felt about the news he'd delivered, but it had driven her under the covers.

"Hey, are you recording in there or can I come in?" Andy's voice came through muffled, but decipherable.

"It's not a recording fort. Just a regular old I-don't-want-to-face-the-world fort."

"Then I can come in."

Actually, no. The world includes you too, sis.

But Lacy said, "Sure. Whatever. Watch the sippy cup."

Andy was already making her way into the supposed-to-be-solitary confinement, so it turned out her invitation wasn't even needed.

"So," she said after she'd settled in. "What's the latest from Lou? When can the tour get back on the road?" Her voice was too loud for the fort. Too perky.

"Never." Lacy would pitch her own tone deep and low to counteract. If they talked at the same time, there would be perfect harmony.

"Are you being dramatic?"

Lacy inched a pillow over her face. "Nope."

Andy jabbed Lacy with her elbow, prodding her to go on.

"Ow!" Lacy rubbed her joint even though it didn't really hurt. Yeah, she was being dramatic. She sighed. "The tour is canceled. Lou texted."

It probably shouldn't bother her. There were only eighteen days left before the tour was supposed to end anyway.

Then there was Thanksgiving. After that she was recording her album. Something she was now looking forward
to. After her block had released, her songs had poured out
like a broken dam. Now she had too many to record them
all in the time she had booked over the next three weeks.

"Oh. Well, that's a bummer." Andy didn't really mean
it though. More than once she'd told Lacy how glad she was
to have her sister home.

And it made sense why she'd want Lacy home because
one week after her studio time ended, was Christmas
Eve. The day of the big "I do." The day that, once upon
a time, Lacy was supposed to have met Folx.

Eli Frank. Not for the first time she wondered what it
would have been like to meet him there at the wedding
reception. She could imagine him in a tux, his scruffy hair
and face giving away his true hipster vibe. He'd smile at
her when he took her hand, his eyes crinkling in that way
she loved.

She missed him so much her skin itched.

That stupid tour ruined everything.

Andy said nothing for a few minutes—which was a
miracle—but she couldn't ever be quiet for long. "Did Lou
fill you in at all about why the tour was canceled?"

Yes. He did. And this was the real reason why Lacy was
under the covers today. "Said the band broke up."

"Damn. Wasn't expecting that."

Lacy wasn't sure what she had expected. She'd thought
through a lot of different scenarios, of course, but all
Sammy or Lou had ever told her was it was a personal
matter.

Deep down she didn't have to be told the reason, though.
She knew.

Like her sister often did, particularly when it was most
annoying, Andy read Lacy's mind when she said, "It's not
because of you. You know that, right?"

The pillow inched back down. "What's not because of me?"

"The band breaking up." Andy sat up suddenly, destroying her side of the fort. "Oh, my God—that's what you think, isn't it? That you're the cause of the Blue Hills breakup?"

"No!" *Yes.* "Dammit, Andy, you messed up the blankets."

Andy gave her a leveled gaze that contained exactly no remorse.

Fine. She sat up as well, her den of solitude now a definite thing of the past. "I don't know, Andy. Maybe I'm not the cause of it. But it's awfully suspicious how the timing of all of it worked out, if you ask me." The coincidence of the tour hiatus happening directly after her fight with Eli, which was directly after his confrontation with Jax— how could it not be because of her? She'd created a rift so deep between the two men that they couldn't even perform together.

No wonder Eli didn't want to fight for her—she was a band destroyer.

"You can't know what it's really about if you don't talk to the guy."

Never mind that Andy's words had some truth to them. It wasn't as if the idea hadn't crossed Lacy's mind, oh, uh, every other minute of the day.

"I told him he was supposed to fight for me, Andy. Fight means, you know, actually try to make things right. If I call him it will just null and void the whole thing."

"Have you tried to see if he's on that Soryan thing?"

"It's SoWriAn. And yes, I did." Every day for thirteen days, in fact. "He deactivated his account after his breakup with LoveCoda, and the status hasn't changed." Man, she was beginning to regret she'd told her sister things, since it required her to *keep* telling her things.

"Would Lou have his contact info, do you think?" Andy sounded more confident now.

No way was Lacy going to just let Andy "fix" things. "Yeah. I'm sure he would. But like I said, I'm not going after him."

"And you have Lou's info in your phone?" The confidence was bordering on slyness.

"Yeah, I . . ." *But why would her sister want to know that?* "Andy! Stay out of this!" Thank God her sister was so transparent. Now she knew to password-safe her phone immediately. Jeez. How humiliating would it be for her big sister to be calling her ex-not-boyfriend and discussing their not-relationship.

"Just trying to be helpful."

Lacy fell back onto the bed with a heavy "humph."

"I know you are." And she really did know that.

She inched up the bed so that this time when she sat up she could lean against the headboard. Then she put a hand on Andy's thigh. "I appreciate it. I really do. But honestly, I think I'm going to be just fine."

Andy cocked a questioning brow. "For reals fine? Or just say-you're-fine fine?

"For reals fine." She wasn't telling fibs like she had in the past either. She'd get through this. She'd survived losing her parents and a fiancé. This was cake comparatively.

Well, not cake. Because she hurt like a mother, every part of her heart broken and rejected. She ached for Eli in a way she'd never ached for anyone—probably because he'd loved her in a way no one had ever loved her.

But she'd given him some good advice when she'd told him to fight for the things she loved. And she loved herself. Not in a self-righteous way, but in a respectful way that made her want to get up every morning no matter how much it hurt. Get up and move on. That was her fight, and even though she was currently moping about, she thought she was doing a pretty damn good job of it.

"You know, Andy, things didn't happen this fall like I thought they would. There were certainly a fair amount of Plot Twist moments that I could have lived without. But the experience helped me move past Lance finally. I got to experience touring. And it gave me a handful of new songs, and I know without a doubt that this album I'm about to record wouldn't be the same if I hadn't gone through all of this." More accurately, the album wouldn't be at all. "So really, in the end, I have to say it's been painfully worth it."

Andy smiled, her eyes full of understanding. "This is one of those suffering-for-your-art things that I'm never going to get, isn't it?"

So much for understanding. "Probably." But even if Andy didn't quite get her, Lacy knew she at least accepted her. And if it ever came down to it, Andy would fight for her, tooth and nail.

There really wasn't anything more she could ask from someone who said she loved her.

"Hey, Lacy?" She opened an eye at her sister. "My bachelorette party's in two hours."

As Andy hopped out, the tent collapsed entirely.

Chapter Twenty-Five

"Okay, I'm the judge now?" Blake asked. For an intelligent, self-made man who owned a highly successful company, the guy was having an awfully hard time picking up on how to play Cards Against Humanity. Or perhaps he was just hoping against hope that they'd switch to Monopoly if he played slow enough.

"I guess if we had more friends, you'd have to spend less time choosing which of us picked the most horrible card."

"Iiiiiiiiiiiii," came a voice. Well, Andy may not have *needed* anyone else, but she'd invited them regardless. Pierce was the recovering alcoholic her sister had met during her brief stint as a bartender. They'd discovered tonight that he was experimenting with pot versus booze. So far, he was just as strange, but stayed clothed. Good enough.

"Why would we need more friends, when we have family?" Blake's hand briefly covered Lacy's. She blinked back tears. Minus the stoned guy in the corner, it was basically just how she'd pictured the night before her own wedding. Well, they'd be around a Scrabble board instead of a card table, but close enough.

Luckily, there was a knock on the door before she could lose her shit completely. She fingered the stone that hung at her collar, a necklace she made out of her engagement ring only that week. After only wearing it a couple of days, she'd already gotten used to the feel of it. It felt a lot lighter than it had when she'd worn it on her hand. And now, when she touched it for comfort, she didn't think specifically of any person.

"Hi friends! And enemy! We brought more booze." Jaylene, obviously, plunking a bottle of red next to the discard pile. Her neighbor was not a fan of Blake, but how sweet that she'd show up for Andy.

"We don't *say* that to people, I don't think." Noah, Jaylene's boyfriend, couldn't hide his grin though. Well, to be fair, Blake probably did have a lot of enemies.

"Okay, I'm going with this one." Blake threw down the winning card, and Andy squealed and threw her arms up.

"Mine! I'm going to beat everyone! Suckers!" Blake smacked her on the ass.

Lacy leaned into Kat and whispered, "I thought your card was better."

Kat beamed and it didn't matter that Lacy had no idea what Kat's card had said or even what Andy's had said. It wasn't exactly an apology—and she'd give her that too, eventually—but this was a start.

Andy was still celebrating her win, so out of curiosity, Lacy peered over Pierce's drooping head to see the card that had taken the round. It read "That's What She Said".

Then Lacy *was* thinking of someone. Eli. Because she missed the hell out of that guy. And tomorrow night, when the group around this table gathered around an altar to

celebrate Blake and Andy's ridiculous, improbable, adorable love, *he* was going to be the one she was longing for.

Lacy pressed her back against the closed door even though
the lock was secured. "We'll be ready in a few minutes,
Tim," she called to the man banging on the other side.

Tim's voice screeched so loudly that Lacy wasn't quite
sure what he said but she thought there was something
about a "schedule to keep" and "splintering wood" and
"not afraid to rip this tux." Surely she was misunderstanding, although she was sadly certain she was not.

"I understand, Tim. But you can't rush perfection." At
least, she hoped that's what was keeping Andy trapped in
the bathroom for so long with the makeup artist. Lacy
didn't know how much longer she could keep Tim at bay.
That girl's tip was going down.

She had an idea, though. "Tim, could you maybe get
us some drinks? You know, to calm our nerves?"

"Drinks *before* the wedding!" Tim's response was
somewhat calmer this time and therefore his words intel-
ligible.

But his voice faded and the pounding stopped, so Lacy
counted it as a win.

After again checking to make sure the door was unlocked (splintering wood was a concern, even on these
metal doors, when Tim was involved), she headed to the
back of the dressing room's private bathroom to in-
quire about her sister. It wasn't actually a dressing room,
of course, but a back room at the Museum of Science
that Tim had arranged to be used by the bride during the
wedding.

Lacy had deduced that it must be a cataloguing station—
long tables with various scientific items sat in clear protective bags stickered with long identification numbers.
They'd signed an agreement to not touch any items, but a

few of the objects were irresistible—a meteor-like rock, for one. Another was a large bone. Yet another, a broken piece of pottery carved with some sort of hieroglyphics. She touched them all. Probably it wouldn't be the final step on her road to hell, but not touching the art was the hardest thing in a museum. And in galleries. And in people's houses. She touched the bone again, just because she could.

It wasn't the first time she'd thought it, and probably not the last, but what a weird place to have a wedding.

Lacy paused at the bathroom door, not wanting to make her sister anxious, but also afraid of the wedding planner's return. After a second, she knocked softly, "Hey, honey. I don't want to rush you, but I think Tim's going to break the door down if we don't let him in soon. Are you about ready?"

"No," she said at the same time the makeup artist said, "Yes." A moment of hushed words followed, then the door opened, and the artist bustled out.

"Perfectly understandable," Lacy said. "I got it from here."

Before Lacy could think about doing anything about it though, Andy stepped out from the bathroom.

Lacy gasped. "Oh, Andy!" Her sister was dressed in a simple gown of white silk, à la Caroline Kennedy. Her auburn curls were down, defined and shining, but about to be covered in a lace-edged mantilla veil that was even longer than her gown. The makeup she had been concerned about was perfect—soft rose and gold on her lids, mascara, and a nude gloss. Andy was absolutely radiant. "You're breathtaking. Really. Blake is going to melt when he sees you."

Andy lowered her eyes, a blush creeping up her neck. "Blake isn't really the type to melt."

"He'll melt today. I promise." There was no way he couldn't. Andrea Dawson-soon-to-be-Donovan was the most stunning thing in the world. Okay, maybe Lacy was a little prejudiced, but, to be fair, she wasn't the type to easily melt either.

And she was, most definitely, melting. The whole of her insides felt warm and squishy and good. With all the crap she'd been through—with all the crap *they'd* been through—seeing her sister happy, ready to walk on to something new . . . well, it was A Moment. One that made up for a lot of shit ones. One that almost made it bearable that when Andy walked down that aisle, she'd be walking out of Lacy's spare room and into her own life.

Lacy reached for Andy's trembling hand. "Mom and Dad would be so proud."

"You think so?"

"I know so." Lacy's throat clenched at the end of her statement. They rarely talked about their parents, but today it seemed apropos. After all, it was never more apparent that they were orphans than when Andy was trying to figure out who would give her away.

Andy waved at her face as if she could fan away tears or heavy emotions. "Stop it. I have waterproof mascara, but let's not test it, okay?"

"Okay. No tears. Just smiles." They smiled at each other with big, matching, toothy grins.

Then Andy dropped Lacy's hand and plopped down on one of the plastic office chairs, her face crumpling.

Lacy knelt at her sister's feet, concern in her voice when she asked, "Hey, what's wrong?"

Andy looked up with blinking eyes, obviously trying not to let the gathering tears spill down her freshly made face. "What the hell am I doing? I can't be a wife."

"What do you mean? Of course you can be a wife." Lacy dabbed at a corner of Andy's right eye with her thumb careful not to disturb her liner.

"Because I'm not wife material." Andy's hand resumed the earlier fanning. "I'm lousy with housework. The first time I had to make ramen by myself, I googled how to boil water. I was worried I'd burn it. Remember in my first apartment when I burned the curtains down with the scented candle? I can barely keep a plant alive. That's a lie. I have never kept a plant alive. The cactus on my windowsill? Has been dead for a year, only you can't tell, so I pretend. What if we have kids? Imagine me with children! I can't stick a kid on my windowsill and pretend! And I can't hold my tongue in public. I'll be such an embarrassment to Blake. What am I going to do?"

It was typical to have jitters of course, but Lacy knew that the banality of them didn't make them any less real. She remembered having them on occasion as she and Lance were preparing for their wedding. Though she'd like to think differently, it was possible that she may have felt the exact same worries on her big day. Particularly about the children. She thought guiltily for a moment about the time she'd killed an air plant. The kind that only needed a mist every two weeks.

She smiled sympathetically and patted Andy's knee. "Oh, silly. You can't embarrass Blake anymore than he embarrasses himself. Remember all the blackmail material you have on him? Besides, it's Blake "Control Freak" Donovan. He knew what he was doing, proposing to you."

She stood and reached for the veil on the table next to them. "So what you're going to do is you're going to get up. I'm going to put this on you. And you are going to marry the man. And you're going to have a wonderful honeymoon. In England, because you are fancy as hell now. Then you'll hire a maid. And a cook. A nanny. You'll have fake candles and fake flowers or you'll buy new cactuses and fake everyone out like you did me. I was always fairly impressed you

kept that thing going." While she spoke, Lacy fastened
the clip to Andy's hair.

Then Lacy straightened the long sheer material so that
it ran straight down her sister's back. When she was finished, she took Andy's hand and helped her to her feet.
"And as for children—you're going to be an excellent
mother. Or at least as good as anyone else because none
of them can do any of the things you think they can. Don't
you know? Everybody's faking it."

Andy squinted an eye suspiciously. "Do you mean that
or are you trying to make me go through with this because
you're scared of Tim?"

"No, I mean it. Everyone's faking."

"Even Mrs. LaRue who lived down our street when we
were little and she had all those daughters and she did their
hair in perfect braids everyday with matching outfits and
even their dog's collar matched and her house was immac-
ulate and always smelled like fresh-baked cookies?"

Lacy was surprised that Andy made it through her run-
on sentence without a breath, especially considering how
close to blubbering she seemed to be. "Yes, Andy, even
Mrs. LaRue. She was definitely faking it. She probably
hated that dog, only had sex in the missionary position, and
drank cough syrup straight from the bottle to get through
her days."

Andy's face twisted in disgust. "Please don't ever let me
drink cough syrup straight from the bottle."

Lacy took a step back and admired her sister. She was
absolutely gorgeous. She turned Andy to see herself in the
mirror that Tim had brought in and propped against the
wall. "Look at yourself. You're stunning."

A shy smile played on Andy's lips as she gazed at her
own reflection. Then her eyes met Lacy's in the mirror, her
brow creased in uncertainty. "You're sure everybody's faking it?"

"Yep. Positive." Lacy hesitated, trying to decide if this was a good time to admit her secret. She decided it most definitely was. "In fact, even I've been faking it. I didn't grieve for Lance like I should have. You know that. And I didn't write a song for more than a year after his death, until the tour, actually, and I pretended I had."

Andy spun to face Lacy directly. "You didn't? What was all that composing time? All the music I heard you playing?"

"Me faking it." Lacy took a deep breath. It actually hadn't been as hard to admit as she'd thought it would be. It probably helped that she was past it now. As Andy would get past her own fears.

Lacy took her sister's hands in hers. "My point is, Andy—I faked it long enough to get me through, and then things worked themselves out. Fake it 'til you make it—that's probably the truest cliché of them all. And that's what you'll do. Because you love this guy, don't you? You *want* to marry him."

Andy nodded. "I do love Blake. And I love you."

Lacy was afraid to pull Andy into a hug and mess her up, so she simply squeezed her hands. "I love you too, sister. More than you know."

Then, because any more heart-to-heart conversation would ruin both their makeup jobs, Lacy let go of her sister's hands and changed the tone. "So you're ready?"

"I suppose I'm ready as I'll ever be."

The next half hour moved by in a blur. There were no more moments to talk or hug as Tim gathered the ladies for their walk down the aisle of the main room in the Blue Wing of the museum. The music began playing—a beautiful octet of stringed instruments that Lacy had worked with at the studio and recommended for the event—and Tim dinged a triangle to cue each woman's entrance.

In what seemed like the blink of an eye, Lacy was at

the front of the room waiting for the music to change and
her sister to appear. And when she started her walk down
the aisle, Lacy glanced toward Blake to see that he did indeed melt.

Lacy touched the diamond at her neck. As she'd expected during the bachelorette party, watching the display
of love before her, Eli was the one who came to mind.
Today was the day he and LoveCoda had originally set to
meet. She'd hoped it would be a beginning for them. Now
her sister would be leaving for her honeymoon and Lacy
would be left . . . alone. At least her tear-filled eyes could
be attributed to the wedding and not her broken heart.

Don't think about him, don't think about him.

But not thinking about him made her think about him
even more. She thought about the way he held her and
kissed her. Thought about how her songs were so much
better with his additions. Thought about the things she'd
said to him and wondered if they meant anything at all to
him. If he'd even thought about fighting for her or if he'd
simply decided it was too hard.

Then right in the middle of Blake and Andy's exchange
of rings, it occurred to Lacy—*she* hadn't fought for *him*!

"Oh, shit!" The words were out of her mouth before she
could stop herself.

All eyes of the wedding party turned to her. The minister scowled. "Pardon?"

Lacy felt her cheeks redden. "Sorry, sorry. I, uh—"
Nervous, she fumbled the bouquet she was holding, nearly
dropping it before she recovered. "Um, I'm just so happy
I couldn't keep it in any longer." *Only a partial lie.*

The excuse seemed to go over well—Andy beamed, a
tear sliding down her cheek, and even Blake's mouth
turned upward in a half smile. The minister's glare lingered
a second more on Lacy, but soon enough he returned his
attention to the couple before him.

Whew. And also, damn, what a time for an epiphany. Why hadn't she realized before now that she needed to apply her own advice to herself? What kind of a hypocrite was she to say that he had to do all the work in their relationship while she simply waited and moped?

The situation had to be remedied immediately. She had to go after him, had to find him. Would Andy notice if she skipped the reception? If she didn't, Tim certainly would. Maybe if she snuck out the minute the ceremony was over, during the chaos . . .

Her eyes danced around the crowd looking for the wedding planner so she could devise her escape. He was sitting in the front, crying like a baby. Typical. But after they left Tim, they found another familiar face. There, in the second to the last row, in the last chair, his own eyes glued to her was Eli.

And if she wasn't sure it was him or if her eyes were playing tricks on her, she had no doubt when he lifted his hand and gave her a tiny wave.

What the . . . ? How did . . . ?

Dammit, Andy!

Except, not really *dammit, Andy* but *I love you, Andy* because she couldn't think of a thing that Andy had ever done for her that pleased her more than inviting Eli to the wedding. Maybe Andy wasn't quite as self-centered as Lacy always said.

Also, she was a better matchmaker than Lacy gave her credit for. Andy had realized that Eli was the person for her long before Lacy had. He really was too. Seeing him like that, even across the room, made her head spin and her stomach flutter and warmth spread through every nerve in her body. He had to be there because he wanted her, right? Why else would he come? Andy wouldn't have invited him unless he was going to try to fix things between them.

God bless Andy!

When the minister pronounced the couple man and wife, after Blake kissed the bride, Lacy grabbed Andy and gave her the biggest hug she could muster, not caring anymore if she messed her up or not. Lacy was full of emotion. She had a million words she could say, but nothing that would ever express her love and appreciation so she just clung and hoped Andy understood.

"I love you too," Andy whispered in her ear before letting Lacy go and taking the hand of her new husband.

Yes, apparently Andy did understand.

Chapter Twenty-Six

With the ceremony over, the chaos had just begun. Lacy, unfortunately, lost sight of Eli during the recessional. Then she was swept away by a sobbing Tim for photos. After that there were the wedding toasts, followed by a weird thing where Andy stood in a cagelike contraption that made lightning bolts when she touched the metal edges.

"So this is the advantage of a Museum of Science wedding?" Lacy asked with more than a note of sarcasm.

Tim nodded and sniffled. "Isn't it simply spectacular? God, I just can't take it. Weddings are so emotional. Where's the bartender?"

The first break that Lacy got, she looked for Eli, hoping he hadn't left while she'd been wrapped up in wedding formalities. She'd understand if he had—it was likely pretty boring stuff for an outsider. But she thought it might mess her up something awful inside if he'd gone without talking to her.

Thankfully, she didn't have to find out. She found him instantly, watching her across the dance floor. With his guitar in hand.

Andy stepped up to the microphone. "While the DJ is on break, we have the special treat of hearing from an up-and-coming solo artist. I haven't actually heard him sing personally"—she found Lacy's eyes—"but my sister vouches for him, and any of you who know Lacy know that she has excellent taste. I give you now, Eli Frank."

Guess I forgot to password-protect my phone.

Or maybe she hadn't forgotten at all.

Eli moved to the mike, and her pulse picked up to a happy/nervous rate as he returned the smile she gave him. He positioned his hands over the strings and began a song she hadn't heard before. Though she always listened to lyrics, she paid close attention this time, certain they had meaning for her.

Seems I'm not the person I
Thought I was
Scared, coward
Sitting on the sidelines of my life
Didn't know it mattered
Till I met you
Now I want to be
Anything you need

I watched you walk away
But I've got something more to say

There you are
Here I am
I got nothing to offer
Except for my hand
You wanted a fight
So I'm taking a stand
For you

Blake and Andy swayed together in the middle of the floor, but Eli and Lacy were the ones having the moment, their eyes locked as he continued with his second verse.

Seems you're not the person I
Thought you were
Scared, wary
Looking for the answers I can't give
I knew that I would love you
When I met you
What I didn't know
Was how much I'd hurt to let you go

You tried to walk away
But I've got something more to say

There you are
Here I am
I got nothing to offer
Except for my hand
You wanted a fight
So I'm taking a stand
For you

I'm making it right
I'm taking a stand
For you

At the end of his song, all the guests applauded, except Lacy. She was too overwhelmed to do anything but clasp a single hand to her chest and hope her knees didn't give out. When she'd asked him to fight for her, she never imagined he might fight like this—with his heart and soul, in front of so many people. It was the single most romantic thing anyone had ever done for her.

She went to him then—how could she not? She took her time walking over, though, enjoying the way he surveyed her every step. Besides, she wasn't sure what she wanted to say to him yet, and she hoped the extra seconds would help her come up with something.

As luck would have it, she was still unsure when she got to him, but unlike the other times she'd been blocked, she knew the words would come. In fact, the words that came out were his—the ones that used to greet her online. "Hey, you."

Eli smiled, his eyes creasing in that way she adored. "Hey, yourself." He cleared his throat. "You look incredible."

She blushed as his gaze and compliment heated her inside and out. "Thank you." But now he'd flustered her and she didn't know what to say, so she scrambled. "Uh, you sang! It was nice." *Nice.* Geez that was a lame compliment for the most amazing thing she'd ever heard. "I didn't know you did weddings."

"Thank you. And I don't. At least, I hope this isn't what my career will be now." He looked into her eyes. "This one, well . . . I only came for you."

"That's what she said." God, had she really just responded with one of those? She was failing miserably.

He laughed genuinely. Man, she'd forgotten how much she loved that sound. It relaxed her. Reminded her how easy it was to be with him.

"Ah, Lacy, I've taught you well." Eli's smile turned somber. "And *you've* taught *me* well too."

Well, that was intriguing. "Really? What have I taught you?" She was suddenly nervous that he wasn't there to claim her after all. Partly because he hadn't yet touched her—and she was aching to be touched—and partly because a "lessons I've learned" speech seemed a little more like the kind of thing you said with good-bye.

She bit her lip anxiously while she waited for his response.

"Uh, lots of things. But mostly, you taught me how to fight." His forehead wrinkled and he rubbed at his jaw. "I'm not sure what Lou told you about the band breaking up or what happened with the tour—"

She broke in. "He didn't tell me anything. I worried . . . was it because of me?" Her voice squeaked with the question and she hated herself a little bit for it.

"No!" *That's something at least.* Except then Eli said, "I mean, yes, but not directly." He shook his head, as if trying to erase what he'd just said. "Actually, first it was Jax. He had an . . . accident."

Lacy's stomach dropped. "Oh, no! What happened? Is he okay?"

"Yeah. He, uh, you know, I'll let him tell you what happened the next time you see him. Anyway, he had to have surgery and has to take it easy for awhile, but I think he's going to be just fine."

"And that's why the band broke up." Of all the reasons she'd imagined why the tour had ended, she'd never thought it was because someone had been hurt. She felt awful for having been so egotistical to think she was the cause of it.

"No. The band broke up at my suggestion. That's where you come in." He took a step toward her. "You, Lacy, made me realize that I needed to fight for the things I love and one of those things was my music. Another one of those things was Jax. I think he needs some time to get some focus. And I need some time without him murdering my songs. Hence the announcement that I'm now a solo artist."

Her throat felt tight. So that's what his song was about, what he'd chosen to fight for—Jax and his music. And here she thought he'd chosen to fight for her. She was shattered with disappointment, but she forced herself to keep smiling.

"That's great. I'm really happy for you. You'll be a much better artist on your own." She felt her eyes starting to pool with tears. "Uh, if you'll excuse me, I see someone—"

She started past him but Eli grabbed her wrist. "Wait, Lacy. Don't go."

A jolt ran through her, not just from the spark at his long missed touch, but because he wasn't letting her walk away. Was he trying to tell her what she hoped he was trying to tell her?

She was afraid to get her hopes up. "Why do you want me to stay?" She didn't turn to him, just let the question fall over her shoulder.

"Because I'm not done telling you what else I have to fight for." Still holding her hand, he walked closer to her until his front was nearly pressed along her back and his mouth was near her ear.

Lacy could barely breathe, her voice a whisper when she asked, "What's that?"

"You."

He turned her so she was facing him, and though her eyes were downcast, he tilted her chin up until she gave in and met his gaze. "I love you, Lacy."

Her pulse sped up.

"I meant it that day when I said it, I meant it months before when I only knew you online, and I mean it even more today than ever. I wanted to follow you that day, wanted to come after you so many times in the weeks since, but I knew that I couldn't until I was free of everything that would get in my way of fighting for you the way you deserve to be fought for. So I made sure that Jax was settled and band stuff was tied up, and I swear I was headed to find you—Lou told me where you lived—when your sister called and invited me to do the wedding." He cocked his head. "A Christmas Eve wedding, huh? You planned our first date to be a wedding? Seems pretty serious, if you ask me."

She gave a guilty smile, but smiling made her feel more vulnerable so she quickly covered by saying, "It was convenient. That's all."

But Eli knew her. "Uh-huh," he said, skeptically. "Anyway. When Andy asked me to play, I thought it was perfect. It gave me a chance to keep my promise to meet you tonight. I couldn't stand the thought of breaking that after I'd already broken your trust in so many other ways."

"Not *so* many other ways." Not too many that they couldn't work through it. She hoped.

"Maybe not *so* many. But enough. So I wrote you that song—well, I wrote you about twenty songs, but that's the one that said what I needed to say most."

Her heart flipped. But she played it cool. "Twenty songs? I think I need an encore."

"Later. I promise." He smiled in a way that had her guessing that he meant his next performance to be sans clothing.

Or maybe she was just hoping that.

"Anyway," he said, "despite the promise that I'd meet you tonight, it took every ounce of strength to wait until today to see you. But I figured you'd be busy with the wedding preparations otherwise."

"You mean that Andy asked you not to come until today because *she* was worried about being busy with preparations." Lacy put a finger to Eli's lips before he could protest. "Don't defend her—I know her well." If it weren't Andy's wedding day, Lacy might have decided to be irked at her sister for that. Or maybe she wouldn't since she was too happy about Andy's matchmaking to think about much else.

Except now all Lacy could think about was how nice Eli's lips felt beneath the skin of her finger. How much she wanted to kiss them and lick them and suck them.

Eli grabbed her hand and kissed her finger before

moving it from his mouth. "Yes, Andy asked me to wait until today." His eyes crinkled with worry lines. "Was that okay? Did I mess up on fighting for you by not ignoring her? It did seem appropriate since today was the day we were supposed to meet originally. Besides, I didn't want to disrupt your recording time. I know how you musicians get when you're cutting an album."

She chuckled. "It is appropriate. And no, you didn't mess up. You did just fine, and I appreciate that you gave me time to focus while recording. You're right about how we get. How I'm sure *you* get too. I finished fourteen brand-new shiny songs. Only regret is that I didn't have a professional mandolin on any of the tracks."

"If you want to add it later, I know a guy who's recently gone solo." He winked.

"I do too it seems." Her smile faded as she took a deep breath and gathered courage for what she really needed to say. "About us . . . I didn't fight for you either, Eli. I didn't realize it until today, but I let you walk away too. More than once. After that night, I knew I wanted you. I didn't even care if Jax was Folx—I wanted *you*. But then I read your note . . ." She couldn't use his brush-off as an excuse, though, either. "I could have fought then, but I didn't. I let you go."

Eli shrugged. "Then we've both made mistakes."

"Are they mistakes that we can get beyond?" Her lip quivered and her body itched to press against him.

"I'm here. So what do you think?"

"I think we can too." He pulled her into him, finally, and she melted into his chest. "Eli, I love you. Thank you for being the man noble enough to fight for me."

"There's no one else in this world I'd rather be." He put his hand beneath her chin and tipped her face up to his. She leaned in, and touched her lips gently to his. The sparks were still there when they met, but now there was something more. A sense of completion. He pressed more firmly against her, and her lips parted. But just barely. *Church tongue*. Her hands came up and held his face, the familiar scruff, then moved up and through his hair.

She wanted to make it last forever, this kiss, but eventually Eli pulled away to ask, "So now what?"

That was certainly a loaded question. Because she really wanted to say "now we find an empty closet and get it on," but Andy had just caught her eye as she twirled around the dance floor, so sneaking off wasn't an option.

With sex off the table—for the time being, anyway—there was only one other thing that made any sense. "Now we dance!"

Lacy tugged Eli behind her to join the crowd in the "Macarena." For the next twenty minutes, they danced and laughed and grooved to the music. Lacy was happy to find that, like her, Eli wasn't the best with his moves, but he didn't let that inhibit him.

She was tired and sweaty by the time the DJ turned on something slow, and Lacy was more than ready to be pulled into Eli's arms.

They swayed together for a whole verse without speaking, simply enjoying the pleasure of being in each other's arms without any guilt or regret to mar it. After a bit, Eli asked, "Did your sister walk down the aisle to the theme from *Downton Abbey*?"

"Wow. You know *Downton Abbey*? Is there something you need to tell me?" She'd love the man, but she wouldn't be forced to watch the PBS turn-of-the-century British drama.

"I know the theme song. Not the show. But if you want me to watch an episode—"

"No," she cut him off sharply. "That's okay. We can let the Donovans be the fans of that one." She paused, letting her sister's new family name settle in her ears. *The*

Donovans. "They're really good for each other. Perfect, actually. You should see their groom's cake—it's in the shape of a pinball machine."

Eli pulled her closer so they were now dancing cheek to cheek. "Please tell me we aren't that strange of a couple."

"We're not. But honestly, we might be faking that."

He chuckled. "God, Lacy, I love you." He kissed her ear softly, sending all her hormones into overdrive. She racked her brain trying to remember—was the office they'd dressed in still unlocked? Maybe they could sneak in there for a quickie. Surely the dinosaur heads and Mayan remains wouldn't mind a little frolicking in their vicinity.

Eli pressed closer, and she wondered if he was thinking what she was thinking. "Would it be too soon to say this whole event has me thinking about the future?"

So maybe not thinking what she was thinking. Unless "the future" meant the next five minutes and involved a loss of clothing. She decided to ask, though, in case they were totally on separate tracks. "It depends. What exactly are you thinking?"

"A proposal, of sorts."

Lacy tensed in Eli's arms. Jesus, they really weren't thinking the same thing at all. And that was bad. Not bad that their minds had been in different places, but bad that he's said that scary P word. Because she loved him—she really did—but it was way too soon to be talking marriage. She'd lived with Lance for over two years before she even let him start to talk about wedding bells. Yes, Eli wasn't Lance. She knew that. And she could see herself with Eli—like that—but way off. In the future. After more albums and more tours and more time getting to know each other.

"Relax," Eli said at her ear. "Not that kind of proposal."

Thank goodness. She let out the breath she'd been holding, relieved.

Then her chest sank. Didn't Eli think of her as the type of girl he'd want to marry? Sure, it was too soon, but she still wanted to know that it was a possibility one day.

And, yes, she recognized that she was being a very complicated girl with her internal reactions, but that wasn't the point.

Reading her mind as he often did, Eli pulled away to meet her eyes and said, "Of course I want to marry you, too. One day. Not too far away, but not quite yet."

Her skin tingled everywhere as goose bumps shot up on her arms. "One day, though."

"One day." He smiled. "But for now I have a different proposal for you. See, I'm a solo artist now. And while I don't mind not having a band, I'd much rather do this whole music thing with someone by my side. Someone even more talented than me who writes the most gorgeous songs and creates the most beautiful melodies."

"Eli. Are you asking me to make music with you?"

"Yes, Songbird, I am." He lowered his eyes, seeming suddenly embarrassed. "You can take your time and think about it if you need to."

"I don't need to. The answer's yes. Definitely yes."

Lacy laughed as Eli spun her around quickly. Her glance shifted to her sister who was dancing with her new husband, then back to the man gazing at her with love in his eyes. She had so many major milestones to look forward to. A future filled with good times. Albums to record, songs to write, babies to make. A husband to love.

And with a lifetime of days left to live, it was probably premature to label any particular one as such, but she felt pretty confident when she said that this one was *The*. Best. Day. Ever.

Acknowledgments

Laurelin Paige:

To Kayti McGee—This road is so much easier to walk when I'm not going it alone. Don't ever leave me. I can't adult without you.

To our editor, Eileen Rothschild—You were so patient with us through this book. Thank you so much for believing in it when it was hard for us to see the finished product.

To the team at St. Martin's Press—I never want to work elsewhere. 'Nuff said.

To Bob Diforio for hooking us up with SMP and Rebecca Friedman for being AMAZING. You are my patronus. I love you.

To Shanyn for bossing me around, Melissa G. for keeping me online, Candi Kane for assisting and fanning (you're my favorite!), Carly H. for hours of data entry, and KP for InkSlinging me. What a crazy team!

To Bethany—This was the book that never ended and you were there through it all. You deserve a vacation. Cancun?

To Lauren Blakely for teaching me how to market these books. You're a genius. Actually, you're better than that— you're Lauren Fucking Blakely.

To Jen Probst for saying such nice things about our book. I'm delighted to have you on our cover.

To my husband, Tom—I'm sorry I didn't read this one to you as we wrote. I'll owe you. Thanks for enduring me and the other woman. I'm struck with love for you daily.

To my children—Better than song babies are my real babies. I hope you learn to make your own music and sing it loud.

To Mom—You inspire me. Thank you for encouraging me to find my own words.

To my Maker—When I forget to look up, you remind me. Thank you for everything.

Kayti McGee:

As always, a million thank-you's couldn't be enough for Laurelin. You're the best work-wife ever. Bethany and Mel, I couldn't do anything without you guys. Cancun forever. The Order, of course, for endless encouragement, entertainment, and Tom Hiddleston gifs.

Bob, for brokering this shebang. My agent, Natalie, who is awesome. Our editor, Eileen Rothschild, who made this book a hundred times better—we are so lucky to have you. The team at St. Martin's—Erin, Michelle, Heather, Jenn—you guys work so hard and I am so grateful. *dances out backwards*

M. Pierce, you're the Jaime to my Cersei, and I love you more than Dornish red. Jen, Ang, Tarah, Sheri, and Psuka, Whitney, Kelly, Bethany S., Sara, Shea, Leah, my family . . . your encouragement means the world to me. Our readers and bloggers make all of this possible and I puffy heart every single one of you. And of course, Frank Turner provided the soundtrack and inspiration—thank you for your unwitting role. The next round's on me.

Don't MISS Laurelin McGee's previous novel
of delightful romance

Miss Match

From St. Martin's Paperbacks

And look for her e-novella

MisTaken

www.stmartins.com